# WHEN SHADOWS DANCE

## CLAUDIA R.E. SYX

PublishAmerica
Baltimore

ISBN: 1-60474-155-4
PUBLISHED BY PUBLISHAMERICA, LLLP
www.publishamerica.com
Baltimore

Printed in the United States of America

# Author's Bio

Born in Milford, Connecticut, in 1952, I have been writing since the second grade. Although sporadic through the childbirth/rearing years, I became serious about my writing again approximately ten years ago and to date have finished three complete novels, the first of which is *When Shadows Dance*.

I have three grown daughters, with the two eldest living in Phoenix, Arizona, and the youngest close by in Connecticut with her husband and my beautiful grandson.

I live in the small town of Naugatuck with an outrageous little Pekingese who has been my own special guardian angel. There are also two black cats, Baby and Sinamin, who are not entirely welcome, but accepted.

I hope that this story sets some hearts aflutter and some minds to deeper thoughts, and I hope that my second and third novels will also find their way into people's homes.

I am currently working on fourth novel, *Penon*, as well as my fifth novella.

# SHADOW DANCE

Shadows dancing
   ever prancing, hiding from the light
silent calls down endless halls
   opening to the night

Darkness drawing
   scraping pawing, to ready the attack
fear comes creeping
   steadily seeping, leaking through the cracks

Coils unwinding
   comes the binding, taken by surprise
hear the screams
   of shattered dreams, to watch the world's demise

In empty rooms
   of growing gloom, the night begins its dance
infected foes
   a sickness grows, like a boil to be lanced

Night upon night
   allows no light, where shadows are between
alas the play
   end of day, while the movements stay unseen

Chains that bind
   inside the mind, to a depth beyond sane thought
hear her scream
   lost in dream, what disbelief has wrought

Beware the voice
   without choice, that lies with promised pleasure
have faith in proof
   by hidden truth, awakening the treasure

It comes to see
   as gentle plea, to join in hideous rhyme
an offered hand
   from nowhere land, a place of empty time

She challenges you
   oh enigmatical hue, inside the dark of light
nocturnal surrender
   can't remember, freedom from the night

Shadows dancing
   ever prancing, fearful of the sight
hiding well
   in nighttime dwell, phantoms dead delight

Through tests and trials
    and endless miles, the learning was delivered
no one to find
    her distraught mind, as it is slowly slivered

A war unseen
    in worlds between, one small angel to prevail
but win she must
    with naught but trust, with no allowance can she fail

Through darkness deep
    still they creep, insatiate shadows breed
forever night
    undeliverable flight, implanted insane seeds

No one is freed
    from evil deeds, and at endless corners glance
poor angel caught
    her heart was taught, beware when shadows dance.

# CHAPTERS

# PROLOGUE

The entity stood alone. Surrounded in an aura of pure white light, he watched intently as a nurse gently placed a newborn child into its mother's waiting arms. The watchful being was momentarily interrupted when another circle of light carouseled into view, and joined him. As if turning a dimmer switch, the lights around the two beings became less and less until it revealed, at first glance, what appeared to be two very ordinary-looking men. The first one stood nearly a head taller than the one who joined him, and was dressed in a simple light-colored robe. He turned to face the second man, his light gray eyes holding a strength and wisdom never known to any man who had walked on mortal soil. The man who joined the first looked upwards at his elder with a deep reverence and respect, waiting as always, with an impatient patience for the elder to explain the reason for his summoning.

"She is a very small child isn't she?" The younger waited, knowing that although a question was asked a response was not required.

"This is the child that we will protect until we have need of her services. Before you ask me why, which I know you will, I will tell you that the exact reasons are not yet clear to me. I do know, however, that there is going to come a time in her life and ours, when an evil upheaval will turn both worlds upside down, and threaten our very existence." The younger absorbed the words of the elder, and then formulated his first question. He knew his allowance for questions was limited to two, so he had to be very careful in the choosing. He continued to watch the bonding of mother and child while he too took pleasure in the miracle of birth. He sensed there was something special about this child, but there also came an underlying sense of uneasiness with that knowledge.

"Her light is bright for a human child, the brightest I have ever seen, but there is something else. I sense a small piece of dark that thinks we cannot see." He did not pose his verbal observation as a question, but it required an answer.

"I saw it as well, and as sad as it will be, we will all need the strength that she is going to find in that darkness." This response caused the second to brighten his aura for just a moment as if the light was helping him to decide his second and final question. It wasn't that they were not allowed to ask questions, it was simply that this particular guardian would continue to ask them, never being filled with enough answers. His curiosity put to test even the patience of the eldest of them all, so out of necessity, he always limited the younger to only two.

"Are you sure, great guardian, that she will stand to the test that is going to be set before her?" The eldest of all the ancient guardians raised his hand, and laid it on the shoulder of his most favored.

"David, you know as well as I that the road traveled between light and dark is a road always traveled alone. The strength is there, born to her, everything she will ever need to brave that dark path is already inside." The younger returned to watch the newborn child as she slept comfortably in her mother's arms, feeling a slight tremor of fear. He knew that not only were her life's tasks going to be set as a tremendous burden, but so would her fight against the darkness that hid inside of her. The aura surrounding the ancient guardians grew bright as they moved away from the woman and her child. The mother placed a light gentle kiss on the baby's forehead, and she held close to her heart the child she lovingly named Darien.

# CHAPTER ONE

# THE BEGINNING

The child stood alone in her backyard, her small little three-year-old mind totally fascinated with the way the snake undulated through the brown dirt moving itself delicately through the dry earth without the help of legs to make it go. The little girl followed it slowly as the snake made its way towards the man-made stone wall that separated her home from the adjacent piece of property. It slithered proficiently in between the rocks, and disappeared from her sight. Not one to be daunted from wanting to see more, the child began pulling stones from the wall, becoming quite excited to find out just where the snake had gone.

"Darien," the voice called to her, but it did not come from her house where she could see her daddy sipping liquid from a brown bottle, and talking with their neighbor. Her chubby little hand rested on the smooth dark stone, while hidden underneath a nest of snakes grew restless with the disturbance from above.

"Daddy?" When her father did not acknowledge her, she turned around and started to remove the stones one more time. When the voice came again it sounded like there was someone standing right next to her and the voice itself was gentle in its persuasiveness as it sounded her name.

"Darien." Her hand moved away from the stone just as a large snake appeared from underneath. At that precise moment, her father looked up and saw a dozen snakes emerging all at once from under the stones directly behind Darien. His beer bottle fell onto the cement stairs and shattered brown glass flew everywhere just as his wife appeared at their back door. Her eyes immediately followed her husband's Olympic run through the backyard. He went around the swings, jumped over the tricycle, nearly falling as he traversed the wading pool, finally snatching Darien up in his arms. Her mother came running up through the yard behind him, her breathing labored, her heart pounding at triple time, as she struggled with the extra weight of her seventh month of pregnancy. Darien's father kissed the top of her curly brown head, and handed the child to her mother while both of them just stared at all the snakes that lay basking in the warmth of the heat held by the stones.

"Oh God, Dennis, are they poisonous?"

"Yeah, I think so." His neighbor joined him in the backyard, and handed him a pointed shovel.

"Take Darien and go back inside." A warm breeze blew across the yard lifting her brown curls away from the little innocent face as she smiled over her mother's back at her father.

"Mommy, I see an angel."

"Your guardian angel, my little love," her mother whispered as she held her most precious gift next to her heart, and carried her to the safety of their home.

# PART ONE

Darien hated riddles.

She had always hated riddles, they were just too hard for her to figure out, and she hated trying to understand things that she was just not capable of understanding. Life was like that with Darien, one big mother fucking riddle that she could not figure out and one that she had given up hopes of ever finding an answer. In spite of that, she still walked through life trying to understand the whys, wherefores, and hows that produced the full circles, which made life exist on this place we call home. There were times when trying to understand the riddle that it would make her thought process run askew from terms that a psychiatrist would refer to as "normal" and Darien had always felt as though she did not belong, anywhere. She could be in the middle of changing a diaper on her daughter when she would suddenly drift off, entering what she fondly referred to as the "zone." In the zone, fragments of her past mistakes emerged, and the wonders of "why did I do that?" and more often than not was her most pondered question of "where do I fit in?"

There came a time in her adult life when everything began to fall apart, while at the same time, it all came together. If you were to ask her to give you an exact date as to when it actually started, would have been impossible, because it seemed to Darien as if her life was always falling apart. However, if you were to ask her for a date when everything finally ended, she would be able to recite day and time, down to the last second.

In addition, if you had a couple of hours to spare at the diner, she would tell the most fantastic story, while taking you on an adventure, which for the most part, had become a part of history. Moreover, if you were really lucky, at the end of her story, she might allow a small piece of the sun to shine.

Her young life was not that unusual. She was born to Dennis and Kathy in nineteen hundred and fifty-two, robust and strong, with lungs that could drown out an opera singer. For the first three years of her life, Darien did all the baby things, as all babies did everywhere, and it is a time in everyone's life when there are no recognized differences. We all cut teeth, cry when we are hungry, and are fed milk by either a fake rubber nipple or a genuine teat. We all messed our pants, and we all learned as we grew and if we were lucky, the first thing we learned was the soft warm smell of our mother, along with the sweetness of her love.

Then we learned differences.
We learned what gave us rewards.
We learned what did not.
We learned from our peers, the difference of color.
We learned hate.
We learned not to overcome hate and fear, but to succumb to it, and in the end
We learned despair and desperation.

Darien had a hard time understanding all of those differences. When you die, when we are sent to a final rest in the ground, and the worms come to feast upon our empty bodies, there are no differences. Therefore, the biggest riddle of life would become all encompassing to Darien until she was made to see the answers to who and what she was.

Somewhere in the early years was when it all started, and somewhere during her adolescence Darien became lost. She grew up without guidance, without love, and this would leave any person hard pressed to grow into responsible adulthood. It was a viable excuse as to why she ended up the way she did; however, one could also use it as an excuse not to be responsible for their actions.

It could have started the day her mother died. Darien was only four, and her father in the year of nineteen hundred and fifty-six had no idea how to care for his four small children. In those times, cooking, cleaning, and raising children was left to women. Men worked, brought in the money; while on the other hand, women stayed home and accepted their role as homemaker and mother. This was never disputed or argued, it simply was an accepted way of life. So instead of life with their father, the children of Dennis and Kathy were sent to live with a cold harsh grandmother who believed in beatings as a form of discipline and love. There was a plentiful supply of swats to go around, which allowed the children to share equally in the learning process of respecting your elders. Darien never knew what it was like to receive a hug from someone out of pure affection, or to receive a kiss of appreciation or words of praise. It seemed as though the grandmother was as devoid of hugs as she was of feelings. When Darien's father remarried, it was to a woman who hid her alcoholism until they had gone several years into the marriage. Darien gained a quick education in learning exactly what that word meant. This new education process became the time in her life when she would hear, and forever remember what it was like for someone else to be on the receiving end of a beating. It was unfortunate that although those kinds of screams can be put into a kind of holding tank in the back of your mind, they are never forgotten.

Darien would also always be able to recall the nightmares of her father when he screamed in the middle of the night, jarring the family awake with a heart-thumping jump. She would remember the chills that traveled through her body when he woke the family with these cries of despair. The thing that puzzled her most was that although she did not know what caused the nightmares, she knew that the nightmares were the reason that he became an alcoholic. It would not be until many years later when visiting her grandmother that Darien would find out about her father's experience the day Pearl Harbor was under siege. The elderly woman would reveal how the explosions on the ship trapped her father in the engine room of the SS *California*, nearly losing his own life as he escaped from the unprovoked attack. Darien finally understood how the nightmares had become so haunting, and why the continuing battle to retain a degree of sanity was such a fragile delicate fiber. In later years she found herself wishing that she could have understood her father just a little bit more, but then, in her younger years she had never really cared. There were so many parts of her past sadness that continually haunted her, and some of the darkest memories were of her father's and stepmother's descent into an alcoholic's hell.

When her stepmother binged, Darien quickly learned to stay out of her way, because if you did not, then several well-placed slaps would help you to remember. However, there were times when confrontation was unavoidable, and it was after one of these violent attacks that she ran away into the woods and remained there until the sun started on its downward path. She did not mind sharing space with the bugs that lived among the leaves that she sat on, or the ones that hung from the branches in the bushes and trees. Actually, she took contentment in playing with them all afternoon, not caring about going home and definitely not caring if her father missed her. She watched the ants carry on with their daily life, and she wondered what it would be like to shrink down to ant size, wanting desperately to run and hide away from the world inside one of their tunnels. Her lazy contentment was interrupted when she felt a strange scratching on her leg, and instinctively she reached down to swat away whatever was disturbing her. Imagine her surprise when looking down and instead of a minute crawling insect, she was staring at a little toady-faced man who was poking her with his cane. She was not frightened or even startled, but more there was an acceptance because it just was, and the toady face was so tiny that it made Darien more curious than anything else.

"Darien," he said softly to her, "it's time for you to go home."

It could talk!

"I don't want to go. I don't like my house, mean people live in there."

"You can't stay in the woods all night; it will be too cold for you."

"Will I freeze?"

"Perhaps," he said with a comforting smile.

"Will I die?" she asked with wide-eyed child innocence.

"It is possible," he answered with growing concern.

"Then I want to stay."

"Darien, death is so cold, so final; there are too many great things ahead for you. Your father cares, and he is very worried about you. Please, let me help you to find your way back."

"Bullshit, Mr. Toady Face, my father doesn't care. He's probably pouring a shot of whiskey right now for him and my stepmother. They'll get drunk, and he will beat her and then tomorrow it will be my turn. I would rather sit here and die."

"He loves you."

"No he doesn't, he loves his drink." Mr. Toady Face sat down on the small rock behind him, appalled at the language. However, Darien had already lived more than most other girls her age, her life's education having put her far beyond the ten physical years that she was. The little crooked man pondered this for just a moment before deciding to take another route.

"Do you like playing games?"

"Sometimes I like 'em. When we all go outside at night and play 'Red Rover, Red Rover, let Bebe come over,' or the one that we want to catch." The little man listened with rapt attention, smiling and shaking his head in agreement, as if he had played the same game many times himself.

"Oh, and sometimes we play hide n' seek in the dark, or we raid the neighbor's peach trees, and did you know that they put in an alarm on account of we were stealin' too many of them. Nnnnn sometimes we do other bad stuff, but most of the time it's good."

"Won't you miss all of this if you stay here?" She had been smiling and animated while talking about her friends and playing together, but now that he mentioned going home, she grew quiet.

"I guess."

"You guess you might miss it?"

"Well, maybe a little."

"Come, Darien; let me help you find your way home." The young child did not realize just how far into the woods she had run, and was secretly glad that he offered to help her find her way. The tiny man had nearly disappeared into the encroaching darkness, and if it were not for the little light shining from his lantern, she would have lost him altogether.

To someone Darien's age, the walk seemed longer than it really was, but Darien still did not want to return to a home that offered her nothing more than pain. She suddenly voiced her reluctance at having to do so.

"Toady Face, can I go with you?"

"You already know the answer to that."

"Will you come and see me again?"

"If you really need me I will be here, not always where you can see, but I will be with you, or I will send someone who can."

"Like a guardian angel?" Darien quickly became excited as she told the crooked man about the time when she was little, and the snakes came, and her mommy said that her guardian angel saved her. (Not that she could really remember at age three, but it had become a favorite family story.)

"Are you him?"

"No, Darien, I'm not your guardian angel, but you do have one."

"It's my real mom isn't it? She comes to help me doesn't she?" Darien looked down as the strange crooked little man began to fade.

"I want to be with my mom."

"One day you will, but not yet. She wants you to live and to be happy; death is not always a quick way to being free."

"Wait, don't go, you said we could play a game." The little man was popping and crackling and fading in and out like a bad connection on a television set.

"You are playing a game, Darien, and the game is called life and it will be the grandest adventure that you will ever have." The little man disappeared completely and Darien was left puzzled by his game and his riddle, to her they seemed to be the same. But she knows that riddles are games, and Darien prepared to enter her game of life and her riddle for living. At age ten, Darien already knew all the swear words, and she thought how cool she sounded when she said aloud:

"Stupid fucking riddle." For the second time in her life the voice came to her, and using soft gentle tones it called her name:

"Darien" was all it said and she heard it as if he was standing right next to her, speaking directly into her ear.

"What?" she asked, feeling just a little anxious as she looked around. There was a glimmer of hope that the little man had come back, but she already knew that this voice was different than that of the toady face. It told her the beginning of another riddle that would end up being the puzzle, and the answer to her life.

"A light warm wind, a gentle breeze,
Is how it all begins
Then it will come as shadows creep
And bind the seraphims."

At first, she was not sure if she heard the riddle because it faded so quickly, leaving only one word in her mind, and that word was seraphim; however, before she reached her home that too would also fade. Darien did think though, that for whatever reasons, there was more to the riddle. It would be many years before the toady face would return, but when he did come, he would bring her solace and a sense of peace.

Her father was waiting for her when she stepped into the garage and as he started towards her, Darien believed for a moment that he was going to grab her and hug her to him, genuinely happy that she had returned home unharmed. Instead, all she received was a quiet gruff voice that asked if she was okay.

"Yes, Dad, I'm fine."

"Your dinner is on the table." That was it, not another word was said about why she had run away that day, where she had gone to, or the reasons behind it. However, from this point on she began to defend herself against the beatings, and when she couldn't hide away physically, she would hide away inside, and unknowingly she gave birth to the different personalities of Darien.

The years quickly passed, and as she became older, Darien would automatically tune out her immediate surroundings every time their arguments started, and following the arguments would be the inevitable beatings. It wasn't long before she started spending less time at home, staying overnight with any friend who would have her. The prolonged absences from home continued well into her sixteenth year, when Darien's life would take another drastic change.

At sixteen she became of working age, found a job, earned her driver's license, and shortly afterwards purchased her first car, a nineteen-sixty

Corvair. It was an amazing thing for her to accomplish, or so she thought, and when she drove into the driveway, her pride of accomplishment showed in her smile. Imagine how astonished she would be to find that in nineteen ninety-four her old oil-burning car would have become a collector's item. With her first car, and her first job and her first paycheck came her independence. How grown up she was at sixteen! Her friends took her out, and she learned to follow in her father's footsteps, and shortly thereafter was able to experience her first drinking and vomiting binge. Darien very slowly and very deliberately set upon a path very similar to her parents' that would begin to lead her very close to her own self-destruction. So while her father and her stepmother sat at home drinking, Darien would be out and about drinking and driving. In the late summer of her seventeenth year, her stepmother died from alcohol and drug abuse. Four short months later she watched helplessly as her father followed, leaving Darien alone in a world of darkness and pain. She searched diligently for acceptance with her friends, with their families, and with anyone who showed the slightest bit of interest in her, and it was during her first big crush and the inevitable breakup that Darien realized the personality of Sibby.

Sibby was annoying, and she had an insatiable hunger for affection, craving attention, any kind of attention. So when attention from boys meant giving them what they desired, Sibby gave willingly, endlessly, without question, and believed inside her heart, that these boys or one of these boys would eventually like her.

The next two years passed in a confusion of realities, while Darien searched for someone that she could hold onto, someone solid instead of the dreams that were her only solace in a world of loneliness and pain. Her own drinking reached proportions that would have staggered even her father, and she spent seven nights a week in the local taverns building a reputation and catching the disease called alcoholism. Her fear of being alone for the rest of her life grew with each passing day; her fear of not having a place to call home scared her even more.

She gave up her virginity to the first boy who said he loved her. This boy, or rather, nineteen-year-old man, abused her, beat her, and then said he loved her. Sibby cried when he left, calling him relentlessly begging him not to leave her, to take her back, promising that she could do better, that she would be better. In the end, he left her anyway, due more to the never-ending whining from Sibby than from anything else.

Darien would be vaguely aware when Sibby was in control, but was unable to control her appearance, forcing whatever partner she had at the time to become disgusted with the clinging dependency. Eventually he too would scorn the whining Sibby. Intermittently Darien would return and take control back from the sniveling whiner. She would stay strong for a certain length of time, but as soon as the next man showed even the slightest bit of interest, she would immediately accept him to her bed, release Sibby, and never quite understand why they never came back. At age nineteen, a short three years after losing her virginity, Darien slept with nearly sixty men, believing that each time a man touched her it would be because his feelings for her were real. She believed that each one truly wanted her for herself, and not for what he would find between her legs. Sadly Darien never learned the lesson of why they never came back, and it was incomprehensible to her that men wanted sex and nothing more.

Two short years of continued drinking without proper nourishment quickly took its toll on Darien's young teenage body. In an unfortunate turn of events, she became physically ill and ended up at the local hospital waiting to undergo emergency life-saving surgery. Her mental anguish outweighed her physical pain and in the end, her hopelessness and desperation consumed her. It was time to give up, time to join the rest of her family who waited patiently on the other side.

"Let me be free," she whispered to the only doctor who came to help her, "let me be free to fly." The sympathetic look on the face of the physician was more than Darien could understand, so trembling uncontrollably, she forced herself to sign the consent form that allowed the hospital to call the cold harsh grandmother. For twenty-four hours Darien drifted between leaving and staying, and during that time, the voice from eight long years ago came to her while her mind slept, and her body began to heal.

"Darien," he called softly to her, "I am here for you."

Darien opened her eyes and saw a tiny man sitting comfortably on the bed close enough to be seen, yet far enough away so as not to disturb her.

"I remember you," she said softly. He smiled at her and there were tears in his eyes. "Mr. Toady Face."

"I knew you would."

"I've been sick," she whispered to him as she slowly closed her eyes. He carefully walked up the side of her bed, and placed a soft kiss on her forehead.

"You're going to be okay."

"I wanted to die and they wouldn't let me." He sat down next to her head, laid his hand on her cheek, and watched as she drifted in and out of sleep. Her eyes rolled under closed lids, as her mind drifted through years past punctuated with nightmares of pain. The dreams brought her out of sleep, and she smiled when she saw the toady-faced man had remained steadfastly by her side. He recited the same riddle told to her many years earlier.

"A light warm wind, a gentle breeze
Is how it all begins
Then it will come as shadows creep
And bind the seraphims.

Do not fear the shadows dark
For they can be brushed away
Fear more the twisted evil thoughts
You think have come to stay."

"It is more than before, a harder riddle," Darien said softly to him.

"Yes," he agreed.

"Let me sleep now, little man, please, without dreams, without riddles and without pain." Mr. Toady Face gave her what she requested, and then lightly touched her forehead. He watched as her face smoothed out, and his magic left only healing sleep for Darien. Several weeks later, when she was feeling better, the hospital released her back to the care of the cold harsh grandmother and the defeated grandfather who came to take her home.

As soon as she entered their house, her mind flooded with childhood memories and Darien became that small child once again. She wandered into the living room, and without asking, her grandfather started a fire in the fireplace. Darien drew in the familiar odors of her grandparents' home, and despite the abuse of her earlier years, she began to relax, realizing that as an adult, the physical abuse was no longer an option for them. Unfortunately, the good feelings did not last long because her grandmother quickly reminded her that abuse comes in different forms. She could not do anything right, and Darien had a difficult time understanding why her grandmother had brought her there. However, whether one wants it or not, with life comes education, and eventually Darien would come to understand what the word martyr meant, and how her grandmother used it to her own benefit.

Only four short months later the continuing verbal abuse took its toll, forcing Darien from the only real home she ever had. A constant barrage of "you can't cook right, you can't dust right, for God's sake you missed a spot on the rug, don't touch my washing machine, you got the wrong brand at the store and why don't you go look for a job?" She returned to the only life of survival that she knew, and began to sleep with whoever put a roof over her head for the night. She also restarted the steady downward spiral of drinking, and among the bar crowd the men always knew who would part their legs for free sex, if you knew the right words. Deep inside Darien knew what she was, but continued to hope that a caring man would come, rescue her, and give her a home. There were fairy tales about knights in shining armor, about the rescuing of fair maidens, and somehow Darien kept hoping that there would be a truth inside the tale.

Instead, Darien realized the personality of Mary. She emerged as the experienced woman hiding inside the young body, and this personality knew her job well. Mary became the seductive, sensuous side of Darien. She knew how to walk with just enough swing on her round little bottom to attract a man's attention, and she knew how to be a rapt listener, as if no one else on earth was as smart or as intelligent as the man she was talking and listening to. Mary knew how to lean in towards a prospective partner, and accidentally touch her breast to his arm, letting him have a brief example of what was yet to come. Mary was also particularly attracted to married men; they always seemed to make the best partners, and excited her enough to comply with all of their wishes.

Mary, the giver of free love, wanted to fuck them all, and inside Sibby would start to cry, already feeling the pain of separation that would inevitably come when that man would leave her bed never to return. Poor lost little Darien wanted only acceptance, to be held, and to curl away safe and warm inside someone's arms who really cared about her. Someone who would love her for who she was. The married man that danced with her that night wanted her to spend some time with him in his car, but it was raining outside and Darien needed a place to stay. Mary emerged to become the center of attention, playing and flirting while all the time looking for a prospective bed partner, and that was when she met Jack. He would become her knight, but his armor was far from shining. Darien was always attracted to taller men, and for her that was anyone over five foot five, considering that she herself was barely five feet tall. Even with a lack of height, she always stood out in a crowd, her achievement being that of her brightly dyed red hair. The second reason was that Darien was also partial to men with lighter colored hair, usually light brown to blond and brown eyes, and she especially liked it when their bodies were lean and hard. Darien herself came in at one hundred and eighteen pounds, a little overweight, but she was solid and strong. She was also very experienced at finding and seducing the type of man that excited her.

Jack came into the bar on a rainy Friday night, and he watched her from the bar, intrigued with the young woman who so openly flirted with all the men. He approached her, asked for a dance, and during their conversation Darien found him to be as lonely as she, but he lacked the physical appearance to which she was accustomed. Jack was a short man, leaning towards the heavy side with long dark brown hair, and blue eyes. Nothing appealed to her physically, but he did have a place where she could sleep for the night, and she would pay for that dry room with her body. So when Jack asked her if she wanted to go to his apartment, Darien answered "yes" gratefully.

The strange part in all of her experiences at seducing men to her, or rather their beds, was that neither Darien nor Mary (when she stayed out) ever experienced an orgasm. Darien spread her legs, which she knew they expected, but as far as wanting the excitement to continue, there was none after penetration occurred. Oh, they all bounced, and pushed, and exploded and collapsed; however, while all this grunting action took place Darien would just lie there and wait for them to finish. She did not know that she was supposed to move; if she had known, then maybe she might have become excited. Or maybe the movement would have come natural if they continued the excitement. So until Jack opened her to oral sex, the only way she ever experienced an orgasm was through her own masturbation. Despite her excellent ability to seduce men, Darien had no idea what a satisfying relationship should be. In the end, the act of intercourse or making love, or for her, having sex, simply became "The Fuck." There never was anything else.

Jack and Darien ended up together through an unusual series of circumstances. There was no actual dating, but more of a hanging around through mutual friends. They continued to share of themselves, but never mentioned love. Eventually they fell into a relationship, shared an apartment together, and Darien decided to stay with Jack. She had a permanent roof over her head, found a job, and she stopped drinking. She worked ten-hour days, six days a week, and came home on Friday and Saturday nights to an empty apartment. She grew tired of the bar scene, and wanted a life at home with Jack, and Jack wanted a home, but he also wanted someone who would clean and cook for him. Darien likened it to Free Maid Service, with a fuck thrown in. However, she also reasoned that it wasn't so bad, because after all, Jack did give her the first orgasm through oral sex. He had also stayed with her when no one else would, and that alone must mean that he loved her. Darien honestly thought that this was how love was supposed to be. How could she have known any difference? This is how it ended up, after twenty-five years of marriage, that she never verbally told Jack, once, that she loved him. Her life with him became a simple acceptance in what was.

Eventually Darien decided that she wanted to have a baby. She had been very protective of herself in all of her wanderings, and in all the shameless nights of finding a place to sleep, she made sure there would be no babies. Having a baby without understanding the responsibility was the last thing that she had needed, but with Jack, it became all she could think about. Darien wanted someone who would be waiting for her when she came home, someone who genuinely needed her love and support, and she wanted desperately to have someone who would love her in spite of who and what she had been. Without telling Jack, Darien deliberately became pregnant.

The first time the nurses placed the warm bundle on her belly, it burst the dam releasing a flood of emotions. Protection was first in her thoughts, accompanied by a surge of love that was so strong it threatened to overflow and break her apart. The tears came for the tiny baby that turned her inside out, and she did not understand all of the changes that she immediately began to go through. She silently vowed to keep her child as safe as possible from the hideous outside world of drinking. She vowed to be there for them, not like her parents, and not like Jack. Darien found drugs to be a waste of time, and it scared her to even think of experiencing what others her age had done. She would do everything that she could to keep her child safe for as long as possible. Darien's daughter became her life, and every place she went, in everything that she did, the child came first, and nothing else mattered. In her need to nurture, to protect, and in making the child her world, she pushed Jack further away. As unintentional as this was, it would inevitably have a lasting effect on their relationship. When the time of recognition finally came, the result would be irreparable.

Darien became pregnant for the second time when the first baby entered her second year, and it was during the second pregnancy when the nightmares returned. Darien would often get up in the middle of the night, partly to relieve the extra pressure on her bladder and partly to splash cold water on her face after one of her nightmare attacks. This second pregnancy was making her physically ill, the first child relentlessly demanded her undivided attention, and of course, Jack never helped. He still went out for his Friday night drinking binges, never being able to stay away from the bar, and Darien despite her life education, never fully realized how overwhelming it would all be.

It was the middle of winter and on a particularly cold night she woke at four a.m. A sudden blast of bitter wind rocked their house, and Darien shivered unintentionally as she walked slowly down the stairs. The fire flared in the old-fashioned gas space heater, and it brought some warmth to an otherwise emotionally cold home. The flames cast shadows on the bare wall, and they moved, intertwining in a dance of ups and downs. She watched in total fascination because it appeared as though there were human shapes hiding inside those shadows. They moved, but not with the burst of flames, but in a pattern that they were creating on their own and she stood thoroughly entranced by the twisting turns of the intricate dance. Darien absently pulled out a dining room chair, and sat down heavily with the swelling in the sixth month of her pregnancy. She watched the dance of the flames, nearly hypnotized with their erotic actions, and she absently rubbed her belly while her mind drifted and she entered the "zone."

She was sixteen again, still an innocent, and her boyfriend, John, held her hand as they walked through a large apple orchard. It was late September, but the night was warm, and the air heavy with the sweet smell of over-ripened apples. Darien's little heart thumped, jumped, and skipped a beat when Johnny suddenly turned and pulled her to him. He kissed her deeply, and she was lost in a sea of rampant feelings that at sixteen, she was not emotionally ready to deal with. John laid her down on the ground, and covered her body with his and she trusted him completely. There were no thoughts of right or wrong, there were only feelings, and Darien was running an emotional high as her body responded to his mouth and to his touch. Suddenly John stood and moved away from her, and Darien sensed his absence before she opened her eyes. He stood with his back to her. He did not move, didn't turn around, and it was only his voice that drifted across the space that separated them.

"I have never seen anyone become as lost in their feelings as what you just did, and I could have done anything to you that I wanted, but I won't. I care too much about you to ask for something I don't think you're ready for."

"I don't know how to answer that." He finally turned around, and the bright light from the full moon seemed to cast a warm glow around the young man, who, if it had been anyone else, would have educated her in the importance of a man's penis. Instead he held out his hand, helped her to her feet, and then put his arm around her as they walked slowly back to her car. Darien was at a loss to understand the reasons why John stopped his advances only because this was all new to her and to the feelings he began to arouse. She had been especially surprised at the way her body responded to a man's expert touch, almost as if it were no longer hers to control.

Two months later John died in a car accident, and Darien lost the only one in her life at that time who honestly loved her. Her thoughts of love and John brought her out of the zone, and she became aware once again of her swelling belly as the movement inside reminded her of the growing life. Her heart fluttered each time the baby kicked, and the bond of love and protection for her second child grew as strong as the first. The shadows that only moments ago resembled human shapes that danced along the walls were now nothing more than a reflection of normal flames, and her stomach rolled with the relentless nausea of her pregnancy.

Darien hoisted herself from the chair and walked slowly to the bathroom while trying to swallow down the dinner that threatened to erupt from her stomach. She turned the old cracked knob to run cool water in the white chipped porcelain sink and splashed it on her face. As she reached for the towel, her reflection in the mirror caught her attention. The water droplets seemed to freeze halfway through their drip, and Darien became fascinated with the image that looked back at her. Her lips and face were slightly swollen with the water retention caused by being pregnant, and she stared at eyes bloodshot from a lack of sleep. She stopped coloring her hair the signature bright red, and at twenty-four, going on forty, she discovered the first few strands of gray. A year earlier Darien found a full-time job in a factory, but the insurance money they provided didn't even come close enough to help her pay the impending hospital bill. She wondered what her life was going to be like with two babies, a full-time job and how they were ever going to have enough money to get through it all? She raised her hand and touched the mirror image that reached up and touched her in return. Her hopelessness in the situation threatened to overwhelm her, and all Darien could do was sigh and shake her head. Her children had no grandparents; there was no one to help them. Darien was with her children on a constant round-the-clock basis, and her husband—well, he was still running around with his friends when he should have been at home. Darien slowly forgot who she was as a person and the more she stared at her mirror image, the more she became convinced that she would never really know.

The face that looked back was hers, but only for a moment, then it started to waver and change, becoming that of a small little man. It was the same miniature man who sat on her bed nearly six years earlier, the same little man who convinced her to fight for a life meant for a different destiny.

"I remember Mr. Toady Face." He smiled at her, a smile that she remembered and was grateful for.

"Have you come to finish playing the game with me?"

"Your game has barely started, Darien."

"Sometimes I feel as though we need to finish."

"I know that it's been hard for you." Darien shrugged her shoulders in recognition of life being what she made it.

"Why don't I ever remember seeing you, until I see you?"

"Now you're making riddles. That answer lies inside you. I have no power to block myself from your memory, but I have come with a warning of what is yet to come. The next part of the riddle has begun, and you would do well to try and remember it; however, I can't force you, I only ask that you try." And with that warning he began to recite:

"A light warm wind, a gentle breeze
Is how it all begins
Then it will come as shadows creep
And bind the seraphims.

Do not fear the shadows dark
For they can be brushed away
Fear more the twisted evil thoughts
You think have come to stay.

In the past you made a few mistakes
For which you will atone
But they must not rule the here and now
Stop hiding in the 'zone.'"

"That is a stupid fucking riddle and by now you must know how much I hate them, and it's still not finished." Mr. Toady Face started to fade away in exactly the same way that he had done before, with a crack and distortion of the same bad connection.

"You're right, it isn't finished, but Darien, you must try to remember, you must try to remember, you must try to remember…" His voice faded away, and she was left seeing her mirror image once again, and that image was beginning to border on hating what it saw.

"Stupid fucking riddle, stupid fucking Toady Face." She went back upstairs and fell into a troubled sleep of dancing flames that touched but did not burn, and the pregnant woman danced inside those flames, a touch of dark evil growing from its beginning implantation. Her hand roamed and caressed the swelling of her naked belly, while her mind tripped inside the dark, her thoughts of sexual perversion brought the shadows who danced with her, daring her to answer their deformed persuasion. She dreamt of different worlds where only her mind could fly and the Toady Face riddled her with words of puzzlement. Darien had long since buried Sibby and Mary, refusing to allow them the privilege of her children and upon waking the next day, Mr. Toady Face joined the ranks of her dreams along with her buried personalities.

In the meantime, the chores of everyday living took precedence in her life and Darien began to wish for twenty-eight-hour days. It was good that her love for her children outweighed any obstacle that fell into her path. She loved holding, bathing, feeding and hugging her babies, and the words "I love you" flowed freely from her mouth to their ears as Darien knew these words encompassed true feelings coming from deep inside, where her love for them was genuine. Jack and Darien married, and she was happy to have a wedding band on her finger and a committed father for her children. She also honestly believed that Jack would change with that commitment, but in the matter of her home and her children, life became harder. It would be many years later, when her children were grown and ready to go out the door to begin their own lives, that she would give them a warning she never had.

"Find the right one, make sure he is everything that you need and want in your life, because you will never be able to change him."

Darien continued working a full-time job and had to recruit a stable babysitter for her daughters. She grew into an overprotective mother, and wherever she went that was not work related, her children went with her. Her husband, Jack, still did his barroom thing, staying out late on Friday nights and sometimes on Saturdays as well. Darien spent many sleepless nights wondering if he would be able to drive home, wondering who he was with (possibly a she) and as the early morning hours crept in, she would wonder if he was ever coming home. The years went by and Darien and Jack drifted further apart. They were never a couple in love, so their drifting didn't really come as much of a surprise as she thought, more just an acceptance. Her attention to her children never stopped, but as she stopped caring about Jack, she also began to stop caring about herself.

In all the time they were together, Jack never even asked her if she would like to go to dinner. He never said to her:

"I think you need a break Let me find a sitter and we'll go out tonight." He never asked her to a movie or tried to provide any kind of relief for her, and Darien wasn't even sure if she would have gone out with him because every free minute she had, she wanted to spend with her children. As her daughters became older, Darien missed not having that small soft bundle in her arms so she actually asked Jack how he felt about her having another baby. He merely hummphed and replied:

"Do what you want, Darien, you always have." Darien became pregnant for the third time, giving birth to another healthy baby girl, and finally she felt her life complete. The children's activities kept her busy, too busy to think about anything else but them, and the day-to-day living became automatic as the years flew by.

The gray hairs started to become more noticeable, and Darien began slipping further and further onto her own side of the bed, wanting to have nothing more than a good night's sleep. She substituted food for the missing affection in her life as she started to realize that hugs from her children were not enough, and not the same as hugs shared between a man and a woman. In the end, sex joined the ranks of a household chore, rather than the pleasure of sharing between two people. However, she was still determined to hold her family together at whatever cost to her own emotional stability, simply because they are her family. The result of her overindulgence in the spoiling of her daughters was to push Jack even further away, and in retaliation, he became verbally abusive with her. His mean spiteful words were used intentionally to cut deep emotional pain. This abuse peaked with ugliness when her best attempts to look nice were greeted with his lastingly haunting words:

"No matter what you do, Darien, you will always be ugly." Verbal slaps came natural to him, and he seemed to delight in battering her with a constant barrage of belittling words like "stupid" and "idiot," in front of their children. None of it made sense because Darien went back to school, earned her high school diploma, and had even started taking some college classes. Still Jack never missed a chance to shame her, whether it was at home, in front of their friends and family or out in public. She doubled her resolve to remain strong for her children, and tried to steel herself against his constant criticisms, but eventually those criticisms began to crumble her wall of resistance.

Christmas remained Darien's favorite time of the year, and she loved the wonder of the holiday. Her house filled with the good smells of holiday baking, and the excitement generated by the children's expectations was catching. Then there was Jack. Darien refused to let his sullen attitude dampen her exuberance at this magical time of year. It was also at this time that she relaxed and enjoyed the comfort she found in her little home, enabling her to block out the nightmares that were now coming alive to haunt her waking hours.

As the months passed, Darien's mind refilled with self-doubts, and then her children felt free to verbally abuse her the same way their father did, and calling her "stupid" or "dumb" became an everyday occurrence. This repetitious abuse started to find a permanent place inside her mind, as it had many years prior, and she wondered if her life was worth anything at all? The decisions that used to come easy for her before were now difficult to make, and once made, even more difficult to do.

Her nightmares continued, and her past came back to haunt her more than ever. Now every time Darien looked in the mirror she saw an ugly, worthless human that had fucked up her life so bad that all she deserved was punishment for her sins, or perhaps not to be at all.

The nightmares increased.

There were dreams of flying, dreams of falling, and then waking just before she crashed upon the stones of her wasted life. There were dreams that gave over to thoughts of finally being free from a life that was only a cumbersome chore. These dreams haunted her continuously throughout the daily drudgery of being factory laborer, wife, and mother. She was rushed, totally overburdened with normal day-to-day living, and the face that looked back at her from the mirror was pained and lonely.

Trapped, with no way out and nowhere to go.

Darien put out a good impression, but it was the thoughts running rampant through her mind that pulled her apart. Her daughters grew into the strong, independent girls that she wanted them to be, but they also grew away from her, and she fell back into desperation to hold someone to her that she could love.

The years continued to fly by and it was nearly twelve years since Darien first entertained herself with thoughts of dying as she lay on the emergency room cot. She remembered being barely able to see as the burning pain rocked her body to trembling. Once again, she looked to her mirror image, and this time she saw a tired, worn-out, exasperated, overweight woman that really was worth nothing. She put her hand up to the mirror that held her, for just a moment, in fascination of how much twelve long hard years of working changed her features. She began once again to have thoughts of death and dying and those thoughts came every time she saw the old frazzled woman who stared back at her from the other side of the mirror. It turned into a face that Darien hated to see. Then one morning, much to her surprise, the face that looked back at her was not her own. She was not frightened as she beheld the strange little man whose features were slightly crooked; instead it reminded her of an old nursery rhyme.

"There was a crooked man who had a crooked house."

"Hello, Darien." He spoke to her and Darien was not at all surprised because she already knew that she was taking a road trip to the other side of sanity.

"Hello," she answered as she began to wash her face. The voice of the little man sounded familiar but she could not quite place it.

"Dumepa, dumepa, dumpadedo, I have got a riddle for you."

"Hey, you're not toady face, you're an Oompaloompa."

"I'm here to let you know there's more to your riddle."

35

"I'm not good at riddles and you're not real, so it doesn't really matter does it? Besides, I can't even figure out my own life, which is one big idiot riddle." She returned to washing her face, hoping that the stupid little man would be gone when she looked back up.

"Darien." Her head snapped up from the sink, her face dripping with soap and water.

"I know that voice. Who are you, and why are you in my mirror?"

"You have always been quite forceful, intrusive, and independent, but now you must listen to me, and listen well. You must remember what I say to you." The voice that came out of the little crooked man's mouth was soft, gentle, persuasive, and it had a hypnotic effect on Darien.

"If the sun should fade away and die
The world would breathe and empty sigh
In a silent realm devoid of light
An evil grows from endless night

Unless you remain to be seen
Through pleasure/pain for little queen
The endless night becomes the day
And all of humankind will pay.

The suffering bequeathed will know no bounds
And screams in pain-unholy sounds.
Become the light you are meant to be
A savior for humanity.

Save them, Darien, save them all
A crumbling empire set to fall
The light flows out from within,
The release of Paul's Sweet Serephims."

"Remember the riddle, Darien, because a path of greatness lies before you. Riddles are simply puzzles that interlock to reveal a hidden picture in much the same way that the pieces of your life will eventually interlock and reveal your secrets. You must be strong, and you must survive. You must believe in yourself, and in the end you will understand."

"It's a different riddle than before."

"It is all connected, but you must figure out how." The crooked man faded and fizzed like a bad connection on their cable box.

"Wait, don't go, tell me who you are."

"When at last we meet, you will know me." Another damn riddle! He fizzed out like their connection was suddenly broken; leaving Darien staring at her own worthless image while the riddle, once again, faded to the back recesses of her mind. She was, however, able to hold onto the last line that kept repeating itself in her head.

"The release of Paul's Sweet Serephims."

"What the hell is a seraphim?" she asked aloud. Darien ran from the bathroom, dripping water and soap as she went. The books on her children's shelf seemed to jump out at her as she pawed through them all looking for the one that would give her an answer. She could feel the pull in the tightening of her skin as the bubbled, caked soap dried on her face. She found it finally, the kids' dictionary. She opened the large tome and repeatedly pronounced the word as she hunted for the meaning.

"Ser, ser, sera…" Her finger followed down the words as she scanned the page hunting for the meaning, and she stopped at seraph and began to read.

**Seraphs – aphs – or aphim – or aphin 1. A celestial being having three pairs of wings.**

**Isaiah 6:2**

**2. One of the nine orders of angels. See ANGEL**

Darien quickly flipped the pages of the dictionary to the a's even though she already knew what an angel was, everyone does, but she looked at the definition anyway, and her eyes grew wider with each word that she read.

**1.** *Theology* **An immortal spiritual being attendant upon God.** (She had expected that, but the next line she did not). **In medieval angelology, one of the nine orders of spiritual beings (listed from the highest in rank to the lowest) serephin, cherubim, thrones,**

**dominations or dominions, virtues, powers, principalities, archangels, and angels.**
 **2. A guardian or a guiding influence.**

Darien read the meaning two, three, four times over. Nine orders of angels. God made ranks for his angels according to what, the value of their service? A vague thought came to her, and she remembered something about an army of angels, but she could not remember if she had heard it somewhere, perhaps from a time when her father made her attend Bible school, or if the knowledge came from reading. To Darien there were only two ways in life, one was good and the other of course being bad, and that was all. You either made it to heaven or you didn't, there was no in between, and now she saw that apparently there were different levels of good, so did that make different levels of bad? Did Lucifer have an army of demons to face off against God's army of angels? But wasn't he an angel of God before being cast down? What about the war between the angels? Darien was starting to rouse a real thumper of a headache, one of her special ones that would sit in one place and just thump thump thump thump thump in her head. She stared at the dictionary still tightly grasped in her hand and suddenly threw it as hard as she could. She watched as it nearly took flight, skimming across the desk, taking out pencil, pictures, along with a few shelved dolls.

"What a bunch of shit! Serephims my ass!" The downstairs clock played its melody of chime time, and Darien left to pick up her children from their various after-school activities, and amid the screeching and yelling her head would continue its thump thumping. Jack would come home, pop a beer, and then settle in front of the television to wait for his dinner. Darien, after her own eight hours of working, would continue her hectic schedule as she cooked, cleaned, washed clothes, made the girls bathe, helped them with their homework, and listened to their stories from school.

In between Jack would scratch his balls, pop several more beers and continue with the evening's televised entertainment.

Thump Thump

Darien would crawl into bed around elevenish, and Jack would reach for her. Nothing had changed, and just like so many years ago she would spread her legs while wishing that it were over.

Thump Thump Thump Thump Thump Thump

However, instead of nightmares tonight as she slept, her dreams would be full of light, full of softness, and full of gentle touches. The angels had come, the serephims who would touch her heart. The angels brought her a sense of deep abiding peace, and then suddenly they all began to fly away.

"Don't go," Darien whispered.

"Don't go." Her eyes squeezed shut and a single tear rolled out.

"Don't go," she whispered inside her troubled sleep.

"Please don't go." But they did go, they were free to fly, they were free to fly away from all that was terrible in life. Darien ran after them, begging them to stay for just a little while longer, and she found herself wishing desperately for her own pair of wings.

# PART TWO
# PRESENT DAY

It was morning again, almost as if it were not supposed to happen.

Darien heard the repetitious sound of the hair dryer, knowing it was time to get up, yet wanting to stay in bed forever. The drapes kept her room dark as she tried to push back the beginning of the day. It was the same dream, always the same dream, and in that dream Darien was always falling. However, it was not in a state of screaming horror that one would think constituted falling in a dream. She was falling fast; her hair stood straight out from her head, and her nightclothes followed in the same direction as her hair. Darien knew why she wasn't afraid, and that was because she had heard many times before and had often told the same story to others, that if you ever died in your dreams then you would die in real life. Darien wanted to fall, she really wanted to hit bottom, and never wake up.

There were many dreams and nightmares for Darien, and as she lay quietly in her bed she remembered that she had dreamt one time of war, of an invasion that reached her home. The soldiers were not of any "official" type army because they did not wear traditional fatigues. They wore black pants, shirts, and wool caps, resembling movie rebels that hide in secret, a known part of the underground. Darien came running down the stairs, worried for her children's safety. She suddenly came face to face with the invading rebels, and immediately shocked herself in place on the bottom landing, terrified. When one of the rebels turned to look at her, she slowly backed herself into the farthest corner of the small step down. What she saw in his face set coldness in her, as cold as any death could be. He saw her with eyes that reflected nothing more than total indifference. Everything began to happen in slow motion as the rebel raised his weapon, took aim on Darien, and slowly began to squeeze the trigger. The gun belched its bullets and Darien watched it spit deadly fire. Suddenly she was standing beside the rebel, watching as one, two, three, four bullets entered the Darien still standing in the corner. It was as if her soul had left her body, and she watched in terror as the Darien in the corner moved in continued slow motion. Her head flew back on impact, her shirt ripping where the bullets tore through her soft skin, blood emerging from the fresh wounds. She looked up the stairs and saw her children staring in mute horror as the penetrating bullets flung their mother about like a stuffed rag doll. Her body bounced against the walls at the bottom of the stairs, and when the gunfire finally stopped, she fell, crumbling as a lump on the landing.

Darien woke with a startling jump, her soul falling back into itself, and she opened her eyes to see the ceiling circling in her bedroom. She waited for her breathing to slow, and for her temporarily dislocated thoughts to ease their way back into her reality. She blinked her eyes while the quiet that was so prevalent in the middle of the night settled in around her, and it seemed that even with her children and her husband, Darien still became victim to an intolerable loneliness. Her nightmare left her heart beating just a little too fast, and she rolled onto her side only to find herself staring at her husband's back. She started to reach for him, and then suddenly stopped. Darien could never talk to Jack, and he never to her, so when all else failed she gave up and settled into a life with just her children. Jack worked every day, came and went as he pleased, talked to her sometimes, and fucked her when he needed, but neither of them knew how to love each other. There had at one time been kissing, and holding, but that time had passed, and now it was just repetition and release. Such a sad thing to lose between two people and yet he stayed, as did she, but then where was there to go?

She lay still in her bed remembering that nightmarish night until she became aware once again of the hair dryer, and now on top of that she heard the shower door slam shut. Darien threw back the covers, swung her legs out of bed, and sitting on the side, she thought of how nice it would be just to lie back down for another hour or two. The morning urge to pee came upon her, and it was putting her in a position that would not allow her to fall back asleep. She pulled the warm flannel nightgown around her short stocky body. It was warm and soft, reminding her of a hug, and Darien practically lived in it during the winter months. She sighed and glanced over her shoulder at the sleeping, snoring form under the comforter. The years seemed to have passed in a blink, and she wondered when they had drifted so far apart. Were they ever happy with each other?

"Where do you go when you're so far away?" she whispered under her breath. Darien pulled herself to her feet, slipped her nightgown over her head, and standing half-naked in the middle of the bedroom, she sighed as she looked down at her body.

"When did you stop caring about the way you looked? When did he stop looking?" She slid the plain white underwear down over her ample hips, and opened the top drawer of her dresser. Lined up inside were neatly folded rows of panties, and she thought that it was too bad that life couldn't be as neatly folded as this. But then where would the excitement be? Darien shook her head; sometimes things were just too confusing to have any reason. She slid on a pair of the clean plain white panties, and after hooking up a plain white bra, she moved it around until it comfortably cupped her ample breasts. She sighed again—plain, everything plain like her life. Her daughters started an argument downstairs, and the escalation in volume was in direct response to their escalating tempers. Every day it was the same until it pulled at her last shred of sanity and threatened to send her screaming into a safe sacred place of darkness. Darien turned her arms over and stared at her wrists knowing that she could never do what she was thinking.

"Mom! Come on!" The voice came barreling up the stairs. Darien looked at her breasts again touching the few stretch marks that still survived from one of her pregnancies. She stared at her reflection in the mirror for a few minutes trying to smooth down the ends of hair that stood out from her head.

"Is there any beauty left for anyone to see? Was there ever any at all?" She quickly pulled on a T-shirt along with warm jogging pants, and then she quietly opened and closed the bedroom door. She heard him snort through the closed door, which let her know that he was awake, but not ready to deal with the problems below. By the time Darien made her way down the stairs and entered the small but efficient kitchen, the usual arguments were already taking place.

"You're in my way."

"Well you're in mine."

"I was going to use the milk."

"I'm using it first," came the sarcastic answer.

Darien stopped and smiled. *How does anyone use milk?* she asked herself, and quickly decided against saying anything to them because no matter what she said to defuse the situation, the argument would only get worse. She reached for the coffeepot, the brewing already finished on the automatic cycle, and she sipped carefully on her much-needed eye-opener.

"Mom, brush your hair or do something before you take us to school." Darien put down her coffee, and went obediently into the bathroom, but not before she playfully stuck out her tongue at the one who had commented on her hair. She ran the warm water, quickly soaped her face, rinsed, while a quick glance at the image in the mirror showed her far more than she wanted to know. Darien left the relative sanctity of the bathroom, and entered back into the morning activities. She slipped her glasses on with one hand, reached for her coffee with the other, and grimaced as the sugary sweetness hit her mouth.

"Okay, who put the sugar in?" she asked. All of her children sat grinning at her, even the oldest who would often put herself above this kind of prank, being a mature sixteen-year-old, and nearly an adult. The middle one pointed to the youngest one.

"Did not."

"Did too."

"Yeah, well you told me to!"

"Okay, okay!" Darien could see this escalating into another full-blown argument and wanted to stop it before it started.

"Let's get going before you're all late for school, and I'm late for work."

She piled her daughters into the car, and after dropping them off at school, she returned home to take a quick shower before going to work. Darien turned the water on and waited for it to run steamy hot before stepping in. She anchored her feet firmly on the sides of the tub and put her head back as the water cascaded down her body. She quickly washed her hair, and then with a heavily soaped washcloth Darien scrubbed her arms, her breasts, and her fully rounded belly. Looking down she brought one leg up onto the ledge of the tub so that she could wash below. Imagine her surprise when the realization came that somehow, through the course of the morning, she had become excited. Damn, when did this happen? She could not remember the last time she felt this way. Usually if she felt like masturbating, it was because she was bored or tense, but never because she was actually excited. The funny thing was that Darien almost never masturbated with her hand, and she supposed the reason for that came from the "forbidden book" she read all those years ago. The book taught her all about masturbation, and how it related to the powerful explosions known as orgasms. After all these years she still remembered the name, *Deliver Us Annie*. It had been chock full of educational insights into the exploits of one Annie Matter, who learned at a very young age about man's importance to the world, and her deliverance into it. The book showed why women should rejoice in the strength of a man's penis, and according to the author, what a wonderful gift it was to women everywhere. She recalled the plain deep purple cover, how the tattered pages gave credence to its obvious overuse. After reading the smutty novel and conducting her own experiments, using her fingers for self-pleasure was something that she just never did. But this morning in the shower she felt different, and ever so slowly her hand crept inside, parted her labia, and quickly found the "spot." She marveled at the amazing little pleasure nub, and thought what a fascinating little thing this piece of excitement was! She held her breath as the tremors passed through her body like small jumps of electricity, and she could not help herself as her hand moved lower, her need rising and she gasped aloud. Suddenly there was a loud banging on the shower door, scaring Darien, causing her to cry out.

"What the hell are you doing in there, Dee? You got this place filled with so much fucking steam I can hardly breathe."

"Nothing, nothing, Jack. I was just getting ready for work." Darien felt her face burn hot with shame.

"You're going to be late, you're going to make me late, now hurry the hell up." Darien heard the toilet seat go down, and the bathroom door close. She quickly finished washing, and then shut the shower off. If she was excited before, she certainly wasn't anymore and Darien quickly dressed for work, almost forgetting the shower, almost.

Her day was hectic, and she was glad when four-thirty came so that she could grab her car keys and go home. Today though, more than ever, the thought of going home became extremely depressing. Darien pulled into the local grocery store already impatient with the idea of having to wait in long express lines. She always ended up behind people who accidentally picked up five items too many, or those who never brought enough money, and now had to cash a check. Darien grabbed one of the small baskets kept by the door for middle-of-the-week shoppers like her, and she moved quickly from aisle to aisle quickly picking up exactly what she needed. She checked her basket one more time to make sure that it was all there, and then headed for the express lane. A large man stepped directly in front of her cutting her off, and she had to bite her tongue to keep a string of profanities from leaving her mouth. She took two steps backwards to get out of his way, which in turn caused her a near collision with a small boy.

"Hey, lady, watch out!" he yelled at her, and suddenly Darien felt completely unbalanced. She gritted her teeth as she stood in line, and then as sharp as could be she heard someone call her name.

"Darien." It was said directly in her ear, as if someone was standing right next to her, and she turned to answer.

"What?" Unknown to Darien was that while she became lost inside of herself another express lane had opened, and the whole line behind her had moved over so that there was no one behind her. Who had called her? She turned back to her line thinking that there was a vague familiarity about the voice, so just to be sure she turned around once more to check, just in case someone she knew was there.

Darien started to think back into her childhood, as she did every time her stress level became close to intolerable, and she began to enter what her family fondly referred to as the "zone." She could vividly hear her stepmother arguing with her father. The words sounding as sharp and as shrill, as if she were once again a young girl standing in the living room. Darien remembered watching her stepmother wash down her Valium with several shots of whiskey, taking her into a high that would help her find the courage to begin the arguments with Darien's father. The stepmother would antagonize the poor man to the point where her spiteful words about Darien's birth mother would become unbearable for him to listen to. Then because of her viciousness, her father would beat the stepmother to make her be quiet. There was a time that he had so viciously attacked the stepmother that he ended up putting her head through the wall. While reliving all of this, Darien put her groceries up onto the conveyor, remembering her stepmother's screams. She took money out of her purse to pay for her purchases while hearing the hard slaps and punches along with the woman's agonizing groans. She picked up the grocery bags to leave the store, and realized that she did not remember doing any of it, except that the voice in her ear had sounded so real.

"Darien" was all it had said, but it had been deep and strong, definitely male. She left the store and headed for her car, the well-worn but practical eight-year-old four-door family sedan. Standard riding for the standard family. As she neared the car, she noticed movement near the right front fender, and to Darien it resembled a shadow, but it was a shadow that moved of its own volition, and seemed to change its shape. The closer she walked to the car the more she watched in fascination as this strangeness in the play of dark undulated, and the longer she watched, the more curious she became.

*Maybe,* she thought, *it's just a difference in the way the light is hitting against the curb as the sun goes down, or the shadow of the bushes moving with the wind. What else could it be?* Darien put her bags into the car, and then went to open the front door while looking around the parking lot. She was amazed at the variation in the clothes that people were wearing; some of the braver ones were wearing shorts trying to hold back the winter, while others were already wearing winter coats in preparation for it. The trees were nearly bare, and the quietness of the cold months yet to come was already settling down around them as nature began putting the earth to rest. A kind of melancholia crept into Darien, and she felt a chill of the wind sweep through her. It left the kind of chill that came and settled into you with a cold found only in the deepest of winter. Darien opened the car door and stood quietly with one leg in the car and one leg out. Her thoughts drifted with the odd sighting of the moving shadow, and suddenly she wondered what it would be like to take the highway home at seventy miles an hour, and just run her car right into a bridge abutment. It was this idea, this thought that gave vent to more shadow play, and for just a moment she thought she saw the same shadow shift. She watched intently as it deliberately changed direction, and suddenly Darien felt a soft gentle breeze, and the warmth of a hand that rested briefly on her thigh. As quickly as it all happened, it was gone. She shook her head, not even sure of what she had seen or thought she felt, and after climbing into her car, she quickly locked all of her doors and drove home.

The fighting at home between her daughters was a constant given, and she was so tired of everything. In the kitchen she put her head down and counted to ten while clenching and unclenching her fists. In this tense position, she zoned into another flashback. Her father was away, working far from home, while Darien herself was working at a local restaurant, putting in ten-hour days. The pizzeria where she worked had been extremely busy that night, and it had taken her forever to get all the dishes done, making it nearly midnight when she arrived home. Putting her key in the lock, she went to push the door open only to find that it was jammed from the inside. Darien sighed audibly as she put her shoulder against the door and pushed as hard as her tired condition allowed. She could barely move the object that was against the door, but she was able to get just enough room to squeeze inside. The dim light afforded her little sight; however, as her eyes adjusted she could see the outline of an overturned chair. Darien righted the chair, returning it to its proper place, and felt a chill creep down her back when she recognized the still form of her stepmother lying on the floor in the corner. Darien walked over to her, totally disgusted because she knew that the woman would be high on pills and whiskey again. But this time, what she saw caused a ripple of fear to run through her body. The woman was completely naked where she lay, and she had pulled a pole lamp over on top of herself. Her body was so still, and Darien leaned over repeatedly calling her name. After a few minutes of this, the drugged woman finally responded. She begged Darien not to be angry with her as the young girl helped her off the floor and guided her to bed. Darien covered the stepmother with a blanket and then she stood watching until she fell asleep. Once Darien was sure that her stepmother had finally fallen into a deep sleep, she left the bedroom, opened the refrigerator, and she took the first step to a path of her own self-destruction as she popped open and chugged a beer. She remembered her stepmother's funeral a few months after this event and of her father's funeral only four short months later. His passage into death numbed Darien, firmly planting the belief that no matter whom or what you loved, in the end, they would eventually leave. Darien was seventeen and alone. Her older and younger brother already lived with her grandmother, her sister was married, but none of them had any room for her, except that the state of Connecticut said differently, at least until she was eighteen.

Darien blinked her eyes, becoming aware of her youngest child by her side, and despite everything that was happening in her life, Darien deeply loved her children. It was overwhelming in its emotion, although she believed that she was slowly losing her grip on reality. It neared the time for her husband Jack to come home for dinner. He worked full time at night, and was too cheap to eat out and too lazy to make a sandwich to take to work, so he came home every night expecting a hot meal on the table. There was never a break for her from all of the cooking and cleaning, never a vacation, and the understanding of wife and mother became lost to her.

Later that same night after all the mundane repetitious chores were finished Darien sat down for a few moments' relaxation. She turned on the television and slowly leaned back into the softness of the sofa. As she began to relax she also began to remember what had happened in the parking lot, and as she put her hand on top of her slacks, she was surprised to find an extraordinary warmth making its way through the thin cloth. Darien quickly stood up and dropped her pants expecting to find, at the very least, a red mark. There was nothing to see, however, there was a spot that definitely felt warm to her touch. She moved her hand to another part of her leg, and it felt cool, well normal, and then back again to the same spot. It wasn't her imagination, it really was warm!

"What the hell touched me back there?" Darien switched off the television, and lay back onto the sofa as she closed her eyes. This was too much for one day. Her breathing slowed as she let the quietness of the night settle down around her. Darien's relaxation gradually deepened, and a line from a riddle told to her long ago came to the front of her mind, and she recalled the words said to her:

A light warm wind, a gentle breeze is how it all begins

The warmth on her leg was moving, no, not moving, it was spreading. She remembered the shower that morning and her hands started to move down her body traveling in much the same way as they had done earlier in the day. She ran one hand into her underwear, back in between the place that she so seldom touched. Darien lifted her T-shirt, and put her hand inside her bra, finding her nipple already aroused. Could it be that she was just cold or was she actually excited, or maybe it was a little of both? Her body came alive with feelings while her hand moved almost as if it weren't her own. She slid her fingers in between her labia, wishing again that both her fingers and her arm were longer, and she pushed hard on the same small nub of excitement. Tingly feelings jumped down her legs, and her breasts strained against the confines of her bra. The administrations continued until she released a quick orgasm, shuddering as she turned onto her side, almost closing her legs while making a small aaah sound followed by a little nmmp noise. She lay there for a long time feeling her pulse pound through her body, while the after effects of the orgasm pulsed in her place of release.

In the corner of the room, a shadow moved, and through the darkness there came a voice and it sounded directly in her ear:

"Darien."

It sent chills through her body.

Someone or something was watching.

\* \* \* \*

The next day was Saturday, and she considered it a "free day," usually hers. Darien was alone most all the time, but it was by choice, because she had closed herself off to everyone. She found that it made no sense to let anyone into her heart knowing what would happen if you did. Darien loved her parents despite the problem of alcoholism and drug abuse, and neither of them had cared enough to stay. She also loved her grandparents even though her cold grandmother had driven her out of the house with her old-fashioned ways of discipline and love. They too had not cared enough to stay. She mistakenly thought she loved her husband; however, instead of leaving, he took an alternate route, and locked her out of his heart. Darien loved and was deeply committed to her children, but all too soon they wouldn't need her either.

She thought about these things as she walked through the park, enjoying the quiet calm of the early morning. The stillness of the pond drew her attention, and she ended up sitting by the water feeding the ducks the scraps of bread she always brought with her. Dark obscure thoughts suddenly invaded her mind, and she was unable to keep them from taking over. They caused her to wonder what it would be like just to fall into the water, to keep sinking until there was nothing left but blackness and complete peace. She remembered her dreams of falling, always falling, but never reaching the bottom, and Darien really wanted to crash against the stones to know if dying in dreams was a real way to die. What if death brought final coldness, and there was never again any warmth? But no, she refused to believe that, because out there was the mother who gave birth to her, the mother who died when she was only four. Somewhere out there was the mother who could hold her, love her, and dry her tears while telling her that everything was going to be okay. Up until Darien gave birth to her own children, she did not realized how much she missed not having a mother. She became deeply occupied inside her own thoughts that when the voice came, she wasn't sure at first that she heard it, until it spoke again. The same deep voice caused her skin to give rise to goose bumps.

"Darien."

She turned slowly around and saw a shadowy shapeless blob sitting on the ground right next to her. She hitched backwards on the ground and it moved and rolled after her, not unlike a small dark cloud. Darien sat staring at the thing next to her, and instead of being afraid, she felt a sudden sense of sadness for it. It was a shapeless black shadow, and she was not afraid, and then for reasons unknown to her, she felt compelled to speak to it.

"You have been following me haven't you? What are you anyway? I know your voice, I've heard it before. Can you speak to me other than to just say my name?" There was a long silence while the shadow thing rolled over and into itself, and then a voice came from nowhere speaking directly into her ear.

"I am a part of you, Darien, and I have always been with you. I have walked beside you for many years, and I have watched you run away from your life for as long as I can remember. However, now it's different, and your considerations to ending that life have become too real. As the need for this unnatural release has become stronger I have become more visible. You need me, Darien, and I can help you." Darien sat in stunned silence. She had expected yes, no, maybe, but not this degree of intelligence, and from, of all things, a shadow! How could any of this even be real?

"Help me? Hell, I don't know if you are real. What I really think is that just sitting here and talking to you could very possibly prove that I am losing my mind. This really must be happening. There's no other explanation."

"If that was true do you think you could feel this?" A part of the shadow thing brushed against her arm, and she immediately felt another warm spot.

"That was you in the parking lot by my car! Well, maybe I shouldn't be so surprised. You know there is a possibility that I'm hallucinating, and you're nothing more than a part of my hallucination." She sat staring at the strange shapeless black shadow wondering if she should continue to talk to it at all and then she wondered if it would really matter so much if she did. After thinking about this for a few minutes, trying to straighten out in her mind what was really happening; Darien decided that it really would not make any difference because when you're lost inside madness anything is possible.

"You know I sometimes fall into a place that my family has nicknamed the 'zone'. It's where my mind encounters flashbacks of my childhood and my teen years. How do I know that you're not just a forgotten part of my flashbacks?" She stopped and looked at the shapeless shadow blob that moved and rolled beside her. It brushed up against her side while bringing to her a slight warm breeze, and Darien felt a sudden kinship for this shadow thing, almost like it was becoming her pet. Instead of mistrust or not believing in a stupid mental illusion that she was trying to make real, she instead found herself saying, "I must really be out of my mind to tell you this, but I guess it will be okay if you want to hang around for a while. I suppose having you to talk to is better than not having anyone to talk to at all, even if you are only in my mind." Darien shifted her position on the ground so that she could look directly at the small shapeless blob.

"So shadow thing, have you got a name, something I can call you other than shadow thing?"

The shadow thing let out a burbling noise that sounded somewhat like a laugh. "Call me Ishmael." Darien laughed at the strange-sounding name. How odd, she thought, that it should pick a name like Ishmael. It made the laughing sound again, and then it said to her, "If it's easier for you just call me your friend." Darien laughed once more, and the shadow thing burbled, and for reasons not completely clear to her, she felt happy.

The shadow friend started to become a frequent visitor in her home, and always when Darien was alone. She would find it hiding in the corners, and sometimes when she cleaned it would brush its warmth up against her if only to let her know it was there. But most of all it talked to her. Darien began depending on him (she decided by the deep tone of the voice that it had to be a him) and knowing he would be there whenever she needed. When she closed her eyes at night and her dreams took her to the place where she was falling, she no longer wanted to crash at the bottom to find out if the dying was real. The best part in finding her shadow friend was that she was happy when she woke, there was more music played in her home, and Darien started to smile, a lot.

About a month after the shadow and Darien met, Darien's husband made the decision to tackle the much-neglected chores on the house and he sent her out to his shed in the back yard for a hammer. Darien could not find the damnable thing, and she slowly became nervous, fearing that she was keeping Jack waiting too long. She kept moving, putting and placing things rapidly back and forth until she felt herself becoming anxious and a little afraid. She didn't want to call him because he had already insisted that his hammer was out there. Darien was looking for a good fifteen minutes when suddenly the shed door flew open with Jack standing before her in a total rage.

"Christ sakes, Dee, how long does it take to find a goddamn hammer?" He bent down and moved a few rags that were lying on the table, and there it was.

"What the hell is the matter with you? Are you that stupid?" He looked directly at her and made a disgusted noise. "And how many times do I have to tell you that no matter how much make-up you wear you are never going to look any better." Jack turned around and walked back to the house, and Darien couldn't help it, the tears started to flow. Huge streaks of black mascara ran down her face, and wiping her eyes accomplished nothing more than to make herself look like an oversized raccoon. Then she saw it, a small pair of outside snips that she used for pruning. Slowly she reached over and picked them up. She picked up a large clump of her hair while moving the outside snips closer to her head.

"You don't deserve to have anything, Dee." She snipped off a large clump of hair and threw it onto the plywood floor. Her mind zoned into a place where even her own thoughts were gone from her, and picking up another handful of hair she said aloud, "You are so ugly, Dee, no one would ever want you." And she snipped again. She began crying so hard that she couldn't see anymore, and she just kept grabbing hair and snipping. Then without realizing it she called aloud for the shadow thing.

"Please come, I need you," she said to him between her sobs, and suddenly there were arms around her, big strong solid arms folding her inside, holding her while she cried. Darien pulled the shadow around her, a blanket of safety, and she held on. It continued to change, the torso becoming solid, and it began having a vague resemblance to a real person. It used its shadow hands to dry her tears and wipe her face. Darien reached up and put her arms around its neck and before she knew it the shadow thing kissed her cheek while pulling her back into its secure safe folds, and it was there that Darien stayed until she cried herself out.

"Dee! Get in here and put these kids to bed!" The angry shout came from inside the house and then Jack opened the back door.

"You put them to bed; they're your kids too!" The back door slammed shut, Darien jumped inside its arms, and the shadow thing that was becoming a man held her tighter.

"I don't care if you're not real, I don't care if you're just a part of my imagination."

"I am as real as you are," the shadow thing said softly to the mother of three.

"What are you?" Darien whispered inside of its warm softness.

"I am whatever you need me to be." The shadow man turned her face to his and placing one hand on each side of her face, he held it there while looking into her eyes.

"You are a beautiful woman, Darien; don't ever let anyone tell you anything different." He brought his newly formed lips to hers, giving her the barest taste of a kiss, and Darien quickly pulled away from him.

"I'm sorry, it's not you, it's just that it's been so long that I don't think I remember how. This is all so strange. I want to hold you, to kiss you, I really do, and you have been so kind and understanding. But I'm still having trouble with the fact that you might not be real, and I really could be crazy." She felt the shadow thing move, and then it swept around in front of her, stirring her hair, her clothes, creating a gentle breeze that left warmth everywhere it touched.

A light warm wind, a gentle breeze is how it all begins

"Darien, listen to me. There really is a beautiful woman inside of you. The outside is but a shell, and when that shell is gone your heart and soul go on. I can see to that beauty inside. I can see it when you touch the pictures of your children, when you look at the world around you and when you let your dog lie beside you. You need to find that wonderful you hiding somewhere inside and I have come to help that happen. There is an old Chinese proverb that goes, 'In order for others to love you, first must love self.'

"Oh, and did Confucius say that?"

"No," replied the shadow, "Mr. Miagi." Darien burst out laughing, and kept on laughing until her side hurt. The shadow man floated nearby smiling down at her while listening to the light freshness of her voice.

"Your laughter is a thing of beauty," he said to her, "as beautiful as you are. I think Jack might say those things to you only because he is afraid another man might find that out." Her smile vanished immediately as she quickly answered him.

"Nice try," she said sarcastically, "but I find that hard to believe."

"Believe it," he said to her, "I would never lie, and you have three lovely children who still need their mother. Eventually when they become mothers, they will be glad that you were there for them."

"Well, that too could be debatable." Darien looked at her shadow man, and he knew what the question would be without her asking.

"I can't help you with him," he said nodding to the house, "some people go beyond understanding and cannot open their hearts no matter how hard you try to help them. Your life with your husband is something where only you can make a decision."

"Can I come and stay with you?" she asked.

"You're not listening to what I'm saying, Darien, you are only hearing what you want to hear, and blocking out everything else. Listen to me; your children still need you."

"And I need you," she whispered to him.

"I will stay as long as you need me, but I don't want you to worry about that, because first we will work at making you strong again."

"What happens when I no longer need you, if that time comes?"

"Don't think about it, Darien."

"No, come on, that's not fair, you have come here to help me, and you've just told me that there will be a time when I will be better. So when that time comes and I no longer need you, I want to know what will happen to you." The shadow man floated down, and sat directly opposite Darien on Jack's workbench. The bottom half of the shadow's body moved in a circular motion, like a mini-tornado, which suspended the solid top half above the bench. He was grayish white in color, with the features of a man, reminding her of the fairy-tale bottled genie, and Darien wondered when and how the illusion became so real.

"Your question does need an answer. I will return to the place of shadows where the dark loneliness that we absorb from the ones we help is released. When we come to people like you Darien, we bring with us the warmth of goodness and a light of strength to help you heal from the inside because that is where the healing must always begin."

"You speak of we, so there are more? Are you a guardian angel?"

"I guess a guardian angel of a sort, and yes there are many of us. If it is easier for you to think of me in that context, then I will be your guardian angel. Do you remember when you were young, and fell off the raft at the swimming pond?" Darien shook her head yes as she remembered the previously forgotten memory.

"You came up under the raft, hit your head, and it caused you to become disorientated. I took your hand to lead you out, and I also protected you when the boyfriend you latched onto wanted you to sniff the brown bag full of airplane glue. I'm the one who made him pull it away before you permanently harmed yourself. I was there to protect you when your father died; you could have been hurt a lot worse than what you were. Remember all the nights when you were desperate for a warm place to sleep, and remember the motorcycle gang members that you met when you were eighteen? There were so many times in your life when you could have been seriously hurt or perhaps killed. As much as I wanted to, I couldn't protect you from everything, I couldn't stop everything from happening, but I did try to make them not as bad, except when you married Jack, I did my best to stop that from happening."

"You did?"

"Don't you know why he couldn't get the ring on your finger?"

"But we already had a baby and she needed her father. Jack even got up and walked the floor with them at three in the morning when they had colic. My shadow friend, I know Jack is a good man, and I know that he tries the best that he can, same as me. He goes to most of their school plays, and he has never ever hit me." She was quiet for a few minutes and said softly, "I know there have been times when I made him angry enough that he wanted to."

"And when, Darien, have you made him that angry?"

"I don't want to answer that." Darien lowered her head and refused to look at the shadow thing that had become her only friend.

"When was it?" he asked her one more time, his voice becoming a gentle persuasion.

"When I," she looked at him with tears shining in her eyes, "when I refused him sex." She lowered her head and looked away from the half-shadow man, embarrassed at having revealed such a personal painful choice.

"And why did you refuse him?"

"Because," she looked back at him, and the tears were no longer shining in her eyes, but they began to fall, "because there is no love." Darien looked at the shadow man, her eyes overflowing with sadness, and the tears came again, allowing her to release a great deal of emotional anger and sadness.

"Because," she said softly again, "there is no love." The shadow man became completely solid, and stood before her, a figure of sculpted beauty. His eyes were the deepest russet brown, and his smiling mouth gave her comfort in the midst of her despair. He swept Darien up into his strong arms, into the warmth of himself.

"I have that love for you, Darien, all that you need and more. You have lived too long without it. I can teach you to love; I can show you the amazing pleasure that can exist between two people. There is so much more waiting for you than what Jack had given. Please let me take you where we can learn again the secrets of your body, and in return you can learn the secrets of mine."

"But won't he..." Her sentence went unfinished.

"Don't worry, he will sleep for the night. You must trust in me as you have been, and in your heart you will see and understand that I will never hurt you. You know that I only want to help. This is, after all, why I am here."

Darien buried her face in his neck as he held her close, and the shed in which they were standing, along with her home, slipped slowly away until a sea of rolling clouds completely enveloped them. Darien felt no movement, she felt no wind, but the shadow man cast his shadows in every direction. She watched the clouds from the safety of his arms, feeling just a touch of fear tickle the pit of her stomach.

*What are you doing, Darien?* she asked herself. *Not another man has looked at you in twenty years, let alone touched you. Is he even a real man? Is what is happening to you real? Are you living a dream? Maybe you are really home in your bed and soon you will be falling, with the stones at the bottom coming closer and closer then just before you crash...*

They stopped.

Shadow man released Darien and she stood on solid ground.

"Where are we?"

"I have brought you to a place of dreams, schweet heart."

"Bogey, right?"

He smiled and nodded. "This is a place where you can rediscover the Darien that you've buried inside. I want you to release yourself to me. Let me inside of you so I can warm your heart and leave you open to experience all that you have denied yourself. Come with me, Darien, trust in me, and I will lead you into an ecstasy that you have never had before." He took her hand but suddenly she stopped and pulled away.

"I need to call you something besides Ishmael or shadow man."

"You mean you want a name, a human name, right?"

"Yes."

"Then choose one for yourself. There are hundreds, Darien, pick one, it's not that hard." Darien felt humbled by the shadow's most generous offer, but a bit frightened as well, and she could not deny the excitement he was evoking inside her.

"I will call you David. Not Dave, or Davie, for that you could never be."

*(She knew his name as if he had been with her from the very beginning.)*

*David.*

"It will do," he said with a smile on his face. "Wait a minute." He turned his head to one side. "I sense that your husband is waking." David looked at her a little hurt at what he was finding.

"You still do not trust me."

"I'm sorry; it's just that I'm afraid."

"Afraid? We've been together now as shadow and friend for many months and you are still afraid of me?"

"I'm not afraid of you, I'm afraid of what I might feel." She looked at the shadow thing that was becoming a man. She loved the brown eyes, and his mouth so full, so sensuous. Darien could almost feel the softness of those lips touching hers. Slowly she reached out and placed her hand on him, caressing where she touched, becoming mesmerized with the smoothness of his skin. He seized her arm and pulled her to him in one quick movement, sweeping her up into his embrace, and if she had never experienced this then she would not have known that you could actually faint from excitement.

"Give yourself to me and I will drown you in love," he whispered fiercely in her ear. Darien tried to answer but found she had no breath with which to speak. Finally, she was able to take in a deep breath and answer him.

"How could I do otherwise?" she said.

David walked over to one of the two pieces of furniture in his room of dreams. The first one was an oversized bed made just for the love he was going to give her, and the second was a giant fireplace to relax and to help keep her warm. He sat her gently on the bed, and then disappeared only to reappear an instant later. David told her to close her eyes and extend her hands. Into these he placed a single red rose, and around her neck he placed a necklace adorned with a rose pendent. The fireplace sprang to life bringing relaxing warmth into the room.

"The fire in the fireplace is to bring warmth into your life, because you have spent too many years lost in a cold and empty world. The red rose signifies the rebirth of your new life, and as you wake, so shall this flower begin to unfold. The silver rose that I place around your neck is to forever remind you of the woman you will become."

Darien held the rose in her hand and for the first time in her life felt a great rush of love and affection, it was real, and it was for the shadow man she named David. She turned quickly around and flung herself onto him and he held her tight as she whispered in his ear, "Why must I learn to live without you?"

"Trust me, Darien; there will come a time when you will no longer need me."

"I hope that doesn't happen for a very long time." David was becoming more solid, more complete, and as the minutes passed by Darien could not help but notice everything that was developing.

"Oh my," was all she could say. David laughed and Darien smiled.

"That's for me?" she asked with a huge smile on her face.

"Yes, but you are not ready, not yet." He started to lift her sweater while Darien raised her arms like a small child getting ready for bed, and she felt like she had found life in permanent dream as the last of her resistance disappeared.

"Trust in me, let whatever happens, happen, let whatever emotions you have lead you into your most inner self. This is going to be a total experience of feelings for you because we will awaken all that has been buried for so long." While David talked to her, he touched her everywhere, and she watched him, memorizing his soft warm features. She watched him as his eyes traveled over her, and soon she was nearly naked. Darien raised her arms to cover herself, because she had suddenly become humiliated in her nakedness.

"Don't be ashamed of yourself, Darien, you have had three children, that's not an easy thing for any woman."

"Other women have children, sometimes a lot more than three, and they take much better care of themselves."

"Other women have not been through what you have." David took her arms and moved them down to her side.

"Before I can touch you, before I can help you, you must free yourself of all your inhibitions, all your old self-doubts, and you must trust in me completely. Can you do that, Darien?"

"All I can do is to try." He put a finger to her lips.

"The word 'try' has been stricken from your vocabulary. There is no try, there is only do, but first there is another place that you must go, so close your eyes and remember that once before in your life, there was another."

Darien closed her eyes and let her mind fly back in time, almost like she was in the zone, but this time it was different. It was early fall when the leaves were just starting to change and her young sixteen-year-old body was just starting to wake. She had just acquired her first serious boyfriend; his name was John. He taught her how to kiss, how to soften her lips and return that kiss with just the right amount of pressure. He also was the first boy who gave her the luxurious taste of a tongue, and he was the first boy she allowed to touch her young, inexperienced body. They were sitting in an apple orchard, face to face, cross-legged, and the overpowering smell of ripening apples was everywhere. The strong odor overwhelmed her senses and she felt herself falling into a deep dark place where no one could touch her, no one could reach her, except the young man that she loved.

John reached over and unbuttoned her shirt, sucking in his breath as he opened her blouse, seeing how the low-cut bra flattered the swelling of her young breasts. At the same time, the older Darien sat across the room from David, who also pulled in his breath as he marveled, not at her young breasts but at the available ample adult bosom. John let his hand move softly across the top of the swelling, and Darien in the dream place mimicked him as she touched her own breast. David watched her intently, and his eyes softened as they took in the super-imposed picture. Slowly both Dariens put their heads back as the explorations continued. Her hands were in juxtaposition with his hands, both sets running simultaneously up her neck, and through this, Darien finally began releasing her inhibitions. She started to lie back on the bed while at the same time Darien the younger was lying back onto the blanket in the middle of the orchard. David, her shadow man, her beloved guardian angel, helped to ease her gently down.

"Remember; give yourself over to feelings, and to trust," David whispered softly.

"Remember how it felt to love, to give him yourself freely, remember the sensations as they flow through you, and remember how you opened yourself to him." John leaned over her, and placed his lips on hers, kindling her body into a torch of hot passionate fire. It was as if there were no thoughts left in her mind, and she lived only through the emotions, responding to the love she felt flow through her body. David watched as her hands traveled slowly over her own body. Her lips parted slightly, her breathing slightly erratic. Johnny leaned over her gazing tenderly at her face as he put the palm of his hand to her cheek, and then the young Darien started to fade as did Johnny. She was still Darien, just older and even more aware than ever of her body's reawakening.

"Don't stop to think, only feel." David's face replaced Johnny's, and Darien gave herself over to him. As his lips slowly touched hers, all of David finally became real, solid, and whole.

"I am for you, Darien, and you alone." He breathed these words into her mouth as he captured her tongue, and played with it until Darien gave up trying to keep up with him, and just let him explore her mouth. David took his mouth away from hers so he could place small tender kisses on her face. His hand continued to explore her body and he placed it over her breast, moving and playing the nipple between his fingers, and suddenly Darien's hand covered his.

"David," she whispered to him, and he leaned over her putting his lips by her ear.

"You must trust in me, my littlest angel, for if you do not, then I cannot help you and you know in your heart that I would never hurt you." He placed a kiss by her ear, and then slowly down her neck. He left lazy, slow kisses, and sometimes he left kisses with little tongue trails. Darien gave her body to him, literally responding to David with a passion that she had never known before, with a passion that she would not have believed was possible. And for just a brief moment she wondered where this guardian, this innocent protector of the human race gained such insightful experience in the way of a woman's pleasure.

"Open your eyes, Darien, and watch me love you." She did as requested, watching his head move down towards her breasts. Her small pink nipples were flushed with excitement, and she shuddered as his tongue played with each one before nibbling softly on them. Her head went back with pleasure causing her back to arch, and pushing her breasts up towards his mouth while at the same time her breath slowly hissed out between her clenched teeth. His tongue drove her, fielding her emotions into a boiling cauldron ready to bubble over the sides, and crash down around her. David's hand traveled lower, sliding down her thighs and then moving back up between her legs, which she automatically parted. His large hand cupped her passion, and he held it buried inside his palm. Darien placed her hand in David's hair and made a fist to hold on while his mouth followed down her body to where his hand lay. She held him back with a gentle pull to his head, wanting him to place his cheek against her lower belly, while she marveled at all the new feelings. In the meantime, his fingers began gentle explorations below. David parted her nether lips, and tickled the same amazing little spot as Darien had done many times before, but somehow it was different, more exciting when someone else did the exploring. She shivered without control. His fingers moved further down, found her secret opening, and he teased her there before pushing inside. She cried aloud as David expertly moved his fingers around until his thumb rested on her nub while his fingers remained inside. There was a word for her journey into finding this part of herself, and with David's help, Darien knew that her experience reached ecstasy. He used his tongue to make small wet circles on her belly, and then small wet kisses as he traveled downwards, replacing his thumb with his tongue, nearly causing Darien to jump from the bed as her body rocked with her newfound passion. David pulled his mouth away from her, and kneeled between her legs. He took one side of her labia in each of his hands, and spread her open. He bent his head closer. Darien grabbed onto the bed sheets, both hands automatically curled into fists, as small moans involuntarily escaped from her throat. His tongue licked though the middle of her to that wonderful place, and he was insatiable as he nibbled softly on her excitement. Without a break in between, his finger replaced his tongue and his tongue moved to where his fingers had been. He brought her to the peak of delight only to pause, and then begin again. David delighted in his feast as the reawakening of Darien's passion brought to him the same excitement.

"David," she said to him as he kept on feasting, and she called softly to him for the second time: "David."

He lifted his head up, and moved towards her face, as she lay open under him, her heart pounding with delight. He stretched himself over her and she could see that he was ready to enter her. He gently kissed her mouth, allowing Darien to know her own taste. She felt the tip of his hard excitement as it barely touched her, resting just outside her opening, the very center of her self. David moved forward and entered her, filling her all at once, completely, totally. He withdrew and pushed again, diving into her again so deeply that he hit her nub. He was large enough to reach every part of her. David rose to his knees and pulled her up to him, onto him.

"David," she cried for him.

"David!" she cried for him again, tears streaming down her face, her body rocking with his force as she wrapped herself around him. Darien buried her face in his neck and he held her down on his swollen member while together they burned within the mini-revelation of how much they needed each other. Darien's entire body came alive as she shuddered and called his name, while David the shadow-thing turned man, her guardian, erupted inside of her, his release a match for her own.

"My angel," he said to her, quietly, affectionately, holding her close, enveloping her in his scent, kissing her mouth fully, not being able to get enough of her.

"Oh God, David," she whispered sweetly into his mouth, "what have you done to me?"

"I, my smallest, sweetest angel, have given you back yourself, and showed you love." David gathered her into his arms, holding her in his comfort and security, while the riddle came to her, no longer blocked from her memory. With a renewed faith in herself and in who she was, Darien recalled Mr. Toady Face, and a riddle from a long time ago:

"A light warm wind, a gentle breeze
Is how it all begins
Then it will come as shadows creep
To bind the seraphims

Do not fear the shadows dark
For they can be brushed away
But fear more the twisted evil thoughts
You think have come to stay."

*Are you a part of this, Mr. Toady Face? Did you send David to me? Will you let him stay?* She snuggled closer to the warmth of her David burying her face in the softness of his skin, and as he kissed the top of her head, Darien could not stop the tears of happiness. Normally full of questions and not enough answers, Darien quietly wondered if all the guardians who arrived for an anguishing woman brought such an amazing experience. How does one ask another woman if they too were favored by such a wondrous being? Suddenly Darien realized that she had cheated on her husband. But if David is not human, is this real at all? She decided that for just this once, she would not ask her questions and maybe, just this once, there were no solid answers. Darien closed her eyes, and delved into the peace and sanctity of her guardian.

# PART THREE
# MIRROR IMAGE

She woke groggy from her late-afternoon nap.

Darien rolled over and found herself nose to nose with her small-breed dog.

"Poor thing must really have to go bad to brave the wrath of Jack and enter the bedroom." She reached out to push the dog's muzzle off the bed but was not quite quick enough because the dog was able to deliver her a wet lick anyway.

"Okay, okay, I'm up." Darien stood and stretched in the late-day sun that shone between the blinds and cast the dancing shadows on the green-carpeted floor. There was a fascination with shadows that Darien had never fully been able to understand. They danced for her, always dancing, and they mesmerized her into near hypnotic trances. Sometimes Darien wanted to join them, to become as dark and semi-shapeless as they. At times she truly wished for a loss of self, to join the mindless dance where no one could find her, and to let insanity take her to a place of no return. What is in the dark shadows that call to her? Her thoughts slowly returned, and she looked around her small bedroom, so neat, so orderly, so much like the rows of white underwear lined up in her drawer, then in a sudden surge of emotional emptiness Darien started to cry. The last encounter with her guardian was nearly three months ago. Three long months since she talked to him, and she could no longer hear his little burbles when going about her daily routines. Darien repeatedly searched the shadows in her house, but this too proved futile, and she desperately wanted David to return. She ached for his touch, she ached for his arms to hold her, and for his lips to touch hers as she remembered the taste of her most amazing guardian.

"Was he ever real?" she whispered to herself. Darien raised her arms towards the ceiling in her empty house and looking upwards she said aloud:

"Where are you, my lover? Have I done something wrong? David, please, you promised that you would stay as long as I needed you, so where are you?" Darien lowered her arms and walked slowly down the stairs to the emptiness below. It was so quiet in her house; her husband had gone out and the children were visiting with various friends. She slipped a shirt over her nightgown to take the dog outside to do her business, and it seemed as if the quiet was going to become overwhelming in its capacity to encompass the silence of her life. The dog realized the reason for Darien getting dressed, especially as she slid her small feet into her husband's sneakers left by the door, and the dog wagged her tail hard enough to send her spinning into a circle.

"Okay," Darien said looking down, "let's go." She paused, looked around just long enough to see the mess the children had left behind, opened the door, and headed outside.

The thermometer on the outside wall of the house read thirty degrees. It was the end of November, but Darien welcomed the cold wind as it bit through the light shirt, while the season's second snowfall swirled around her. She looked towards the darkened clouds that signaled a heavier snow was yet to follow. In a way, this would be a welcome relief because the previous one had already turned an ugly crusty brown from all the sand and salt that was sprinkled on the road. Soon the city would be covered in another beautiful blanket of crystal white, and that made her happy. The mother of three stood waiting patiently for the dog to finish, not feeling the cold as she stared across the street at the large empty factory, deserted now for almost ten years. The gentle sprinkling of snow had increased its rate of fall, almost as if the clouds had reached their capacity, and the wind was picking up speed. They seemed to her to be in a kind of challenging race, the wind beckoning to the snow to fall faster and thicker than it could blow it away.

The small half-breed dog felt the chill, and nearly knocked her over running back to the security of the house. Darien smiled; Katie had never liked the cold weather. She opened the door to let the dog back inside, and then turned to look across the street. The snow became erratic in its fall, moving in many directions, giving way to the strong blustering winds, and as Darien stared at the factory through the building blizzard, it appeared to be taking on a different shape. An illusion formed through the frozen water crystals that filled the air, and in between the snow's mid-air dance, the factory began to resemble a Norman Rockwell painting. It took on the appearance of a small winter cabin set in the middle of the snow-covered woods. A trail of smoke issued from the stone chimney, and a small wooden door opened to reveal inviting warmth shining from inside.

Darien felt herself lifted by the snow swirls, and carried much farther than just across the street; deposited at the entrance to the cabin. She stepped cautiously over the threshold, and was not particularly surprised to find that the inside of the cabin was as rustic in appearance as the outside. There was also a roaring fire blazing in the stone fireplace. As far as even being real, or for her to question what her eyes were seeing, well, she stopped questioning reality ever since David entered her life. Besides, this was her most favored daydream. She used it as a guard from entering the zone, and she longed to spend her time with David in a cabin that brought peace inside of her. Darien turned to watch the shadows in the fireplace flames that danced behind her in reflections on the wall.

"They have always danced for me, these strange ominous shadows." And it brought to mind the one who first arrived as nothing more than a shadow on the ground.

"David," she said as she stared at the flames, "where have you been?"

David didn't answer, instead he just smiled as the shadow walked towards her and she opened her arms to welcome him. He was almost there, ready for Darien to touch, and ready to love her when suddenly everything disappeared, and the lonely woman was left standing in her driveway still holding the door open with the dog sitting on her haunches watching her from inside. She could not believe the unexpected intense sense of loss accompanied by a sudden flow of unwarranted hatred for her home. As if in an amazing revelation, Darien suddenly realized that she had come to hate living in the center of town without any peace or privacy, and she hated cleaning her home day after day, finding it to be a burden. The pride she used to take in her accomplishments had fled. And even though she didn't want to admit it, there were times when Darien just didn't like her children very much. It was hard for her to understand how she could feel this way, when she knew that she loved them more than her own life. She lifted her foot to step inside the house when she thought she saw movement in the shadows. However, it turned out to be just a strange play of shadow and nothing more. Darien filled with a deepening disappointment, and an even deeper loneliness as she entered what she now referred to as "the house of doom."

There were jackets, papers, library books, shoes, and dishes littering the downstairs. It had become such a cumbersome chore now to pick up after her children, and Jack being the big help he was, would spend most of the weekends hiding downstairs in the basement or watching sports on the television. This of course left Darien, the same as it always had, to do all the cooking, cleaning, washing, and all the other chores of keeping a house. It was a normal home, but the mundane routines caused Darien to again become restless, unfulfilled, and feeling unwanted.

Trapped.

And alone.

A few months ago, a few days after the last time she saw David, a surprise event came about when completely out of character for him, Jack become more attentive. He was a little more loving, and had actually taken her out to dinner. Even more surprising was when they woke the next day; he suggested having breakfast out with the entire family. What had changed, what had happened? *Maybe he does care about me and love me after all,* she had thought to herself, but unfortunately the attention did not last, while neither did his attitude. Darien was at a loss to understand any of it.

Her daily routine beckoned her back to what lay before her as she began walking, thinking, and automatically hanging up the jackets in the closet. Then she turned her attention to the kitchen. After putting the plug in the sink she spun the knob on the faucet to its highest setting for hot water. Her actions were automatic as she absently reached for the dishwashing liquid and squirted it into the running water. All these years of washing dishes in nearly scalding temperatures didn't affect her as she dipped her hands into the hot soapy water. She fantasized about David standing behind her, pressing himself into her back as he reached around from behind her to help her wash the dishes. He too dipped his hands into the water, trailing soapsuds up her arms, and then he bent to nuzzle her ear. She could feel his warm breath touching the light hairs on the back of her neck, and it so easily roused her passion. Her breath caught deep in her throat, and she closed her eyes against the longings that she felt while wanting his shadowy touch to became real.

A light warm wind, a gentle breeze

All of a sudden the years of frustrations that Darien held back came exploding from inside of her, and in a rush of wild anger the dishes started to fly. She broke glasses and plates throwing them at the door, where they shattered, sending slivers of glass everywhere. Her nightgown fell off her shoulder, and her hair went askew with the remnants of her wild temper, her eyes went dark and empty as the world slipped away, and she zoned into a final place of shadowy dancing nightmares. Slowly Darien staggered into the bathroom, caught a glimpse of herself in the mirror, and staring back at her was a strange wild woman that she didn't recognize.

"I hate you!" she screamed at herself and the mirror image screamed back. "I hate you!" at the same time. Then before she could stop herself, her fist came up, and the blow to the mirror shattered the glass, embedding small shards in her hand. She watched unblinking as the blood formed into little droplets and fell into the sink. The initial shock to her body deepened as the blood started to create little rivulets that trickled down her arm. Darien stood and stared at the miniature red rivers as her mind bordered on remaining permanently in the zone.

"Darien," the voice came to her, floating on the warm wind that circled her body.

"Darien," it said again, but she did not acknowledge its presence.

"Darien," it came a third time, and David was becoming frantic in his concern for Darien. He could not form, he could not become solid for Darien unless she called to him, and David was seeing that she had finally zoned to a point where even he might not be able to reach her.

Slowly she turned from the mirror in the bathroom, and the shadow that swirled around her feet hitched a ride with her as she carried him up the stairs to her bedroom. Darien stood before the large mirror that decorated the wall directly over her double dresser. She was looking straight into and then past the mirror image that looked back, and after several long minutes she blinked her eyes as a small look of recognition came across her face. This caused David to burble happily around her ankles. Darien still did not acknowledge the mini-tornado as he spun in excited desperation. What she did next, she did so quickly that David could not have stopped her, even if he had been solid. Darien raised her fists, and at the same time her mirror image raised its fists. She clenched her hand so tightly, that it enabled a continuous pulsing free flow of blood down her arm. The large jewelry box that sat on her bureau captured her attention, and in her dream state she picked it up, and then threw it fiercely against the mirror that made her see what she had become. The bedroom mirror exploded on impact, and pieces of the thick glass flew everywhere. Darien stood still, waiting for the penetration of the large shards, never even trying to avoid them as they flew out across the room. One jagged piece embedded itself in her arm while several smaller ones targeted her face. Her body stood rigid absorbing the impact, and the pain within her mind strained to the breaking point while her dream state threatened to take her beyond sanity. There was one name that she called, one person who could bring her back, and she said this now, in the barest of whispers.

"David." Her desperate plea to him shattered the quiet house, the birds downstairs that were normally chattering became instantly still, and at the same time, her dog howled for the first time in all of its twelve years. The cats scattered to the safety they found in the corners, becoming as indistinct as the shadows themselves. Blood covered most of her clothes, and Darien started to shake, but her call for David broke the invisible barrier, and he was finally there. He started to uncurl as a dark vaporous trail rising up from her feet, swirling like a mini-tornado around her. His hands were there to hold her when she started to fall, and he wrapped himself around her, pulling her to the safety of his arms, and holding on tight.

"David," she whispered quietly.

"I'm here." Her body went limp as she fell completely into his arms. He held her in his embrace while waiting for the whirl of cloud that he was to finish forming so that he could become a solid entity for her. David carried her downstairs to the bathroom and set her on the edge of the tub while he ran the warm water. He gently dislodged the pieces of glass from her body as she sat unflinching on the cold hard fiberglass surface. David then carefully cleaned the oozing cuts and bandaged them, taking great care to make sure that there would be no infection. Once that was done, he undressed her, picked her up, and placed her into the warm water. The shadow man stood up and stepped into the tub, easing himself in the warm water behind her. David put his hands on her shoulders, and with gentle pressure, he pulled her backwards until her head was resting against his chest and he was once again able to surround her in a blanket of warmth. He held her there, secure in his arms until he could feel the tension leave her body, and she relaxed against him.

"David," her voice was soft and luxurious, "where have you been, my guardian?"

"Does it matter where I've been? I'm here now, and this is what is important."

"No, I guess it doesn't matter." She looked at the many cuts on her hands and arms and at the shattered mirror on the floor, her violent fit a blur of memory, causing a vague puzzlement. Her brows knitted together as she tried to remember, and it felt as though it had been someone else, someone who looked like her that broke the mirrors.

"David?"

"Yes, Darien."

"I love you."

"I know." She turned around and softly caressed his face, and he gently pulled her to him so their lips could touch. Darien felt the tears begin to gather under her closed eyes.

"I've missed you."

"I know this too, and I'm here now to love you for as long as you need." He stood up, the warm water sliding easily from his body. He encouraged Darien to stand, and then he lifted her into his arms. Suddenly they were upstairs, and as the house fell away David stepped through the shattered mirror that had once been over her dresser. Against unwritten law, David took Darien to the other side.

The darkness that surrounded them was only temporary and Darien shivered despite the heat David generated for her. Out of the stillness came the warm winds and a light appeared over their heads allowing Darien to see that she was in what appeared to be a tunnel. She looked down at her feet, and saw hundreds of tiny, whirling, miniature tornadoes dancing a strange circling dance spinning wildly at their feet, and generating the warm winds she felt.

"They are all guardians like me," David explained. "This is where we wait, in the light of the tunnel, until we are called upon to go and help people like you, Darien, people who need us." His voice was only a whisper yet it sounded loud in the light humming of the whirling winds. The breeze was so warm that it felt like a mid summer's day, and it created a softness that was its own caress.

(A light warm wind, a gentle breeze is how it all begins)

A hundred caressing arms, a hundred warm breezes helping make David strong, and he held Darien close to him while the little whirling guardian tornadoes lifted, and carried them out into the full light. A peace entered her body, capturing her soul, a peace known to her as her guardian David.

"My heart cries for you, David, and I love you more than I can understand, why is that?"

"Sometimes there are no answers, Darien, sometimes there are only feelings."

"Tell me why you went away."

"I will, but give me a few moments."

"Are you going to go away again?"

"Not for a long time." He took her hand in his, the surrounding area came into focus, and Darien found herself on a white sandy beach where the warmth of the sun replaced the warmth of the disappearing tornadoes. David let go of her hand while motioning for her to sit on the blanket already spread out and waiting for them.

"Please sit down and I will tell you some of what has happened." He motioned to the blanket, and Darien obediently sat down, unashamed in her nakedness. David floated over the sand, and came to rest directly opposite her. He looked down at the small woman that he had watched come into the world, and he knew then that he loved her from the beginning. The guardian took her hands in his, brought them to his lips, and kissed them ever so softly.

"We, meaning the guardians, do not appear to just anyone, you know that." She nodded her head in understanding. "We also have just one purpose when we do come, and that is to help the people who need us. We can love you for as long as you need us to, and when all is right within your world and your life is put in order, we move on to the next person who needs us. Of course we don't always appear to those we come to help, and there are times when the 'miracles' we perform are how you know us. Despite our reasons for being here, and the abilities we have to interfere and alter some lives, we still have to abide by certain rules. Your rules are written so that you can actually read them; you call them laws. The rules of the guardians, although not written, are rules nonetheless, and we are subject to follow those rules. Darien, because we have the ability to change the course of lives, the guardians have to pay strict adherence to those rules much more than anyone in your world would have to, do you understand this?"

"I am trying to, David."

"That is all I can ask. Unfortunately for me I have broken a few of these rules, and the 'elder' guardians, the ones that I have to answer to, they are the ones who called me away."

"What did you do, David?"

"Don't you know, Darien?" She shook her head no, and looked at him with the same wide, innocent eyes that she had first seen him with when he had called to her all those years ago and saved her from the nest of snakes.

"This is hard for me to say, Darien; it would be easier if you understood. My 'job' was to help you, to ease you through a difficult time in your life, and to turn your thoughts from suicide to thoughts of happiness."

(Fear more the twisted evil thoughts, you think have come to stay)

"In doing what I was sent to do, I have broken the first rule of the guardians and that was to fall hopelessly in love with you, so much so, that I wanted to bring you here with me, through the mirror, to stay." He moved closer to his little angel, gathered Darien into his arms, and the tender voice that she knew spoke softly to her now, and his eyes filled with tears as he said to her:

"I have never wanted to be with anyone before as much as I have wanted to be with you, because I have fallen for you, totally, hopelessly, and helplessly. I have loved you from the very first day that you entered your world." He held her tight inside his arms, kissed her so skillfully, so tenderly, that it made her quiver inside. Their tongues entwined in a taste of warmth and sweetness until David finally broke the kiss, allowing one small tear of happiness to fall upon his fingers.

"Guardians never cry, my sweet Darien." He placed a kiss of love and tenderness on her forehead, then her cheeks, and could not help himself as he continued down. Darien guided his mouth down her neck, thrilling to his touch, excited to a point beyond what she thought was possible for her to experience. His hands brushed nipples that were already aroused, and he played them skillfully between his fingers. David's breath was hot on her chest as his mouth curled around what his fingers had just had, and Darien let out her breath in a great moan of anticipation. His hand caressed her side, her hip, and then finally to her thigh. Darien parted her legs, and David's hand slid between them. He smiled with his mouth still secured to her nipple; his tongue was hot and teasing. Finally he slipped his fingers inside and filled her so full that Darien cried out.

"You are ready, my lover," David said to her, "but not yet." He withdrew his hand, and she cried out again, this time from the emptiness.

"It's okay, I'm here. I'm not going anywhere." David sat back, took Darien's hands, and he pulled her up and into his lap, surrounding her with his lean, hard body. She buried her face in his chest, breathing in deeply of his scent. His hands moved over her body, softly touching, almost absorbing her with his caresses, taking inside of him a part of her, while taking pleasure in the oversized contours of her body. He touched her bottom, and smiled when she moved against him, and he began to knead her back there, gently, slowly, exerting more pressure until it separated at his touch. Darien opened her mouth and gasped in great mouthfuls of air, not realizing that up until then, she had been holding her breath. He continued to tease the small opening back there, and Darien once again moved against him. David slid his finger back inside of her, moving it until it was thoroughly lubricated with her excitement, and then returned it to her other small opening. He teased her one more time around the small opening and exerting just a slight pressure, he began to push his finger inside. She gasped aloud with the wonderment at the new feeling that took her. David then separated his fingers and entered one up inside her while placing his thumb on her ever-excitable nub. Darien's head went back, and her body stiffened as David laid her back upon the blanket, never loosing his grip on her. Darien gave herself completely over to him. Suddenly his hand was gone, and he had risen up over her. The guardian who had become her only lover was ready for her, and as Darien lay open for him, he looked deep into her eyes as she returned the same.

"My guardian, my David. I could not love you more than I do right now. You have become my life, you are all that I am, and I will forever be your Darien." He let his weight fall upon her, pushing himself until he buried deep inside of her, and she rose to meet him. He kissed her lips, tasting sweet Darien, and he reveled in that taste.

"My Darien, all that I am is you, for now and for all that is yet to come. I will love you ever, as I have always loved you, my littlest angel." He moved against her, she against him, his size filled her, nearly overfilling her, and they became each another, crying, holding, and loving. They were complete, and they were whole. For Darien and David, they felt as though it had finally become as it should be.

They lay on the beach, the warm sand heating them from under the blanket, with their bodies locked around each other, afraid to let go, afraid that if they did one of them would disappear. As far as could be seen there was nothing but beautiful white sand and the few palm trees that offered them a comfort of shade. In all of her searching, she never thought that she would find such quiet, bringing an almost unnerving peace. Darien spoke first, breaking the silence of the deserted beach where he brought her.

"What is going to happen to us, David?"

"Oh, my littlest angel, if I knew the answer to that, it would already be done. I would take you away and spend my days loving you."

"And I you. Hold me, David, and never let me go."

"I love you, Darien."

"I know."

Inside the mirror where David had taken her, the home of the guardians filled to its capacity. The tunnel usually full of the waiting guardians was now empty of the small whirlwinds, and the light of their goodness filled the great hall. The eldest of all the guardians looked over his charges, the great guardians that stood vigil to the species known as man. He breathed a deep sigh of exasperation in his weak attempt to hide the ever-growing concern about the one called Darien. How could the Gods have played such a hand in their never-ending game? They create the worlds, they create the species, and then bring them to the point of madness just for their amusement. The part that bothered the eldest guardian of all was that now one of his own was involved, and he had to ask the one named David to lead the human woman straight into a path of evil with a possibility of self-destruction. Unknowingly, David had already begun her training, and the elder angered as the Gods used one of his own He feared too, that his involvement would eventually have to become known to her.

It was a harsh play in the game.

# PART FOUR
# DAVID AND DARIEN REVISITED

Her headache had been escalating all day.

It was difficult, at times, for Darien to remember exactly what singular event started the whole thing. A self-absorbed person, drowning in her own self-pity, she believed that her life was the only one filled with hardships and heartaches. She had come to the point, where to continue living the life she chose seemed to be impossibly hopeless. Darien had begun to think that the only solution, the only escape from the life she could make was a permanent one. With these thoughts, her silent plea for help was heard, and that was when the guardians sent her one of their own.

He picked her up and took her to a place she had never been before. David took her to herself; he tried to help her see to the inside, he tried to help her find the beautiful person that she hid away from everyone. Darien had always been afraid to look, she had always been afraid of the kind of answers that waited there for her. She ventured into dark and scary places with fragments of nightmares that frightened her almost to the point of madness. Who was the person that walked through life disguised as Darien? What was she looking for when she entered the zone? Through all of this, David stood beside her, and encouraged her to find the answers that she so desperately sought.

David helped her to face the in-between time, the time Darien referred to as the "before Jack time." She was able to tell David about the time she fell victim to the three men who raped her, but what she did not tell him was that she entered the house where it occurred of her own free will. Even though she allowed some of the memory to surface, there were parts that still lay hidden, therefore she still felt guilty that somehow it had to have been her own fault. There were other facts that she kept hidden from him, and one of those was Matthew, the man who lied to her, the man who pretended to care about her. He duped her into thinking that he was her boyfriend while all the time there were two other men waiting for them at the house. They forced Darien to drink liquor and to smoke marijuana so she would get high enough to relax so she would not protest what they were about to do. Several weeks later when she had reflected on all that had occurred, she became convinced that they had laced the marijuana with something else, quite possibly a hallucinogen. Matthew took her into a separate room, where he laid her on the floor and proceeded to perform the act known to Darien as the "fuck." She was not aware at the time, that while she lay with him, his brother and a friend (the two men who had greeted them on their arrival) brought a camera into the room. A few minutes after they entered the room Matthew stood up, walked over to the corner, and offering Darien up to his older brother, and then watched.

He hid inside the obscurity of the shadow dance allowing it to grow, and extend its dark reach towards the helpless woman.

She struggled briefly trying to push him off, but the joint she smoked left her too weak to do much against this large overpowering man. They bound the helpless Darien without ties. They raped her. He raped her physically with his own body, and when that was not enough he began to rape her using different objects. At the same time the other man who greeted them upon arrival stood in the corner empowering his own erection, while filming the degrading positions they placed her in. Matthew finally emerged from the relative safety of the corner when he could no longer keep himself in control. The wine bottle that they had previously drank from became the only object that she remembered seeing and feeling, and even years later when Darien drifted into zone, she could never recall the other objects that were used, only that they had been. One thing that she did remember was trying to get up off the floor, and that was when Matthew whispered to her.

"Don't move or you'll hurt yourself." His voice had sounded heavy, emotional, full of guilt, and she could almost feel that he had some remorse, but still he did nothing to stop the degrading rape. The part that saddened her most was the trust that she placed in him as her boyfriend, and the fact that if he really wanted to, he could have stopped them. Instead he perpetuated it, encouraged it, because deep inside Matthew wanted it to happen. Darien obeyed him and slowly lay back down. She was alone in that room despite the men who abused her, and she lay quietly staring at the ceiling while holding back her tears.

After they were satisfied with the filming, Matthew's brother took another turn, as did the man who held the camera. He had no name; she never asked and she could not remember if anyone said it aloud, and he was destined to remain in her thoughts as just the "other man." She didn't know when the filming stopped as the rape of her body continued. Darien could not cry, her mind became too numb to cry, and she still believed for all of this to have happened it was her fault.

It was weeks before her fears settled down, and she made a final decision. If she continued with the life she was leading, it would only bring her pain and suffering, so when Darien met Jack she made the conscious decision to turn things around. The men who raped her continued to look for her, but Darien was clever when it came to hiding away. She hid herself, her husband, and her daughter and most important, she buried the bad Darien. She settled down, worked hard on being a good wife and mother, until that too began to go wrong. Her mind zoned in and out of these thoughts as she pleaded with the shadows to release David and let him come to help her.

"I know they can't hurt me anymore, David, I know they are only memories, but how do I stop them from coming back to haunt me? I want to let them go, but I don't know how, and sometimes the nightmares are more than I can bear." Sibby the sniveling whiner, the annoying miserable baby suddenly returned, and she cried with the pain of her separation from David. Darien sat crying in her house as the walls closed in on her, and she called for David so persistently that he finally came, but he was angry. The guardian of infinite patience was overcome with loathing at her self-pity, and she had never seen him that way before.

"This is enough, Darien, I can't do this anymore. You try even the patience of a guardian. You have to learn to stand on your own, that has been the whole purpose of your leaning experience, that is the whole purpose of the guardians, to teach you to let go, to be independent and strong."

"But I have been strong, David. For twenty-two years, I have been strong. I don't know when I lost control; I don't know when I let everyone run over me. I taught my children to be strong and they are. I let my husband do whatever he wanted to do, and never questioned any thing that he did, even when I knew he was seeing other women. I guess something inside of me has finally broken and I am falling apart, David, even with all of your help, I'm falling apart and I'm begging, just for once, let me be happy! Let me do something for me! And I was happy, with you, David, I was happy. We talked, we made love, and I started to regain my self-respect, then that too started to fall apart and I still don't understand why. I know I told you to go if you wanted to, and then I called for you and you wouldn't answer me anymore. David, I'm so scared, I don't know what to do. My body shakes without control, and my fear of losing you scares me to the point of just ending it all. Thinking I lost you made me cry, and Sibby came out, well, she came back. My nightmares started again in a rerun of the persistent endless stream of the men in my life who have hurt me. And they haunt me even when I am awake, silhouettes of black featureless faces that laugh at me. They make fun of me, and I think, 'My God, how could I have been that stupid?' I wish that I could have been smarter, and then maybe my early life would have been different. It sometimes seems that the only thing that I will ever be capable of is stupidity." David sat down on the sofa emitting a large sigh of frustration.

"Darien, slow down and take a deep breath. You know that I've heard all this before. Let it go, let go of it all. Haven't you learned yet that it is no longer a part of your life, that those men can no longer hurt you? Your life is here, it's now, and what you did in your past no longer matters. You're letting it destroy you, and I can't watch anymore."

"God, David, don't you see...I CAN'T." Darien fell down to her knees sobbing hysterically. "I swear I want to, but I don't know how."

The guardian stood up, totally exhausted by her demands, and for the first time, he turned his back to her.

"I want to be strong again, I want to take control of my life, and most of all I want to stop needing you the way that I do," she told him between sobs, "I just don't know how. David, how do I stop loving you? How do I stop needing you? How do I stop wanting you to touch me, to bring me the passion, to bring me the desires that you woke?" The patient guardian turned back around to face Darien.

"Darien, I don't have all the answers. I am a guardian, and my love for you, although pushed to the limit, is still there. Why haven't you realized yet that love is not supposed to hurt? I have loved you in all the ways that you have wanted, in all the ways that are possible for me. I have stood by you while you cried, I have stood by you while Sibby whined, and now I have to go because there are others who need me as much, if not more than you do. No one ever said that the love was going to be a forever love. I cannot stay, Darien, you know that."

"You will leave me even though I am not ready?"

"I told you, Darien, sometimes even the guardians fail. We can't always help everyone, and it has become apparent that you need something more than I am capable of giving you. You need the help of someone who understands the inside of your head and that is not me, that is a doctor."

"So you are telling me that I'm crazy, right?"

"That's not what I said."

"My kids say that I'm crazy, my husband says I am not right, it appears that everyone thinks I have lost my mind, including me!" Darien was very close to losing the little edge of sanity that she had been holding onto. She closed her eyes, and felt the room turn into a swirling black void. The black shadows let loose inside her mind dancing within the hell's fire that burned inside her thoughts, and they pulled her into a deep dark insanity. The wall in front of her began to crumble, pieces flying out into nowhere, and she started to scream while holding her hands to the sides of her head, squeezing and pulling on her hair.

"I'm not fucking crazy! I'm not fucking crazy! I'm not fucking crazy, David! I'm not, I'm not!" She pulled on her hair, and the tears came, a tremendous flood of them while she cried and screamed… "I'm not FUCKING CRAZY!" Two large pieces of hair came off in her hands and the raw bald spots quickly filled with blood that spilled over and dripped down the sides of her head.

"Darien, don't." David went to her, and pulled her up from the floor. He folded her into his arms, and she immediately lost consciousness, having totally exhausted herself in the encroaching madness. He picked her up, and like so many times before, the floor fell away as David took her to the place of guardians, the place where the whirling tornadoes waited for their call to help others in her world. With one exception, for Darien there would be no volunteers. David walked through the miniature spinning vortexes, and he could hear their thoughts, he could feel their pity for him, and for the woman that he could no longer help. There was another man waiting for him at the end of the tunnel, and the brightness of his luminance pushed him towards transparency. He was extremely tall, taller than even the largest of the guardians, and as David walked by, he sent the guardian his own silent plea for help. David laid Darien on the bed in the room that had once been full of dreams, but now even the fireplace had become as cold as Darien's heart.

"I have failed her, sir." David stood with his head bowed, unable to face his failure. The transparent man laid a hand upon David's shoulder and the transparency gave way to warmth as the being gained solidity. He was stronger than all who would stand before him, guardian and man alike, and it was David's turn to be comforted.

"You have not failed; you must understand that Darien is beyond your help."

"There must be something I can do."

"David," he said patiently, "sometimes love is not enough. There are too many things about Darien that she has not told you, and until she unburdens herself of all the guilt she has locked away, she will never be free of the demons that live inside her mind."

"How could she raise her children, live all of these years, and seem so normal until now? Even as we speak she carries on with an appearance of normalcy without anyone knowing any different, except her husband, and even then he does not know everything. Can you explain that to me?"

"No, I can't explain it to you, David. I can, however, tell you what I know from my own experiences. It all comes down to the fact that the human mind works differently from ours. They can hide many thoughts inside the complexities of their mind, and they can forget things inside those complexities. For most humans it is easier for them to do that, to hide it away, rather than deal with the problem. I have also found that when they hide those things away, they stay hidden until they pass from this life into the next. It is difficult to understand why, but for Darien as well as some others, these problems can resurface with a vengeance. It is apparent that upon this resurfacing, and the continuous reliving of these past events, presents a problem that some humans are unprepared to deal with. After her mother died, Darien, along with her siblings, was forced to live with an emotionally cold grandmother, who believed in beatings as a form of love and punishment. The beatings were not so bad as to leave visible scars, but they did leave mental scars."

Completely exhausted, David sat down in a chair that suddenly appeared out of nowhere.

"Her father punished her on several occasions but in those days, it was considered a normal punishment. However, her stepmother, ah there was the one who tormented and deliberately hurt her. Darien has suppressed most of this, and the process of recall had not been easy. She watched her stepmother drown her life in pills and whiskey, and when Darien tried to help, her father told her to leave it be. He was waiting for the woman to die. He knowingly made the decision that rather than help the woman who was his wife, it would be easier to let her die. Fortunately, when it did happen, it was a blessed relief for the sick woman. The father's mistake was in telling Darien he cared so little for life that he was willing to stand by and do nothing. You cannot tell this to a seventeen-year-old child without knowing it could have possible repercussions later in life. My instincts tell me that as Darien reaches a turning point in her life, coming close to the same age as her parents, she feels that it would be easier for her to die, as her parents did, rather than to fight. The young man that she gave her virginity to abused her, consumed drugs, and he too was an alcoholic. He forced himself upon her, and rather than saying no, she accepted this form of closeness as opposed to nothing at all. In all of the times that she relinquished to the demands of men, all she ever really wanted was for someone to kiss her, to hold her and most of all to love her. The entanglement became greater when she fell into the wrong hands living in the town where she met the man named Matthew."

"She told me that she was raped," David offered.

"It was so much more than a rape, David, it totally blew her away, and in my opinion, Darien had been steadily raped for most of her young life. When she met Jack, the only man to ever offer her a home, she was so grateful to have a roof over her head that the thought of saying no to him was something that never occurred to her." David sat in the chair shaking his head, he was already aware of most of Darien's younger life.

"Wait, David, there is more."

"More, how could there possibly be more?"

"You know yourself that there have been many times that you were not able to watch over her, and did you realize that of her own free will, she slept with any man who would buy her a drink and take her home? The men of her world took advantage of her vulnerability, and never cared for her feelings. As far as I am concerned, the men who took advantage of her innocence raped her just the same as if they had forced her. To put it bluntly, she just did not know any better because in her poor twisted mind, she thought that eventually someone would love her. She is overwhelmed by guilt that she can no longer deal with the pain. The two years in her life when most of this took place are the years where she gave herself willingly, and it was simply for the touch of another human. Does this make sense to you, David?"

"No, not really, because there are people on the earth who go through so much more than her. People who lose families to snipers, to war, even to people that they thought were their friends. There are women who live in the streets covered with filth, not knowing where they are going to find their next meal, except maybe in the soup kitchen. Darien feels sorry for herself, and she has so much more than these others do. I am at a loss, much as Darien herself, to understand why."

"It is like you have already told her, David, we don't always have the answers. Darien has become lost to you, and what is worse, Darien has become lost to herself. Depression does strange things to the human mind, but if you truly wish to help her, and I think that you do, you must convince her to see the only person that can help her."

"She needs a doctor, yes I know, and I have already suggested this to her, but look what happened, look what she did to herself. I don't think she will go."

"She must go, David." The guardian paused for a moment before proceeding with the next question because where David and Darien were concerned, he was about to walk on very unstable ground. David must not become aware that her entire life had been in preparation for what she still has to face. The elder knew that if David found out, he would do everything he could to prevent it from happening.

"Do you love her, David?"

"Yes, despite her being so demanding and so exhausting, yes, I love her still."

"Then you must convince her there is no alternative."

"Or?"

"Or she will die, and the consequences of her death will have repercussions throughout all of their civilization, and ours."

\* \* \*

David sat on the bed beside Darien. He had taken her home and she was deep inside a sleep that the elder guardian put upon her. David brushed the hair back from her face, and wished to all that made him that his feelings for her were not real but he could not deny the surge of protection he felt. She needed someone to be strong for her in the way she stayed strong all those years, while nurturing and caring for her family. David, the guardian angel who came from the shadows to help Darien, felt at this time to be so helpless. All he had to offer her was the love that they shared, and it hurt him to know it was not enough. She opened her eyes, and then slowly closed them again, while reaching for his hand. She held tightly to his hand as she slept, as if she knew it was finally over for them. David leaned down, kissed the lightly freckled face, and quickly lost himself in the light fruity scent that always dominated her. He closed his eyes and laid his hand over the small hand, which completely disappeared inside his. The door opened downstairs, and as the dutiful guardian, he merged with the shadows sensing it was the husband who arrived. David wanted desperately to defend Darien to Jack, but this was forbidden, so instead he bristled like a caged animal, and stayed hidden in the shadows.

"Darien, you lazy cow, where the hell are you? Are you sleeping again?" Jack shouted as he started up the stairs, the impatient anger in his voice already rousing Darien. She put her feet over the side of the bed, and held onto the nightstand. Her thoughts remained fuzzy, her eyes still heavy with sleep but her awareness of Jack's anger was vividly apparent. David started forward, but she waved him back into the darkness, safe within the shadows where Jack could not see, and she heard the heavy footsteps coming up the stairs for her. The clomping of the heavy work boots brought a tense flinching to her already stressed mind.

"Darien, damn, I don't understand you. Why the hell don't you do something with yourself? I'm sick and tired of coming home, and finding your ass laying around." He came into the bedroom, and suddenly stopped, totally amazed when he saw what she had done to her head.

"You're a stupid fucking crazy woman, you know that?" David watched as his words relayed into the same effect as if he physically struck her.

"I'm sorry," she said timidly. "I'm just a little tired."

"You're always tired. If you weren't so fat and lazy then maybe you wouldn't need to sleep all of the time. Christ, Darien, I'm so sick of it, and what the fuck did you do to your hair? Didn't I tell you to keep it short? Well didn't I?" He was shouting at her again, and she cringed from his harsh words.

"Sibby did it."

"Fuck Sibby and stop making excuses for what you did by blaming it on a person who is not real." The tears came, without control, and Jack did not disguise his disgust for his wife.

"Put it away, Darien, I don't want to talk to the person you pretend to be, and don't start crying. You need to take the blame for your own stupid actions." Darien choked back the tears, and brushed the hair out of her face.

"I'm sorry, Jack. You know that I don't mean to do this, it just happens."

"Yeah, yeah, tell it to someone who gives a fuck. I'm going out. Joe will be here in a few minutes to pick me up, and we'll be up to the lake fishing for bullheads. So clean yourself up; go take a shower or something. Your kids are downstairs, they need their dinner. I'll eat when I get home."

"Okay." He stood in the bedroom staring at the slovenly overweight woman that still shared his bed. There was a look of pity that crossed his features, but it was quickly gone, replaced by disgust.

"What the hell happened to you? I can hardly stand to look at you anymore." He slammed the door on the way out of the bedroom, and then again on the way out of the house leaving Darien to herself upstairs.

"I don't know, Jack, I just don't know." David fumed in the corners, rolling and blending in the shadows. Jack didn't have to insult her, he didn't have to verbally abuse her; all she needed was a little self-confidence. Why couldn't he try to give her that? Darien rose from the bed, looked at herself in the mirror, and then she smiled a very scary smile. There was an evilness about her, so much so, that even her features seemed to change. It made David shiver. Darien walked down the stairs, ignoring the snide comments made by her children about her hair. She walked deliberately past them into the bathroom where she opened a drawer and retrieved a pair of scissors. She began to methodically snip away at her hair until there was only bristle-like stubble left. "He wants short fucking hair; well he's got short fucking hair."

David sat impatiently in the shadows wanting to help, but the rules were and always had been that he could not help her unless she called for him. Her eyes squeezed shut against the depression that threatened to overwhelm her and as she lowered her head, David easily recognized the beginnings of a Sibby headache. When she looked up again, David was not surprised to see her crying. Everyone that knew Darien hated Sibby, even Darien herself. Sibby was the part of Darien that drained even David of all of his patience. She whined and clung to him like a small annoying child. Actually, Sibby annoyed everyone. Suddenly her face changed again, and the strange look reappeared on Darien's face, the one that had scared David only moments earlier. This was a new personality, and in a brief span of only a few minutes, it became the second time that he saw it.

"Who are you, Darien?" he whispered from the shadows. She didn't hear him and she picked up the scissors again, staring at her mirror image while she imagined all the swirling tornadoes on the other side even as David swirled around her feet. Slowly a smile spread across her face, and she opened her mouth to speak.

"Hello, Cynthia, you slut. Where the fuck you been?" David was beside himself. This was someone new, and he didn't know this side of Darien. Was it possible that this personality was the one who broke the mirrors? A fourth personality named Cynthia who despised her mirror image. When had this new personality begun?

"By all that I am, Darien, who are you?" he whispered once more remaining in shadow, softly caressing her ankles, appearing as nothing more than a play in light. She held the razor-sharp scissors over her arm, and then slowly brought them to her chest. Darien opened her shirt exposing the breasts that David so loved. The scissors slowly separated, and Cynthia readied to cut off Darien's nipple. David held his breath, and his agitation showed in the way he rolled and boiled at her feet. There was a sharp knock at the door, and just as quickly, the slut disappeared, allowing Darien to regain control.

"Mom, we're hungry. Are you cooking dinner tonight?" David was not overly fond of Darien's children; they were self-centered, spoiled, rude, and verbally abusive to their mother. Suddenly the front door opened and closed announcing that Darien's husband returned home. It had been a very short fishing trip. Jack looked for his wife, wanting to speak to her, to say something kind, maybe something that might help. He sighed; there was nothing left to say; he should have stayed at the lake.

"Darien, how about some damn dinner?" he demanded more than he asked. Darien slowly walked out of the bathroom and David recognized the "zone." Her safe place of refuge, especially when all of them became too overwhelming. Darien left the bathroom and through habit alone, went about preparing a simple dinner. Only David knew as the knife came down into the head of lettuce what Darien was thinking. She cut up the red pepper, the cucumber, and put them in the salad, but wait, where was the red onion? Jessie liked red onion in the salad, but Jack hated onions, and as she added some romaine lettuce Darien put in a couple of slices anyway. The iceberg lettuce was already cut, and she dumped it all into the bowl, topping it off with some croutons and a few bacon bits. She methodically took down the salad plates, and walked into the dining room.

"I hate onions in the salad, Darien."

"Jessie likes them," she answered, and then she stood in the doorway with her back to them mouthing the exact same words as Jack said them.

"Does Jessie pay the grocery bill around here?" The simple compromise would have been to set a few slices on a small plate, and why this never occurred to her was just ignorance. Instead Darien shook her head encouraging his anger, and went back to the kitchen. They all sat at the table waiting for their dinner, and Darien had long ago stopped asking for help because they would help no one but themselves. Finally, with dinner on the table, she picked up her purse, along with her keys, and headed for the door.

"Where are you going?" Jack asked her.

"Does it really matter anymore where I go?"

"Well, you never fail to let me down, Darien, with your stupid fucking answers. Go on and go, what the hell do I care?" As she turned to leave, the hardened street woman returned. It wasn't Darien who walked out the door; it was the destructive one, the one who could take Darien on the last final step.

Cynthia cranked the four-cylinder family sedan up to ninety as the six-lane highway lay before her. She opened the window letting the cold air hit her full in the face, and Cynthia bypassed the slower-moving vehicles like a veteran race car driver. The toughened streetwise juvenile was in control. She felt exhilarated at being in control, a different kind of excitement as the car jumped to her demands; bringing a temporary sense of finally being free.

David was there. He swirled around her ankles, trying to protect her from herself, but without her call he could not form for her, so instead he rode with her while attempting to find a way to help.

Twenty minutes later, still doing ninety, Cynthia suddenly began to slow the car so that she could pull out of the fast lane and into the breakdown lane. She shut off the engine, got out of the parked car, and walked around to the front where she proceeded to lift the hood. She put on a good show of touching and pulling a few things on the engine to make it look as though there was a genuine problem. David already realized that potentially Cynthia could be a very destructive personality, and he was very afraid for Darien. He also knew at that moment who had taken Darien through all the hard roads of her life. She is the strongest one, the one whose wild, uncontrolled thoughts bordered on suicide. And now she was in control. Cynthia is the one who fought back when it was necessary and up until now, she kept a very low profile. David had never had to face her before, and he was not sure how to handle this new personality of Darien. He watched in apprehension as she left her car, walked over to the side of the bridge, and looked down at the rapidly flowing river five hundred feet below. First one foot, then the other went up and over the side of the bridge. Darien sat on one of the beams, her hands caressing the cold hard steel as she bordered between leaving and staying. Cars skidded wildly on the pressed pavement, but Darien couldn't hear them, and Cynthia didn't care.

"Hey, lady, stop!" It was too late as Cynthia threw herself over the side.

David's love was all encompassing for his guardian life, but Darien had brought him a passion that, despite all of the teaching in the ways of the guardians, he was missing. For the first time in all of their existence, a guardian's love was stronger than all the rules. David solidified and he caught Darien! Everything fell away as they journeyed to the other side, and those who stood watching swore that the woman fell into the water below.

\* \* \*

Darien woke to the sounds of an intense argument. As soon as the guardians became aware that she heard them, their voices hushed, and David came out of the shadows into her view. He waved his hand impatiently at the fireplace, and very quickly a large blaze warmed the room causing Darien to smile.

"You do know what I love you, don't you, David?" Now it was his turn to smile at her, and his voice softened to nearly a whisper when he spoke to her.

"You should have died, Darien, but I saved you. I shouldn't have been able to and now I have to answer for that."

"There were other times when you were able to help me without me calling for you, like that time at the lake under the raft. I can't believe that you have to answer for the fact that I'm alive, when it's been your job right along to keep me that way." Her voice sounded so cold, so convinced, so smug.

"So what was all of this, a test? Were you testing us? Testing me, Darien? You do not do things like that when you truly love someone. Haven't you learned anything?"

"I don't think I was in control."

"Maybe not, but there are some things that you can learn to control. I could help you before, because they were small helps, more like guidance than anything else and at that time, without your knowledge, you did call to me. It was different then, and now because of your carelessness and selfishness, I have to answer for what I've done."

"You answer to a strange person. Aren't they glad that you saved me?"

"Darien, don't you understand?"

"Do I want to?"

"You always did ask too many questions" David did not attempt to hide his frustration, but despite the overindulgence of her personality conflicts, he loved her still.

"If I tell you, you must promise to keep Sibby and your new side Cynthia under control. Can you do that?"

"Yes." But she really couldn't be sure.

"The ones that I answer to believe that above all else life is sacred. To live is a gift, Darien, and anyone who does what you just did, tries to take their own life, does not deserve the privilege of being saved.. We face very difficult decisions when we have to distinguish between a cry for help, and those of you who do not deserve the privilege of continued existence. The fact that I was able to become solid without you calling for me, well that miracle alone has given way to a hundred questions among the guardians. You have violated that which they hold sacred above anything else, deliberately trying to destroy a human life, your life, Darien. If it had not been for me, you would have succeeded." David could see the personalities inside of Darien fighting for control. At first, the tears came from Sibby the whiner. Then Cynthia emerged, and the hatred for herself that came alive in her face scared David. Mary made a brief appearance, but her sensuality was not needed, and she left just as quickly. Darien was the last to emerge but David found himself wishing for Mary, the soft, sensuous, gentle one, and he despised the way his mind was working.

"Who are you really?" he whispered as he gathered her into his arms.

"I wish I knew," she answered back, "because I can't find me anymore." David placed one hand on each side of her face, and looked into her eyes.

"I love you, Darien. Let me find someone to help you heal."

"You mean a doctor don't you?"

"Look at me, look at the love I have for you. How could you think that I would ever let anything hurt you? I'm not one of those people from your past, Darien, I am you're here and your now. Please let me love you one more time, and then let me help you heal, and if that's selfish of me as your guardian, I don't care."

"I don't want you to leave, David."

"Let's not talk about that now." He softly kissed her lips. "I want to make love to you." She put her hand up to hide her head and looked away from him.

"It doesn't matter how you look to me, Darien," he said as he turned her face back to him.

"I love you, Darien, and nothing else matters." He kissed her again, and Darien turned sensuous as Mary emerged. Her emotions went into overdrive, and she fairly lost control. Her lips pressed to his, and she made the little noises in her throat that he loved. She kissed him fully, pulling his tongue into her mouth, the taste that she missed for so long. He leaned over her, and she lay back onto the bed so David could make a series of kisses down her throat, and then back to her mouth. Their feelings overwhelmed them and Darien cried, Mary disappeared, but the sensuous feelings remained. Sibby tried to hang on, crying hard for dominance, but then she too slowly started to dissipate. Darien felt his hardness on her leg, and she longed to have it inside of her. He became rough in his caresses, and she reveled in the strength that he showed. His mouth traveled over her belly, and she let him roughly push her legs apart as she gasped and pulled in her breath. David took his thumb and ran it lightly down the side of her labia, and then into the velvety smoothness inside. Her secrets swelled with excitement.

"God, David," she whispered to him. She quivered under his touch, and as his mouth descended into her nether region, she lost control. Her hips thrust upward into his face while he bit and nibbled at the very center of her being. His large fingers pushed inside and so great were her feelings that she was unable to hold herself back. Slowly David turned himself around until they lay side by side and Darien gathered all of him up into her warm moist mouth. She feasted on David. Her mouth was open, wanting, slowly releasing, and then pulling him back inside. She rolled over, and David moved her legs until she was positioned over his mouth, and he pushed his tongue deep inside causing her to swallow him even more. Still it was not enough.

"Darien, please, I want all of you." She obediently waited for him on all fours as he slid out from under her. She opened herself to him, for him and David pushed into her from behind.

"All of you, Darien, all of you belongs to me." His body shivered, as he withdrew and then pushed back into her crying out with the pleasure of the friction caused by her tightness. Suddenly he shuddered, and poured himself into her. David collapsed on her back, and then immediately reached around, pulled her open, plunged his fingers inside, and she exploded on his hand with a hot wet orgasm. David gave out small moans as he climaxed again, filling her once more with his pleasure. Together they shuddered and lay on the bed while he kissed the back of her neck, until she turned her face to his so that he could kiss her lips, taking delight in the salty taste of them both. He rolled her over to kiss her breasts knowing how much she liked to have him pull her nipples into his mouth. Darien arched her back, and felt the weakness in her legs start to spread through her body. Slowly he opened her labia and held it open gently moving his fingers up the inside; taking his time with the silky softness that he found inside. Darien shivered, overcome by exhaustion, but he continued caressing her until she responded. She moaned as her excitement began again. David took her leg and placed it over his so that he could enter her one more time and Darien was amazed at his ability to become erect so quickly. He slowly teased her, until he knew she was ready for him, then he pushed the most amazing part of his body fully into her, and she cried to him.

"David, please." He kissed her face, her lips, and her closed eyes.

"I love you, Darien, I have always loved you. Now what I need is for you to be whole for me. I need you to heal, but not just for me, for yourself and for your children."

"I don't want to heal, David, because then you will go away, and if that's being selfish on my part, then like you, I don't care."

"I promise, Darien, by all that I am; I will never leave you again."

"David, do you really want to stay with me?"

"Darien, I want to stay with you more than you could ever understand."

"And more than anything I want to stay strong for you."

"I love you, Darien, and I swear by the Gods who created me, I will always love you." He entered her, and she knew that despite what he said, she would loose the battle to stay with him. She could feel her personalities cry out, and as the crying began to fade, Darien knew that sweet David, without the help of doctors, wanted to begin her healing. He was her guardian, her lover and he was saving her from herself.

They loved and they climaxed together in continued unison of unbelievable passion. They aroused each other with an incredible appetite for lust, until finally exhausted they lay asleep in each other's arms. Darien held David to her; refusing to allow him to return to the shadows, and David for all that he was, loved Darien, and refused to go. He finally realized that he could love because he wanted to, without it having to be a part of his duty as a guardian, and it was a new feeling for him. Unknowingly, Darien had captured the true love of a guardian.

The elders watched them, and shaking their heads in despair for they know how self-destructive Darien is, and that the result of this would be to drag David down with her. As much as he loved her, and as much as he wanted to stand by her, they were not going to allow it. She was truly beyond even their help. It was quite a quandary, because the final effect in taking David away would most certainly push her over the edge. How could David completely heal her, how could he help her find herself, when she was so unstable? Who was Darien? One thing was certain; Darien did not even know who she was, not anymore. The real puzzlement in the continuing episodes of the two was how it had become possible for David to become real for her when she had not called for him. This could only have happened if his love was a real love. Allowing this to continue could possibly cause David's destruction, and stopping it might hurt them, resulting in a negative effect on the outcome of Darien's training.

Fully content, the two lovers lay in each other's arms, but even in the midst of her deepest sleep, Darien's face was changing. Her eyes moved rapidly underneath her closed eyelids, and her grip tightened on David, as she drained him of his strength.

"Take him out of there," the older one demanded, as he felt the life force draining from the guardian. "Now!" So even while she held him as tight as she could, David began to fade, and his power of love could not match the power of those who held command over him. Darien woke. David was staring at her, scared, and astonished that they had actually come for him.

"David, please don't go."

"I can't stop it, they are too strong."

"David," she pleaded softly as he faded from her view, and the tears glistened clearly in his eyes, becoming the last thing she was going to see. David's voice echoed through their dream room, and as the clouds rolled in to take her home, she heard him whisper just one word. It was said directly into her ear, making it sound as if he was still lying beside her.

"Darien."

"Oh God, David, please no."

Her pleas went unnoticed, and Darien stood alone in her cold empty living room. She called to him one last time, her voice a whisper, her heart truly broken, her mind holding onto a small sliver of sanity; it was all that remained as she said his name from the depths of her self-made despair.

"David."

The silence that surrounded her became oppressive, and her mind shattered into a hundred pieces as she fell to her knees totally lost to herself. The dark insanity reached for her and from this point on the shadows did not dance for her.

Darien danced for them.

# PART FIVE
# PLAYING THE GAME

Her life is an explosive reality.

The continuous pain sits in one corner of her head while the small demons with the miniature fire hammers keep pounding away at the giant pointed spikes. Each blow delivers the bolt of searing heat that sparks the pain, and ignites the nerve to jump and leap in response, leaving her with tears that flood her eyes while causing her head to jerk to one side. She reaches up to pull on her hair to alleviate the pressure they were creating, only to find it gone. Darien pulled so much out that it left only bleeding patches of skin and the nurses had no recourse but to shave her head. They left her nothing to pull.

Darien spreads her fingers wide and places her hands palm down onto the patch of sun sitting on the floor. The spot is warm, and it sends shivers up her back. Her hands absorb the heat, letting it bake into her aged skin. It was her preference to call herself aged, feeling as though she has lived for centuries, even though she has not yet reached the classic definition of middle age. Her head jerks towards the bed as another hammered blow pulls it to one side making her eyelids flutter with the delivered pain. There is movement at the door; Darien had been expecting this because it is his day. It's time to play the game he likes so well. She watches him out of the corner of her eye so that he won't know she watches him. He sits on her cot, and she stays kneeled where she is, letting her hands gather the heat that allows the spreading warmth to ease throughout her entire body.

"Do you know what day this is?" The voice that speaks to her is deep, very masculine, and seemingly sympathetic. Darien won't answer him, what would be the point? She leans backwards extending herself from the waist, rear in the air, flexing like a very smug, satisfied feline. The nerves in her head jump along their path, and her eyes squint against the tortuous blows of the fire hammers.

"Still having those headaches?"

*Don't answer him Darien. Play with him, you already know how much he likes to play this game.* She relaxes, stretches again, and then she stands up in the single patch of sun that falls inside her empty cell. She walks towards him as she disrobes. The caged woman kneels before him, and raises her arms wide over her head bringing her breasts up for his scrutiny. Darien leans her head backwards and it jerks again against another delivered blow. The doctor gets up, picks up her clothes, and dresses her, slowly, carefully buttoning the night shirt so that he "accidentally" touches her naked breast. She reaches out, grabs his penis, and hangs on; smiling when she finds him erect. She squeezes tighter, making him make a grunting noise. He, in turn, reaches down and slowly uncurls her fingers from around him, and Darien returns to kneeling in the sun patch while he remains on the cot. Darien knows this game so well, and she turns to look directly at him.

"Do I know you?" She speaks! He raises his eyebrows in surprise. This was a new twist in the game, Darien has never spoken before.

"Yes," he answers, "I am Dr. Holmes." Well of course, she knew he was that, maybe she should disrobe again, he likes that game, or maybe she should continue with the new one. "Well," she decides, "let's see what plays will be made with this new game."

"And you are?" she asks him.

"I told you, Dr. Holmes. I tell you every time I come to see you."

"Dr. Holmes is who?" She smiles inside of her head, thoroughly convinced that she is confusing him, hoping he would like it better if she did not speak. She studies him, staring into his hazel eyes knowing that he studies her at the same time. Darien can see the little imps running around inside his head, and they too are looking for their fire hammers. He is going to have a bad one, but at least he can dissolve them, hers need to be pulled out, but they had taken away her hair. This lets the demons run free and now they hammer the spike almost all the time. She reaches up and hits her head as hard as she can with her fist, jarring the little fuckers, knocking them over. They'll stay down for a while. Lucky for her they are stupid demons, and it will take some time for them to find their hammers again. Darien opens her shirt.

"Want a taste?" She missed sex.

"No thank you." He remains sitting on her cot with his legs spread wide apart, and she can see that inside of his pants, he is still erect. It had felt big. One of the despairing demons suddenly found his hammer. Bang! Darien's head turned quickly, her eyes shut tight, and she hits her head again with her fist.

"Get Out!" she screams. One of them falls over, and it seems to shrink a little while the movement of her head causes them to roll around inside. She feels immediate relief, although it will be brief. Why didn't they know? Why weren't the doctors who came to see her able to stop the demons from pounding her with their fire hammers? Darien stands and walks seductively to the doctor, and placing her knee in between his legs she straightens her back, which causes her breasts to rise up even with his face. This time he does not close her blouse, instead he kisses the space between them, and she feels the little demons begin their endless thoughtless search.

"Bite them," she whispers harshly to him. He does, almost hard enough to leave teeth marks, but not quite. He pulls down her pants, and plunges his hand inside. Her wetness floods him in response. She throws her head back as his mouth and his tongue target her large pink nipples. His erection bulges in his pants.

She unzips his pants, and reaches inside so she can wrap her hand around his erection. She squeezes him again, and then she pulls him from his underwear. His hand never releases Darien, and as he lies backwards onto her cot, he takes her with him, but it is Darien who pulls his hand from inside her, anguishing for just a moment at the emptiness. She brings his fingers to her mouth. The taste is a bit salty, but it adds to her passion while encouraging the pleasure waves to beat back the demons. She licks his fingers, and then she places her lips on his.

"Taste me," Darien whispered into his mouth. She lowers herself onto his erection, and their mouths meet as he penetrates her.

"Fill me," she encourages him, and he takes her hips to push her down, while at the same time he pushes up. Euphoria overtakes her demons, and she cries aloud. She furiously pushes down, sucking him up inside, catching him with her opening, and holding him there. A feeling of fullness starts to settle inside of Darien, and she is having trouble breathing. He teases her lips with his tongue until she raises herself up over his face and he once again captures her breasts with his mouth. He holds onto her, and she pushes down as if trying to hold him inside forever. Darien's movements are fast, and she silently demands that he keep up with her. She explodes onto him, and he in turn becomes wet inside of her. He heaves and grunts while she rides his sex. Finally the doctor is spent, as is the patient and she leans forward to lie on his chest. Her head rises and falls with his heavy, labored breathing while he rubs her back with his hands.

"I want to take you home with me." She does not like to play this part of his game. Darien immediately leaves his embrace, and begins to dress.

"Don't, Sibby; please don't shut me out again." He replaces his exposed part, and gets up to run warm water in the small porcelain basin that is a permanent fixture in her prison. When the basin is full he places a washcloth in the water, and Dr. Holmes soaps it fully. He takes down her pants and washes away his evidence while humming softly to ease Darien's tortured spirit. It is a wonderful feeling, and one that she loves for him to do. He kisses her from behind, and his hands roam over her. She makes the strangest sounds deep inside her throat, then suddenly a huge pain sears the inside of her head, and her hands reach up trying to grab onto the missing hair. She screams once more, lunges sideways hitting the back of her head against the wall. The doctor jumps up and tries to cushion her head with his hands, but not before Darien reopens old wounds. The culprit demon, riding on a stream of blood, slides out of the reopened wound. The creature slips in the stream which causes the miniature being to slide across the floor towards the doctor's feet.

"God, Sibby." His voice is full sorrow as he pulls her pants up with one hand while cradling her head with the other, trying to keep it away from the wall. The door flies open crashing, and echoing loudly in the nearly empty cell.

"Get me bandages," he orders as Darien slumps against him. He picks her up, carries her over to the cot, and lays her back down. The orderlies who had opened the door return and Dr. Holmes quickly bandages Darien's head. She watches in growing horror as the little dislodged demon regains his balance, and heads back towards her.

"NOOOO!" she screams.

It comes at her smiling, and she covers her ears to try to keep it out. It fools her and climbs straight up into her nose. Darien's eyes roll back in her head, leaving only the whites of her eyes showing.

She convulses.

It found its way back in and it has brought a larger spike along with an even larger fire hammer.

BANG!

Her head jerks sideways and she lets it go as it follows the slam all the way into the wall. The demon falls over inside of head. Darien feels something prick her arm, and the sunspot on the floor starts to fade. She will sleep, the game is over for now. Dr. Holmes is ready to leave the room, and two days from today, it will begin again. He comes three times a week to play this game.

"Let me take you home," he says to her, but if she did, then the demons would get him too. She did not want that to happen, so they all played the game his way.

The demons howl with laughter that rocks her soul.

Dr. Holmes is erect again as he walks down the corridor.

He is also smiling.

Darien sleeps and she dreams wonderful dreams of flying, dreams of warm soft lights, dreams of guardians, and dreams of funny crooked men that live inside her mirror.

# PART SIX
# FOR THE LOVE OF DAVID
# DARIEN RETURNS

Darien closed the door of her new room.

Privileges here were a joke, besides what made THEM think THEY could make her normal. She had never been normal, not for as long as she could remember. Darien had started to recall many things about her past, especially about the teen years where she should have been enjoying dates and dances, but ended up just trying to survive and worse yet, she had to re-live all of her past mistakes for Dr. Holmes without hiding in the zone.

(In the past you made a few mistakes, for which you will atone.)

Unfortunately, for Darien, the hospital decided to bring in another doctor, the infamous Dr. Marris, and she hated him. He was short-tempered, insolent, insulting; full of himself as a man and a doctor, and he pushed her until the demons came that pounded the stakes and made Sibby cry. Up until he interfered, her headaches were getting better, and the little fuckers that pounded the stakes only came once in a while. Then Marris had decided to change all of that even though the paperwork showed positive progress with Dr. Holmes. Darien tried to enlist the help of her husband, but her personalities were too complicated for him to understand, and he left his wife's problems to the doctors.

Despite her condition, Jack still kept every Saturday as his visiting day, and on this particular Saturday, he was actually being nice to her. Darien was aware that pig-headed Marris was probably setting them up; standing in observance behind the one-way mirror. She had been wondering why they were allowing Jack to have so much "alone" time with her today. She surmised that Marris was probably hoping her husband could get one of her personalities to emerge for his personal entertainment. Her husband continuously tried to kiss her hello, but she kept turning her head. She frustrated the poor man who tried repeatedly to get close to her. Rather than giving in to anger, Jack finally admitted defeat and went home. Darien's children never came to see her because they were too embarrassed to admit to having a mom in a "crazy" house. They were afraid one of their friends would see them, or find out, then the inevitable adolescent teasing would begin, and the entire world would know. They told people that their Mom was in the hospital, which she was, so in essence it really wasn't a lie. Dr. Marris entered the room, and Darien quickly turned away. She hugged herself close, and despite the warmth of the summer, she started to shake. She was not afraid of Marris, not really, but she dreaded the touch of the slimy doctor. She could feel his anger without having to see him.

"Darien." His voice was stern, full of the power that came with his position. She would not answer him, and her head began to hurt.

"Fuck you," she said to herself.

"Darien," he said to her again, and she shivered harder than before, hugging herself even closer.

"Fuck you!" she said harder and deeper inside her head. The demons started to dance wildly, and they pounded the stakes harder than ever before, causing Darien's head to throb but also causing her to become angry. Dr. Marris was pushing all the right buttons, the ones that would cause her to seek the separate personalities that she had promised long ago to heal for David. The cold, unfeeling, dominating doctor saw the effect that he was having on her, and he was pleased.

"Sibby!" he shouted at her. Unknown to Marris was that he was unleashing an uncontrollable anger to replace the whimpering crybaby attitude, and it was not Sibby or Darien that faced Dr. Marris with a rage surpassed only by his lust for her total destruction. This is what he does with some of his strong, challenging female patients; it gave credence to his power and brought him an undeniable high. He tore apart their minds, destroyed their free will, and then he would rebuild them into the case studies that he wanted them to be. There was no way that he could know that in the undoing of Darien, the result would be the release of Cynthia. This is her strength, her strongest personality, the one that Darien herself once referred to as slut. Marris pushed her beyond her limits, and she turned on him with a vengeance.

"Fuck you, cocksucker!" she screams at him. Dr. Marris had read all of Dr. Holmes' reports and he knew the details of Sibby, the weak one, the one who is clinging, and who cries at every little mishap. Then there is Darien. The mother of three strong, independent daughters, and the wife of Jack. Darien spends most of her time in the zone, and of the three documented personalities, the doctors considered her the one most often in control. Finally there is Mary, the slinky seductress (Dr. Marris's own personal favorite) and he liked it when she decided to emerge. But, according to Holmes, there was no report of this strong one. Whom had Dr. Marris found? What had he found? Had Darien hidden this personality from everyone?

"I would like to talk to Sibby," Dr. Marris said to her in an even monotone voice while purposefully looking at her chart.

"Well she's not here, and I'm not letting her come back." The headache was on a wild rampage, running out of control. Instead of the demons driving the spikes with their little demon fire hammers, her head was caught in a vise resembling two strong hands that were crushing her skull. Those hands belonged to Marris. She looked at him from under the stringy dirty hair that had finally grown in, and she could barely see Dr. Marris through the rage that was churning inside. Her body shook with the exertion it took to hold back an anger that threatened to explode and become the hardened woman named Cynthia. If Cynthia came into control, to have voice, and access to all that transpired, there was no telling what could happen. However, it was too late because the voice that came out of Darien's mouth was low and hard as she strengthened herself against the doctor who would rape her body and mind.

"Fuck you," she said firmly. Darien finally stopped shaking and Cynthia had nearly gained total control.

"That is not nice, Darien."

"Neither are you, Marris."

"Dr. Marris."

"You call yourself a doctor, I call you what you really are. I know why you're here and Darien is not in control anymore and now you have to deal with me." Dr. Marris pulled out a chair and sat calmly down at the table as Darien glared at him from the corner of the room. Marris calmly flipped through the papers that lay in Darien's file, thinking perhaps he had missed something, but the records were exacting, always recording the same three personalities. So who was this?

David knew who it was.

Although allowed to watch over Darien, the guardians forbade his direct interference, or any actual contact. He had kept an eye on her through the mirrors, and his heart ached for her touch. When the guardians took him away, and Darien had her breakdown, he could not go to her, and now he despised what the doctors were doing. David knew all of her personalities, and the only one that frightened him was Cynthia. He knew what would happen if Marris kept pushing her, he knew that Cynthia could put an end to all of their paperwork.

Unknown to Dr. Marris, Dr. Holmes had entered the room on the other side of the two-way mirror and he was watching the events as they unfolded. Paul Holmes raised his eyebrows in surprise when he saw a person in the room totally unknown to him, while at the same time patient-loving David undulated in the corner of room, hidden inside the ever-present shadows. He remained in the corner, part of him in the world beyond the mirrors, but without anyone knowing, he was able to slide part of himself into the room where Cynthia sat with Marris. His movement in the corner was a dance in shadow that Darien had seen before, and he was hoping that she would see him now. If only he could give her back part of her faith so she would know that he had not totally deserted her. Both Paul and David watched as Cynthia fully emerged from Darien and David could not help but feel partially responsible for her current situation. The guardians should have been more cautious when they chose to help Darien, because for the all centuries they have lived, there should have been more wisdom in their choices. They should have had more knowledge in the understandings of the human mind, and in this instance, it might have been better if they left Darien alone. He did not understand all that the eldest told him when Darien first arrived in this world; he only understood his own position in relation to her. His true feelings for her were something no one had planned.

"Who are you, Darien?" David replayed the question over and over in his mind.

"What have we done to you, and worse yet, what have we helped you do to yourself?"

Dr. Marris sat quietly going over the papers, focusing more on Mary, the sensuous one, the one who stayed hidden most of the time. He liked it when Mary came out. She was only eighteen years old, portraying the innocence of a young girl, but with all the experience of an adult woman. Marris was after that experience, the one who would be able to play his body into sick erotic fantasies. On paper, anything created from Darien's disturbing mind, Marris would record as her delusions. Delusion! What a wonderful word! It was such a neat place to hide his sick eroticism with his disturbed female patients, of which Darien was just one. He turned another page, and glanced through the reference that she made to the guardian she named David. She gave such a detailed profile to a nonexistent entity that upon reading it, one could almost believe in the fantasy with her.

Dr. Paul Holmes shifted his feet, clearly nervous that Dr. Marris would find out about the game that he too played with Darien, but unlike Marris, Paul preferred Sibby. He was fond of her weak side, the side that needed nurturing, and the side that needed more healing than the rest. After all isn't this what doctors were supposed to do, heal the sick? So now, two wanted to play games with Darien, very unaware of each other's designs, until now.

Dr. Hugh Marris removed his reading glasses and quietly observed Darien's body language. He watched in amazement as the personalities talked to each other, overrunning into and onto one another. There were actual noticeable face changes as the different personalities emerged, and then took shelter back in the farthest corners of her shattered mind. She talked to herself, argued within her differences, and all the time he watched carefully for Mary. The argument suddenly stopped, and Darien walked away from the wall towards Dr. Marris. She pulled out a chair, flung it around backwards, and swung her leg over the back, never taking her eyes off the face that she wanted to destroy.

"We have decided that no one talks to you but me."

"Who are you?" In his calm simplistic approach to this new personality, it appeared that Dr. Marris was clearly undisturbed by this turn of events.

"You smart-ass doctors are supposed to know everything; why don't you tell me."

"Be realistic, Darien, how would I know? Everything is hidden deep inside of you, and all we can do is to try to help you bring yourself under control. I am here for advice and guidance, but in the end you must heal yourself."

Darien sat quietly for a few minutes thinking about what he said. He was no doctor to her; he was just another man who wanted the fuck. She knew his type; she could smell a horny bastard before he even got close, and Darien had known what Paul had wanted even before he did. The only difference between Paul and Hugh was that Dr. Holmes might actually care a little bit, but in the end, it would all come down to the same thing. He too was after the "act," same as all men. Her husband Jack, who she thought different, who she thought sincere when he offered her a way off the streets and who in the end, was no different than any of the other men that became a brief part of her life. Love had never entered their relationship, and she accepted that for many years, until completely frustrated, she knew there had to be more. Sibby appeared after many years of being repressed crying constantly for someone to take care of her, someone to tend to her needs because she was so tired of tending to everyone else's. Dr. Marris enjoyed bringing Sibby out as a form of punishment to Darien, especially because he sought Mary.

Sweet Mary, with all the innocence of youth and the experience of a woman caught between two stages. She wanted desperately to recapture a past before her life experiences, yet she still tackled each new day with the blind innocence of seeing all that is good in the world. Mary presented herself as clean and wholesome, open to brand-new learning, and shy within her knowledge that she could knowingly seduce men with the pretense of just having wakened to her body's emotions. Explore me, learn me, teach me, but do not love me, for when love comes so does Sibby. It was here that Dr. Marris longed to go. That sweet innocence of youth combined with the knowledge of an older woman, safe within the confines of his fantasy, his perverse life, hidden inside this hospital and inside Darien's mind. He wanted this more than anything, and Darien knew that it would all come down to the act she named "THE FUCK." Was there anyone left, any one person at all who cared enough for her as a human being who could help her?

"You are a lousy black-bearded piece of shit, and you know it." The man across from her slowly blinked his eyes, giving a small hint to the fact that she pegged him. He was cool though, she had to give him that.

"I'm not afraid of you, Marris." She wasn't, not really, not this one. This one was mean and hard; made strong against men from all the years of abuse. Dr. Marris repeated the question he had asked earlier.

"Who are you?"

"Does it really matter who I am? What matters is that I am here now, and everyone else is sleeping, and you have to deal with me, Hugh." She said his name like it tasted bad, a sour, bitter taste. "But just to satisfy your curiosity, my name is Cynthia, and I am the one that holds them all. I don't think that we've met." Hugh Marris put his glasses back on, and continued reading through the report, ignoring the new arrival, hoping that his indifference would cause her to retreat into the recesses of Darien's mind, from which he had unknowingly released her.

"I'm not leaving, Marris, if that's what you're thinking." She was cool and calculating, and very strong. Dr. Marris started to think that maybe conquering Cynthia to find Mary might be worth the ride. He decided on another approach, and in the room behind the mirror, watching quietly, Dr. Holmes was totally absorbed in the new twists and turns in the world that is Darien.

David disappeared from the shadows.

He whirled and twirled in the darkness, bumping and jostling with the thousands of other mini-tornadoes. The elders made him small again, putting him back into the holding area with the other guardians knowing that if he went to Darien it could mean an end to the caring guardian. He released wave after wave of Darien's despair into the darkness, and the other guardians rolled and tumbled as his discharge of anger and desperation threatened to overload onto some of the oldest guardians themselves!

It has been known to happen, in the rarest of instances, that a guardian can and does fall into a real love with a human. The only thing that keeps them returning to the place on the other side of the mirror is that eventually the guardian realizes that he needs to help others for himself to survive. This is the guardians' sole purpose for life, the very reason for their existence, it's the reason for their creation, and it's all that they have ever done. The elders mistakenly thought that the love between Darien and David would wane; simply because that is the way it always happens. However, nothing could have prepared anyone for the passion that the two would release. It came with such an outpouring of emotions that it even set some of the older guardians' hearts to flutter! When it came to Darien, they all had a problem distancing themselves from their feelings. Wave after wave of devastating despair reached tidal proportions, flooding into the world of the guardians, and David was ready to explode in his frustrating efforts to break free from the restrictions that held him partly in his world. He needed to return to her as a solid being; to free Darien from herself, and from the men who would harm her.

In the meantime, Dr. Marris was pondering which way he wanted to take Darien. He had seen the anger and the hatred in the eyes of Cynthia and he knew that he was getting close to where he wanted to be. After studying the new personality that emerged, Dr. Marris had to admit that even he was a little afraid to pursue the one Darien called slut, but then again, overcoming this one could be rewarding and exciting. Cynthia was well aware of his intentions, and she decided to release just a little bit of Mary. Dr. Marris reached across the table and touched Darien's arm, causing her to shiver noticeably

*God, he is nasty,* she thought to herself. He had a way of making her feel so dirty, however, she knew that the only way she would be able to draw him in would be to draw him out. Mary was the best at seduction; it is her finely tuned quality. Set them up, bait them, watch them take the bait, and then reel them in. She did know that all men, when prompted, used only the brain between their legs, and that women are the brain-eaters.

He touched her arm again and she shuddered from that touch as he used his fingers to trace little nonsense patterns over her arm.

Paul moved closer to window, not believing what he was seeing. How could he? Darien was his, how could she?

Hugh continued tracing the patterns over her arm as Cynthia steeled herself against him while trying to keep the whimpering Sibby under control as she cried for release. Behind it all Darien became the silent, stern observer. Mary responded. Cynthia let her out with just enough advantage to do what she did best, and together they all sat inside of Darien's head, secretly wishing for release, and for an end to the pain that her life had become.

From where he was in the place behind the mirrors David felt her despair go to an even deeper level, and with his mounting frustration, a power began to build.

He started to grow.

In her need for him, and in his love for her, the guardians could not hold him back, and David began to spin, drawing the warm winds to him, along with the winds of the other whirling tornadoes around him.

Paul Holmes stood with his hands pressed up against the glass, silent in his inability to help, not wanting to ruin his career by revealing his own not too ethical doctor/patient relationship. Dr. Marris was completely unaware of what he was about to release.

The doctor rose from his chair, and slowly walked around the table, never letting his fingers leave her arm. He mistook her shaking anger as fear, and stepped one more step into the trap she was preparing for him. Cynthia smiled as Marris took the bait, and she rose from her chair as he approached her.

Mary was awake and ready to reel him in.

Cynthia, however, was in total control.

Sibby as always, whined and cried.

Poor Darien, all she could do was to sit and watch it all happen.

In the place beyond the mirrors, where the guardians lived in the light of warmth and goodness, a whirling vortex grew. Building, spinning, and gathering strength from an incredibly powerful bond that David had formed in his love for Darien. He swept the other guardians up into his fevered efforts to break free from the invisible ties that bound him to this place. David pulled on their strengths, and they could not stop him as he broke their metaphysical ties, growing to a tremendous proportion unlike anything ever seen in their world. He pulled them all into his vortex, as the power of his love for Darien consumed them all. David carried them with him, gaining strength from the righteousness that the guardians were, have been, and always would be. His efforts escalated as he went to save the one person who belonged to him alone. Their love made her a part of his soul, and he erupted violently from the place beyond the mirrors, shattering the unwritten rules that govern both planes.

David came for his Darien.

Cynthia struggled to suppress her anger, and hatred of all men, which threatened to boil over into a single attack on Dr. Hugh Marris. He was behind her now, putting his arms around her and she leaned seductively into him. She could feel his body relax against hers, and his breathing shortened, becoming heavy in her ear, as his lips delivered a kiss of lust on her neck. He pressed his hardness into her back, and she immediately knew his style. He would be like an animal in heat; holding her down to ravage her body from behind, bringing her under his domination. Mary was emerging, she liked sex, and she loved men, and the struggle continued as to who would dominate in Darien.

In the room behind the one-way mirror, Dr. Paul Holmes joined in the game. He unzipped his pants to release the center of what drove all men. Holmes stroked himself until he stood out as hard and as ready as when he was with Sibby. He was ready to masturbate until he climaxed with whoever Darien would become. He smiled slightly as he remembered a saying that he had once seen on a novelty T-shirt.

"The One With The Most Toys Wins." Holmes emitted a grunting noise as he pulled down on himself and the doctor felt that there should be only one saying on novelty T-shirts and they should all simply read: "Men Always Win." He laughed aloud as if it were the funniest thing he ever heard, and as he watched Marris with Darien, he knew this was true. Paul could not wait to fuck Sibby again. He pulled down on his hard penis, slowly lingering over the top, and the reaction caused him to pull in his breath between tightly clenched teeth. Damn! What she did to him even at this distance was incredible!

Mary moved her body back against Dr. Marris, he brought his hands around in front of her, and before she knew what had happened, he pulled her arms up pinning them behind her back. He placed his free hand on the back of her neck and pushed her down onto the table. Darien turned her face turned sideways, feeling the crumbs left over from someone's snack cookie scrape over her cheek. She quickly pulled her legs together as her gown fell open in the back to reveal the plain white underwear that the patients wore. Marris leaned over her, and she felt his hot breath on her back, his free hand playing over her soft skin. His hands were large, and he was able to hold her wrists together over her back while she desperately struggled to break free herself. It was the struggling that fueled Marris, giving rise to an even greater need to dominate the personality of Cynthia. He ripped her panties off, and stood for a moment enjoying the contrast of her pale skin against his finely tuned tennis tan. Finally, he forced his foot between hers and moved her legs apart. Darien heard his zipper go down, and she started to fight against him one more time.

"Go on, fight me if you must but you can't win." His breath was hot on her back, his hand cold against her body, and it made her cringe and fight him even more. Marris made his last mistake when he just could not resist gloating over his final victory. So, with his male ego in place, convinced of certain victory and with sarcasm in his voice, he sealed his own fate.

"So Darien, where is your guardian now? Where is the ghost that helps you in your times of crisis, the one you call David."

Thoroughly engrossed in the proceeding, watching from the other side of the one-way mirror, Dr. Paul Holmes could not hold back any longer. He ejaculated his release all over the wall as he stood watching Dr. Marris rape his patient.

With all the strength and all the hatred of all the men who had hurt her in her lifetime, Darien released that anger and threw her body backwards up off the table into Dr. Marris. Taken by surprise he fell backwards onto the floor, hitting his head on the dark green tiles, and Darien looked down at the comical picture he made as he held his head with his deflated ego hanging out of his pants. She stood over him, burning with hate, and lifting her foot she brought it down directly onto the part of his body that he wanted to please. Marris screamed, and rolled over onto his side, clutching himself with the sharp pain. Cynthia turned around and picked up one of folding metal chairs.

"You stink, you fuck, you know that?" Her anger overrode all common sense, and suddenly everything went out of control.

Dr. Holmes yelled from the other side. "Oh shit!" He pressed the alarm button while quickly stuffing himself back into his pants, not even taking the time to wipe his pleasure from the wall. The alarm sounded down the hallway causing the attendants to burst out from their languid afternoon routine.

Darien raised the metal folding chair over her head while the women inside her head clamored for dominance. She stood there poised on the edge, ready to end the life of one Hugh Pukey Marris, when all at once Darien realized that the demons who drove the spikes were ones of her own creation. There were no real demons inside of her head, there were no fire hammers, nor were there any spikes. As these years went by, and she refused to confront the problems that she found to be so insurmountable, the migraines created by her own refusal to accept and deal with everyday life. The simple fact is, if you only need to take your time to find a reasonable solution, then everything else falls into place. The door to the room burst open, and Darien dropped the chair, grimacing as it made a clanging echo throughout the room. She backed herself up against the wall to face the enemy. She glared at them through dirty hair that hung in wild strings down across her face and she braced herself against the struggle that was yet to come. With the appearance of the male attendants, fear replaced her anger because she could not win, and Darien's desperate battle to stay afloat in a sea of dominating males was slowly sinking. She took a defensive stance, her hands flat against the wall behind her as the attendants approached. One of the nurses entered the room behind them with a straitjacket, and Darien called loudly for the only person who could help her now.

"DAVID!" she screamed, but would he come? Would they let him? Would he be able to find the strength to respond to her, or had she, in her inability to accept unconditional love, destroyed everything that they once had? The attendants held her, forcing her into submission, bending her arms at unbelievable angles to get them into the jacket. Dr. Holmes avoided Darien's eyes while he dealt with his own guilt feelings as he helped the attendants put Darien into the straitjacket. But even the guilt feelings were not enough to allay his thoughts because at the same time he was also plotting what his next move would be in playing the game where Darien always lost. The nurse who supplied the jacket was helping Dr. Marris to his feet, and he stumbled backwards a few steps while holding onto the starched white uniform to regain a steady footing.

"Take her to Number Three," he gasped to the men that held her, and his voice could not conceal his pain. Paul's head jerked up from where he was buckling Darien's arms behind her.

"Dr. Marris, I don't think…"

"I don't give a damn what you think, Paul, she is totally out of control. Do as I say and take her to Number Three!" Dr. Marris limped over to where Darien stood in total submission to the men she so hated, and he whispered vehemently in her ear.

"I'll teach you, you little piece of shit, no one does this to me." An odd stillness suddenly settled into the room and then a small warm wind moved in and around the hospital staff. Darien looked up and gave Dr. Marris a slight half smile. The pages from the lengthy report that lay scattered across the floor rustled slightly as the air brushed by. She lifted her head into the wind, letting the warm air fill her with his love, letting the tenderness of their feelings calm her, bring her peace. Before he could reach her, she felt his touch, and in that touch there was comfort. In that touch, there was safety, and in that touch was David.

"A light warm wind, a gentle breeze is how it all begins"

She turned and looked at the people who surrounded her in an aura of pain and their faces showed a perplexity at the unknown breeze and where it could be coming from. Darien laid her head back on her shoulders, closed her eyes, and smiled once more.

"He's coming for me, Marris, but more importantly, he will also come for you."

"Take her down!" Marris demanded, and unexpectedly Darien lashed out at them again, fighting with the power and determination of all that she believed in while they dragged her down the hallway. Darien fought against them as they removed the straitjacket and strapped her to the table. The nurse fastened electrodes to the sides of her head while at the same time one of the attendants buckled a leather strap across her forehead.

"David, please," she whispered, and the tears trickled from the corners of her eyes while at the same time, she widened them in response to the fear growing inside. Then with all the strength she had left, and by all she held inside for the one man in her life that loved her despite what she was, Darien cried for him one last time.

"DAVID!" Dr. Marris looked at her as he forced a flat piece of rubber between her teeth, and he bent over her again so that she could smell his wintergreen breath, deliberately making his face the last thing she would see, and the first thing she would recall.

"You won't even remember your precious David after this, you little bitch. You'll be lucky if you remember your own name." He looked at the voltage Dr. Holmes set on the machine.

"Turn it up." Dr. Holmes backed away, refusing to touch the controls, so Marris walked over and turned it up over three hundred.

"You'll kill her," Paul said in stunned surprise.

"It won't kill her, but it will shock her into a complete and final submission," and he added under his breath, "then I can finally have what I want."

Outside the hospital cars were swept into the air, disappearing, absorbed into what would become the largest tornado in recorded history. A white tornado of tremendous proportions twisted with record-breaking winds, pushing everything out of its path as it headed straight towards the Fulbright Hospital for the mentally disturbed. The guardian that he was, forever diligent in his never-ending job to help protect and guide those appointed to him, now headed on a very different path. He created a path of destruction to reach these cruel and unjust human males. David was going against every rule, every reason as to why they even existed, and he pulled his strength and power from the other guardian entities. In doing this he forced them to leave their pre-appointed charges, leaving them open to despair and hopelessness. David surged onwards, blind in his mission, heedless to the demands for his return and pulling away with a strength brought on by one thing and one thing alone.

His love for Darien.

Hugh Marris stood with his finger paused just a mere fraction away from the bright green "ON" button, when a disturbing wind rippled through the room. It lifted every one's hair, almost like a small charge of static electricity, and all of their heads turned as Darien continued struggling to break free.

Outside the building, it became nothing less than a mass uplifting of anything in the tornado's destructive path, cars flipped over, uprooted trees crashed into each other, and debris from the outer rim of the tornado filled the air, blocking out the sun, before falling to the ground. David's anger with the men who imprisoned Darien went far beyond the reach of those trying to control him, and he raced with unabated fury towards what could only be the end of David, brought on in his love of Darien.

The two doctors, the two attendants, and the nurse were totally unprepared for what happened next as the tornado blew out the entire side of the building. It was a miracle (or so the papers reported) that no one in their offices flew into the intensity of the whirling storm. The nurse hung onto Paul Holmes, while both he and Marris, and the two attendants clung precariously to the tables bolted to the floor. The force of the wind ripped away the small flat piece of rubber placed in Darien's mouth, and she wept without control, calling to her guardian above the hurricane-force winds.

"David!" Those who remained in the room watched in stunned silence as arms that were nearly transparent emerged from the spinning vortex, and when they neared Darien, they started to solidify and gain color. Slowly he stepped from the center of the violent maelstrom and undid the straps that held his beloved to the table. Resembling a small child, Darien climbed into his arms, and David made ready to strike down the evil that was Hugh Marris, but as much as Darien also wanted an end to this man, she stopped him.

"As evil as this man is you know it's not right for anyone to take his life, especially a guardian. Let them live with what they have done for the rest of their lives; I think it will be punishment enough." She hugged herself to him, nestled in the safety of his arms as they prepared to re-enter the white tornado that stood spinning and waiting for them both. David would take her away, he would take her to the place where dreams come from, and neither of them would ever come back.

Holmes and Marris lay exhausted on the floor, not fully understanding what they witnessed or perhaps not wanting to. The nurse and the two attendants lay unconscious next to them, and they too would only remember the side of the building crumbling to the ground. There would be no recall for anyone of the mysterious entity who emerged from the twister.

"What did you see, Paul?" Dr. Holmes looked at Marris, he himself still weak and dazed at having fought against the pull of the winds.

"I didn't see a damn thing, except one of our patients being sucked out of the building when the tornado ripped it apart."

"Same thing I saw." They never spoke again of this day to each other or anyone else, and Darien's file became lost in the storm. Under the threat of David's possible return, neither Dr. Marris nor Dr. Holmes ever touched another female patient.

* * *

Darien sat patiently on the bed watching David sleep. He had exhausted himself and he lay so still that Darien frequently put her palm against his chest to see if he was still breathing. She covered him lovingly with the blanket, and then bent down to kiss his full sensuous lips.

"My sweet David," she whispered softly, and a fire sprang to life in the fireplace to warm the chill that had settled into their room of dreams. It was then that she became aware of another presence joining them in the room, and her eyes never left David as she spoke to it.

"He sleeps too deeply, doesn't he?" She was unafraid as she addressed the new entity, because in these beings she knew there was only the good side of all that walked in her world.

"Yes, he has nearly exhausted his life. There is a powerful force in hatred, also a very destructive one, and guardians are here to help, to guide, and not to hate. In allowing that emotion to have dominance, David has gone against everything he was created for."

"Is there no way back?" The eldest of all the guardians stood looking at Darien, studying her, wondering what it was that tore David apart in his quest to save this human from her torturers. He never told David the full reason of why they needed her, so that left only one reasonable explanation for his actions. It proved that his love for her was real. The elder continued to study her as she tended David, seeing for the first time that she really is a plain, average human; however, he could sense a change in her that was not there when they originally sent David to her.

"There is only one way back, Darien, but first let me say to you that I can see a difference in you, a sense of self, of oneness." Darien smiled at him, a smile that radiated warmth much like the guardians themselves, and from her memory came two lines of a riddle that jumped into the middle of her thoughts: "But they must not rule the here and now stop hiding in the 'zone.'" Then as quickly as they had jumped in her head, they too were gone and without hesitation, she answered the guardian.

"You are right, great guardian, I am different. I do feel healed. David has done so much to help me. I love him more than my own life, and I know that this is where the answer lies." She looked at the elder with great big brown eyes filled with tears of love for David, and for all the guardians. Then suddenly the clarity of a vision exploded into Paul's inner thoughts, and the enormity of Darien's quest became known to him. It staggered him, as he looked to the small woman with great sadness, and it took all of his faith in who he was not to pick her up and take her away. Instead, he spoke to her with a vague reference of her destiny.

"Your true beauty, Darien, lies in what you see inside of all human nature. You see to the strength inside where only your love can help you to surmount any obstacle that may block you from your chosen path. It is from this strength that your greatest challenge is yet to come. In knowing this I must ask you one more time. How great is your love for David?" Darien looked at David, and saw in him, not a supernatural being that swirled like a mini-tornado, not a being who had the power to call the winds. She saw the gentlest man she had ever known. She also saw a man who knew when to be strong and aggressive, when to be passionate and tender, everything that a woman dreams of, but seldom finds. She tenderly took his hand in hers, and his fist closed around her palm, and she smiled as her diminutive hand disappeared inside of his, then she looked up to the guardian that humans sometimes mistakenly called angels.

"I love him with all that I am, with all that I ever will be."

"And what must you do, Darien?"

"For David to survive, noblest of all the guardians, I must release him from his duty to me. This is the only way it can be, and I will do this for him, because I would not be able to live myself if he died, even more so if the fault were mine." Darien tenderly caressed his face, and the fire that burned hot in the room where he had made her dreams real, burned inside of her and David. As if sensing her agitation, he stirred for just a bit, and then fell back into the deep healing sleep.

"He won't remember me at all will he?"

"We cannot allow that, you have seen what he can do."

"But I will remember him?"

"Yes."

"He cannot come for me ever again, can he? Wait, don't answer. I already know that everything will end here."

"Darien, you are strong again, you don't need David anymore, but there are other people who do. It is time for you to take charge of your life, put yourself and your family in order, and let the future become your home. Trust in me, Darien, when I say that you will love again. Your husband waits for you, as do your children. There is no right or wrong here, only what is."

"I agree with you. I know I will love again, for no one knows my heart better than I. However, it will never be as strong or as passionate as my love for David."

"Ah, Darien, in time David will be but a remembered dream for you, for you cannot have what has never been real. Do you understand what I'm saying?" Darien slowly nodded her head yes.

"Please let me stay just a few more minutes, let me stay by his side, and touch his lips to mine just once more." The guardian never replied, he never said goodbye but instead he started to fade, and as she had asked permission to do, she very gently kissed David. She drew in the texture, the shape, and his taste, all that would help her to remember. She touched his hair, ran her fingers over the softness of his skin, and touched one last time his passion for her. She smiled, not at all surprised to find him ready even in his sleep.

"My David," she whispered to him, "you are such a part of my life, my body will ache for your caring hands, but I cannot bear for you to die. So with all my love, I release you from your promise to be there for me, and in time, I know that you will be nothing but my remembered dream. I also know that as happens so often with dreams, there will come a time when I will wonder if you ever were real, or if you were only just a shadow in my thoughts."

The room fell away and the last thing that Darien saw was David waking to a reality that he was needed elsewhere, that someone else had called for help, and he would become guardian to that new him or to her. What Darien could not have known was that David did sense the deepest loss inside his soul, but the exact memory of what that loss was, was gone.

\* \* \*

Darien climbed up from the side of the hill, and followed the path out of the woods that surrounded Fulbright Hospital for the mentally disturbed. She heard the ambulance and the police sirens announcing their approach. She crested the small hill, stepped into the parking lot, and tripped over television cables and fire hoses running over and on top of one another.

"Oh great, the TV news trucks are here already."

Then someone yelled, "Over here, hey, I found her!" Jack reached her first, and gathered her up in his arms.

"Darien, I thought I lost you." He had genuine tears in his eyes, and Darien thought to herself, *This is not Jack.*

"Mom!" It was her youngest daughter putting her arms around Darien. Her other two daughters were there as well, and seemed just as happy to see her. It was a touching moment, but she had to wonder how long it would last. Suddenly a newscaster appeared beside her, desperately pushing a microphone in her face.

"We heard that the tornado pulled you right out of the building. Is that true?"

"Yes, I guess you could say that." (The arms that had held her, so warm, so strong.)

"It's amazing that you survived at all." Suddenly more reporters clustered around her and Darien paused, not quite sure of what she was going to say.

"What is it like being inside a tornado?"

"I really don't remember, it happened so fast."

"How did you survive?" They were all crowding around her, and Darien had to back up a few steps to compose herself before answering.

"I guess you could say that I have a guardian angel on my side." Jack put his arm around her shoulder, and her daughter was holding her gown closed in the back, because she was quite certain that her mother did not want to reveal all of her secrets.

"Come on, Mom," her oldest one said, "we're going home." Darien was suddenly beginning to feel like her old self, and it was a good healthy, whole feeling.

"I remember you," she said quietly, "I remember Darien."

"You don't need this place anymore," Jack said as he walked her over to the car and opened the door so Darien could slide safely inside. She rolled down the window and watched the shadows by the TV van, where Darien alone could see the shifts and changes in the darkness. A paramedic was passing by their car, and Darien called out to him.

"Was anyone hurt?" she asked, her voice full of concern.

"No, no one as far as we can tell, but we're still checking to make sure everyone is here. Considering the force of a tornado, it's a small miracle that no one was killed. We were extremely lucky today." There was a man standing nearby, and as he approached her, he inquired about her earlier statement.

"You said something back there about a guardian angel, and I'm curious, Mrs. Sharnell, do you really think you saw one?" Darien looked at the man, wondering if perhaps he might be one of the reporters who helped to fill the grocery store tabloids. She thought a minute about not answering his question, and then decided that sometimes when people have lost all of their faith they need to believe in miracles, much as she had. Of course there would be skeptics, the ones who will say "Prove it," but how does someone prove a faith kept alive in the heart? That is exactly what her faith was, the ability to believe beyond any doubt, without the proof.

"Yes, I really saw one."

"Is he here now, can you see him?"

"No, he's gone, he has gone to help others that need him."

"Do you think he will come back?

"I don't think so, he has done what he can here, but I trust him and I believe in guardians. If you want the truth, then let me tell you that in some way there is a part of him that will always be with me, in here." Darien pointed to her heart, and then started to wind up her window to avoid having to answer any more questions, and she had to smile when she saw Hugh Marris standing near a huge oak tree, puzzling about how his car had ended up caught between the largest branches.

"You're lucky you live, you fuck," she said under her breath.

Darien gazed out the window of her car, watching as the reporters moved from place to place, still looking for more miracles in a sea of sirens and confusion. Darien watched the shift and dance still cast inside the shadows, and suddenly she felt a gentle, invisible hand laid on her shoulder, and a voice that said softly in her ear: "You did the right thing, Darien." Then it too was gone, and Darien felt it leave while looking towards the heavens to find the first star in the encroaching darkness. She found herself thinking of the old nursery rhyme, "Star light, star bright, first star that I see tonight." And she made her wish, and her promise.

"When the first snow falls I will think of you, and the passions we shared by the warmth of the fire. Maybe one day things will change, and I will be allowed to see my beloved guardian, my most gentle lover. You will always be my David. As I release you from your bond take a part of me with you, and remember I will remain forever, as you have known me. I will always be your Darien."

# CHAPTER TWO

# THE BINDING

Born of despair, it had awareness.

No one knows why these things happen or how, only that they just are.

What are some of the thoughts that come with awareness? There was but one that it knew.

It had life.

Like all newborns, it had an insatiable hunger and it craved despair and destruction to fill its mind and its belly. In their ignorance, the guardians fed it all the despair it could consume, and out of this ignorance there came a shape of darkness that grew as twisted and as evil as the despair that fed it.

Its eyes opened, resembling shining green stones, and it recognized that the darkness was its mother. It succored him within the security of the womb, and made it feel safe. Its food became the blankets of captured hopelessness, fed to it by the great guardians themselves as they continuously penetrated the dark liquid womb. The guardians who were so wise and so knowing were so completely oblivious to the evil growing almost inside their own home.

Through the eons, the food to help it grow became endless. It continued to mature until with its thought of "I am," there finally came reason, and its only reason was to conquer and control the guardians themselves. It wanted to bring more and more of them to itself until with its evil it could bind them to him eternally. It had grown to tremendous proportions having become a Titan of dark madness, and so it gave itself a name, Tianato Morebind.

As its reason came, so did its capacity to learn. It was as simple as extending its consciousness to absorb everything that it touched. As it fed off the despairing empathy continuously released into his liquid pool of surreal nurturing, the thing grew as twisted as the emotions that fed it. Its eyes glared with the hatred of its imprisonment and for its physical deformity. The bottom half of its twisted torso was planted as firmly as tree roots into the very ground from which it grew, while the top half reached and stretched through the endless night. At the same time, it longed to be as the guardians themselves, to be with the small whirling vortexes that waited patiently for a calling so they could go and help those who needed their guidance. Tianato wanted to send his darkness out of his prison, out into their world and then beyond. If he could not be with them, then he wanted all of them to be his, to hold, to bind, and to play with as he wanted. It had such a simple reason as to why it wanted them, but being still a child it did not recognize the emotion of jealousy and more importantly, the one of loneliness. It wanted only to belong, to be a part of their world. If the only way to do that was to bind the guardians to him, then that was how it would be. He would own them all, and when the cries for help came from the human world, Titobind would be the only one who would be able to answer them, and like a sponge, he would absorb them all. He would eventually have the whole world for his own and they would all serve him or live forever inside of their worst nightmares. Therefore, it watched, it waited, it fed, and over the years as it continued to grow, it continued to learn.

* * *

The eldest of all them called for a convening of the great council. The guardians are a great force outside the human world and their only reason for existence is to serve the inhabitants of that world. They are as old as time is old. They came to earth when man began to evolve, and they have watched over him and guided his steps.

As a new species, man had intelligence, the capacity to learn, and a new world to play with, along with the opportunity to evolve into whatever he chose to be. However, he had evolved into a somewhat less than desirable race of beings. In a universe of such infinite proportions, humans were still in the infant stage and they were a selfish, violent race of beings. In spite of that, they did have one thing in their favor, they were still evolving, and some of the guardians had hope for them.

Some of them did not.

This was the reason for the meeting of the great council, and the eldest had to listen and determine what the final decision for this species known as man would be. There were good arguments presented on both sides. While some believed that in his selfish violence, man would ultimately cause their own destruction (and without the guidance of the guardians, this would be inevitable), others argued that their enormous capacity for compassion, love and understanding made them worthy of survival. The arguments presented at council were solid on both sides, and the eldest himself leaned towards Man's survival. He continually found a strange uniqueness in their passionate love and fierce commitment to freedom that he had never seen in any other species. There was also the influence of the Gods themselves, who were as fond of this species as the eldest was, and the creators of all the known universes had great respect for the eldest of all the guardians.

The guardian could also see tiredness among his chosen that he had never seen before, almost a desperate futility from the overwhelming cries for help. The screeching that barreled into the guardians' minds at an accelerating pace was becoming a never-ending tirade of give me and I want. These humans, as they called themselves, pulled on the very fabric of the guardians' beings, to a point that was capable of tearing them apart. Of course, they all knew their existence was to guide any given species through the course of their evolutions, but there had been times through all of their eternities that whole worlds of beings had catapulted themselves into oblivion. The preternatural beings feared that this was going to happen to the species that called itself man. For every hundred souls that they saved, thousands more clamored for help, and the eldest was aware of the evil growing from their despair. However, the extent and the maturing of the being he did not know. Man's hopelessness along with the continued floundering in their deepening despair became unparalleled to any other species, and never before did the guardians have to handle such loneliness and depression, which kept growing, spreading across the world like an incurable disease. A hatred for each other also grew among these beings, and the escalating violence among their own differences were astounding. The greatest of all the guardians was extremely tempted to leave them to their own destruction, except for one thing; a birth in their world had drawn his attention. Whether intentional or deliberate was yet to be decided, for no one could predict or know what moves the Gods would make or why.

This one birth kept Paul from sweeping up all the guardians, and carrying them away to a new world. One of these humans was born with a destiny that would directly affect the guardians, something that made her special above all of them. She possessed a unique inner strength that went beyond what any human had the capacity to understand. She was the one her mother cradled with so much love, kissed her softly on her little forehead, blessed her, and then named her Darien.

The guardian who took the human name Paul knew that the child was destined to greatness, but that would only happen if, as a species, they could survive. Paul already knew that Darien Denton would lead a tumultuous life, so he bequeathed her with a very special guardian. He sent David. This guardian had been with her from the first day she came home from the hospital, and he continually floated in and out of her life when most needed. Paul would occasionally observe the twists and turns that compiled the life of Darien, and at times, the guardians would stand together and watch the humans with hopes that the violence of their race would change; however, their sadness grew when it kept escalating.

Now they had come to this, a council of guardians who could not control or destroy the evil that this despairing world helped to create. It was beyond the guardians' capabilities to destroy any living things, so destroying the growing evil was not open to discussion. However, to recruit and prepare Darien to destroy it for them was something they could do. Did this deceit make them as evil as the entity humanity had created? This reasoning was also a part of the argument set before the council, and it had been the very center of all of their discussions for the past eight years, when Darien first saw David.

It was on the day, beside the small pond, when Darien had thought that she could simply "float free," and to finally be "at rest," that Paul relinquished, and allowed David to become real for her. This strong, towering, wise guardian could not foresee the destruction that would eventually emerge from their tumultuous affair. When Darien had nearly destroyed poor gentle David, Paul wanted then to tell her about her destiny, but he could not. Even in the world of such magnificent beings as the guardians, there were still rules that commanded each step taken. Through his own preoccupation with Darien, and from the relentless calls for help that issued forth night and day from the other desperate humans, Paul remained unaware of the enormous proportion and strength of the evil entity. The day Titobind took the guardians was a day that Paul could not stop, only because he had begun to see Darien as a savior to her own species, to her own race of people, but doubted the danger to the guardians themselves. They would use her yes, they would help her, but no one realized that the Titobind had fooled them all.

* * *

It waited and watched so patiently through the years, steadily growing every time the guardians flew overhead to release the human despair down into his everlasting night. He greedily accepted the nourishment that made him stronger, more powerful, and when Paul convened the great council and called all the guardians home, Titobind released his evil.

He moved quickly and quietly through the darkness, sending his myriad of tentacles before him like a giant squid moving through an ocean of night. Titobind kept hidden in the shadows much as the guardians themselves stayed hidden from man. He swam undetected into the castle that served as home to hundreds of whirling tornadoes waiting for assignment. It slithered along the walls bringing darkness as it came, pushing back the life-giving warmth from the inner lights of their goodness. So while the body of guardians discussed the education of Darien to help with the expulsion of the Titobind, he prepared to strike against them. He tightened his circle around them, and sprang from the shadows, releasing the appendages that took them all by surprise. He literally burned his cold evil through the guardians, extending his black soul to reach inside, burying his tentacles in deep, feeling the pleasure as they penetrated and clung to their bodies. Screams of agony rose from the council and their subsidiaries as they tried to spin, and call the winds to run from the pain of his reach. They were, however, too late with their attempts at escape. The guardians were quickly defeated, and bound to Titobind's twisted torso. Paul alone remained the only one strong enough to bring the winds to carry him away.

Titobind doubled, and then tripled his grotesquely misshapen form as he pulled and dragged the guardians into himself. The dark clinging pincers growing from his appendages were deeply embedded inside each guardian as one by one he brought them to him, binding them to his body. They cried out for Paul to help them, screamed for him, and begged him to stop the pain. Their bodies burned inside as they felt the tentacles reach for their souls, and the tiny tortures of the pincers kept breaking into them, until they had no choice but to bear the pain in silent agony.

Paul watched from afar, staring in silent horror, listening helplessly as all of his beloved guardians became captive. He could not keep the tears from his eyes when their cries for his help had to go unanswered. His heart cried with them, and his mind became lost in his inability to stand against the evil, so he sat in hiding and watched hour after endless hour as Tianato Morebind tightened his hold, until he had pulled them all in and secured them against his cold body. Paul looked at the empty castle, and at the hundreds of furrows in the ground where Titobind had dragged the guardians through the cold dark earth.

Thunder bellowed through the dimension that existed on his side of the mirror, and the beauty in Paul's dimension that grew through the years, now withered and died. Tianato's little creepy crawlies danced as they came alive, and cold fires sprang up everywhere as Titobind prepared to release his hell on an unsuspecting world. However, there was an unintentional flaw in the plans. He was ignorant in his overconfidence at how easily he had won, and he reasoned that Paul's binding would simply be a matter of time.

Tianato Morebind pulled his gelatinous appendages back into his disparaging distorted shape. He attempted to bind their minds as well as their bodies, but in this attempt, he failed. In the binding of the guardians he had inevitably bound David, and the intense agony had reawakened his sleeping memories, and now he was recalling everything that been so diligently put to sleep. It overwhelmed his senses and then overflowed into the other guardians. Just one thought overpowered everything else, and out from the darkness through their collective pain, calling with intensity even the binding could not stop, David remembered, and their voices became one as they cried:

"Darien!"

From her home on the opposite side of the mirror, Darien screamed and covered her ears against the thunderous cry. She felt the blood dripping out between her fingers as she moaned and dropped to one knee, while at the same time recoiling from the blast inside of her head. She staggered back to her feet, knowing that something terrible had happened, knowing the voice she had heard was not one voice, but the sum total of all the seraphims. A riddle told to her by a little crooked man who sat inside her mirror came back to haunt her and she finally had the sum total, all of it, and David, oh God, poor David!

A light warm wind, a gentle breeze
Is how it all begins
Then it will come as shadows creep
And bind the seraphims.

Do not fear the shadows dark
For they can be brushed away
But fear more the twisted evil thoughts
You think have come to stay

In the past you made a few mistakes
For which you will atone
But they must not rule the here and now
Stop hiding in the "zone."

A destiny still waits for you
Of good and bad beware
To reach out and find the truest path
And stop the binding in his lair.

For if the sun should fade away and die
The world would breathe an empty sigh
In a silent realm devoid of light
An evil grows from endless night.

Unless you remain to be seen
Through pleasure/pain for little queen
The endless night becomes the day
And all of humankind will pay

The suffering bequeathed will know no bounds
And screams in pain, unholy sounds
Become the light that you are meant to be,
A savior for humanity.

Save them, Darien, save them all.
A crumbling empire set to fall
The light flows out from within
To release Paul's sweet seraphims.

Darien closed her eyes, screamed aloud, and held the sides of her head
as the tears came with the extreme pain. David called to her, the other
guardians echoing his voice, and it was no wonder her head felt as if it was
ready to explode. Their collective effort to reach her caused her to fall to
her knees with an explosive shock. When Darien took her hands away

from her ears, she found her palms covered in blood, and she had the beginnings of the mother of all headaches.

In the meantime, with all the children of the world still looking for the basic goodness of Paul, Titobind decided that he wanted to create something that would be exclusively his, his children, so he began to form and give birth to the twins. They strained up from the ground, growing from his planted seed and nurtured by hate and despair, they had but one purpose, and that was to serve and worship their life-giver, Tianato Morebind. He pulled them from his womb of darkness, and the liquid night that still succored him, kept his children safe as well. They held no mind, and had no thought, save the one that he gave them, and that was to find and deliver the one that the guardians called for, the one small human named Darien.

He would make her suffer untold indignities, indescribable tortures, and in the end he would make her serve beside him as his personal play toy for all the eternities yet to come. The guardians should not have called to her, but then Titobind reasoned that he would have eventually learned how to access their thoughts anyway, so finding her would be inevitable. The Titobind, with its reasoning also knew she might pose a possible threat merely because this had been the only person they called. Not to the greatest of all guardians, Paul, but instead to one puny little human, a small woman who existed on the other side of the mirror. He extended his appendages to wrap around his homegrown Myrmidons, and he pulled his seedlings from the ground. If they could have recognized pain, then their screams would have been horrendous; instead, they flopped, like fish out of water, bending their human-like bodies into non-human contortions.

He made them stand.

He made the walk

He gave them one single thought:

Do not kill; do not harm any part of her.

She belongs to me.

The one called Darien.

# CHAPTER THREE

# THE DECISION

Darien sat alone in her empty living room.

The scrapbook that her children had assembled lay open on the coffee table in front of her. Some of the pages were already old to the point of yellowing around the edges, although not many years had passed since the "event" had happened. Of course she received tremendous support after her miraculous survival, and it had been documented in all of the most prominent magazines and some not so prominent, and she had been featured on the cover of *LIFE* magazine.

"Woman Survives Worst Tornado in Recorded History." Numerous news people interviewed Darien, and numerous medical doctors poked and prodded her, making sure that she was in good health. Then much to her surprise, invitations to make the talk show circuits arrived by the dozens. These were readily accepted. Most of them were more interested in her claim that a guardian angel saved her, rather than the fact that she had actually survived the tornado. Darien found it exciting to be the center of attention, and it kept her so busy that the reality of releasing David from his duty to her had not been as sad as she thought it would. Television stations called her sporadically for almost three years, and it was enough to keep her mind busy. She traveled across the country and television producers used her delusions and her case history as a basis for a movie of the week. Initially she had trouble revealing her multiple personality disorder to the entire world; however, payment for her cooperation was substantial, and of course seeing herself portrayed on television was thrilling. The movie had ended with her survival of the tornado, but it also left the viewer wondering if she had been "cured" of the multiple personalities. Darien herself was not even sure if she had been "cured" of her disorder, so the accuracy of the ending was based (somewhat) on the truth.

It was a little bit of a puzzle as to how her medical records had mysteriously reappeared, especially when Marris and Homes swore to her they were permanently lost. She never told anyone about her treatment, except for when the doctors tried to shock her, and the tornado came. Neither did Darien emphasize how David appeared from inside the tornado, nor did the doctors; they only confirmed what was recorded, not the details of the event as they had lived them. She could have gone public and ruined their careers, but Darien knew her nationwide publicity was enough to keep them strictly to patient/doctor relationships; besides, they were family men with children. As much as Darien hated them as men, she had no desire to ruin the lives of their children. There was a good side to what had happened. After Darien's release, the staff dismantled room number three. There would never be another patient in Fulbright Hospital treated with electroshock therapy.

In the meantime, her two eldest daughters finished their college education, starting into their own lives nearly two years earlier, and more recently, the youngest one moved from home, ready and eager to embrace all her life had to offer. Darien was alone and lonely. It was strange that even though she had always felt alone, never finding a place to fit in life, when her children left it became even worse. It did not take long for her husband to slide back into his old habits, but with Darien so caught up in the excitement, she never really noticed or cared. Eight long years had passed since that day, and as she looked around the quiet empty house she thought about David, and she sighed her discontentment. Darien never tried to call for him, and his absence from her life at times became nearly unbearable. Sometimes Darien thought she would again need the hospital or at the very least, counseling. She had not thought it would be possible for her feelings about the past to resurface again, however, she allowed it to happen. Darien was more embroiled in her emotional past than ever before, and the zone seemed to attack her at her most vulnerable, when she was alone. The chaotic feelings flowed in and out of her body like the ocean retreating from the shore; allowing enormous waves of regrets to come crashing in with the approaching tide of her realities, eroding away a little at a time, the very essence of her sanity. As before, everything became mundane, repetitious, and in the same day-to-day routines, she functioned like a normal human being, accepting her role as mother, supplier of sexual release for her husband, clothes washer, and general errand runner.

Darien repeatedly replayed all the events in her mind, trying to justify her actions with David, and wondered what would have happened if instead of things going wrong, they had gone right. She felt that if it had been less wild and crazy, and she adjusted faster, then he would have left her so much sooner, and maybe not have loved her at all in the way that he had. She hated herself for almost destroying the beautiful guardian that was David, and felt that whomever she had to answer to when she made her final crossing to the other side would not be as forgiving with her as the eldest. Darien started to buy every tabloid paper that mentioned angels or the appearance of angels, and she added all of those articles to her scrapbook.

"That was so wonderful," she would say when someone had a miraculous save, "It must have been David who helped." Then she would lovingly paste the story into her scrapbook. Slowly she started to return to her old ways, and become as obsessive about David as before, and she would force herself to remember every detail of their time together. She remembered the great passionate fires that he lit inside of her, the fires she still allowed to glow and burn, like the remaining hot embers after the flames go out. Darien leaned back onto the sofa, and closing her eyes, she slowly let out her breath to relax and draw back into herself. Her conscious slid deeper and deeper inside, and she rode her thoughts to one of the many hidden places where David released her inhibitions. She hugged herself tight, feeling his arms around her, loving her, showing her how wonderful something as simple as a touch could be. Suddenly the phone rang, jarring her out of the nearly hypnotic state in which she had pushed herself. Through much cursing and grumbling Darien moved her tired body off the sofa, and made for the clanging interruption of the phone. She fumbled with the portable handset, finally pushing the talk button, and the voice that penetrated through her lingering reverie sent chills down her back.

"Darien."

"Yes, speaking. Who is this please?" She felt as though someone had touched an icicle to her spine; and the cold began creeping down into her bones. The terror generated through the voice terrified her quicker than anything ever had.

"He's lost" was all that it said and she could hear the evil there, the instinct that everyone has when every fiber that holds a person together just knows when something is wrong. She knew immediately that the only "he" that could be lost was David.

"Darien." The voice was raspy and it gurgled at the same time and Darien knew, she just knew that it wasn't only David who was lost. It came to her then, the gentle pressure of a hand that calmed the fears that the evil voice started inside of her. Her hand automatically hung the telephone in its cradle, and the room started to fall away leaving her with a memory of screaming agony raised in a chorus of pain crying for release.

Darien stood alone in the middle of fine rain, amazed as it passed through her body without making her wet, and the voice that she heard was gentle, kind, and soothing. It put to rest all of her fears, and it generated a peace that calmed her troubled soul.

"They are all lost to me, Darien." She recognized the voice of Paul, the eldest of the guardians, and the one who told her that giving up David was the only way to ensure his survival. He came towards her, as just a ripple through the mist, and as his body started to solidify, he became more visible. Darien was startled at his size; but the look on his face brought tears to her eyes. Never before has she seen anyone whose eyes held such extreme sadness and defeat. He approached her, a mere shimmer of his former self, because the guardian, despite his greatness and his strength, was slowly dissolving.

"I don't understand what you meant when you say they are all lost to you. What has happened?" The guardian sighed so deeply and so hard that Darien shivered with his effort to hold himself together.

"An evil has grown in our home, and its strength is so great that it has captured my guardians. It binds them to itself in such painful agony and they cry to me for release. I cannot help them for I too am losing my strength. This evil thing acts like a giant leech. It clings to them, sucking away at the very base of our existence, and draining from them the goodness that holds us together." Her temples began to throb, a memory erupted inside of her head, and it came from a time long ago when Darien faced herself in the mirror. The image was one that she could not escape from, not even when her personalities threatened to overwhelm her. Now in the quiet of the clouds, through the gentle mist of rain, she finally remembered a poem told to her, which she now repeated in what she thought was its entirety.

"A light warm wind, a gentle breeze
Is how it all begins
Then it will come as shadows creep
And bind the seraphim.

Do not fear the shadows dark
For they can be brushed away
Fear more the twisted evil thoughts
You think have come to stay

In the past you made a few mistakes
For which you will atone
But they must not rule the here and now
Stop hiding in the 'zone'

A destiny still waits for you
Of good and bad beware
To reach out and find the truest path.
And stop the binding in his lair."

The guardian listened, watching her stumble through the riddle and as the understanding came to them both, they looked to each other in stunned surprise and it was then that Darien realized the riddle was not finished.

"Many years ago, I ran away from home, becoming lost in the woods, and a small crooked man came to me and told me that riddle. I remember him now; I called him Mr. Toady Face. He's been with me for a long time hasn't he?"

"I don't know who this person is, Darien. Your revelation to yourself is also new for me. We, meaning the guardians, have not been in your life continuously, but you have been closer to us than any other human ever has."

"Once before you called me human; it was when I released David. I am guessing that although our outside appearance is the same, that inside you are not human." She smiled to herself thinking of how wrong that statement could be, because for her, David had been very human. This was a thought and a privacy that she kept to herself. Darien looked up at Paul and as always, spoke her mind.

"And now you are telling me about this evil, and there is this riddle about the binding in the lair. It all sounds more like a story from a novel; I fail to see where beings such as you would have need of a 'human.' I have always had this burning desire to understand where my life is going, but most of all I need to understand. Where has this evil come from, and why?"

"Ride with me, and I will take us to a safe place, and try to explain to you in a way as much as I possibly can." It was a long time since Darien felt the warm winds of the guardians, and it is a wonder of warmth not forgotten. The wind filled and lifted them through the clouds, and she found herself in a place as familiar to her as her own home. She entered the room of dreams where safety and comfort are given in large unlimited doses. She stood in front of the fireplace as it came alive; generating welcoming warmth, which for Darien was nearly as loving as David. The guardian watched her with great solemn eyes, and she waited for him to speak.

"We have only a theory as to why this evil has evolved, Darien, and it is all we have to help us understand. In recent years, the despair generated by your civilization has increased a thousand fold, and I know now that the releasing of the despair into the darkness has given form to an evil that I cannot begin to describe. I am the last free guardian, Darien, and the painful cries of the captured ones as they call for my help is steadily weakening me. I am the last connection that holds them to the light. If the evil succeeds in binding me as well, then all of the guardians will disappear."

"All of you will be gone, with no way back?"

"Forever gone, Darien, and once we are gone," he looked to her with unbearable sadness, "nothing will survive in your world."

He let the impact of the words fill her senses and Darien too overflowed with such an immense sadness that she felt also on the verge of breaking apart. She looked up at the guardian with eyes that already knew the pain involved in the loss of a guardian, and yet she had a feeling that the elder was not telling her everything. Wait a minute, Darien, the loss of the human race is not enough? What are you thinking? But I just know he's hiding something; this is not quite all there is.

"Why have you come to me?" His sighs of sadness shook the entire room as he faded in and out of her sight, while the effort clearly showed at how difficult it was for him to stay with her. However, Darien already knew that it was going to be an even greater effort for him to tell her.

"Remember when I told you that we have, well, one of us, at one time or another has kept an eye on you." Darien smiled at him.

"I have felt the pressure of your hand, along with the guidance of your voice from time to time, and I guess I knew that someone would always be there, even if it wasn't David."

"He has fulfilled many obligations and has helped more people than you could have ever realized."

"I'm glad."

"I can see in your face and most of all in your eyes that you still love him."

Her eyes never wavered from the guardian; her voice, her entire being had never been stronger with commitment to David when she answered, "I never stopped."

"Sit, Darien, please, make yourself comfortable." A large chair appeared beside her, and she took comfort in the solace of the guardian as she climbed into the oversized seat, taking the role of the child that she has always been. Paul's face held the wisdom of the ages, and Darien could not help but wonder exactly how many centuries he had lived. As if he could read her mind he said softly to her, "In answer to your unasked question, I am nearly as old as time." He smiled at her, giving her a gift of truth and beauty that no human has ever received.

"Let me tell you why I have come. I am here because we need you, and in my weakened state I am no match for the evil that binds the guardians, but you can find him, Darien. You have the ability to defeat him." He continued talking, ignoring the look of astonishment on her face.

"There is a road that you can take, but only you can decide if it is a road that you want to travel. I will advise you that it will be a dark and dangerous journey, and you can very easily become lost to yourself again. But I fear if this were to happen, then there would not be a way back for any of us. You will need to draw on all of your faith, and on all of your love to free them. Do you love him enough, Darien, to do this for David and for all the guardians?"

Darien thought of how tender David was with her, and of how loving and patient he was when he drew her from the shell she created around herself, the shell he cracked and slowly opened. David who loved her without question, David who accepted her with all of her faults, accepted all of her problems, unconditionally, and without question. When she answered Paul, it was with a conviction that almost drew her to her knees.

"Never in my life have I ever loved someone as I have loved David."

"I know the words you speak are true, Darien."

"Greatest of all guardians, it is because of this love and because of your understanding that I will do as you have requested. I will try to find David, to free him and all the other guardians."

"I am going to ask this question, Darien, not because I want to, but because I have to. Do you fully understand the consequences of what will happen if you are not strong enough?" She looked at him with eyes that no longer held any secrets.

"I understand." The guardian became very quiet, and Darien thought for a moment that perhaps he would decide the task was too great for her, and he would change his mind. Instead, he rose from his sitting position and the warm winds that were the very essence of the guardians themselves came at his command. They lifted them and Darien relived the thrill that raised her spirits every time David came.

"Our continued existence depends on you, Darien. I will help you on your journey when I can because you are about to enter a very dark and dangerous world. Hold tight to your memories and remember your love for David, and the reason that you go to seek the one called Tianato Morebind. He holds the night to him, it is the blackness of his soul, and it is in this darkness where he binds the guardians. There are evil men who walk in your world that worship him, and they know him as the 'Titobind.' Instead of physically bound, these men are mentally bound to him, but it is a permanent bond just the same, and they do his bidding." The guardian's voice was heavy, nearly remorseful as he spoke these words:

"It is through one of these men that you will find him." The guardian wavered in and out, much like the static-filled disappearances of Mr. Toady Face. The ghostly form summoned what little strength he had left, and carried Darien home. She was again standing in her empty living room, in the quiet of an empty home that echoed the emptiness inside of her.

"Remember and keep alive your love for David. I fear, Darien, that it might be all you will have." The voice faded away while her eyes and memories played tricks on her and she could almost see the shift in the shadows, and hear the happy little burbles that had been her first contact with David.

"No one has ever loved you more," came the whisper, and it sounded directly in her ear.

"I know," she whispered back. "I will free all of them for you and for myself, or I will die trying." Darien quietly climbed the stairs to pack her bags, not knowing where she was going, only that she must go. There was nothing left for her in this home, nothing to keep her tied to this place, and Jack her husband, well he could take care of himself; besides, what he needed her for, he had a strong right hand for that. Mr. Toady Face had been right when he had said to her that the grandest adventure was going to be her life, but there was no way anyone could have prepared her for the events that were about to unfold.

\* \* \*

Darien decided that if this were going to be a new life for her, then everything in it would also be new. In recognition of this fact, she had packed only the basics of what she would need, and then decided to take one last walk through her home. The small black dog that was her faithful companion for fifteen years died two years earlier and Darien cried almost as if Sibby re-surfaced. Even though her personalities were under her control at all times, there were a few instances where she could tell there remained an inner struggle for dominance.

She looked around her little house, at the rooms that were her life for twenty-five years, and sighed in frustration at all the time she wasted being lost in the worst of her depressions. Darien suddenly decided, there could be no regrets for the past, she could not change what had happened, but she could control her future. The first step was walking out and closing the door behind her without any feelings of guilt. She would leave Jack a brief note even though she knew he would just rip it up and throw it away. Maybe after she was gone Jack would be able to find someone who was better for him, someone who could give him the love he deserved, because Darien just did not have that for him anymore. She still loved her children more than her own life, but as they had become older, they became more arrogant, and even more self-centered. Darien was not worried about them, she knew their father would still be here if they needed him, and she would write or call, but not until after they had time to digest the fact that she was making a new life for herself. Just before she walked out the door, she turned around for one last look and then closed the book on this chapter in her life.

Her first stop would be the local bank where she was planning to withdraw her entire life savings of sixty-eight thousand three hundred eighteen dollars and forty-seven cents. Most of the money had come from the TV movie they had made, some from her most recent job, and there was a lump sum sitting in a 401K rollover that Darien left alone. She would convert the withdrawal to traveler's checks, keeping her cash to a minimum. It took a little over two hours to go through all the transactions, and Darien was becoming anxious to be on her way. She carefully wrote down all the serial numbers on a separate piece of paper, and mailed them to her oldest daughter. She also enclosed a short note for them to look in on their dad from time to time, just to make sure that he was okay. With the traveler's checks safely tucked into her suitcase, and her little compact car in excellent running condition, Darien headed up onto the highway with a feeling of freedom that put her close to euphoria.

Several hours later, Darien was still riding the crest of her elation, and the music she played on the radio reflected her mood until she suddenly realized that she had no idea where to go. Even though the freedom was there, and along with wonderful feelings that she wanted to last forever, an underlying current of fear surfaced and rocketed through her senses. She would face anyone or anything for David, of that she had no doubts, but how does one find an evil thing that has the name of Titobind? She played the name over, and over again in her head, like a needle stuck on a scratch in a record. She rolled the name around on her tongue, and vocalized it aloud in the car. The separations in the pavement under her tires that usually gave way to the familiar, ker-klunk, ker-klunk, ker-klunk was now sounding like Tii-Toe, Tii-Toe, Tii-Toe.

Her car fairly ate up the miles as though it too had been hungry for a journey, and Darien finally decided as long as she started heading west instead of south, that she might as well keep heading west; better yet, combine the two and head southwest. She smiled to herself when she thought of the guardian and how he did not give her any specific direction, leaving it all up to a test of her faith. How does one track down evil? There were no street signs that said, "Caution Dark and Dangerous Journey This Way" with large red arrows to direct her, and neither were there any flashing red lights warning "Danger, Danger." And she definitely could not find any signs that read, "Proceed with Caution, Titobind Approaching."

Darien yawned, suddenly realizing that she had been driving for nearly five hours straight, which put her just into West Virginia. Suddenly filled with an overwhelming urge to pee, she quickly decided a break was definitely in order. There were usually eateries off the exits, at the very least a McDonald's, where she would be able to get food, and free indigestion, which was always an added bonus. A road map could also prove to be useful, so maybe a trip to the local shopping center should be a consideration. There was no way she could get around the reasoning that no matter how free you thought yourself to be, you would end up needing somebody for something. She was making her way on instinct alone, and instinct told her to head southwest. After taking the much-needed stop and having a bite to eat, Darien took some time to study the road atlas she purchased at the local bookstore. For reasons unknown to her (which were becoming commonplace), Darien targeted Texas.

Four days later, she crossed the border into the state where everything is bigger and better, and she could not help but wonder if that was also true about the men of Texas. As usual, she had over-extended her driving time, and was currently shaking both legs in an effort to hold off the threat of wet pants. The next available exit was not for ten miles so Darien pushed her little car up to eighty-five, knowing already that it was going to be a long seven minutes. The exit sign came up, and she pulled off, slowing her car as she went down and around the ramp, until her speedometer targeted the recommended exit speed of thirty-five miles an hour. Darien hit the brakes quickly as if the stop sign at the bottom of the ramp had actually taken her by surprise. She looked to her right, saw a small dimly lit diner, and turned her car towards the place where she would find relief for the problem that was putting pressure on her kidneys. She screeched into the diner, jammed her foot on the brakes, which caused her body to rock back and forth, as she put her car into park almost before she had stopped. The learned lesson from seventh-grade science class briefly skirted her thoughts, "For every action, there is an equal and opposite reaction." This caused her to smile, while the pressure on her bladder pushed her into greater urgency.

Once inside the diner she ordered a cup of coffee, and then practically ran to the ladies' room. There was a tremendous gush of release, and Darien slowly closed her eyes while she relaxed, breathing in deeply of the bathroom's disinfectant. Behind her closed eyes, she had sudden flashes of unbearable torture, terrified screaming, lots of screaming. She quickly opened her eyes, finished her business, and then stood patiently at the sink washing her hands. She stared intently at her mirror image as she tried to remember what it was that kept drawing her to stare so intently at her reflection. It seemed to her that there had to be a reason that she was so curious about mirrors, and the strangest thing was that at times, she actually expected to be able to see through them. The screams that she had heard in her head only a few moments ago became very real screams, and they were coming from inside the diner. "What the hell is going on?" Darien rushed from the bathroom straight into a young mother frantic with fear.

*"Mi bebe, mi bebe, por favor, mi bebe!"* The woman was nearly hysterical as she grabbed Darien's arm. Darien looked around and saw a small child sitting in a high chair whose little face was slowly taking on a bluish tint.

*"Por favor,"* the woman pleaded, *"verga haga algo."* Darien turned and looked at one of the servers.

"Call 911, now!" She made her way to the baby and lifted him from the high chair.

*"Por favor, por favor, ajude a mi bebe."* Her plea was desperate and that came across in any language.

*"Si, si,"* answered Darien. She remembered a little Spanish from her high school days, but just one look at the child and Darien knew he was not breathing.

The woman put her hand to her own throat and said, *"Abregardeu."* Darien needed no interpretation for that; it was obvious that the child was choking. Darien turned the child over onto her knee and gave three sharp slaps to its back. Nothing happened, and whereas only seconds before the child had been lying stiff in her lap, he suddenly went limp, and Darien knew there was no time. The woman cried to her again, *"Mi bebe, por favor, senora, ajude* him!"

Darien quickly turned the little boy over and opened his mouth to look inside, and she could see deep inside his throat there was some kind of pink obstruction. It was apparent that the few sharp slaps had brought it into view, but not enough to release it. Darien knew that reaching in for the object could possibly force it further into his throat, but there was no choice, he would die if she did not. She held his mouth open with one hand, and with her thumb and forefinger, she felt for the object. She had it, latex? A balloon! She grabbed it and pulled. The balloon stretched open and you could hear the little bubble of air that had trapped the balloon make the funny squeak as it escaped from the narrow latex opening. The balloon snapped out and hit her fingers like a released rubber band, however the little boy was still not breathing. Darien quickly covered his mouth with her own, and then breathed deeply into his mouth, watching for the rise of his chest. Three more times, and the baby finally drew his own breath and then gushed out a loud scream accompanied by a torrent of tears. Everyone smiled and clapped and Darien beamed from ear to ear as she handed the baby to his mother.

*"Gracias, senora,* thank you," the crying woman said as she held her arms wide for the wailing child. The ambulance arrived, and the EMT team began to check out the baby. Once assured that his condition was stable, the paramedics decided to take him to the hospital just to make sure there were no more pieces of balloon in his throat. Amid the thank-yous and the congratulations, Darien slowly made her way back to a booth, slid into the seat, and a steaming cup of coffee seemed to appear magically in front of her. The waitress waited patiently as she took her first sip.

"Anything you want, honey, it's on the house."

Darien looked at her, surprised at her generosity. "Are you sure?"

"It's what the boss said. Hey, you deserve it, you saved Manuel's life."

"Manuel," she said softly.

"Yeah, and he's a cutie pie. So what'll it be, dinner, lunch, you name it."

"Well, I am hungry. How about the meatloaf special with a large glass of milk."

"You got it." Darien was very much aware of all the glances back at her while she tried to act as nonchalant as possible, even though inside she was ready to burst apart with pride at having saved the little boy's life. A shadow passed across her table and she looked up to find that Manuel's mother had returned. This time when the woman spoke to Darien, it was in broken English.

"Thank you, senora, for save my baby."

"You're welcome. How is he?"

"He will be o-kay." She reached out, took Darien's hand in her own while smiling down at her with gratitude.

Darien felt she should partake of this woman's goodness, her love for her child, and the happiness in the smile she offered to her. She took the gift deep inside for safekeeping, watching as Manuel's mother turned around, and walked back outside to where the paramedics waited. Darien continued to watch as the EMT personnel helped the woman step up inside the ambulance, and when they secured the doors behind her, Darien took comfort in the loud boisterous cries of the baby. It was almost as good as the comfort she felt when the waitress placed the old-fashioned meatloaf special in front of her.

The plate was steaming hot, and ketchup topped the baked hamburger, her own favored way to cook meatloaf. The potatoes were on the creamy side, not entirely lump free, with a well of dark brown gravy centered in the middle. Just by looking at them, Darien could tell they were homemade. The bright green broccoli was steamed just enough to allow the vitamins to stay inside, while making the vegetable a little less than crunchy. It could not have been more home cooked than if Darien prepared it herself. She lifted the fork to her mouth, and the first bite told her she was more than just a little hungry. After cleaning her plate, the waitress brought her a slice of homemade apple pie, with a spoonful of whipped cream on top. As full as she was, Darien could not resist the tempting smell of the fresh pie, and another cup of fresh coffee.

She smiled as the waitress picked up the second empty plate, and then Darien turned to glance out the window as she slowly sipped from her cup. She was curious but not alarmed as she watched a large black sedan pull up to the diner, and two well-dressed men emerged from the car. Both were dressed in suits, ties, and shoes polished as bright and shiny as the black car they were driving. They stood next to the car, staring at the very same window that she was looking through. How strange. Was she being followed? Jack would not hire private detectives to follow her; hell, he would not even open the phone book to find one. She shook her head, and silently admonished herself for being so paranoid. There came a sudden flash of being swept away into a vortex, an actual feeling of spinning out into the middle of a purple desert surrounded by dark purple mountains. Darien blinked her eyes, the image disappeared, and she realized so had the large black sedan.

Now Darien was still prone to small wanderings inside her head and although the zone was a place that she sometimes still escaped to, she tried not to fall inside without awareness. Dr. Holmes told her that entering the zone was harmful to her mental well-being, and that much of his diagnosis for her illness, she believed. Yet sometimes it still happened, and at these times, she had a tendency to see through whatever was in her line of vision, almost as if it wasn't there. Therefore, there was a chance, a very small chance, that perhaps this car and those men had not actually been there. "No, not possible, I watched them pull into the parking spot. No, that's just silly; no one who looked like those two would have a reason to come for me." The new anxiety caused her mind to drift, and a new headache developed. Darien was suddenly gone, entering deeper into the zone than she had been in many years.

She was a little girl again, living in a warm loving home with her mother, father, older sister, and brother. Darien and her sister shared a bedroom upstairs and she remembered waking in the middle of the night. The little three-year-old sat up in her bed with her big brown eyes as wide as they could be. Against the wall at the far end of the room was an old-fashioned steamer trunk banded with staves of metal. On top of this trunk stood a doll made of a hard molded rubber, decorated with a painted-on skirt, and much to Darien's surprise the doll was doing a Hawaiian hula dance. She remembered how frightened she was by her play toy, a painted Minnie Mouse doll, and she slid deep inside the safety of her blankets, daring to peek out just enough to see if the doll was still dancing. Imagine her surprise and terror to find that not only was the doll still dancing, but it had also moved onto her bed. Darien quickly pulled the covers back over her head, and being only three she lost herself in the night as sleep came to take her back to the land of dreams.

The next morning she told her sister about the dancing doll, her sister told their brother, and they poked fun, laughing as only children can. However, her sister Denise made the decision that bad dolls needed punishment, and that form of punishment was going to take place as a surgical procedure. Darien did agree with her sister that the doll was bad, so she let her take the scissors and cut off the tip of the doll's nose along with three of its four fingers on both hands. After surgery was completed, Darien held her deformed doll up in front of her. Rather than be satisfied that Denise implemented the proper castration, she instead broke into tears of sadness for the injuries they inflicted on the poor inanimate piece of rubber. Despite scaring her with the dancing, which she was sure happened, of all her dolls, Darien loved Minnie best. Her mother tried to glue the severed appendages back on, but they kept falling off and she remembered putting the doll away, never touching it again.

Darien blinked her eyes and focused on the old-fashioned wall jukebox in her booth. She sighed aloud from the vivid memory, and using the metal L-shaped levers on the bottom of the music box she began flipping through the metal pages. The pages hit each other, clack, clack, clack, and she wondered if either of the suited men along with the black car were ever there. Darien rose from the booth, stretched her cramped muscles, and while slipping into her light brown jacket the strangest thing happened. She watched in amazement as the pages on the wall juke continued to flip themselves over, clack, clack, and she felt an abnormal sensation begin a slow crawl through her body. Clack Clack Clack, clackity clack, louder, and louder, clack clack, and then suddenly they stopped. She picked up her purse, hoisted it to a secure spot on her shoulder, drew in a deep breath, and let it out slowly.

"Thanks for dinner, it really was good," she said to the approaching waitress, who seemed oblivious to the previously loud clacking pages of the wall juke.

"It's nothing, honey, you can't put a price on what you just did."

"Thanks anyway." The waitress nodded her head, and Darien made her way through the diner and out the door.

The music of the crickets filled the night with a symphony of chirping, all of them in perfect cricket pitch. Darien leaned up against her car wondering just what in the hell she thought she could possibly be doing. Jack was going to think she had totally lost her mind, not that it mattered much now that she was gone. If it was not for the spot on her leg that David touched, where the heat was first generated, a spot that never cooled, even in the coldest winter temperatures, if it wasn't for that, she would agree with Jack about the mind part. Hell, the doctors all agreed that she had lost the proverbial senses she was born with, but then had Darien ever really been "normal"?

As she stood by the car, new and different kinds of questions were coming, questions that put her on edge about the dark and dangerous journey Paul was sending her on. This thing, this Tianato Morebind, what kind of a thing could it be? She could not refer to it in her mind as anything other than an "it," because something called a Titobind could not possibly have any human qualities. Darien wondered if she would have enough strength, enough of whatever she needed, to do what she had to do. How does one find pure evil? How do you find a Titobind, and know how to defeat it? The guardian said that she would have to travel into its darkness, a dangerous path; well it was dark right now. Darien humphed at the feeble attempt to joke with herself. She stood by the door to her car searching for the keys that were always lost inside her purse when her eardrums suddenly felt as though they were going to explode. The scream that erupted in her head was not her own, but voices that belonged to a thousand captured souls.

"Darien!" She closed her eyes, and held the sides of her head as the tears came with a pain so extreme it caused her to scream as well. He called to her with the other guardians echoing his voice, and it was no wonder that her head felt ready to explode. In their collective effort to reach her, the thunderous shock of the voices caused her to fall to her knees. Darien took her hand away from her ears and found her palms covered with blood, prompting her to realize that she had the beginnings of the mother of all headaches.

"Oh God," she muttered.

The world became strangely silent; she could not hear the song of the crickets or the cars as they raced by on the straightaway. Darien pulled a tissue from the inside of her pocket and carefully swabbed at her ears while the quiet of the world settled down around her. With shaking hands, she reached up, inserted the key into the lock, and opened the car door. She slid behind the wheel and found herself immediately comforted by the familiarity of her car. It was funny how something as cold and impersonal as a piece of metal, transformed into a small miracle of transportation, could become so comforting. While she sat there trying to regain her senses, and hopefully her hearing, inside her head she could still hear the lusty cries of a very disgruntled Manuel. Darien carried a sense of accomplishment from having saved the life of the small child, giving him the opportunity to grow into whatever he wanted to be. She put her key into the ignition, started her car, and smiled as the noise of the engine came to her, faint, but audible. She put her car in drive, pulled out into the nearly deserted street, and followed the signs back to the highway. If only she knew where she needed to go, then perhaps the going would not be so difficult. Then again, maybe it would make it worse.

It became a world of questions, a world of vagueness, and in this deepening paradox of playing the game, the divorced middle-aged woman could not help but wonder if she would ever solve the riddles. Darien felt something drop onto her shoulder, and put her hand back to her ear only to find that it was bleeding again. She pulled several tissues from her pocket and put them up to the side of her face. She kept the pressure on until she was sure that it finally stopped. Darien reached over and turned the button on the radio, needing something to take her mind off what had happened. She listened to the music while concentrating on driving. It wasn't until Darien found the need to turn on the headlights that she became aware of how far the day had gone. As the night closed around her, and her tired body forced a yawn, the would-be savior decided it was time to find a place to sleep. Nodding off, jerking her head up, and finding herself driving on the wrong side of the road only added to her decision. The next exit promised "phood, phone, gas, and lodging. "Phood." Ha ha, very funny, very creative for a bunch of kids wondering what to do with the white paint they found in their neighbor's garage. She finally arrived at a grungy cheap motel, about six miles off the exit with a flashing sign that advertised:

"ACANCY."

"Well, I'm not surprised," Darien grumbled to herself when she saw the missing "V," and she just hoped that the "NO" was not missing as well. Not only was she tired but she was cranky as well.

She was able to rent a room, but continued grumbling all the way there, and wrinkled up her nose in disgust at the heavy smoking odors that hung in the drapes and seemed to have actually permeated into the walls. All she needed was sleep, and despite the lack of cleanliness, the bed looked inviting. Darien decided against pulling down the blankets, not knowing what kind of little nasties might be lingering in the sheets. (God knows when the last time was that they took the time to change them.) She found an extra blanket in the closet, and lay down fully clothed pulling the blanket up tight around her chin.

It did not take long for her to fall into a deep and troubled sleep punctuated periodically by nightmares of falling. As she fell, dancing shadows appeared by her side, sticking out their tongues and laughing. Her mind would not let her rest in the deepest of sleep, and it forced her to dream of David. She felt him, so lost, in so much pain, and all the other guardians as well who cried out to Darien. The woman in her dream was someone who was running and running, searching to find and free the guardians from the Titobind's prison, and Darien felt as if she were sitting and watching herself in a movie. However, in the movie/dream, the quest for David was proving futile, and her frantic journey was taking her deeper into the depths of his capture. Suddenly, out of the shadows stepped a large hideous creature that appeared to be made of solid night. It towered above her, looking down with bright green eyes that glowed inside a shapeless face. The thing raised its right arm, and its captive dangled helplessly in front of her. It was David. Darien could see movement around David's neck, and she knew that the thing held him in a tightening noose, and as she watched, it pulled him up into the air. The creature grasped David with huge claw-like pincers, which drove and ground their way into the guardian. A scream began as the creature of darkness began to pull his body in four opposite directions, and then Darien screamed as David started to separate.

Her eyes opened.

She found herself standing in the corner of her motel room with the scream still issuing from her mouth. Darien was afraid to move, terrified that the dark monster of her dreams was waiting for her somewhere in the shadows of her room. When the cold dampness of the night settled around her, she ran and jumped back into bed, knowing that eventually even blanket safety would not keep these shadow demons away. Sleep came to her again, slower this time, lighter than before, and when a persistent knocking came to her door, she was instantly awake and aware. Through the parted drapes, she could see a dazzling display of light that was so brilliant it was bringing day to the nighttime sky.

"Christ, what the hell is going on now?" She stumbled to the door, opened it, only to throw up her hand against the sudden onslaught of the bursting white and yellow lights. There were streaks of lightning illuminating the night sky as they exploded like Fourth of July fireworks, and began a free fall gently towards the ground. Halfway through their downward flight it looked like they hit an invisible barrier, causing them to explode again in the darkness, showering the immediate area with the brightness of a hundred miniature suns. One of them reached the ground, and the sparks bounced back upwards, disappearing in the sky. There was strangeness about this display of unexpected light, and the spectators stood unafraid, finding a beauty to behold from this great spectacular show. All of the people were standing close together, still in their bedclothes, having become the temporary residents of Motel 6. There were no ooos and ahhs that normally accompany a fireworks display and Darien sensed in all the motel neighbors that stood around her, a touch of sadness. She saw Gramma and Grampa on their way to visit their children and grandchildren. There was a young couple possibly doing "it" for the first time, along with the cheating spouse doing "it" for the nth time, wanting to recapture a lost passion. There was also the family who had traveled too late to find a vacancy at the Ramada Inn with a heated pool, and where children under twelve stayed free. She observed the man who stood outside the immediate area, possibly not wanting to be recognized. She wondered if he was a local big shot who had a taste for something in women just a little bit outside the norm.

"Hey, lady." Darien looked down; saw a little girl with pigtails, and an upturned freckled nose staring up at her with child like innocence.

"The man said to tell you…" A sudden burst of yellow lit the sky in a stunning performance of sparkling light, and Darien looked up at the brilliance. She felt the tug at her shirt, and before she returned her attention to the girl, she watched the display a little longer.

"He said to tell you…"

"Who said?"

"That man, he said for me to tell you something."

"Tell me what?"

"He said for me to tell you that Tito is bringing a guardian down." Darien quickly looked back at the sky as a deep-seated terror took hold. The lightning cracked, and the bursting fireworks continued their explosions until she realized what the breaking of the suns meant. That thing must be pulling the guardians in tighter, binding them to him, bringing them down to his level, and making them a part of his soul. Darien looked back down and found that the little girl had disappeared.

"He already has them bound," she whispered to herself, "is that not enough? Why does he have to consume them as well? Greatest of all the guardians, giver of peace and comfort to all who walk in this world, has he found you too?"

"Not yet." She turned around to find the person who spoke to her, but there was only a shift and change in the shadows.

"He is close, Darien, but as you can see, he has not yet taken me. What you are seeing is the final death of one of the eldest of guardians."

The last lightning streak broke the night sky, and the last sun burst in the darkness. The guardian that had only a moment ago hid in the shadows was now gone, and out of the darkness came a moan of unimaginable sadness and loss. The power of his moan carried through the surrounding woods, bending the trees with its force and sounding like the howl of a powerful wind. Then it began to rain as the last free guardian wept while one of its own died. Darien too let the silent tears fall, her first since David had left, her first since she had set him free nearly eight years earlier. The trees bent again as the continued moan of loss whistled through the woods, and the warm gentle winds that had always been the guardians was now a cold hard rain. Such sadness filled her, and Darien felt her resolve to help David start to crumble. Listening to the guardian weep was almost more than she could bear and only Darien knew the real reason for the rain. She stood outside the motel room long after the others had gone inside, and as she absorbed some of Paul's warmth and his smile only a week earlier, she now took inside his sadness and his tears.

Someone threw a towel around her shoulders, led her to her room, and after opening the door for her, she stepped inside. That same person closed the door behind her, and Darien walked over to her bed where she sat alone, cold, wet, and shivering under the standard white motel towel. Finally rising, she went to take a warm shower, with each step becoming heavier than the last.

"Be strong, Darien, I am still here." She smiled when the shadows shifted and moved in the corner, instantly elated knowing that the eldest was still with her, but then instantly depressed. How long would he be able to continue to fight against the evil? How long before that thing, that Titobind captured the greatest one? The voice came to her again, and in that voice was strength, a power that Darien felt traveling across a vast distance to reach into her, and to pull her together. The voice that spoke was one filled with love, filled with devotion for all of man.

"How great, Darien, is your love for David?"

She thought of the sacrificed guardian, the display of light and brilliance that brought her a sadness that traveled beyond her depth of understanding. When she answered, she was careful in choosing her words. "It is greater, my guardian, than the glow of a thousand suns."

"Then use that belief, Darien, and make it work for you." Suddenly a tiny sparkling sun appeared, glowing at her feet, shimmering with goodness and laughter. Darien bent down and picked up the sun, mesmerized by the warm glow. She played with it in her hands, watching it try to hide between her fingers, playing peek-a-boo with her. She laughed with delight when the sun rose above her head, and she felt a deep reverent respect when it shattered into a thousand fragments, which fell into, and became a part of Darien.

✳ ✳ ✳

The road hummed under her tires as she drove her car down the interstate. She could feel the vibrations in her teeth, and she gritted them together against the constant annoyance. She asked herself for the hundredth time where she thought she was going and for the hundredth time she could not answer. Darien had been gone from her home nearly two weeks and she didn't know if it was a good thing to try and call, but she gave it a try nonetheless, if only to let them know that she was alive and well. Of course, their reaction was as she expected it to be, her eldest daughter hung up on her.

"No one wants to talk to you, Mom." Click and silence.

Darien thought to herself that at the very least, one of them should have a little concern for her. However, in an odd way, it also eased her mind. Although the reaction from them was expected, she was relieved to know that despite her unexpected disappearance, they were okay. Darien had always been an overly concerned wife and mother, however, they were all adults now, and she could not find a reason why they should not be able to take care of themselves. She was hoping that maybe one of them might be just a little worried about her. Darien sighed. Obviously, the family was not ready to forgive her for leaving, nor could she ever explain why.

She glanced at her watch and saw that it was four in the late afternoon and early evening traffic, the prelude to the expected rush hour, already had her bottled in. They were moving at a record-breaking thirty miles an hour and Darien knew she should be glad they were moving at all. She wound her window down to try and get some fresh air circulating in her car, but all she received were the noxious fumes of bumper-to-bumper traffic. Suddenly the traffic ground to a halt, and Darien was startled to see an older woman running haphazardly through the stalled traffic on the other side of the median. Unexpectedly she stopped, and stared directly into Darien's face and then she made a cranking motion with her hand to have Darien roll down her window.

"Please, can you help? It's my husband; I think he's having a heart attack."

Darien's first reaction was "Cheesh, lady, why me?" However, rather than leave the woman to find someone else, she dutifully exited her car, climbed the median and sprinted after the woman who had already begun to walk quickly back through the temporarily stalled traffic. Darien could not believe how many cars there were between them, and the elderly woman had been on the other side of the road as well. How was it possible for this woman to run so far without one of these people offering to help her? How in the world did she find her way all the way back to Darien? Darien looked in the windows of the cars as she passed by, and all of the faces inside held the same exasperated look of being stuck in the traffic jam. The woman suddenly stopped, which very nearly caused Darien to collide with her. She leaned over, reached through the car window, and tenderly touched the very quiet, very still body of a man who was very close to her own age. The man's face was ashen gray in appearance and his lips were already turning color. Darien knew immediately that the man was dead, but the silent plea in the eyes of the woman who had loved this man for almost half a century made her want to help.

"What's your name?" Darien softly asked the exhausted woman.

"Gladys."

"And your husband?"

"Henry."

"Gladys, go find someone with a cell phone and have them call 911. I'll see if I can help Henry."

"Is he going to be okay?" she asked with tears in her eyes.

"I don't know. Go and find a phone," Darien turned back to Henry and very quietly said, "I'll see what I can do."

"Okay, Miss..."

"Darien, my name is Darien." Gladys touched her hand briefly, and then wandered back into the idling traffic. Darien opened the car door and reached into the back seat to retrieve a folded blanket. She dropped this onto the pavement, and then she pulled Henry from inside the car. His head rolled back, his mouth opened, and Darien could not help but notice that his fingernails were turning the same color as his lips.

"Well, I guess I at least owe it to her to try." Darien kneeled beside Henry, who was best known as the other half of Gladys. She remembered her CPR training and leaned down to listen for his breathing, then two fingers up the side of his neck, there, the little indentation for his pulse. No pulse, not that she had really expected to find any. As if she did this every day, Darien followed his ribs up to the center of his breastbone, placed her palm next to her two fingers. She laced her fingers together, and then locked her elbows as she leaned up over him. She cringed before she pushed down, remembering how one of the men in her CPR class had told her that when you give the first initial chest compression on an elderly person, usually some ribs cracked because they are so brittle with age. She pushed down and sure enough, she heard the cracking.

"Oh, damn," she said aloud and pushed again. She was not a doctor, but she was sure that not only were they cracking, but that several of them were breaking. She could not remember the technical amount of compressions that one is supposed to give, she just counted, one and two and three and four and five and six, going all the way up to ten. Then shifting positions, she gave him one long breath, and then back down to his chest, tracing, locking, counting, one and two, then starting all over again. Shift; breathe, trace, lock, and count.

Darien felt again for his pulse, and to her surprise there was one, a weak one, but a pulse just the same. She sat back on her legs in amazement as old Henry's eyelids fluttered and then opened. Gladys, the other half of Henry, was walking back down the highway towards the car. Even more amazing was that the traffic had finally started to move and Darien could hear the scream of the ambulance siren. Gladys knelt down beside Darien and mouthed a quiet "Thank you" as she gently smoothed back her husband's hair. The cars began speeding up, and Darien was surprised and pleased to see that someone had stopped to help direct the cars away from them, and allow the ambulance through. The paramedics quickly administered oxygen to a very tired Henry, who could only lie still, blink, and watch. Gladys stood with her car door open ready to follow the ambulance back to the hospital, and Darien turned to walk back to her car, suddenly remembering that she had left it idling in the middle of traffic.

"Darien!" She turned back around, and squinting against the sun, she saw a very grateful Gladys gracing her with a huge smile.

"God bless you!" she called out.

Darien smiled at her and waved back as she mumbled under her breath, "Somebody sure as hell better bless me." Darien waved goodbye then continued walking in the breakdown lane and had just about reached her car when the cars that were passing her started to accelerate to dangerous speeds. She looked up ahead and saw a tow truck hitching up a twisted black piece of metal that used to be her little car.

"What the hell is that mess? What the hell happened to my car?" she yelled as she went running towards the operator of the tow truck.

"How the hell should I know? All I did was get the call to move this crap outta here."

"Christ," Darien said as she was buffeted around by the wind from the speeding cars. "Can you at least give me a ride into town?"

"No riders, lady, I'll get fired."

"Oh, for crying out loud, what the hell am I supposed to do? Just stand out here and hope I don't get hit, or try to hitch into town? No one is going to stop for me on this highway. Come on, mister, please, who am I going to tell?" He must have felt sorry for her, because he reluctantly relented, and let her climb on board. Darien sat inside the dirty, smoky cab of the tow truck, afraid to touch anything in her immediate vicinity, afraid that even just sitting there would give cause for the grease and dirt to jump on her.

"What's your name?"

The question brought her out of the "Just what the hell am I supposed to do now" thoughts, and she turned to look at the coverall-covered truck driver.

"Darien Trenton. What's yours?"

"Milton Rose, call me Milt, or Rosey, nickname don't bother me."

"I like Rosey." She smiled at him and he smiled back showing perfect white teeth surrounded by his grease-covered face.

"Sorry 'bout your car."

"Yeah, well what are you gonna do, Rosey. I saved two people's lives in the past two days, hardly measurable against a twisted piece of metal."

"Two lives?"

"Yep, yesterday at a diner and then just now, an old man with a heart attack."

"Well fancy that, a real-life hero in my cab."

Darien shrugged her shoulders. "Heroine, but I'm hardly that. Right place, right time."

The cab grew quiet, and they rode the rest of the way in silence. Darien finally rolled down the window when her stomach revolted against the smell of smoke and grease, not that anyone would notice a little vomit in its acquired filth. She watched out the window as the huge bustling city came closer and closer, and she was surprised to see that it was a lot larger than the other small towns she passed through. Huge cement buildings loomed in the distance, and then after going over the bridge, the buildings seemed to close completely around the truck as they entered the large metropolis. It was not until they were approaching the third city light that Rosey told her she would have to get out. Darien thanked him and slung the book bag over her shoulder, and grabbed the worn-out handle of her old suitcase. She was lucky that they had been in the passenger seat rather than in the trunk, otherwise they would be gone. She was also very lucky that no one opened her glove box and stole her traveler's checks, not that they were irreplaceable, but the hassle of getting them replaced was something for which she had no patience. Just before closing the door, Rosey leaned over and handed her his business card. This surprised her.

"For your insurance company, they'll total your car, trust me, I've picked up enough wrecks to know there's no salvaging this one." She watched quietly as Rosey drove away, and suddenly felt more alone than ever before.

Darien stood on the corner watching all the people rush by, so busy carrying on with their mundane, boring daily lives. At the same time, all she could think about was that she had to enter a dark and dangerous place, find the evil Titobind, mortally wound it, and set the guardians free! Piece of cake. Well, at least she had a purpose, yeah well go figure.

The first thing she had to do was find a place to stay, and then she could spend her time wandering aimlessly down the streets looking for the signs which would be invisible to all but her, advertising, "Dark and Dangerous Journey This Way," in bright flashing neon lights. Darien really had started to wander aimlessly while these thoughts rambled through her head, and she had almost entered the zone again when she walked right into a man coming across the street.

"Christ, lady, watch where the hell you're going."

"I'm sorry, it was my fault."

"Damn right it was your fault," he said with a sarcastic voice as he bent to retrieve the magazine dropped during their collision. She watched as he picked up the "forbidden fruit" and tried to hide the magazine under his jacket, but not before Darien had been able to read the title, and what she read sent shivers up her back:

*Bondage for Beginners*

She thought that perhaps the physical bondage of one human by another could not be any worse than the mental bondage that had kept her defeated and chained inside her own mind. Suddenly Darien found herself wondering if the Titobind was so evil and so bad that maybe, she should start looking for him in places where this sort of stuff occurred. A city as large as Corral, Texas, was bound to have its share of underground, most cities usually do. Besides, the guardian had told her that she needed to find the men that lived here, in our world, who were bound to the Titobind. Where better to find evil, bad things than in places where this type of decadence takes place? Darien was aware that some people considered this way of life as normal, and as it was in all ways of life, different people do things to different degrees. Just how it all worked out or how it was all put together, she had yet to understand.

A sharp squeal of tires brought her out of her thoughts just in time to see the collision of a car with a bicycle messenger. The bicycle lay crumpled under the front end of the car, while the messenger lay sprawled nearly twenty feet away. Pieces of the car's shattered windshield lay across the road like iridescent slivers reflecting the blood that had, on impact, burst out of the rider like an exploding water balloon. The force of the hit spattered his blood all over the car, in the road, and the large puddle under the messenger was growing larger even as she watched. Traffic stopped moving, and quickly bottlenecked exactly like the traffic on the highway.

"Three times in two days," she said aloud to no one in particular, and her heart nearly broke in two when she heard a loud moan come from the crumpled body in the street. Suddenly she realized that with the guardians gone, who was there to protect them? Who was going to help the ones taken before their time? This young man, the messenger, she knew it was too early for him, and she knew with this one, there would be no second chance.

Darien walked over to where the man lay on the ground, and someone handed her a blanket, which she quickly placed on top of the bicycle rider. She looked down at open eyes that spoke to her in a silent plea of "what happened?" The mouth moved slowly, allowing a very quiet voice to speak.

"I can't feel anything." Darien kneeled down, and softly smoothed the blood-soaked hair away from his face, and she said to him:

"Don't try to move, there is an ambulance on the way. Hang on, okay?" Without really thinking about what to do or not to do, Darien talked to him.

"What's your name?"

"Tommy."

"You hang on, Tommy, help is coming. My name's Darien and I'll stay here with you until they get you in the ambulance." The young man slowly closed his eyes, and then they flew open again as he looked out past Darien.

"My mom is here, I heard her call my name. I can see her; she's behind you." Darien bit her lip to try to hold back the tears, while at the same time she clasped Tommy's hand. Her pants had begun to soak up the blood that continued to seep from the boy's wounds. She could not help him, and that moment, the helplessness overwhelmed her, and she knew how difficult a guardian's duty truly is.

"Are you happy, Tommy, have you been happy with your life?" He shook his head yes.

"Do you have any regrets?" He shook his head no.

"Then go and be free with her." Tommy, bike messenger, looked at Darien and smiled. His smile radiated complete happiness, along with a serenity that she found overpowering in the love that he shared with his mother. Tommy closed his eyes, and died quietly in the street. Darien felt his soul push up out of his body, his energy passing through her in an effort to reach the outstretched waiting arms of his mother. For a few brief moments Darien was living Tommy. She took his first steps, experienced his first kiss, languished for a moment when he lost his first love, and experienced his final resolve within his own self as his body terminated, and his soul was set free. She reached out and touched the nearly invisible hand, and it clasped strongly around hers. The touch was enough to allow her to see the passing of a very decent, hardworking young man.

"May your next journey be a longer one." Then he left Darien with a continuing sense of loss, and the voice that spoke unexpectedly in her ear was noticeably weaker.

"It's not supposed to be his time, Darien, too many are dying." She drew the blanket up over the lifeless body, hiding him from curious onlookers. She whispered softly to Paul, trying not to draw any more attention.

"I am trying, my guardian, but there are times that I feel lost."

"Look to your heart, and you will find all the answers you need." The voice faded away, the sound of the siren cutting through the murmuring crowd, and Darien felt a brief déjà vu.

The man behind the wheel of the car came staggering across the road falling down when he tripped on the curb, and vomited his liquid lunch all over the sidewalk. He was not even aware of the wonderful life he ended. Darien turned away in disgust, and she slowly backed away from Tommy until her own heels hit the curb. She stumbled backwards, her arms pinwheeling to help her keep balance, but the momentum brought her down hard enough on the pavement to ricochet the shock through her body. Darien rubbed her rump with one hand while watching with quiet interest as a shiny black sedan pulled up to the intersection, and two men, impeccably dressed in very expensive-looking suits, got out of the dark car. It seemed as though they had decided to wait outside the car until the traffic cleared around the accident sight. They appeared to be the standard issue of morbid curiosity seekers, except to Darien. She was sure that they were the same two men that she had seen at the diner (not seen), and the most obvious question was, were they really following her? In addition, if they were, what could they possibly want?

She sat and observed the paramedics as they loaded Tommy's body into the ambulance, not really thinking about the bloody jeans that were drying and sticking to her legs. She watched quietly as the fire department washed the memory of Tommy from the street and soon, for his family that was all he would be, a memory. Darien decided that the last thing she wanted to be was nothing more than a memory and yet, that was how everyone ended up. The world was comprised of nothing more than memories, and that only happened if you were lucky enough to have lived a life that even warranted being someone's memory. This realization brought such a strange sadness to her and she suddenly found it difficult to stand. Her legs were somewhat cramped, her arms aching from having helped the elderly Henry, and the short walk to the Army and Navy store that she had spotted across the street proved to be a chore. Darien wanted to get rid of the stiff, dried pants that were now giving her nothing more than a memory. She pushed open the door at the discount store, and it seemed as if the proprietor had been watching and waiting for her.

It did not take long to replace the jeans, and she talked with the man who ran the store. He voiced his feelings on how she knelt beside the poor boy that did not deserve to die. First Darien told him how glad she was that no one had taken her things while she comforted the messenger, and then she commented to the owner about the intolerable condition of the man who drove the truck.

"That driver was so drunk. He couldn't even stand up and then he practically fell out of the truck he was driving."

"It happens all the time." Darien did not expect the store owner to become so solemn, and so resigned when he spoke to her about the way life had become.

"We all live in so much fear of each other; it never used to be like that. Where does all of this violence come from? When did things get so out of hand? When did we all stop caring about each other?" The elderly man's eyes filled with tears as Darien handed him the stiff and bloodied jeans that he promised to get rid of. Their hands met over the counter, and Darien gave his hand a little squeeze, causing him to smile gratefully at her. She pulled her hand away, suddenly uncomfortable, made a fake little cough, and then asked him if he knew of a cheap hotel close by. Imagine her surprise when his entire demeanor changed and the man in front of her miraculously transformed himself into an expected textbook Texan.

"Well gal, there's the Corral Conquest next block over, but it could be a might rich for you all, but the further out of the city you go, the cheaper they git. If'n you go 'bout four blocks straight down out of Corral Center, go left fer two blocks, and then right fer one more'n you'll happen on the Triple Dove. It's cheap and not in a very good part of town, if'n you git my drift, gal." Darien looked at him and it was all she could do to keep from bursting out laughing, however a few giggles did manage an escape.

"Don't worry; I can take care of myself."

"Yep, I jest bet you kin, but you be careful jest the same."

"Thanks."

He winked at her and whispered, "Tourists expect it you know." Darien gave him a huge smile as she practically ran out of his store. She could not hold in the laughter, and as the door slammed shut behind her the man inside smiled as her laughter reached his ears (and the warm shadow that floated around his ankles unfurled itself, glided across the floor, moving on its own to become lost inside the darkness, hiding in the corners of the store).

After the intense day, Darien felt her nerves begin to relax a little, as the good hearty laughter had been just what she needed. She even took the time to look upwards at the red sun that cast its evening glow as it drifted down behind the horizon. The air had just a little chill, but not too much for it was mid April, and in southern Texas, that meant it would soon be summer. The directions he gave her in typical southern drawl stayed in her head, and she had no trouble at all finding her way to the Triple Dove Hotel. As she walked down the sidewalk, his remembered words made her smile, even putting a little bounce into her step while more than a few people smiled back. It wasn't until she actually reached the hotel that she finally stopped to take in her new surroundings. The man had been right, she could tell immediately this was not a very safe neighborhood; even as she watched, the drug deals were taking place right in front of her, and she could easily see the weapons hidden underneath their light jackets. There were bars crowding both sides of the street with bright colored neon lights that drew her attention as they cast strange colored glows from inside, temporarily highlighting those who passed by. Laughter drifted into the encroaching night, occasionally punctuated by screams of delight, and screams that she did not want to know about. Darien quickly entered the hotel, suddenly grateful to be inside.

She looked around and recognized the lobby of a hotel, but where was the registration desk? Her eyes quickly scanned the large entry area, and finally Darien spotted a small, wizened man sitting behind a window, protected by "jailhouse" bars. What kind of place was this? She walked over to him, and he barely acknowledged her presence. She got his attention though, when she asked him for a room for the night.

"In here most folks want rooms by the hour," he said to her. "You alone or you expectin' someone?"

"No, I'm not expecting anyone. I'm sorry, but I don't understand what you mean by rooms by the hour." Loud boisterous laughter overhead captured her attention, and when she looked upwards several well-dressed men were descending the staircase. They looked neither right nor left, and they purposefully avoided looking directly at Darien. She followed the staircase back up to the laughter, and saw scantily dressed young women leaning over the railing, blowing kisses at the retreating suits. A brothel, a cathouse, a whorehouse? Is this place for real?

"Well damn, hit me over the head or something," she said to herself, and then to the attendant she said, "No, it's just me and it's just for one night." Then she leaned in close to the man behind the barred window and whispered, "I didn't really think that these kind of places existed, I thought they were only found in movies."

"Personally I think you're in the wrong place, lady, but it's late and I'll rent you the room for one night." He turned abruptly away from her, grabbed some keys, turned backed around, and threw them on the counter so that they slid under the barred window right into her hand.

"Number two thirty-two, for one night. I gave you the room way in the back, away from the noise. Forty dollars, cash." Darien opened her book bag and counted out forty dollars then slid it under the window to the man who suddenly jerked with a coughing fit. The sickly man grabbed for his handkerchief that sat crumpled on the counter, and held it over his mouth while he made a regurgitating sound to bring up the phlegm. She was staring at him, knew that it was rude for her to do so, but for some reason she could not stop. He wiped at his mouth, and looked at her over the top of his reading glasses.

"What the fuck you waitin' for? Your room is on the second floor, ain't no bellhop and there ain't no elevator. Get the hell outta here before I change my mind." That was it, Darien nearly ran up the stairs, and she closed her ears to the noises she heard as she passed the occupied rooms.

\* \* \*

Her room was surprisingly clean, something completely unexpected. The end tables by the bed were dust free, clean linens folded neatly, and set on a brand-new-looking mattress. There was no stale smoke smell like there had been in some of the other places she stayed at, and the rest of the furniture was in excellent condition. Darien made her way to the bathroom, and was again pleasantly surprised. The entire room was scrubbed clean; even the tiles on the floor shined with a coat of clear wax. There were no bad stains in the toilet bowl, and Darien used the washcloth to lift up the lid and was again surprised to find the underneath clean. The shower shined like the rest of the room, and she could not resist running her finger along the top of the windowsill, smiling when it came away without any visible dirt. The windows here were cleaner than her home! Her stomach rumbled, and Darien realized that she had not eaten since her good deed on the highway. With all the excitement, who could remember to eat? She was not sure if she wanted a hot shower and bed, or a hot shower and a meal. The night was quickly closing in, and the Darien began to think about which problems would need immediate attention the following morning. She would first deposit her money at a local bank, and then put in a call to her insurance company and find out what she was supposed to do about her poor little car. Darien walked over to the curtains, opened them, and looked down into the city that held a different life at night, another world, where good folk like Darien usually didn't go. The bright lights were merely lures, promising cold warmth inside a place where for a few short hours, people could forget the outside world.

"Is this where I have to go, down to a place like that, where women sell their bodies to please the cravings in their veins?" Darien blinked her eyes; she could not imagine doing drugs, even at the lowest times of her life. However, at one time, there had been the alcohol. Her hand strayed absently to the silver rose that hung around her neck, and her body flushed with a remembered touch from eight long years ago. Darien really had made a mess of things, but then most of her life was a mess. Aside from the earliest days, she had always been spiraling downwards, reaching occasional plateaus when she had given birth to her children. At those times she seemed to level out some of her life, but her past always came back to haunt her. She began to wonder if any of the decisions she made in her lifetime were the correct ones, and if this current decision could be a mistake despite the eldest guardian's determined resolve in making her savior to the world.

It was going to be one hell of an adventure.

On top of everything else, she still had to decipher the clues from a riddle that she detested. Darien released the drapes, walked back to the center of the room and stood in exasperation and confusion, not sure which way she should go. Her mind began to wander, bringing about the familiar tug of the zone, but it was unlike any other zone she had linked into before. Usually she went into her past and let it dominate her present life, but this time it was different. Darien had her arms outstretched, and she was spinning in a circle, picking up speed, twirling faster and faster creating a mini-vortex within the room. Dust was following the spinning circle of air, and several loose pieces of paper along with some tissues were spinning in her little tornado. She had absorbed the Mexican woman's fear, Gladys's misgivings and in the case of Tommy, she allowed his soul to pass through herself to reach the other side. All of this, she now spun into release, accompanied by a great cry of relief. She kept to herself all of the smiles that she had collected, hidden deep inside of her, knowing without any doubts that there would come a time when they would be needed. Darien fell exhausted onto the bed and slept deeply, without dreams, for nearly fourteen hours. The next day when she woke her decision to descend on the dark and dangerous journey had become her only path, and she instinctively knew that everything inside of her was changing.

# CHAPTER FOUR

# A CHANCE MEETING
# ON THE INTERSTATE

There was a certain truth in the saying that "two halves make a whole." And that certainly held true for Harry and Gladys, who are just two people, but together they complete each other and it makes their lives whole. Especially now since they have come nearly full circle, and are entering the twilight of their years. They had lived through generous helpings of healthy children, comfortable situations, and have had to deal with their share of the ones that were not so comfortable. They were blessed with better lives than most, at least they saw themselves that way, and anyone would agree with them having seen what they have accomplished.

Harry and Gladys were on their way to welcome their sixth healthy grandchild into the world, a baby boy, their second grandson. Although the child was already eight months old, Gladys and Harry had postponed their visit because the harsh winter months in the northeast caused both of them to come down with bronchitis. Of course, there was also the fact that they were in their early seventies, prone to viral infections, and it was normal for them to have a slightly longer road to recovery. Then there was Gladys's reasoning, "God forbid they should give the new baby an infection." Therefore, they had been content with pictures until they felt one hundred percent healthy, and able to travel safely

So it was on the day that Gladys, who was the best half of Henry, and Henry, who was whole only when his Gladys was there, happened to be traveling on the same interstate as Darien, except they were headed in totally opposite directions.

Henry lay full fist on the horn, and blasted the speeding driver that nearly swept him from his lane. Gladys hated it when Henry allowed an insensitive driver to block out all of his common sensibilities. He stepped on the gas, and pulled carelessly into the passing lane, nearly causing an accident himself, but he was determined to catch the driver of that car.

"Henry, what are you going to do when you do catch him?"

"Unnh, what do you mean?"

"I mean exactly what I said, what are you going to do with that driver when you catch up with him? How are you going to make him pull over? Or are you going to follow him all the way to his home, get out of the car and then punch him. What good is any of this doing?" Henry looked at his speedometer, and saw that he was pushing eighty, but it was not even putting a strain on the engine of his finally tuned automobile. He looked over at his wife and knew she was making sense, but then she always did.

"I hate it when you're right, Gladys."

"I know, Henry, so why don't you just slow down, and pull over into the travel lane where it's safer."

"No one is safe with loony drivers on this road." Gladys had to clamp her mouth shut, with Henry it was always loony drivers, never anyone else, and never ever Henry's fault. She watched him take off his hat, and set it carefully on the seat, and then he ran his hand through his full head of illustrious sliver hair. She knew that this was Henry's way of taking the edge off his aggravation, rather than taking it out on her.

They both looked young for their early seventies, having kept themselves active with walking and bicycling, and Henry loved to dance. He would catch quite a few stares from the ladies when they went out dancing, and it was not always from the geriatric set.

God how Gladys hated that word! Geriatrics. Ugh!

Who invented that old invalid-sounding word anyway? It reminded her of old age, crippling diseases, and wheelchairs, and a wheelchair was a place that Gladys hoped she would never have to go. Her nightly prayer had changed slightly through the years, and her most recent version went like this: "Let me die before I wake, or at least before I'm debilitated by a stroke." She recited her most current version prayer every night as she lay in bed next to her husband of almost fifty years, and she meant every word of it.

One thing Gladys found distressing as she became older was that she consistently viewed every day as though it was her last. People had sayings and ideas that would play in her head in her head repeatedly, especially the one that said: "Today is the first day of the rest of your life." Gladys had simply changed that to, "Today is your last day," and she changed "Oh God I'm awake" to "Oh God, I'm so afraid to go to sleep," and now as she looked at Henry she hoped she died first and fast, because she could not bear the thought of becoming a drooling helpless cripple forgotten in some nursing home. It that was selfish of her, she didn't really care, and as they crept closer to another year she could not help but be terrified as her slow walk had now become a full-out gallop to the inevitable.

"We're put here just long enough for a taste, a tease of life, and when we have begun to enjoy what life really is, it's taken away." She had said that to Henry a few short months earlier, and he had answered in his typical, sensible Henry fashion.

"Gladys, you have far too much time on your hands. Find something to do besides think about those things."

She smoothed the hat that sat on the seat between them, and as she caressed the brim and felt herself, even now, somewhat sexually excited by Henry, who was and always would be the other half of Gladys. She glanced up at Henry, admiring his strength, the way that he kept his appearance, and the fact that he still looked good for a man in his mid-seventies. Suddenly the traffic started to slow, and they were jammed in during rush hour.

"You know, Gladys, we could have pulled off the highway and had ourselves some dinner, and returned when this time had passed."

"I know, Henry."

"Seems to me I recall someone telling me the exact same thing not too long ago."

"Seems like." Henry smiled at Gladys, and she sighed looking back at him. Henry amazed himself with the sudden realization of just how attractive he still found his wife after all these years. In her day, Gladys was an extremely pretty young woman and even now, approaching the middle of their seventies, she was still very attractive. She did not fashion her hair like the other blue-haired weekly saloned women her age. Gladys kept her hair cut short, a "pixie" cut as she called it, popular from nearly thirty years earlier. She also aged as gracefully as Henry, much like the seemingly ageless movie stars, but without the fancy nips, tucks, and pulls used when trying to stay the normal aging process. Henry felt a sudden rush of love for a woman that had been faithfully his for forty-seven years, and on impulse, he reached over, took her hand, and gave it a gentle squeeze. She returned the pressure, and that was when Henry first felt the squeeze in his chest. He placed his hand on his shoulder trying to move around in his seat as the uncomfortable pressure expanded from where the squeeze in his chest began. Henry was having trouble breathing.

Gladys looked over at her husband, immediately alarmed when the drops of sweat fell from his forehead. The air-conditioning was on, the car comfortable, but Henry was sweating profusely, laboring for every breath.

"Henry?"

"My chest, I can't breathe." Gladys slid across the seat, smashing the hat that only moments ago she had fondly caressed. She placed her hand on the side of the cheek that she lovingly kissed so many times before and found Henry's skin to be cold and clammy. The cars stopped, the elderly couple was stuck in a dinnertime traffic jam, but Gladys knew Henry needed help and fast. He was barely holding on, only vaguely aware that Gladys talked to him, and she sounded so far away.

"Can you hear me, Henry?" It sounded to Henry as if everything was coming through a phone line full of static and it came to him in strange double repeats: "Can, can, you, you, hear, hear, me, me, Henry, Henry?" He was barely able to nod yes.

"Don't you die on me, old man." (Die; die, on, on, me, me old, old man, man.) She squeezed his hand one more time then slid back across the seat and opened her door. Gladys glanced at Henry one more time, and he turned his face to watch her leave while managing a weak smile.

Gladys began to run down through the stalled traffic, tapping on windows asking people for help, and those that did open their windows had the attitude of "what can I do, I'm stuck here in traffic, same as you, old woman." Gladys leaned up against the median trying to catch her breath when she saw a dark-haired woman staring at her from the inside of her car. Gladys made a rolling motion with her hand prompting the woman to roll her window down.

"Please help me, it's my husband, I think he's having a heart attack." The woman hesitated for a moment, and Gladys thought she was going to be like the rest and ignore her pleas for help, but she got out of her car, climbed over the median while at the same time waving her forward with her hand. Gladys sprinted back through the clogged traffic, almost too fast for the younger woman to keep up with her, and they quickly arrived at her car. Gladys looked at the stranger who came to help, and pleaded silently with tear-filled eyes as they both looked into the car at the ashen faced, blue-lipped Henry.

"What's your name?" the young woman asked Gladys.

"Gladys."

"And your husband?"

"Henry."

"Gladys, go find someone with a car phone. Have them call 911 and I'll see if I can help Henry."

"Is he going to be okay?" Her eyes filled again with tears.

"I don't know. Go find a phone, and I'll do the best I can."

"Okay, Miss…"

"Darien, my name is Darien."

Gladys once again moved off into the cars that were compacted into a mass of bumper-to-bumper aggravation. She knocked on window after window holding her hand to her ear like she was talking on a telephone, and people just kept shaking their heads no. Finally a few more cars away a young man in jeans and T-shirt stepped from his car.

"Can I help you?" he yelled across traffic.

"Please YES! Call 911, my husband is very sick."

"What kind of car, lady?" Gladys fumbled for a moment with her thoughts, and then yelled back. "A nineteen ninety Volvo wagon, dark green."

"Okay!" He disappeared back inside of his car, and looking skywards Gladys mouthed a thank you to empty air. She was tired now, all of the terrified running catching up to her, but she still managed to walk quickly back to their car. Her fear lessened when the young woman came into view. She was leaning over her husband, and Henry's eyes were open and blinking. He was confused, that much was obvious, but he was alive. The tears came, uncontrolled, expressing her relief that he was still with her. Traffic finally started to move, and she could hear the distant sounds of sirens.

"Thank God." She turned her face upwards once more and said "Thank you" out loud, not caring who was watching, and definitely not caring if anyone was close enough to hear. Quickly she dropped down on one knee, kneeling beside the woman that had resuscitated Henry. The man who was, and always would be the other half of Gladys. The same young man who called for help on his car phone stopped behind them. He got out of his car, stood nearby, and began directing the finally moving traffic. The paramedics arrived, and went about their job quickly, giving Henry oxygen and hooking up an IV. Their actions were well rehearsed, automatic, and accurate. They lifted Henry onto a stretcher, and then placed him inside the ambulance while Gladys returned to their car. She would have to follow Henry in their Volvo, although she felt some anxiety at being separated from him during such a crucial time. Gladys was just about ready to step into her car when she turned around, and saw the retreating woman.

"Darien!" The younger woman turned around when she heard her name, and saw a very grateful Gladys presenting her with a huge beaming smile.

"God bless you." Darien smiled and waved back at the older woman, who was, and always would be the other half of Henry.

Gladys slid in behind the wheel, turned the key, and started the engine. Suddenly she remembered noticing something very odd when the paramedics placed her husband into the ambulance. There had been two men dressed in neatly tailored suits, standing beside a very elegant dark car, watching them with silent solemn observation. The thing that had made it so curious was that they had not been looking at Henry like the other curious bystanders, but they had instead been watching the retreat of the woman named Darien. Gladys wondered if the woman had noticed them; however, all thoughts were quickly erased as she pulled into traffic behind the ambulance, and her only concern was Henry.

Gladys parked the car in one of the empty spaces reserved for emergency room patients, and quickly walked into the building. She was becoming increasingly nervous because she had to stop several times, explain who she was, where she was going, plus give them the proper insurance information and "God forbid Henry should die and she wasn't there." But no, Henry was not going to die, they were not going to be separated, not yet anyway. Finally, she came to the area where her husband lay on a cot covered with all the little sticky tabs attached to the wires that allowed the doctors to monitor his heart rate. Henry was alert and talking to the physician on duty. Gladys sat down gratefully in the chair next to her husband and allowed more tears of relief to fall unashamed from her eyes. Henry reached for her and she slid her hand inside the one that was so familiar to her. She smiled at him and his grip on her was strong and sure.

"I'm not ready to leave yet, Gladys; it's just a small setback. The doctor said I'll be fine." (But I'll never tell anyone that I know I died back there on the highway.)

"Your husband seems strong and healthy, Mrs. Walsh. However, we would like to keep him here for a few days to run some more tests just to make sure."

"Alright, Doctor." Then to Henry she said, "I think maybe I better go call Jason and let him know what happened." Gladys lifted her arm and Henry's hand still enclosed hers; she rested it briefly on her cheek before returning it to him. She took her purse, slowly left the room, and went to go to the nurse's station to ask for directions to the nearest pay phone.

Suddenly she heard, "Mom?" She turned around and saw her son Jason coming down the hallway with his baby and wife Marisa. He walked quickly up to her, and Gladys's legs nearly gave out from under her as

Jason caught her up in a strong embrace. She held on tight drinking in deeply the therapeutic qualities of a good strong hug from a loved one.

"Mom, what's wrong? Why are you here?"

"You first. Is everything okay? Wait, let's go sit down, and we'll get everything straightened out." Jason helped her over to a waiting area while Marisa left and quickly returned with a cup of water, which Gladys sipped gracefully, not realizing how thirsty she had become.

"Your dad had a heart attack in the car on the way over here."

"Where is he, is he okay?" Jason's voice was borderline panic.

"He's fine, honey," she said as she patted his arm, "But if it weren't for that young woman, he would not have made it. Oh my gosh, Jason, I never even got her last name or her address, how am I ever going to thank her?"

"I'm sure that you have already have."

"She saved your father's life and yes, I know I thanked her, but somehow it just doesn't seem enough." She paused briefly before looking back to her son. "Oh, please let me see my grandson." Jason proudly handed his son over to his mother, and there came an unusual but instant bonding between them. Marisa sat beside her husband, and smiled at her mother-in-law.

"*Como es ta Marisa?*"

"*Bien, gracias.*"

"Good, I'm glad." Gladys proceeded to tell them how they had been caught in traffic, of Henry's trouble breathing, and of her panicky run between the cars until she had found the woman who had helped her. As Gladys retold the story, she remembered every vivid detail, and what she remembered the most was how blue Henry's lips had been, how cold his skin had felt. With a sickening thud, reality hit her, and she knew that Henry had died back there. Gladys sat very quiet holding her grandson tenderly stroking his pudgy little cheek.

"Why are you here, Jason, is everything all right with you and Marisa and the baby?"

"I'm fine, Mom; we're all fine, really. This whole thing is going to seem very strange when I tell you what happened. A few days ago Marisa took Manny on his monthly visit to see her mother, and while there, they decided to get him his first haircut, and the barber gave him a balloon for being such a good little man." Manuel smiled a big drool-filled smile, somehow pleased with knowing he had become the center of attention. "It's a several-hour trip as you know, and on the way home they stopped at a diner for a late lunch. Manny was playing with the balloon, bit it, and the damn thing popped. Don't lecture us about the dangers of giving a baby a balloon; believe me, we've learned our lesson. What Marisa didn't know was that he sucked down a piece of latex and it blocked off his air supply. We're lucky because a woman in the diner pulled the balloon out, gave Manny mouth-to-mouth and saved his life. We're back here today because the doctor wanted to check and make sure that he's doing okay," Jason ruffled Manny's hair, "and he's just fine." Even as he spoke the words about the mysterious woman, they could not help but wonder the obvious. Gladys turned to her daughter-in-law:

"What did that lady, the one who helped you, what did she look like?"

"Ah, brown hair, brown eyes, older than me, but not as old as Gladys. I'm sorry; my English is still not so good."

"It's okay, Marisa," Gladys said, patting her hand, "Your English is just fine. Was this lady short, tiny?" Gladys put her hand up high and then lowered it as she talked.

"*Si, si,* yes, short."

"And her hair too, was that also short?"

"*Si,* Gladys. You think is same woman?" Gladys took hold of her son's hand while at the same time hugging Manny close to her chest.

"I think that for whatever reason, we have been blessed with our own guardian angel." She looked at her son and her daughter-in-law then said, "And now I think we should let Manuel meet his grandfather." She stood up, handed the baby to her son, put her arm around Marisa's waist, and then kissed her cheek.

"We are very lucky, Marisa." The young Spanish girl nodded her head in agreement, and together they walked back to where Henry waited patiently for the one person that helped make him whole.

# CHAPTER FIVE

# DARIEN DESCENDING

Darien released her hold on the small silver rose.

The cool feel of it lying next to her warm skin gave her an immediate sense of comfort. She was distracted at her reflection in the large plate-glass window when she glanced at the neatly showcased novels that ranked number one on the best-selling list. She studied her reflection, the image showing her age, the new wrinkles that she could not hide, and the gray streaks in her hair that were becoming more prominent as Darien's life became harsher. She was beginning to hate, as she had eight long years ago, what she saw reflected in her mirror image. She hoisted her purse to the same comfortable spot that she always centered it in, and continued walking down the street.

Darien spent the better part of the day on the phone. She called the insurance company only to find that when she left the house, Jack had canceled her coverage. It left her without a way to collect on the crumpled automobile, and having to decide if she wanted to purchase another one. There was no way she could know if Corral, Texas, would be the end of her journey, or just the beginning. Looking for answers to questions she could not ask would not be easy, and if there were none here, then the need to find them would push her forward. Perhaps the next step needed to be on foot. Darien had a brief but scary picture of wandering in the desert trying to perform a kind of ritual cleansing so that she would be pure enough to fight the Titobind. This, she quickly rationalized, is a silly thought, otherwise why would the eldest have set me on a dark and dangerous path before a cleansing? She needed to descend to a level that would bring her directly to the monster that bound the guardians. Apparently, there was only one way there, and that was to get out onto the street and find it. The eldest of all the guardians told her that there are men in this world who are mentally bound to the Titobind. So where is the damn blinking sign when you need it? She passed a darkened barroom window, and glanced once more at her reflection.

"Is there a real person hiding in there, Darien?" She did not expect an answer, although she was, at the very least, hoping for reason. She re-checked her pockets, reset her purse strap back up on her shoulder, and taking a deep breath she walked into the bar that boasted topless waitresses along with live entertainment. Suddenly a thought occurred to her about live entertainment. What fun would it be if they advertised dead entertainment? However, it did seem as if topless waitresses should be more than enough entertainment. Well there is the old saying, nothing ventured, nothing gained, and Darien stepped through the door already fated to a path with no return.

It was years since Darien went inside a bar, and her senses were immediately assaulted by the smell of stale beer, while her first breath was smoke-filled. She walked up to the bar as casually as possible, and ordered a drink, something sweet, she told the bartender. He came back with a thick red icy liquid.

"It's a strawberry daiquiri. That'll be five bucks." Darien reached in her purse, handed the bartender a ten-dollar bill, and let the dollar change sit on the bar. It was amazing how quickly it all came back to her. The drink was cold, wonderfully tasty, but Darien drank it far too quickly, and then ordered another one. She hurried and drank half of that one, almost as if she was afraid that someone was going to take it from her. She was feeling a little giddy and slightly tipsy as she spun around on her barstool to watch the crowd. She found herself thoroughly entranced with the way the waitresses' breasts swayed and bounced as they walked and waited on tables. Not that Darien ever had any inclination towards women, but she could understand why the mammaries mesmerized men; after all, she did know what it was like to have them touched. This thought came as a simple understanding, nothing more, but she felt it best to keep that opinion to herself.

Darien continued watching as the "live entertainment" danced and gyrated on the stage, female strippers entertaining the men who stared, and yelled, "Take it off!" She smiled in amusement, having thought they only did that kind of yelling in movies. However, the men who really caught her attention were the ones standing in the back of the room, watching quietly with only the flicker of their eyes to show their response. At least the ones who were yelling and carrying on let you know how they felt, but the quiet ones, well they were the ones that you had to watch for. She remembered one of the old sayings she heard as a young girl, "Watch out for the quiet ones"; she also remembered her dealings with them from her younger bar days. Darien's thoughts drifted, pulling her close to entering the zone, not even aware when one of the quiet ones slid onto the barstool beside her.

"Can I buy you a drink?" He startled her, and she flinched nervously.

"I'm sorry, I didn't see you." She was looking at him through half-closed eyes trying desperately to see what it looked like, but her vision blurred with the effects of her drinks.

"Okay, you can buy me a drink, but make sure that it's a quiet one."

"A quiet drink?" he asked, not quite understanding what she meant.

"Yes, this one is too big and noisy." Darien motioned to the third strawberry daiquiri that had magically appeared in front of her. The man smiled as he got her meaning.

"Tell you what, there's an empty table over there, why don't you go and get a seat, and I'll bring you something a little more subtle." Darien nodded in agreement and as she slid from the barstool, she nearly tipped herself into his lap.

"I'm sorry. I'm not used to drinking." He smiled slightly, and Darien immediately realized that she didn't like his smile. It was a cold smile, and her overactive imagination saw him as an evil person, almost as if two small horns protruded from the top of his head.

"It's okay," he said. "Maybe you do need something quiet." He gave her a small push towards the table, and she obeyed him, giving her good-sized rump a little too much sass as she walked over to the booth. Darien sat down watching the quiet one as he talked to the bartender. She saw the bartender shrug his shoulders and hand the man a bottle of beer and a large glass of water. Darien was having a hard time keeping her head still until she finally leaned it up against the back of the booth. Her mouth felt dry as she ran her tongue around her lips, and then began to pinch them with her fingers making sure they were still there. The man set the drinks on the table, slid in beside her, and leaned over to ask her if she was okay. Darien lifted her head suddenly caught in a moment where she thought her head was still moving when it really wasn't. The man leaned over, getting very close to her face, and asked her again if she was feeling all right. His breath smelled sweet, his after-shave reached her with a light, sexy scent (and given her drunken state it could have quickly made her nauseous), but suddenly she found him quite attractive, in a scary sort of way.

"I'm find, thanks," she answered, and as she reached for the glass of water, his hand closed over hers helping her to steady the glass.

Darien looked up at him after she had quenched her thirst, taking a few minutes to bring her eyes into focus. He really was quite a nice-looking man, dressed casually in jeans and an open-collared shirt. His eyes were a deep brown, the same as his hair, and he wore glasses, which to Darien always made people look more intelligent, even if they were not. Behind the frames she could see the long brown lashes that made her feel more than warm without the use of alcohol. He casually drew one leg on the seat, and she noticed that he wore a brand-name sneaker. He had money; not too many people she knew could just drop a couple of hundred on name-brand running shoes. The man smiled at her, a larger smile than before, but not enough for Darien to drop her shield. She liked his mustache and small goatee, and Darien could tell without touching them, that they would be soft, not scruffy like Jack's had been.

"Really, are you okay?" His voice was deep, but not out of place. He seemed like a nice decent sort of person, with the exception that he had been one of the quiet ones who had been standing in the back of the room. Darien felt that small warning going off deep inside of her, but the warning was too far away to disturb her. She shut off the alarm, and smiled back at the quiet man. Darien had always been able to look pretty when she wanted to, and she had not totally forgotten how to turn on the charm.

"What's your name?" she asked, her words coming out just a little slurpy, more like "Whatchs your name?"

He held out his hand to her: "Jack Trenton."

*Oh lord,* she said to herself, not another Jack. *This is all I fucking need, another fucking Jack, and his last name is the same as my maiden name. This is a little bit more than coincidental to be coincidental.* Then aloud she said to him, "Darien." And she shook his outstretched hand.

"No last name, Darien?"

"Does it matter?" This simplistic way of introduction immediately intrigued him.

"No, I suppose it doesn't." He noticed the wedding band still resting comfortably on her finger, and she saw him looking at it.

"I've have worn it for twenty-four years, and I guess I'm just not ready to part with it. I feel naked without it, and I haven't really been out looking to replace it, although my marriage is definitely over."

"It was that recent?" He knew, well at least he seemed to.

"Almost a month now, and I still haven't been able to decide where I want to live."

"Are you from around here?"

"No, actually I'm a fairly long way from what used to be my home."

"Then you're out exploring." It was Darien's turn to smile.

"I guess you could say that." She was warming up to the old game of bait and catch, finding it a rather fun game to play, one that she didn't know she missed until now.

"Divorcee's have a tendency to explore after a marriage breakup, it's only natural. So tell me, in your recent explorations, what have you found?"

Darien was quiet for a moment while she thought over his question. She slowly realized that there was an even balance returning to her, settling her comfortably back down. She also realized that despite the perfection she continually looked to approve within herself, the world, despite all the hard work, remained imperfect.

"To tell the truth, Jack, I don't know what I'm looking for, and I have no idea if I'm even headed in the right direction, but I think that if I'm lucky, I might learn a few things along the way." Well it wasn't a lie exactly.

"What sort of things?" He had moved in just a little closer, and Darien was mildly surprised because she had forgotten just how persistent men can be once their brains dropped a couple of feet from their head.

(She pictured two little hands coming out of what she fondly referred to as a man's little peeny, and it set a small cap on its head that said "quiet, brain thinking" and as the peeny grew, the cap become tighter and tighter until the brain exploded.)

With this picture in her head, she stared straight at Jack's face, and it was all she could do to keep from bursting out laughing at the man with the little peeny cap. Darien had not been with another man since she had set David free, and despite the picture that she imagined, there were some familiar tingles returning. Suddenly Darien felt such a longing for David that she nearly jumped from her seat and left the bar, but instinct told her that she needed this Jack more than she had ever needed the Jack she had married. As if thinking about his name had brought his attention, the quiet man casually put his arm up across the back of the booth. Darien leaned back onto it, and before long, she had maneuvered her way around so that the back of her head was leaning into his chest. It felt good just to touch another person, a real person, one in the here and now. She picked up the glass of water glass that set on the table and took three big swallows, not realizing Jack had the bartender replace the plain water with liquor. She coughed and sputtered, wiping her mouth with the back of her hand, yet rather enjoying the burn of the alcohol. The music was jumping, blaring out of speakers that were set too loud for the small bar. The noise reverberated inside her head, and her vision became one of blurs filled with flashes of lights accompanied by passing pieces of dancing people. The thumping of bass, thumped deep inside her chest, and the last thing she would remember about the bar would be walking in and sitting down. Unfortunately, her next remembered thought would be that she had let Jack Trenton into her room, and everything that happened after that she would relive nearly every day for the rest of her life. In the end, she would never stop wishing that she could forget. It was at this moment in time that Darien began her descent.

Hidden, as always, tucked away inside the safety of the shadows, the eldest guardian watched as this new Jack mentally prepared Darien's training. In this training, he would inadvertently teach her to find the strength that she would need to hold her own against the Titobind.

* * *

Darien slid the key into the lock of her room. She saw the way Jack raised his eyebrows when she had told him the name of the hotel where she was staying.

"It's just temporary, Jack, as soon as I get a job I'll look for a decent place."

"It doesn't bother me where you live, Darien; I was just a little surprised is all. This hotel is notorious for doing not so legal businesses with not so legal money. You just didn't come across as that type."

"I'm not really; it was a last-minute decision. I was traveling for two weeks, got tired, and needed a place to stay. This is convenient and close to downtown so it would make it easy for me to find a job." They both stepped inside and Jack's surprise clearly showed in much the same way as Darien when he saw the cleanliness of the place.

"Make yourself comfortable, I'm going to use the bathroom." She lost her balance and reached to the wall for support until she was steady. She turned around and smiled at Jack, who sat on the bed watching her. There was no smile, not even an offer to help, and the coldness of his stare caused Darien to hear that same low-sounding alarm going off inside of her, the same one that had cautioned her earlier. However, she is an adult, she knew why Jack came with her, and she knew why she had to let him. She was not completely sure, but there was an underlying suspicion that she was heading in the direction expected of her. Besides, Darien was lonely and it been what, eight years since David had made love to her? It had also been almost two years since her husband reached for her and did his business. Suddenly her stomach heaved up on her, and she leaned over the toilet. It was definitely more years than she could recall when drinking too much caused her to become ill. After she stopped retching, she did feel a little better, if still somewhat lightheaded. Darien reached for the mouthwash and toothbrush. The image in the mirror was stranger than usual; she wondered where this next step would lead. She sighed as she turned from the mirror. Her mind was tired, more tired than she could ever remember it being.

Darien walked slowly back into the bedroom finding that Jack had made himself quite comfortable on her bed. He leaned back, relaxed, and lit a cigarette that filled the room with a smell easily recognized. He offered her a hit on his joint.

"Thanks for making the bed; I didn't mean to be in the bathroom so long. I guess I'm not very good company."

"I barely know you, Darien, and already I can tell that you worry too much."

"My friends used to call me the born worrier."

"Come on up here and let me help you relax."

*I'll just bet you will,* she said to herself, *but this is why I brought you here.* She dutifully climbed up onto the bed, sliding over to where he had made himself comfortable. She laid her head against his chest, accepted the joint that he placed between her lips, and obediently pulled in the pungent smoke. She inhaled deeply only to find her body immediately rocked by coughing spasms. She could not help the spittle that escaped from between her teeth, and Jack handed her a tissue to wipe her mouth, which she did, then she tried to dab at the front of his shirt.

"Here, let me," he said quietly and unbuttoned his shirt, shifting slightly on the bed to slide it off his lean, hard body. What a difference to find this Jack nearly hairless, not like the fur-covered Jack she left at home. Darien could not help herself since it was a long time since she had tasted a man, and as the smoke brought her the relaxing pleasure of the high so did Darien slide into the relaxing pleasures of her body. She began to kiss his chest, slowly at first, then with more urgency. Darien excitedly licked and sucked at his nipples, frenzied in her desire to devour this new Jack. Then without any warning, he grabbed her shoulders, flung her onto her back and towered over her on his knees. Darien was breathing heavily, licking her lips in anticipation. Jack reached down, slipped his hand between the spacing of the buttons on her shirt, and ripped it open. Darien gasped aloud, and felt her desire jump higher than she could ever remember it going. He reached for her, this new Jack, and placed his hand over the silky smoothness of her bra. In one swift movement that nearly pulled her from the bed, he ripped her bra from her body in the same manner as the shirt. Darien watched this quiet one as he unzipped his pants to expose his hard penis.

It was time to take Darien to the next level in playing the game.

Jack smiled, a cold hard smile, and he watched her eyes shine in the semi-darkness with the building intensity of her high, knowing that the little extra he had rolled into the joint suddenly found its mark.

"What do you want, little slut?"

Darien swallowed, and ran her tongue sensuously around her lips. *Which way, which way do I go? What does he want me to say?* Her thinking bordered on panic and her mind raced for an answer.

"Answer me, you little whore, fucking bitch!"

She remembered the magazine, she recalled having read somewhere of dominant men, and suddenly she knew. He wanted her to say the word, words Darien had never been able to say aloud, until now.

"I want your cock." The words felt bad, the entire thing felt bad, and she knew that a little bit of her mind slipped away as she slipped into her role, and she purposely released the only one who could handle Jack Trenton. Darien released Mary. Never before had Mary been so far out of control and so in control. She was the one personality who knew and loved sex.

"That's right, little bitch, you want my cock." And he held it out to her, stroking it at the same time. "Where do you want it?" The one named Mary hesitated, she definitely knew where she wanted it, but she was not able to coordinate her mouth with the words she wanted to say. Jack reached over, squeezed hard on her breast, forced her over onto her side, and slapped her bottom.

"I asked you a question!" This time her mouth worked just fine.

"I want it in my mouth."

"Take off the rest of your clothes, and do it slowly so I can see everything." Darien stood up on the bed, unsnapped her jeans, and then slid them down slowly, exactly in the way he instructed. Mary fully emerged as she proceeded to slide her underwear down over her hips, ever so slowly down her legs, ever so seductively, and Jack caught them at her ankles, nearly knocking her off balance as he pulled them over her feet.

"Now get down here." Much to her surprise Darien obeyed. Her normal personality tended towards stubbornness ultimately determined to do things her way, and the dominant personality of Cynthia proved that. However, Mary was out, and she was responding to this man in a way she never thought possible. In the back of her mind, Darien watched it all. Jack pushed himself to his full height while still kneeling on the bed and Darien crawled towards his straining penis. She saw his excitement glistening on the tip, she could not wait to lick it from him, and that taste was so close. His hand came up under her chin and he pulled her face roughly upwards, stretching her face and neck at a painful angle.

"Do you want it?" His voice was so demanding.

"Yes," barely a whisper.

"Yes what?" Darien was off guard; she was not sure what he wanted her to say.

"Yes...sir." His grip relaxed just a little.

"You can lick off the end." She immediately obeyed his demand, and when she tried to envelop him in her mouth, he pushed her away.

"You didn't say 'May I.'" *(Remember that game, Darien? The game when you always asked "Mother may I? And the lead person would say, "yes you may." It's a game, Darien. Play the game.)*

Mary was very ready for this man and his game was only making her want him more, then without warning her thoughts began to rebel, the personalities went into conflict, and she wasn't sure if she wanted to play this game out. Cynthia descended and the words defied her, bringing an instant angry eruption. Mary suddenly took a back seat, as the strong one pushed her out, deciding for everyone that this game was over. It was not, however, that easy as she answered him sarcastically:

"And I'm not going to."

His response was a slap across her face. Darien was stunned as she put her hand up to the spot that quickly heated up from the sting of his slap. Jack moved to the edge of the bed dragging Darien with him. He drew her across his lap and slapped her bottom as hard as he could with the flat of his hand. Darien gasped as the pain registered, and she knew instantly that there would be major problems if she did not comply with all of his demands. He held her down on his lap with one hand while lighting a joint with the other, and then he handed it to her. At first Darien refused, but another slap to her bare bottom made her take a long pull on the joint.

*Please,* she begged silently, *please let Mary out.* She inhaled deeply, holding it in for as long as she could, and then exhaled as everything in her immediate line of vision began to blur. He was probing at her from behind and Mary succumbed to him, opening her legs, allowing him access to her. He quickly slipped his fingers inside, violently attacking her with his hand and shoving his fingers in as hard as he could. She could feel his penis stabbing her in the belly, while at the same time she felt one of his fingers moving towards her anus. He moved his hand around, pushing, turning shoving his fingers in all of her openings. Jack removed his fingers, and as suddenly as he filled her, she was empty once again. He laid his free hand, still wet with her lubrication, across her red bottom, and then began to do a little nonchalant tapping with his fingers and to her surprise, he began to recite a poem.

"Lay your lover on your lap
And give her bottom hearty slaps."

Whack, whack. Her already red backside shook from the force of the slaps, driving the red even deeper, the sting molding a pain that would open a link to sex that she had never experienced before.

*I don't think I like this,* she said to herself.

"Open wide those sweet wet lips and introduce your fingertips." Darien felt Jack spread her wide from behind, and give a gentle brush against her soft nether lips with his fingers. Somewhere in between, Jack had placed the joint down, while keeping his free hand on the back of her head. Darien was suddenly very afraid. His hand came up inside her with such force and she began a desperate struggling to break free. This only made his purpose stronger, harder, until in the end, she became submissive to his power, and stopped fighting.

"Do not struggle or I will hurt you more,
Be my Darien, my good little whore."

Jack lay back on the bed, keeping his hand inside of her, guiding her, positioning her mouth over his huge penis. Darien thought that she had never seen anything this big, except in pictures. His fingers moved inside of her and despite her fear, she lost control and she flooded his hand with her juice. Her bottom was red and hot to the touch and her body was singing with a desire that she had never known. He forced the joint back into her mouth, and good little Darien drew in deeply, bringing it down to the roach. She drew the smoke inside her lungs, holding, and she closed her eyes as she descended onto her target. The acrid smoke escaped from the sides of her mouth as she quickly remembered the taste that Jack offered her hungry mouth. She devoured him so fully, totally absorbed in pleasing him. He brought her over his face where he held her open looking intently into her eager, wet, open desire. He buried his entire face inside of her wetness. He began to bite at her labia, at her clitoris, and Darien could not help herself as she feasted insatiably upon his member. She became his dirty little whore, and she enjoyed it all. She was lost inside the high, inside the new excitement this type of sex was bringing to her, and her body moved inside a deep rhythm of feelings. Jack harshly massaged her behind and then spread her apart so he could see the little puckered opening. He lathered his fingers inside of her once more and then re-introduced them into her bottom while at the same time he moved her back onto his mouth. Darien moaned aloud, and pulled all of him inside of her mouth, becoming ready for him, ready to explode on his face. She moved with the instinctual rhythm once learned, never forgotten.

Jack removed his hand from inside of her, placed it on her hips, and rolled her off his face. Her mouth was as empty as the rest of her and as Jack climbed over her, he forced her legs as far apart as he could.

"Now tell me what you want!" His voice was deep, and commanding.

Darien wanted to have him inside of her, to bring her into the climax that her body was crying for, and then the game became who she was.

"I want you to fuck me, master." He brought his penis close to her. Darien's lips parted to take in quick panting breaths, her need escalated, and her mind filled with convolutions of colors as her thoughts drifted away from her body, and she sought only a release for her desires.

"Give me what I want." She smiled at him and he descended on her, driving himself into her with enough force to push her up the bed. She opened her mouth to scream, but instead of a scream, a deep moan of pleasure came from inside, and she immediately climaxed onto him. He fucked her furiously, driving himself with the force of his own high, and then he finally stiffened, ejaculating into her while she held him deep inside, contracting her muscles around him, not wanting to let him go. He kissed her hard, vicious in his attempt to secure her obedience to him. Finally, Jack fell from inside of her, and as he sat up, Darien lay in a world that separated itself from her reality. He quickly left her bed, seeming to detach himself from her as hastily as possible. She watched Jack as he dressed, seeing him, but also seeing through him.

"Admit it, Darien, you liked it." Darien hummed softly to herself, as she curled onto her side, trying to hide her body away as her mind transported her to a realm composed of giant marching penises, all demanding her attention. While Darien lay in a pool of their sweat and sex play, the marching penises entered all of her open orifices, and she was lost in imagined oblivion of endless pleasures. Jack tapped her face lightly to bring her back.

"Darien, tell me you like it." Her eyes focused in on Jack and the cloud that had covered her thoughts from the joint that he forced her to smoke started dissipating. However, her body remained hot to the touch, and Mary already wanted more.

"I didn't like it, my master. I loved it."

"Now tell me you would do anything for me." Darien rose from the bed and kneeled in front of Jack.

"I will do anything for you."

"Stand up." She obeyed, and Jack kissed her full on her lips, drawing her tongue deep inside of his mouth. Darien's knees gave out, and Jack held her against him.

"Who do you love?" he whispered in her ear.

"I love you, Jack." He pulled her head back by her hair, licked his way up her throat, taking pleasure in her surrender as he gently bit her lips.

"Who do you belong to, little whore?"

"To my master."

Jack laughed aloud, and threw her back onto the bed. "I'll be here in three days at exactly ten in the evening and I will find you naked and waiting for me. Trust me when I tell you that I will take you to places that you have never been before. We're only just beginning."

He turned and left the room, leaving Darien sitting on the bed staring out at nothing, her mind going into the zone where only she could see. Her hands gently soothed the body still radiating warmth from her recent excitement, and her bottom was still red from the spanking that he gave her. Darien wondered if Jack would really return, and she wondered why she hated and loved what he did to her. She knew that this was a dangerous sex, and allowing it free rein could pull her into a very scary world. Then she heard the guardian's words when he said to her that it would be "a dark and dangerous journey." Was Darien taking a giant leap forward or was this just her first baby step? She wound her arms around herself, and lay back down, curling into the same little fetal-like position. She watched the shadows on the walls, and prayed for David and for all the guardians. Darien felt that she should become part of the shadows as they danced in the lights that flashed upon her walls and she longed for the warmth that was David. She stretched her hand out across the emptiness between her bed and the wall, reaching for a touch of warmth she remembered as her guardian. Her mind still lounged in the lingering effects of the high, and she continued to watch the shadows with a mixture of hope and reborn happiness. There was movement, and the darkness twitched, swirling noticeably as it extended itself towards her hand.

"David?" she whispered.

The shadow touched and crept along her fingers, but it generated no warmth, and the cold dark shadow tried to penetrate her. Darien shook her hand violently, like someone trying to shake off an unwelcome insect, and the shadow clung to her, jumping up and down, following the wave of her hand. She started to panic as the shadow crept along her hand, the cold entering her body, and she gasped as it penetrated through her warmth, freezing her fingers as it do so.

(Outside the hotel, parked on the side of the street was the black shiny sedan that housed two impeccably dressed men. However, for the moment, there was only one, and he stared intently up at Darien's window.)

Darien's strength hid inside, all she had to do was to release it, except her fear was becoming greater than thought, and she was losing her way. All of the reasons that allowed her to draw from that strength were gone. The shadow thing now stood as tall as Jack, it stood without any recognizable shape, and it continued clinging to Darien's hand, mimicking her frantic movements. The coldness of the shadow was moving to the inside of her, and her breath now formed little white puffs as if she had ventured outside in the middle of winter.

(And the man below who was the twin of the shadow above, smiled up at the window as he sensed the penetration into Darien, which would lead inevitably to her domination and then to her delivery. The Father Tianato will be pleased.)

Darien screamed, tried to pull away, and finally self-preservation came on instinct. She released a piece of the sun, a sparkle of the warmth that fell into her from the dying guardian. The dark shadow recoiled immediately, retracting its icy tentacles. A screeching noise filled the air, and Darien covered her ears against the sound. She was bleeding again, the same way as when David and the others had called for her. Her ears dripped red, and she ran into the bathroom to get a towel, settling it under her chin, angling it up to her ears. She turned around and saw her image reflected back at her from the mirror, the frightened face that had nowhere to run. What was it about the mirrors that disturbed her so? The obvious was seeing what she was, but something else scared her more than the shadow that had just danced with her. She walked back into her bedroom and lying down upon the bed, she cried for David, for all the guardians. She cried until the tears would no longer come, she cried until her ears slowed their bleeding, and then she prayed that she would be strong enough to complete the task that the oldest guardian had set before her. She closed her eyes, drifting into a deeply troubled sleep and all the time the little shapes in the shadows shifted and watched, but none dared to approach.

Down inside the dark secrets of the shiny black sedan, the twins sat in silence. They were aware of failure and they knew that there would be punishment for this failure. They were the children of the Titobind, his creations of pure evil. One was as dark as night itself, while the other as pale as the morning sky, and they shared but one thought, and that was the delivery of the one called Darien. It was the only thought that Titobind allowed them to have, and there was nothing else. The result of having contact with the released piece of sun had caused the light colored twin to bleed the black evil from his ears. The pale being sat with his eyes closed, feeling the other's pain as he was pulled away, taken through the mirror in the car. The scream he left behind caused a fresh flood of seeping black to pour from the pale twin's ears. The ebon man's temperature dropped to a level of freezing, and he found himself passing through the mirror to a strange dark land.

The son of Titobind was passenger in a Chinese junk riding on a multi-striped river. There were three visible partitions, and the junk rode on the silver one. However, the water did not flow around his boat; it was more like the three separate canals of water flowed upwards, invisibly forced to follow the river at a slight incline. It was thicker than ordinary water, and on either side of the silver strip that he rode in were canals of blue and gold. The water seemed alive as it undulated, drawing the boat forward, and the ebon man silently observed the things that moved in the water alongside the junk. His face remained impassive during his observation, and he had no reason or thought as to how dangerous they were.

The twin looked upwards to the sky as the giant paddle wheel turned endlessly, its purpose lost to him as well. When the boat banked, one of the paddles extended itself to scoop the boat aloft and set it adrift to sail through the dark sky. The junk sailed on the winds, taking it through a sky of permanent purple night, and it made its way to a floating mountain where the twin would disembark. There it would stand and patiently wait for acceptance into the lair of the Titobind. The one allowed thought was about to be replaced by feeling. In his failure to deliver Darien there would be punishment; in that punishment, the child of Titobind would continue learning the lesson of failure, and pain. Titobind spared no mercy when it came to failure.

There were no remembered thoughts to a time before the Titobind, a time before their singular thought of Darien's destruction. He could recall his surrounding upon creation, his harvesting from the ground. Their growing area surrounded them in darkness, and then a single shade of lighter gray allowed them a view of their magnificent creator. The first thing the children heard were the cries of the guardians bound to the father. Their creator, a growing titan sprouted from a world that stopped distinguishing between the simplistic faith between good and evil. The ebon man remembered watching the father, who was unable to complete the transition to resemble neither guardian or human, because its growth was a perversion of their released corruption and despair. He grew twisted by disparaging thoughts, fed by the hopelessness the guardians had extracted from the human's world. They had unknowingly fed it, nurtured it, and they had helped it grow as large as the darkness that held it in its womb.

The twin shivered, not fully understanding the punishment yet to come, but it began learning fear. Compassion was not part of the Titobind's ritual. He liked the suffering that he inflicted to be as never-ending as the torment to his own twisted body. Even now, he grew stronger as he spread his black despair over the entire town of Corral, Texas, blocking out the life-giving rays of the sun, and feeding on the fear he began generating. He blanketed the city with a growing darkness, beginning in a place where his deviates created the "Pit," the dungeon where they brought victims for their master, the Titobind. Whereas his name previously passed only in whispers, they now openly worshipped him, and began moving him to the Godlike status he so desperately sought.

The atrocious monster would bring them down. The Titan would bring an entire world into darkness, and then he would savor the kingdom of pain that he would release upon them. He also watched with a mild trepidation the one that lay curled into a fetal position on her bed. Darien could possibly present a problem, not a serious one, but he did hold a small concern over the twins' failure to bring her to him. She was, after all, only one small human. Nevertheless, he would cause the twin to learn pain, and then he would send him back to their world. This would be their second remembered thought and next time, they would not fail the Titobind.

The ebon man fell to his knees, and his punishment began.

Inside the room at the Triple Dove Hotel, there was still movement in the shadows, but it was the greatest of all the guardians that rolled and tumbled in a dance of near exasperation. He was losing her; that must not happen, for it was Darien and Darien alone that held the key to their existence! Paul watched the sleeping form, as she lay curled on her side trying to hold herself against the shadow that threatened them all. She was descending to his level, yes, but she was also learning, growing, and becoming stronger. Paul, the last of the free guardians, put all his faith into the one person who carried inside her the greatest gift that anyone in her world could have, the true love of a guardian.

Paul encouraged the release of the hidden dark inside Darien.

# CHAPTER SIX

# JACK COMES BACK

The clock read 8 a.m. as Darien stepped from the bathroom.

She dried her hair and carefully dabbed around her ears. They were still sore from the bleeding explosion she experienced after saving Manuel along with the previous night's shadow fight. The weatherman on the radio station said that it was going to be a hot humid day in Corral, Texas, except as Darien pulled the curtains aside the sun was nowhere to be seen.

It was also the morning of the third day since Jack was with her. Yesterday she stripped the sheets from her bed and went in search of the garbage out back. She was lucky in finding an old-fashioned empty galvanized garbage can. Darien put the sheets inside, sprinkled in some lighter fluid and then burned them with the hope that a kind of soul cleansing could be done. There was no rationalization to what she did, and deep inside Darien wished that she could burn the memory of Jack as easily from her head. Yet in spite of this, here she was waiting for him to return. She had not gone back to the bar, not after that first night. Her anxieties were rebuilding, and her old self-doubts returned to rekindle old fears. Darien needed to go out, she needed to try to hold onto thoughts that would help her remember there were still things good and decent.

She also needed to remember the reasons why she needed to confront the real demon as well as her self-imposed ones.

First she needed to replace the sheets she burned, and the old man who sat in the cage (Jimmy Bigslee) had been upstairs peeking out of his bedroom window, watching her. He gave her a hard time when she wanted to stay another night, but when she paid him two weeks in advance, he relinquished, while at the same time verbally chastising her for wanting to stay in such a place. She left the building quietly, being very careful not to disturb the sleeping nighttime employees of the Triple Dove Motel.

The five and dimes were still plentiful, except now they were closer to five and ten dollar stores, and Darien settled for the local Shop-Mart. Not only did she replace the sheets on the bed, but she also purchased some colorful throw rugs for the floor and a cheap set of matching pictures to hang on her wall. In an odd way, it made it hers and gave it a homey feeling. After putting her purchases in place, Darien decided that she needed more fresh air as well as employment, and when she went back downstairs, the proprietor was waiting for her.

"I know what you're doing."

"Excuse me?"

"You think I don't see what you're doing? You think I don't know? Those damn sheets cost money you know."

"Here." She gave him a shopping bag with the new set she purchased.

"I put some flowered ones on my bed, and those are a replacement for the ones I burned." He stood there staring dumbly into the bag.

"Jest don't bring no food in here, I don't want no roaches, never had 'em, 'cause the place is kept clean."

"I know it's clean, Mr. Bigslee, it's why I don't mind staying here, and the other stuff that goes on, well it's none of my business." Darien noticed a carefully folded newspaper tucked under his arm.

"If you're done with that, I'd like to borrow it to look through the classifieds." Darien could see where her replacement of the sheets and the offering of a mister before his name caused Bigslee's features to soften, along with his gruff attitude.

"Here," he said and shoved the paper at her.

"Thanks, Mr. Bigslee." And she turned to walk out of the hotel.

"Hey," Bigslee called to her, and Darien obediently turned around. "Anyone bothers you, you let me know."

"Okay, thanks. I have to go. I'm going job hunting." He immediately turned back into his old gruffy self.

"So, what? What the fuck you tellin' me fer?" He turned his back to her and shuffled off heading towards his cage mumbling under his breath, but loud enough for her to hear: "What the fuck do I care where you go? Like I could give a shit over what the hell you do."

Darien smiled at the retreating back, knowing that she had conquered him, and she would be relatively safe as long as she stayed on his good side. Everyone has a good side, somewhere, including people like Jimmy Bigslee.

Darien's first stop on her job hunt was Gingers Dinette. She remembered seeing a help wanted sign the other day in the window, and it was conveniently located four blocks from the hotel. A thought suddenly occurred to her that in order to find the "place" that Paul said she needed to go, how could she be sure that a car was essential? After all, there were no road signs, so what did she have to do, drive off the end of the world? Or perhaps Jack would take her on a long road trip through another dimension. How ludicrous that sounded! What a strange sideways trip her life had taken! Darien looked up and saw that she had come to the corner of the block and looking down to her right she found that she had reached the crossroads of Sodom and Gomorrah.

Strip joints and porno shops surrounded Gingers diner, and sleazy bars whose offerings were that little something extra if you knew who to slip the extra twenty to. Unfortunately Darien was about fifteen minutes too late, because Ginger (who was really Gus) had just hired someone. She ordered a cup of coffee, toast, and then made her way to the back booth to look through the want ads. This was not going to be as easy as she thought. Most of the job ads in the paper were for professionals, and most of those jobs were outside of Corral, far from being within walking distance. Darien wasn't opposed to minimum wage or sweeping floors, so she decided the best way to find a job was to wander in and out of the stores. As she walked and maybe if she talked to the owners, she might be able to find a job. What else can you do while you wait for the attack of the Titobind?

It was a good plan; however, she quickly found that when businesses are slow there is no sympathy for an out-of-work middle-aged woman, even if she is a rescuer of guardians. She ended up in and out of dozens of stores until she came, at last, to another small coffee shop. Darien had not been paying too much attention as to where she had been wandering, and now as she looked around she saw that she had come to the worst area of slums in Corral. The buildings were in a hibernating state of permanent disrepair, boasting numerous broken windows, and doors that hung off their hinges. The remains of a torn-down building littered the lot across the street, and keeping the rubble company were rusted-out cars and bags of garbage, enough garbage so that the rats braved the day unafraid. Homeless people draped themselves everywhere, a sad decoration of desolate decadent humans. Darien looked up to see an elderly woman watching her out of a window with a face that was a picture captured inside a frame of jagged, broken glass, her eyes holding the pain of her empty, lonely life.

Darien's thoughts went off into areas of different places, countries that did not educate their people, allowing them to live in poverty and starvation. When did they come to this, why did the human race allowed this poverty to exist? It made no sense to her how people could keep breeding without any thought to how they were going to feed their children. Instead of education, they opted instead to keep having babies. Then the impoverished parent had to stand and watch the children starve to death. Why? Here too, in his great country, the effect was not as noticeable, just hidden better, behind giant invisible doors. You only saw them if you really looked, and most people refused to see; staying safe in their own little worlds.

Darien shook her head in sadness and turned around to make a slow retreat when an OPEN sign hanging in the window of the small wayward diner caught her attention. She crinkled up her nose as she tried to peer through the brown glass window, but nothing was visible through the buildup of grime. She looked again at the OPEN sign, thinking perhaps that it had changed in the past few minutes, or that someone simply forgot to turn it to CLOSED. She stood poised with one hand on the door, and turning around she gave once more backward glance at the gray overcast sky, vaguely aware of the restlessness among the people on the street who looked at the sky with her.

She slowly pushed the door open, and stepped inside.

Darien was not surprised to find the inside of the small establishment as filthy as the windows, and the filth made it darker inside the small eatery than it was outside. She automatically turned on the table lamps as she walked through the diner, and watched in mild amusement when the cockroaches scattered in the wake of the light. She was afraid to touch or lean up against anything. A low phlegm-filled cough from the back of the room caught her attention, and she turned around just in time to see an old man hack a tremendous mound of mucus onto the floor. The splatting noise it made as it hit the linoleum nearly brought up the toast and coffee she ate for breakfast.

"What do you want?" The voice startled her.

"A job," she answered truthfully. The laughter that came out from behind the counter was deep, and it went on for what seemed like forever.

"You serious?" the man finally choked out.

"Yes."

"Come mere, let me get a good look at you, I don't see as good as I used to." Darien walked closer to the counter, and a tall, scraggly-looking man emerged from the back. He wore his hair pulled back in a ponytail, reminiscent of the seventies, and he was so thin that he appeared to be undernourished. However, he looked clean and surprisingly he looked to be about Darien's age.

"You kinda ritzy-lookin' to be slumming in this part of town." Darien decided to ignore his remark, although there was no contempt in his voice.

"I'm new in town and I really could use a job."

"Just what do you think I could afford to pay someone like you?"

"Minimum wage is fine with me." The man studied her as his wiped his hands over and over again on the towel that was tucked into the strings that held up his apron.

"Woman looking like you, coming in here looking for a job. I gotta ask whatcha running from, lady?" Darien decided immediately that with this man, straightforward and honest would be the best.

"Not running from, running to." Her honesty worked because the man's smile widened and she noticed how it set his small blue eyes to sparkle.

"I open at five, close at three, and you will only get minimum wage, 'cause it's all I can afford to pay. As you can see we don't do a booming business in here." The old man in the back sputtered, coughed, and spit again, causing Darien's stomach to flop over when it hit the floor.

"Wheezer, how many times have I told you, old man, not on the floor damn it! Use a paper napkin for Christ sakes!" With that said, he turned his attention back to Darien.

"Menu's plain, eggs, bacon, the usual breakfast stuff, flapjacks and sausage every other day. Lunch is as plain as breakfast, with burgers, hot dogs, fries, chili on Tuesdays and Thursdays, grilled cheese, and soup the rest of the days. I'm closed on Mondays, sometimes on Sundays too, especially if it's been a real slow week. There are times when the mood strikes me and I will offer a special, like meatloaf. Normally food don't sell, so I don't offer the special too often. Got any questions?" Darien shook her head no.

"Wear some old clothes and be here by five-thirty, door'll be open."

"Thanks, Mr....."

"Just call me Tanner."

"Okay, thanks, Tanner." Darien smiled at him and left the diner, genuinely happy to have employment even though it was in that diner. Well, a good cleaning will make a lot of difference. Darien felt good about her decision, and about Tanner, and was actually looking forward to starting her new job.

Tyler Tanner went back to his kitchen, looked at the dirty grill, and eyeballed the filthy oil that he had been cooking the fries in for over three weeks. He started to wipe everything down, made ready to change the oil, and surprised himself when he turned off the blast of the television, replacing it with soft country music. His mind filled with Darien's sweet, light scent, and Tanner smiled and hummed as he worked.

Darien's walk became slower as she neared her home, and she was busy watching the people on the streets running with their heads bent over, scurrying away like frightened little animals seeking shelter against an impending disaster. She looked upwards at the overcast sky watching the dark clouds roll across Corral, as if a building thunderstorm was going to break the sky, except there was no thunder and there was no lightning. The unusual clouds that were blowing through the city suddenly stopped moving, and as she watched they began melding together to form a solid covering of grayish black. The small bookstore she started to pass seemed to call to her, "Wouldn't you like to come inside where it's safe?" Darien looked up, and decided that maybe it would not be so bad to be inside right now, so she went up the three cement stairs, taking advantage of the temporary shelter. The store was quiet, and the newly employed rescuer of guardians watched from inside as people ran by, still resembling those helpless little animals. They all knew, without really knowing, that a change was coming,

Darien turned around, startled by what she faced, and immediately tried to look casual even though all of the sex equipment on display caused her embarrassment.

"Corner bookstore, my ass," she whispered under her breath. One entire wall held a dedicated display of whips, chains, and various instruments used for sadistic/masochistic sex, and/or dominant/submissive partners. Dividing this wall from the paying public was a glass case filled with massage cremes, flavored edible gels, along with crotchless panties, and some things that she could only guess. Darien walked further into the store, and found another entire wall covered with pornographic magazines. There were various pictures of bondage and torture, and she found herself turning back around (several times) and looking at the display while saying softly, "Oh, so that's what those are for." The positions that some of the women allowed themselves to be put into for pictures was so degrading and she wondered how they could do it. Maybe it's not so much for the money, maybe they actually enjoy it.

Directly to her right and up towards the front of the store there was a small alcove. She walked slowly up towards this part of the store to get a closer look at the dozens of vibrators, dildos, and combinations of the two. She was so naïve, and as she looked over the merchandise, she was astounded at the blatant educational merchandise so prominently on display. She lost her initial embarrassment as she studied the exhibited vibrators that boasted clitoris stimulators. (She thought this might be worth checking this out on her own.) There were also various sizes and shapes of "butt plugs" and several different mechanical vibrating vaginas for men. There was one unique item that caught her attention called the "Butterfly," which you strapped on around your waist and then down between your legs so that a piece of it would push and vibrate on your clitoris, while placing the end of it inside your anus. Darien found her curiosity taking over and she became somewhat anxious wondering how that would feel. Then she began to wonder if this really was what the guardian had in mind for her dark and dangerous journey. There are many kinds of dark and dangerous journeys, with some done in the mind alone. There is also extortion, murder, rape, incest, and men who set up and destroy other people's lives. She stood staring at all the gizmos and magazines and she knew, beyond any doubts that she might have previously had, that this was exactly where she needed to go. She would find this evil, this thing called the Titobind at the very center of depravity. In order for Darien to find the worst in humanity, she would have to become as evil and as depraved as it. She would descend to its level, but could she make it believe that she came to it of her own free will. In a way, Darien thought that this would be a good thing, because there was only one person involved, herself. Hopefully it would remain that way.

"Lady?" Darien was deep into the zone, and the voice passed around and through her.

"Hey, lady!" Darien gave a little jump, and slowly turned around.

"You buyin' or what?"

"Yes, but I haven't quite decided exactly what it is that I want." She looked at the odd-looking man that hid behind the high oversized counter. He appeared to be around forty and he surprised Darien when he came down from his perch and pulled a magazine from the multitude that decorated his sin-covered walls. She looked at the man whose deep voice certainly did not fit with his small size while the oversized black glasses reminded her of a cartoon caricature of an owl.

"Here, take a look at this, then let me know what you want." He handed her a magazine that surprisingly, she had seen before. On the sidewalk, only two days ago, an embarrassed and angry man dropped the exact same one, *Bondage for Beginners*. This whole situation, right now, would have been comical if she wasn't so damned scared. Darien thought briefly that perhaps the new Jack might not return, but then she remembered the look on his face. He would come back, and when he did, Jack would continue her education into this darker side of life. She quickly flipped through the magazine, her eyes widening at every turn of the page, especially when she came to the fabricated dildos made to look like dogs' tails. God, how was she going to do any of this? Then she heard the voice of Paul, who had asked her just a short month ago, "How much do you love David?"

"More than my own life," she whispered under her breath, and it was all the conviction that she needed. She lingered in the store, looking the items over, receiving more knowledge and a better education every time she turned to look around.

"For you, David, for all the guardians. Hang on, be strong, and I promise that I won't let you down." She began to choose her purchases.

Twin number two sat in the car with eyes closed and seat reclined backwards while waiting the return of its other half. He could not remember a time before the Titobind, and it knew that the two of them shared in one collective memory, and maybe at one time they were one. Neither one could recall how they had come by the black sedan, only that they were in it, and the knowledge to make it move was placed inside their mind. The one who was waiting became aware of his twin arriving, and he opened his eyes to watch him emerge from the rearview mirror. The child of Titobind came through from the other side like a shadow, solidifying as it slid into this reality. The gray fingers, the same color as the overcast sky, came first, turning real as the ebon twin solidified. He held onto the steering wheel with one hand, and struggled to pull the rest of its smoky form through the mirror. The pale twin put out his arm to give the ebon man another handhold so that all of him could come through. It continued emerging through the mirror into the car, falling forward onto the seat, shaking with effort and the pain of what came close to being born again. He turned his pale eyes on his twin, and a thought passed unspoken between them.

"He said we could come back here and stay, if we bring her to him." Neither twin wanted to return to the dimension beyond the mirrors. It is a place as cold and barren as a desert on an island of emptiness, where almost nothing lives. There is no light, save the light of the cold fire that suspends the home of the Titobind. Little did the twins realize or understand that if the Titobind wins, keeping the guardians bound to him for all eternity, then this world of light and warmth will become a mirror image to the other side. The two lands will reflect each other in dead dark dimensions. They conversed in each other's heads, but their thoughts were nearly simultaneous, as if they shared but one mind.

"He promised to give me a name, and he said it would be mine to keep if we bring her to him. He also said he would also give me a memory of a time before."

"A name?"

"Yes."

"The memory he promised, will it be a good one?"

"He said a memory."

"If we fail?"

"Then he will give us nightmares, and that is all we will ever have."

The twins reclined and rested, because they always knew Darien's presence. Her natural scent came to them in a barrage of odors that were as sickly sweet as a field of flowers, overwhelming and overpowering. It would bring them to full awareness in less than two seconds and they would blend inside the shadows to follow her anywhere.

As they rested and waited, Darien was purchasing the first instruments that were recommended in the small article titled "Getting Started in Bondage." A generously written instructional article, full of how-to knowledge for the beginner. Jack was going to be her teacher, and she would be his most willing pupil. He would start Darien on her descent into the same dungeon from which the twins wished to escape.

It was still early when Darien returned to the busy pleasure palace, and grumpy Jimmy Bigslee almost smiled when he saw Darien walk through the door. She held her little plastic handled shopping bag close to her, and the burden that she carried inside became heavier with every step. Darien opened the door to her room, and the first thing she noticed was the new table with the little refrigerator sitting on it and a note that said, "Don't thank me." There was no signature, but Darien knew who brought it. She threw the package onto the bed, and sat down in the old comfortable chair with sudden and total exhaustion. Her eyes slowly closed, and she hoped that when sleep finally came, it would take her to a place where dreams come from.

\* \* \*

The young girl was standing by the old porcelain sink wiping dry the clean wet dishes while she watched the details of the current revolution on the local evening news.

Hestor Green was eleven years old, and her destiny was to be one of greatness. In the year of Hestor's twenty-sixth birthday, she would lead a revolution of black women in South Africa that would forever change the nations of the entire world. It was a time of great unrest and rebellion as the African nation hurtled towards a stand of independence and equality for all of Africa. Hestor turned back towards the dishes when suddenly sniper fire erupted outside the small apartment that she shared with her family. Instinct made her dive for the floor, as the windows shattered from random gunshot fire. When she looked up, she saw her two-year-old brother headed directly towards one of the open windows. There was broken glass everywhere and in an instant he could tumble and fall onto the sharp shards, or worse, he could be hit and killed by a stray bullet. Hester leapt from her position on the floor; jumping for her brother. She was vaguely aware of her mother screaming "Noooo!" in the background and through the sounds of breaking glass came the continuous sounds of the war.

Darien opened her eyes and found herself standing in the middle of a dirt road accentuated on each side by what used to be clean white picket fences. Some of the pickets were broken, lying in the dirt, while in some places whole sections hung onto the post by only a couple of nails. Darien heard the gunfire, punctuated by Hestor's screams, and before there was even a sane thought as to what to do or where to run, Darien bolted straight down the road into the center of the village and right into the crossfire between the militants and the current governmental soldiers, feeling as though she just walked into a war movie. Bullets whizzed through the air, passing all around her as she walked down the street. Some of them had to be hitting her, but she felt no pain and she had no fear. The only obvious explanation was that she was dreaming. Darien turned as she neared Hestor's house, knowing instinctively that she needed to be there, and the screams coming from inside drew her closer.

The world suddenly went quiet, and even though Darien could see the light blasts from the barrels, the firing guns made no sound. The snipers moved in slow motion as they turned to repeatedly fire their weapons. She watched their mouths move to form words she could not hear, and the world moved so slowly that she could see the bullets as they came by. It was so easy now to move between and around them, reminding her of slow-motion bullets that she had seen in movies. Darien raised her hand, curled her first finger into her thumb, and was actually able to "ping" one of the bullets into a nearby tree. She laughed, obviously delighted with the events unfolding in her dream. Parts of the dream became blurry, as is bound to happen in dreams, and parts of it became so clear that she could see how some of nature had put things together. The leaves to the trees, the petals to the flowers, the grass to its very roots inside the ground, and then Darien heard the screams again followed by a shout of "Hestor, watch out!" She started to run, and there was a brief fleeting moment when she thought she was going to be too late.

Darien turned the knob on the door, and found it locked tight against intruders.

"Well hell, it's only a dream." So with little effort she placed her hands upon the door and with very little thought or effort, she pushed slowly, mesmerized with watching herself as she passed through the planks of wood to emerge inside a house thrown into total chaos. Everything and everybody still moved in slow motion, and Darien slid along the wall, hiding in the shadows watching the scene unfold in front of her. She saw Hestor Green reach for her baby brother as their mother screamed in hopeless terror. Darien saw the slow-motion bullet crash through another window scattering glass in every direction, homing in on Hestor Green's heart. Hestor had a grip on her little brother's arm, and was in the process of pulling him down away from the window. Darien had no choice because even in slow motion she would not be able to reach her in time. She spoke aloud, and her voice carried through the shattering of the glass, through the screams and above the gunfire. She spoke only one word, and when she did, her voice sounded directly in Hestor's ear.

"Hestor." Hestor pulled her little brother down from in front of the window while at the same time she twisted her body around to answer the disembodied voice.

"WHAT!" she screamed above the gunfire, and then the bullet that had been on a pre-determined path for her heart caught the corner of her shoulder and grazed her arm. Both Hestor and her brother fell onto the floor as the blood flowed freely from the wound on her arm. Miraculously, the firing stopped, and the children lay on the floor crying loudly. Hestor's mother smiled through her tears as she went to her children because that crying was the most beautiful sound she ever heard.

Darien moved from inside the house in one fluid motion and she felt as if she was flying, except that it was not really flying, it was more like a spinning motion that carried her through the sky. As she neared her new home, it seemed as if her body was dissipating, moving apart from herself although she was actually falling back in. The small chair in her hotel room was a welcome sight.

Darien was learning to call the winds.

Darien was learning to walk in shadow.

Darien was learning to answer the call of guardian, and now that she was open to hearing the calls, they came to her, by the thousands. She jumped up from her chair covering her ears against the screams of agony as among the voices crying for help also came the collective mind cry from the bound guardians. Titobind quickly silenced them as he drew his tentacles around himself, and bound his captives tighter to his black soul. Darien's ears bled profusely as she tried to cover them against the cries that threatened to explode inside her head. Through her tear-covered eyes, she watched the cubes click on her digital clock to read nine forty-two, and she realized that she had slept for nearly six hours before the cries has wakened her. She reached down to pick up the bath towel that she had left there earlier, and she held it to her head to slow the flow of blood. She fists were clenched so tightly that her fingers were numb, and as she opened her hand, she stared at the bullet that had grazed the shoulder of Hestor Green. The digital cube moved again, and then clicked into place, nine forty-three.

Jack was coming; she could almost smell his expensive cologne. Darien moved towards the bathroom reaching for the little plastic bag that held the secrets of the night that was yet to come. She watched herself in the mirror, mesmerized by her own fluid-like movements, reminding her of watching her body move under water. Darien felt like she was coming apart, and then like she was coming together. Suddenly her action caught up with her reality, and she moved again as herself. She knew without seeing that the little cube was ready to drop down into place to read nine forty-four and downstairs Jack was pulling up to a parking spot outside the Triple Dove Hotel. Now that the dissipation had finished, the voices too had quieted, and the bleeding slowly stopped.

Darien opened her bag and took out the leather outfit she purchased at the Corner Bookstore, the bookstore that held a wealth of knowledge just waiting to be absorbed. She slid off her clothes and watched in total fascination as her movements again caused her body to detach, separate, and then reform. There was no pain and she stared while her body reacted as though someone was passing a bubble wand through her. It was a strange sensation; however, it was not one of disorientation, but more as if she were watching it happen to someone else. Then she came together one more time, and that seemed like a snap, as if someone hit her from the inside.

She calmly took the magazine out of the bag and flipped through the pages studying the way the magazine's model displayed the outfit Darien purchased. First, she put on the leather thong accentuated with two metal clasps at the waist. Then she picked up the package that held the decoration for her breasts. She placed the ring around the aureole the way it showed in the magazine then connected the chain across her cleavage, criss-crossing it across her stomach to the leather clasps on the thong. She fastened the spiked collar around her neck, and then hooked the small leash to the clasp on the leather collar.

Darien looked in the mirror that hung on the bathroom door, and to her complete surprise, realized that her reflection caused sexual arousal, especially with the way the chains looked and felt lying against her bare skin. The black leather thong lay cold against her warm body, but it too was exciting. She looked at the childbearing stretch marks that remained on her breasts, and at how they sagged against her chest. The little potbelly, which she never tried to exercise back into place, protruded outwards from either side of the leather "V." Her thighs were heavy, but still solid, and she sighed audibly. Darien knew that she should have taken better care of herself; however, this was not the time to start regretting an unchangeable past.

She stared at herself, finding that she was beginning to become more than just a little aroused. The entire outfit was outrageously erotic! The mirror seemed to call to her and for just a moment, and she thought she saw movement inside, but that was impossible because it was just a mirror. Darien turned quickly around thinking that maybe it could be a guardian hiding in the shadows, except she found nothing but an empty room.

"Where are you?" she whispered. "Has he at last taken you too?" Darien reached out and touched the mirror. There was something, something about mirrors that drew her forward. A buried memory hid from her, and no matter how hard she went digging through her remembered times, she could not understand her fascination with mirrors. She gave one last glance, remembering that her reflected image showed her someone that at times, she hated. There was a knock at the door, and Darien released a verbal "Oh." Jack was there. She picked up her plastic shopping bag and returned to the bedroom. She took a deep breath, unlocked the door, then stepped back and asked, "Jack?"

"Yes, it's Jack." She recognized the voice. Darien returned to sit in the chair with one leg draped up over the arm, and she answered him.

"Come in, Jack, it's been a long three days." She nearly laughed aloud when she saw the look on his face as she presented herself in her new outfit. She smiled demurely at Jack and moved her leg a little further back onto the arm of the chair. He raised his eyebrows at her relaxation with the roleplay, finding it hard to believe that she had never been down this road before. But then what did it matter? He slipped into his part, ready to be pleased, and to exact the punishment if he was not.

"Who have you missed, little slut?"

"I have missed my master." She swung her leg back around the arm of the chair and stood up expertly in the spiked heels.

"Nice touch," he said glancing at her feet. Darien beamed with pleasure, glad that she was able to make him happy.

"You've been thinking of me, haven't you?" he asked her as he unbuttoned his jacket and threw it onto the chair.

"Yes," she whispered back, head down looking at the floor.

"And you've wanted me."

"Yes."

"And who do you serve?"

"The cockmaster." (The magazine had been full of many helpful hints.)

"And who do you love?"

"No one but you." He laughed, and pulled her roughly to him.

"Tell me what you want." He breathed into her face; his lips close enough to touch hers.

"I want to please you, sir."

He kissed her brutally, making her whimper into his mouth with the force of the kiss. His hand found its way to the small leash that hung from the spiked collar. Jack pulled on the chain forcing Darien to bend down until she was on her knees in front of him.

"Undress me, whore." She unbuttoned his pants and moved his zipper down; Darien could feel him, ready and waiting for him. She slid the pants down slowly, kissing his legs as they became visible to her. He sighed loudly causing Darien to smile. She came to the realization there was probably nothing more a man wanted other than to have a warm, moist mouth wrapped around the real thinking part of his body. His pants came down over his feet, and Darien threw them out of the way. She quickly removed his shoes and socks and he gave a tug on the leash to pull her back up. She dutifully obeyed, licking and kissing her way back up to his erect penis, which now played peek-a-boo over the top of his bikini briefs. Darien touched the tip of it, amazed at how can something could be so soft, and yet be so hard at the same time.

*What marvelous toys we have built onto our bodies, and what wonderful feelings we can hide inside those toys!* Her thoughts were quiet, but with Jack's insistence, her feelings were waking.

Darien licked the very tip of which she most desired as her body came alive with feelings of the erotica. Jack reached down for her and pulled her to her feet, kissing her again, pulling on her collar, crushing her to him, bare flesh to bare flesh. Darien was incredibly overwhelmed, and unbelievably excited. In the course of their kissing, Jack removed the last piece of clothing that had been restraining him, and Darien became lost to herself entering the place where she didn't have to think, where she didn't have to worry, and all that was left were feelings.

*Hide,* she said to herself. *Hide away the part that does not want to see.* Her mouth moved with one purpose, to taste the fully erect object pressed hard against her belly. She spoke directly into Jack's mouth. "Let me please my master."

He pushed down on her shoulders, and she quickly gathered him into her hands and placed her mouth around him. She was enjoying him, his taste, and his excitement in turn became her excitement. Darien could feel the moistness begin between her legs, and she drew them together unable to control her growing desires. Her mouth became more active as she tried to fit all of Jack inside, and when he pulled her off him, Darien nearly cried out at the sudden emptiness. She reached back for him, and he pushed her so roughly that she fell backwards onto the floor.

"Wait." She looked up at him with hurt in her eyes, not understanding why he stopped, because Darien loved having him in her mouth. "I want to see what else you bought."

"Yes, sir." She got up and opened the bag for him, dumped the remaining contents onto the bed, and then obediently backed away, returning to her kneeling position on the floor.

"What have we here?" Jack picked up a small dildo with a long trail of hair hanging out of one end, and as he looked at Darien, he put aside the harness that held the small red ball.

"That is for more advanced sessions, for now we will continue with your basic submission. Now, come over here." Jack sat down on the bed, and Darien obediently crawled over to him on her hands and knees.

"Lay here, over my knees." She immediately rose and lay fully extended across his lap. He brutally rubbed her bottom and without warning, he pulled up on her thong driving it deep up into her, causing an instant response of excitement. He slapped her round soft bottom and pulled up on the thong again, and Darien moaned. His administrations became brutal as he picked up the paddle, and proceeded to redden her large ample buttocks. Jack then moved her thong down over her bottom, pulling it out from inside of her. While she still lay on his lap, he opened her from behind, pushing his fingers up inside of her, making Darien thoroughly excited. Instead of entering her himself, Jack reached for the small dildo and pushed it into her nether mouth of endless wonders, making the little piece of erotica all nice and wet. He then took the decorated dildo and placed it against her small puckered anus. She wiggled upwards, anxious to have Jack push it inside of her. Darien was almost out of control with the need to be filled. He pushed it in slowly, letting her relax against the penetration. He left the "tail" hanging outside as he continued her education using the flat of his hand.

"Don't let it fall out, or your punishment will be worse, little puppy."

"No, master." Her bottom showed bright red against the paleness of the rest of her body. Jack lay down on the bed and yanked viciously on her leash, making her move up over his face. She rose up to her knees and placed herself directly over his mouth. The first contact of his tongue was electric, and as Jack played her with his tongue, while moving the "tail" around inside her back end and Darien exploded onto his face, climaxing hard into his mouth. Jack immediately removed the small "tail," rolled her over onto her back and quickly mounted her. He pushed himself hard and deep, causing a gasp of unexpected pleasure to escape from between her clenched lips. He pumped furiously, exploding inside, nearly shouting with relief. Darien lay still under him, not moving, waiting for instructions from her new master. He lay down beside her and covered her face with small tender kisses. She was surprised at the show of affection from such a brutal encounter, not fully understanding the complete semantics in a submissive, dominant relationship. She also immediately began to wonder what more there was to come.

"What made you buy all of this stuff, Darien?" She really did not expect conversation. Actually, she had thought that Jack was going to just get out of bed, get dressed and leave, giving her instructions as to when he would be back, if at all.

"I thought it would please you. I thought you would like it. Did you?"

"Yes." He smiled as he gathered her into his arms, pulling her close to him, and then he whispered softly in her ear, "It will only get better. There is so more much for you to learn, and I'll continue to be your teacher. You must be obedient, Darien, doing only what I tell you. Next time I am here, we will dip into bondage, and touch the edge of full submissiveness."

*That's what I'm afraid of,* she said to herself.

In the shadows, Paul fumed in anger.

Anger among the guardians was rare, unheard of in one that was as Paul

Yet for the first time, he angered.

He was angry with the Titobind, whose shadowy tentacles reached for him even as he sat in the shadows in Darien's room. He was angry with himself for having to use Darien.

He angered because all he could do was watch and keep faith that Darien could hold her own against the madness that threatened them all. She has to be strong because she is the only hope that they have.

Darien's sleep was restless that night, and it took a long time for her to feel the heaviness of her lids. In her dreams, the room fairly danced before her, the shadows playing among themselves to bring her a taste of what waited for her at the end of her journey. Her hands were bound, her mouth gagged, and Jack encouraged her to accept generous punishment. Her mind generated nightmare upon nightmare, and when she woke; her body was drenched in sweat. Darien forgot that Jack lay quietly by her side, and as the minutes ticked by the clock became her focus; she used it hypnotically until the nightmare-filled sleep came to her once again. The darkness invaded her mind, and she drifted to yet another part of her subconscious where the evil took hold and the dream began again.

It started with the reality of her walking into the bar, finding the man who would take her down, teach her the importance of being a good little slave. Her mind would slip-slide through the evening, and she ended up back in her room with Jack bringing her to his side. The dominance portrayed in her dream was a re-enactment of her reality, and it left her drained, tired, and there was no peace for Darien, even in sleep. Later that night Jack left her bed, and Darien felt so empty, so alone and that was when the things came. In the shadows they danced, the whispery shades of nearly invisible demons. They pulled and tugged on her arms and legs, setting unseen fires everywhere they touched, burning deep into her soul. The hypnotic chanting that droned from mouthless faces was bringing her down and the burden of Darien's sins grew heavy inside of her. They bound her with invisible chains of guilt that weakened her against their attack.

"On you knees! On your knees!" they screamed inside her head. The pain they were causing was driving her even further down as she cowered on her bed. The verbal beating of their words was relentless, endless, and so degrading. Without making a sound Darien began to cry and it was making the demons go, forcing them to retreat into the shadows. Never had Darien felt so lost or so scared and suddenly all she wanted to do was to be free, inside of Darien, she wanted to be free, to feel her soul fly.

Away.

# CHAPTER SEVEN

# WORKING AT THE DINER

Darien walked into the diner the next morning at exactly 5:30 a.m.

She was not sure what to expect as she opened the door. Would there be a mad morning rush as early risers made haste to their respective jobs, quite possibly already being late? But no, there was the same quiet darkness as the day before, and the same phlegm-shooting old man sitting in the same seat. As Darien stared at him, she thought for just a moment that he might be dead, but then he moved and drew in a deep, ragged breath, which caused him to cough profusely. Darien turned her head just in time to avoid seeing, but she could not close her ears against that same splatting sound as it hit the floor. Her stomach rolled, and Tanner yelled from the back of the kitchen.

"Get out, old man!" Darien heard pans clanging, dropping onto the floor, and unexpectedly Tanner burst from the back, his face contorted with an uncontrollable rage as he came for the old man ready to tear him apart. Darien quickly stepped in front of him and stayed in front of Tanner until his anger began to subside. Finally, the old man got up out of his chair and shuffled out the door, completely unaware of how close he had just come to a real death. Tanner looked down at Darien and turned around, walking back into the kitchen wiping his hands excessively on the towel, ignoring the fact that Darien was even there. She let out her breath now that Tanner backed off, still remaining a little bit leery that he was going to return and yell at her for getting in the way.

She went behind the counter, put her purse away, and began looking through the lower shelves until she found another apron. She tied it around her waist in much the fashion as Tanner tied his, and a diligent search through the diner turned up a large bucket, rags and a couple of mops. It wasn't long before she began working on the accumulated filth. The first thing she cleaned was the outside and inside of the front windows. Imagine her surprise when underneath the grease and dirt she found "Tanner's" painted on the window. Darien never stopped cleaning until her stomach rumbled, and when she looked up at the clock, it surprised her that it was almost one in the afternoon. The other surprise was that except for the old wheezer (the one Tanner had nearly killed in his rage), not a single customer had entered the diner.

She smelled hamburgers frying on the grill, and she turned around to see Tanner standing and smiling at her while the sound of sizzling meat filled the empty diner. Adding to the day of surprises was that the entire time she had been cleaning the front, Tanner cleaned out the back. He had vigorously scrubbed all the dishes, put them in order, and he had even cleaned the much-neglected coffee machine. Darien inhaled the aroma of freshly brewed coffee; it all felt so wonderful and warm! More important, she felt at home. Tanner dropped the fries into the hot grease, and the crackle of the cooking brought a smile to her face. She filled two cups with ice and soda then set two plates on the counter next to Tanner. Darien returned to the front of the store, and stood at the window looking out at the dark, deserted street. Normally there would have been people walking to and from work, and the homeless that usually decorated the streets would all be lounging outside. There were also the lost teenagers who had quit school in the hopes of becoming rich selling drugs and running dirty money for the drug lords. However, they too were gone, all of them hiding, as the sky remained overcast, gray and hazy. The air did not move, and a feeling of desolation and despair permeated through everyone and everything.

Inside the diner, Darien opened her arms and allowed a small spark of the little sun its freedom. Its warmth rose in an aura from her body and bathed the diner in a luminescence of wonder and good feelings. It spilled out through the window, casting its light across the street, pushing back the encroaching darkness, and touching the tips of the shoes of the two who hid in the shadows. They had stayed just beyond her range of sight, the twins that came from Titobind. The light fell wider and stretched farther, reaching as far as the window would allow, while the new cleanliness inside helped her light to shine brighter. It also helped to release her inside spirit, the good inside of Darien. She opened her hand, and a little ball of sunlight danced in her palm, happy to be free. She bid the dancing light its freedom, and watched in unabated happiness as the warmth took its place within the inside lights. Tanner placed a plate in front of her, and she grinned at him as she bit into her burger. Then Darien laughed as the bubbles from the soda tickled her nose, and she smiled at Tanner again, because she could not remember ever having had french fries that tasted this good. The door to Tanner's Diner opened, and the old man returned, looking around in surprise, thinking perhaps that he had inadvertently entered the wrong place. He shuffled to what he remembered as "his seat" and Darien brought him coffee along with something to eat, and he looked up at her whispering a very quiet "thank you."

"You're welcome in here any time," she said to him touching his arm, and this brief simple act of kindness gave him a renewed hope along with a reason to live. The next time that he felt the cough coming, as fast as possible he made his retreat to the men's room.

Two more times the door to Tanner's Diner opened, and the people who entered smiled as the warmth of the light bathed them in good feelings, leaving behind the coldness that belonged to the gray outside. Tanner laughed as he threw more burgers on the grill, and Darien kept filling herself with the smiles of those who entered. She lost count of how many times the door opened after that, but the smiles of those who came inside kept the sun shining all day in the diner. It seemed like a miracle, while across the street, hidden in the shadows that crawled along the sides of the light, crept the tentacles of the Titobind. They snaked across the walls, keeping parallel with the light, just outside of its reach they curled and they circled, waiting for a chance to hold another person who had lost faith in themselves. In the meantime, the twin of ebony with the pale eyes, and the pale twin with eyes of ebon waited patiently to capture Darien and take her to their father.

Later that afternoon the diner finally started to empty, and even though Tanner had cleaned out the food cupboards, the customers were reluctant to leave the light and venture back into the oppressing gray. Tanner finally set down the spatula and took off his apron, watching Darien quietly as she put away the last of the clean dishes. "Do you usually work miracles?"

"Not usually." She looked at him with a smile that won his heart.

"So is this a one-time deal, or can I expect the sun to shine in my diner every day?"

"I'll be here won't I?"

He didn't want her to leave, but didn't know how to ask her to stay because he barely knew her. Not wanting to stumble around in awkward feelings, he quickly covered himself as he said, "You be careful going home. I know it's only six, but you never know what hides out there in the dark." She turned to leave and Tanner called to her.

"Hey, Darien. Tell me if I'm wrong, but along with this light that you seem to be generating in here, with whatever magic you hold, could it also have something to do with the darkness over Corral?"

"It could." Right then she knew that Tanner was meant to be a part of her life. She was in the right place. Darien looked at the scruffy thin man suddenly feeling a kinship towards him, and a need. He must have felt it too because his next words were kind and full of concern.

"Hey, you gonna to be okay?"

"Yes, eventually. I'll be back in the morning, you can count on it." Darien slowly closed her fist, and the effect was as if someone was pulling down a shade. She walked over to the nearest table and flipped on one of the lights. His eyes never left her.

"Tanner, don't worry, I'll be fine."

"You sure?"

"Positive. See you tomorrow, okay?"

"Okay."

The twins that waited outside were ready, twisting and writhing as the sunbeam slowly shrank back inside of the building. They were changing now, becoming as a part of the darkness, playing with the evil that grew and moved in and among the shadows.

Darien opened the door and stepped out into the oppressive clouds of all that was wrong in Corral, Texas. She was aware immediately of the twins who watched her with eyes alert to her every movement. Darien herself moved quickly down the street, afraid of the twins and the creepy crawly things that scurried after her. She blended into the shadows as well as David had done, and felt her body begin to dissipate much the same as it had done the night before, just prior to Jack's arrival. She closed her eyes and brought the warm swirling winds. She took pleasure in their comforting safety as they turned her around and around. Darien rose above the ground, spinning a small vortex of protection, and she moved away leaving behind two very stunned entities, again painfully aware of their failure. Neither twin wanted to answer for it because they knew a penalty would follow. They quickly untangled themselves from the shadows, and all they could do was watch the retreating mini-tornado. It moved uninhibited into the air, quickly escaping, but they knew where she would go, because right now the Triple Dove Hotel was the only place Darien had to call home.

Darien stood just outside of the hotel as her body slowed its spinning, and she re-formed from her dissipation. She stood in the perpetual grayness realizing that there wasn't any way to judge the time without the light of the day, so she looked at her watch and saw it was time for the sun to set. Had the sky been clear over Corral, they would see a bright red the sun, a sure signal for the warm day to follow. She sat down on the steps outside the hotel, and much to her surprise, Jimmy Bigslee joined her. He handed her a can of cold soda, and kept one for himself. They sipped them together in silence, as the grayness deepened and the night crept in, causing the shadows within the shadows to become darker than the darkest night. Darien's eyes narrowed, and she could see the movements along the ground spread up the sides of the building, and she knew they were the tentacles of Titobind. All of it was suddenly happening too fast, and it suddenly seemed as if there wasn't enough time. Jimmy drank his cola quietly watching where Darien was watching.

"You bring the darkness, Darien." He gestured at the night. "Or did it follow you?" She nearly choked on her soda, and it sputtered up her throat where several bubbles escaped on the backwash from her nose. Jimmy Bigslee gave her several pats on the back as she wiped her nose with the back of her hand. A braying sound came from his mouth, sort of like a "hemph" and he spoke to her.

"I run a whore hotel, Darien, make a livin' at it, and it's made me a hard man, exceptin' it don't mean I'm stupid. I was damned to figure out what someone like you wanted with a place like this, until now. I know the dark around us is bad, everybody knows it, and I know that there is somethin' growing out there. I can see it every once in a while, real quick like, and then it's gone. You know and I know that it's going to keep growing and unless it's stopped pretty soon, my guess is that the dark is gonna stay. I'd like to think that it followed you, rather than you being the one that's causin' it."

Stunned by his words Darien sat open mouthed, not knowing how to answer him, except as with Tanner, she felt that telling him anything less than the truth would not be fair. Besides, Jimmy would know the difference, and right now she needed all the friends she could get.

"I did both, I'm part of it, and it did follow me here, but it would have followed me no matter where I went. Inside of me, Mr. Bigslee, I'm changing; there is something making me more than what I am. You probably won't believe this but I'll going to take a chance in telling you. Out there, growing inside the dark, is an evil entity that I am supposed to find and fight so it will free the goodness and put the world right again. The problem is that I really don't know to find it, let alone fight it."

"Seems to me like it's right in front of you."

"It doesn't work that way. I wish I could explain it better."

Mr. Bigslee moved over next to her, and totally out of character for him, he put his arm around her shoulders. Darien could smell his sweat mixed with cheap deodorant, and the Old Spice cologne was making her a bit nauseous, but she welcomed the smell as a comforting normalcy inside a building madness. She leaned into him, sighed and then she whispered, "I am so scared, Jimmy."

The voice of Paul came from Jimmy's mouth, speaking to her with a voice soft and soothing. "You must have faith, Darien." And that was all it said. When Jimmy spoke to her again the gruff old man's voice returned.

"That guy you been lettin' come to your room, he's not hurting you is he?"

She thought of Jack spanking her bottom, Jack so commanding, and demanding. He was her master, the one that she answered to, and Darien did not completely lie when she said, "No."

"You let me know if he does, and if you don't want him around, I'll make sure that he stays away."

Darien sat straight up, and smiled at Mr. Bigslee as he wiped away her grateful tear. A huge smile spread across his face, and for a few moments, the shadows drew back while the scurrying little demons stopped in mid-step. Several of the smaller shapeless terrors simply winked out of existence as they felt the pain of happiness. The two friends sat on the steps a little longer sipping their sodas and watching as some of the braver people in the city ventured into the night. These people walked by them at a brisk pace while glancing nervously at the old man who held tightly onto the younger woman.

"Even when people feel the danger, even when they know that it's there, they still come out to dip themselves into their own despair."

He held her at arm's length and looked directly into her face. "If I can help you, I will."

"I know," she answered softly. "Thanks, Jimmy."

"I got to go back inside now. Don't stay out here too long, looks like they're gettin' stronger." He nodded at the shadows. "People would see better if they looked at things more'n with their hearts as well as their eyes, or if they paid just a little more attention to what's going on around them." His old bones popped as he stood, and he muttered a low "Damn" as he straightened up, not quite making it all the way. Jimmy disappeared inside the hotel just as a car pulled up outside. Darien was surprised and a little happy to see Jack step from the car.

"Jack, I didn't expect to see you tonight."

"Get upstairs and get ready for me, now!" he growled at her, turned his back, and then walked down the street. Darien got up and scurried away just like one of the little things in the shadows. She went up to her room, took a shower, and then stood at her window nervously watching the streets while waiting Jack's return.

In the meantime, Jack was at the Corner Bookstore looking at different types of whips along with various vibrators, and a leather vest with cutouts exactly where the nipples should be. He purchased a garter belt, nylons, and a small whip, along with two more vibrators. Jack handed his American Express to the same timid man that Darien had paid, watching closely as he put the purchases into another plastic handled shopping bag. The store clerk then handed the bag to the man who was ready to teach Darien everything that she needed to know about despair and desperation.

Jack was whistling when he left the store, mindless of the extra darkness that was settling into an already dark night, and the little shadow demons left Jack alone, sensing he was already one of them. Darien watched his approach and she shuddered under her towel when she saw that he was carrying the same kind of bag in which the proprietor put her purchases. How strange, she thought, that the bag advertised Corner Bookstore, as if everyone who saw the bag would not know the degrading contents inside.

She thought about her conversation with Jimmy, and the voice of Paul that had said, "Have faith," and wondered if she had heard it only because she wanted him here with her. Her body flowed with the same underwater movement as before, and she readied herself for Jack. She shook her hair slowly while allowing the serenity to infect her and she released the sensuous side, giving rise to Mary. Jack knocked on the door; Darien dropped her towel, and kneeled on the floor waiting for him to enter. The door opened. Jack smiled when he found that Darien had already assumed the expected position, but his smile held no warmth.

"Are you ready, little slut?" And he smiled that cold, unfeeling smile as he shut the door behind him.

"Yes, sir."

"Who do you love, Darien."

"I love only you, my master."

"And what do you do when I tell you what I want?"

"I obey."

Jack opened the bag, removed the whip and Mary sighed with pleasure as he walked over to her.

* * *

Five o'clock came early, and during Darien's walk to work the perpetual night seemed to be thicker, harder to walk through, and it clung to her body, trying to penetrate into her skin as it had tried once before. She recognized the familiar signs that led to hopelessness and futility as they started to return and dominate her. Darien knew that this must not happen, because if it did she would lose in her quest, and if she lost, they would all be lost. She opened the door to the diner and found a jubilant Tanner already serving several customers in a place that was noisy with laughter and good feelings. It was daytime inside the diner although the murky gray fog persisted outside, and the light that shone was giving all who entered a good, safe feeling. When she opened the door to the diner all of the oppression went away, and she was able to shake off the last clinging bits of depressing fog.

Across the street, the impeccably dressed twins once again felt the connection break, and it hurt them every time Darien was able to get away.

They were running out of time.

Darien returned the smiles to the customers, and her pleasure with them was genuine. She pushed up her sleeves and went to work while Tanner expertly flipped eggs and hotcakes. He couldn't help but see several bruises on her arms, but politely kept his mouth closed, and for that Darien was grateful. The diner was busy up until eleven and then the breakfast crowd finally left, giving way to a short lull before the lunch crowd came in. Darien sat at the counter with the newspaper, not at all surprised to see that the old man was clearing and wiping down the tables. Everyone needs a sense of self-worth even if it's just wiping down tables in a diner, and it was ironic the way everything fit together. To a big high-paying executive, wiping tables would probably be a form of punishment, but to an old man with congested lungs and possibly cancer, it helped him feel his own self-worth. Through it all they tied everything together, from the broom pusher to the president, and all the worlds that spun together in between. All of this was in danger of being lost because the evil they created continued to spread, and was showing up in everyday life. As Darien read the paper, there was a noticeable increase in numerous deaths all across the world. She alone knew that it was the connection between the missing guardians, and the despair of the world giving Tianato Morebind his strength. There was no protection, no one to guard them, no one except for Darien.

"There's too many, isn't there?" Tanner slide onto the empty stool next to Darien, and between Tanner and Mr. Bigslee, she did not know who was surprising her more.

"Yes, way too many." Tanner studied her for a moment as she scanned the headlines shaking her head at the increasing amount of accidents.

"You want to tell me what's going on?" Tanner was looking at the bruises on her arms when Darien put the paper down, and turned to face him.

"You and my friend Mr. Bigslee seem to have a lot in common. You see far more than what I ever thought you would, and that surprises me. So why don't you tell me what you know or what you think you know."

"I'm not your enemy, Darien." She looked down at the paper and then back up to the man who had given this new rider of the winds this small but important job.

"I guess that was a little harsh, I'm sorry. To say there is a little strain here is an understatement. Tanner, even if I was to explain everything to you, I don't think you would understand, and I really don't think you'd believe me."

"I'm a good listener. Don't judge me without knowing me. I'm not passing any kind of judgment on you, and it seems to me like you could use some friends." He laid his hand over hers, and Darien felt lucky as his kindness touched her heart.

"You're right, Tanner; people can never have enough friends. So if we had a couple of days maybe there would be enough time to give you the whole story, but as you can see the lunch crowd is coming in, and you know what, I think your meatloaf special is going to sell today." She grinned at him as several customers made their way to the tables.

"Today, after we close, you owe me the truth."

"I know and I'll tell you, I promise, but right now we'd better get busy." Darien slid off the stool and went back to work, losing herself as the little diner quickly filled, and even though it took longer than usual to get their lunch that day, no one became angry or impatient. The good feelings from the day before still shone in this small place of sanctity, and this time Darien did not need the magical little sun to make the light shine. However, it was not quite as strong as the day before and the creatures in the shadows were making a steady advancement.

It turned out to be a long day for Darien and Tanner and when it was finally over, the tired feelings were good ones. The old man was the last to leave for the day and as Tanner said goodnight to the old wheezer, Darien yelled from the back for him to be careful going home.

* * *

Charlie Tanner was much older physically than his sixty-eight years. He had seen pictures of men ten years older and he knew men ten years older who looked younger than he did. It was funny how you can see a path, know the inevitable destination, and follow in the worst possible course that it will take you. Charlie hung out at the diner because it kept him close to his son.. The old man thought about his son, of how he never told anyone his first name was Tyler. Tyler Tanner, how the boy's mother had loved that name! And Charlie had loved holding that woman, and how sad it was when the cancer came and took Elizabeth Tanner. She died when Tyler was eight years old and here was old Charlie forty years later, still missing his wife. She was then, and had remained the one great love for all of his life.

Charlie had no idea how to raise his son because Elizabeth always took care of the boy. From his first day of life, Tyler became her most cherished and prized possession. Charlie had reluctantly taken a back seat but even so, he did not even really mind because it made Elizabeth happy. Charlie Tanner would have done anything to see Elizabeth happy. Thin, scrawny little Tyler looked to his father with great confusion when he tried to explain to the boy what happened to his mother. None of the words seemed to come out right, so he finally gave up, telling Tyler his mother was dead, that she was never coming back, and that was the end of that. Tyler was alone from that day forward. People came and patted him on the head, and said they were sorry about his mother; they shook his hand while all the time he stood stoically next to Charlie taking it "like a little man."

Charlie had watched all of this, knowing the boy needed more, but he did not know how to approach him. He watched Tyler stand by himself at the coffin staring down at his mother, knowing that Tyler could not comprehend her sleeping death. Suddenly Tyler turned, ran to Charlie, and threw himself into his father's arms, weeping hysterically. Charlie had to pry the child off him and tell him to "stand tall and not to be a baby." They buried Elizabeth, and Charlie and Tyler grew more distant from each other, until the gap between them had widened so much that the knowledge to cross it became lost to them both. The two men ended up living in the same house for the next ten years like complete strangers.

At age eighteen, Tyler enlisted in the Army and served his time. Charlie did not see Tyler again until twelve years ago, when at the age of thirty-four, Tyler came home to open the diner in the small city of Corral, Texas. The distance established in their early life kept Charlie from telling Tyler who he was, so instead of trying to dismantle the wall that they had built so many years ago, he simply hung around the diner to be near his son. The advancing emphysema kept him from working while the small government check that Charlie received on the third day of every month gave him just enough money to pay rent in an apartment building that should have been condemned several years earlier. It was, however, a roof over his head and he ended up shuffling through what remained of his time. Then a few days ago, Darien walked into their lives.

Charlie heard Darien yell, "Be careful going home," as he closed the door behind him and limped down the stairs into the approaching night. Whereas just a few days earlier Charlie had found himself wishing for a permanent end to his pain, he now found himself whistling and thinking that being alive might not be such a bad thing after all.

Then the shadows closed in on him and as the fog penetrated his skin, it released a thousand tiny pincers into his weak, diseased body. He watched Titobind's twins come at him out of the night, and he knew that he was too old to run and too weak to fight. They entwined themselves around the sick elderly man and quickly gave him to the tentacles of the Titobind. He saw the evil things' world, they showed him a place so cold and so dark, a place without any warmth, thriving on desperation and death. Charlie Tanner stood watching as the evil twisted thing unwound, and then repositioned his appendages to draw in the guardians, holding them all inside endless nightmares. He watched in horror, bordering on a perverse kind of fascination, as the thing before him turned into a huge gelatinous mass, ready to dissolve and absorb Charlie into his midst. The guardians released a cry of hopelessness, building in volume as Titobind started to undo Charlie Tanner.

Across the dimensionless space their horror went out into the human world, and at Tanner's diner, Darien's ears began to bleed as the howl of despair reached inside of her head. She screamed for Tanner to help her, and then she fell to her knees as the pain crippled her. She screamed again when she saw the black squirming mass of Titobind enter, and then begin to pull Charlie Tanner apart from the inside. His eyes exploded out of his body, and his torture became her torture, his pain became her pain as the cries of the bound guardians overcame her senses. Tanner ran to the bathroom and returned with two heavy towels, which he held to her head and watched apprehensively as they rapidly became soaked through with blood.

Charlie Tanner ceased to exist.

The moans of the guardians slowly regressed until they were nothing more than a whisper on the wind, and Darien could see the Titobind's extensions return into a strange twisted shape that did not resemble anything human or guardian. Her own morbid fascination with being able to see the evil monstrosity made her oblivious to the fact that in return, it too could see her. The realization came too late, the thing looked directly into her heart, and she did not have time to conceal her love for the one bound to Titobind, the one she called David. Titobind left her then, and with the closing of his eyes, he closed her ability to see the shadow of what he was. Darien fell into Tanner's arms, and he held her there on the floor until the violent shuddering of her body subsided. When Darien was able to speak to Tanner her voice was whispery, tired, and full of pain.

"They took him, the old man, he's gone."

"How do you know?"

"I know this, as well as I know he was your father."

Tanner was stunned by her words, but at the same time, he knew what she said was true. Tanner had had a feeling ever since the old man arrived at his diner that he knew him from somewhere, but the same stubbornness that drove them apart at the beginning kept him from approaching the old man.

When Tanner first returned to Corral to look for his father, he dreamed about how he would make amends for their past mistakes. However, despite using his best resources, the attempt failed. In the end, Tyler came to terms with the fact that his father had died, and not once did it occur to look for him among the poverty-stricken or the homeless. The old man who came into his diner never bathed, his hair and beard nearly blended as one, and despite this unclean appearance, Tanner never made him leave. For the most part he simply tolerated the old man's presence and they both had suspected, but remained too stubborn to approach each other.

Tyler Tanner stood up, helped Darien to her feet, and then he swept her up into his arms. He carried her up the stairs in the back of the kitchen to his small apartment, his gaunt figure hiding the strength of which he was capable. He laid her on the sofa, went to get a clean shirt along with a bowl full of warm soapy water, and upon returning he offered to help her to undress. He could not help it when he uttered a soft "damn" as the removal of her shirt revealed the bruise marks all over her body. Darien winced when he accidentally brushed against a few of them as he gently helped her on with a clean shirt. She sat quietly while he cleaned the blood from her face and neck, grateful for his tender administrations. Then she lay back onto his sofa and was instantly asleep while the owner of the diner sat guard against the night. When she awoke several hours later, he still sat in the chair with only the glow of his cigarette to let her know he was still there.

"Tanner?" she said quietly.

"I'm here, Darien." There was a few moments of silence then he spoke again, "Maybe now you wouldn't mind telling me just what the hell is going on." He flipped on the small lamp that was next to where he was sitting, and Darien blinked several times adjusting to the sudden brightness.

"Could I have something to drink please?" Tanner rose from his chair, returning several minutes later with a plastic bottle of self-proclaimed spring water, which he handed to Darien. She sat up on the sofa, pulled her legs under her, and then leaned against the arm.

"There's coffee brewing." He returned to his chair and waited patiently for her to begin.

"I don't know where to start."

"Try, Darien, to start from the beginning." She took several long gulps of water, and then wiped her mouth on Tanner's shirt sleeve.

"It's going to be a long night."

"I'm not going anywhere; it's my house, remember."

She took another long gulp of water and began her story. It seemed as though once she started, there was no way to stop her. She talked on and on about her childhood, about meeting Jack, the most amazing birth of her children and of how her love had grown for them as she steadily pushed Jack away. Through the course of telling this story in its entirety Darien finally began to realize that maybe, just maybe, some of Jack's attitude towards her could have been her own fault. She told Tanner of how David appeared to her when she turned to thoughts of suicide to end her mental anguish. Darien spoke with quiet reservation when she told him of how she had loved David, and of how that love had smothered him and nearly cost the guardian his life. She told Tanner of how Paul had come to her for help because through the centuries an evil entity named Tianato Morebind had evolved on human despair, becoming strong enough and clever enough to take the seraphims away. The only time Tanner asked for a pause in the story was to go and retrieve two cups of the freshly made coffee and to light an occasional cigarette. Darien talked for hours, until they knew it was close to daytime, but not because of the night becoming a somewhat lesser black to gray, but simply because the clock read 6:30 a.m.

Tanner excused himself, went downstairs to make sure no one was trying to get into the diner, and then he checked to make sure that the

CLOSED sign still showed to the outside. Once done, he returned upstairs. Darien was standing at the window watching the city below; barely able to see as it came to life, and she shivered against the dark cold that was taking so much away. Tanner walked into the room and quietly watched her at the window. He could see the writhing darker patterns that surrounded her, but for whatever reason could not touch her and for a reason he could not understand, these strange things brought him no fear. Maybe it was because Tanner had already lived through his own horrendous nightmares, nightmares that were a part of his past forged in the form of a war fought long ago in a place called Vietnam.

"How did you get those bruises, Darien?" This was the question that she had dreaded the most, was hoping he would not ask, but knew all along that he would. She was very grateful for his tolerance and his help with her situation, and she knew that, as before, Tanner deserved a truthful answer. Darien took another deep breath.

"The eldest of all the guardians told me that Titobind lives in the center of our despair and that it was us, the human race, who unknowingly helped it to grow. He also told me that in order for me to find this evil I have to take a long and dangerous journey. No one knows where such a journey begins or ends. I do know that I'm searching for its place of despair, but where does despair begin? I am going on instinct alone, and in doing so I felt that to descend into its growing pit of desolation then I would need someone to show me the way." Darien looked at the man who had become her friend, and nothing changed, except the shift in his stance, and his eyes lost the previous look of tolerance.

"Tanner, you must listen carefully to the next part of what I am going to tell you, and please try to understand what is at stake in this journey. In finding the way in, in descending down, I cannot become lost to myself. I cannot become lost to my purpose, which is, of course, to free the guardians from the prison where he keeps them. In this journey, in seeking to find the worst in man, I must accept these punishments. I cannot allow the Titobind to know the true reason for my coming to him. I have to reach this thing on its own level, and keep everything else hidden. I am so afraid, Tanner, that I will not be able to remain strong enough to release the guardians." Tanner walked a little bit closer to a woman he met only a few days ago, but she had already become a part of his life in a way no other ever had.

"I have seen some strange things in the past couple of days, and if I had not seen the small miracle of sun that you released in my diner, and if you came to me at any other time with this story, I probably would have set you at the same table with the old wheezer." Then he added, "I mean with my father. I can sense strength in you, Darien, and despite how outrageous your story is, I have to say that I believe you. I also believe that you will find your true strength in your love of the guardians, all of them, not just David."

Her voice became solemn and quiet when she spoke next: "David is who I am; he became a permanent part of me."

"Then you must use that love, Darien."

"I know this already, Tanner, I know." Tyler went to her, held her close, and she cried against his chest as she released her fears while making even stronger the resolve to do what she needed to do.

"The world needs their guardians, and the guardians need to protect and serve. This is their purpose and it is why they must survive. Their very existence is to help us, and it has become an added mental torture because they cannot answer the cries that come from the people in this world. These cries of human desperation are exceeded only by the physical torture of their capturing by Tianato Morebind. He binds them to him with the black extensions of his torturous self while continually forcing his agonizing pincers into their bodies, keeping them bound to his evil, twisted form."

Tanner held her quietly while absorbing all her revelations, and wondering what kind of terrible fate was going to fall upon the world if Darien failed. He hardly knew her, and now he did not want to let her go. She was exhausted, that much was obvious, and she needed rest in a safe place, his place.

Tanner offered Darien his bed, and she slept through most of the day, waking only when Tanner crept from his spot to use the bathroom. She was not initially aware that he joined her, but upon his return Darien snuggled up next to him. It felt nice to have a warm soft body next to hers, without expectations, without demands and without fear. Tanner instinctively knew what she needed, and that was just to have someone hold her. He knew loneliness; everyone experiences it at some time in their life, but the total and absolute despair that Darien was seeking, the descent into darkness that she was looking for, that scared the hell out of him.

She woke at four in the afternoon and without looking, Darien knew that the gray murky fog still hung over the city of Corral. She left the comfort of the warm bed and opened the curtains to watch the despairing fog as it pushed against the window. It seemed to be taking on its own life, as if it could enter anywhere it pleased and capture everyone for the Titobind. Darien walked over, stood in the center of the room, and began to move in slow circles, spinning as she had when she was a child, recalling how easily they could spin until they become dizzy and fell down. She moved slowly at first, and then began to pick up speed, spinning faster and faster.

Tanner woke from a sound sleep, startled as the outer gusts of the mini-tornado pulled a small-framed picture into the air, and then smashed it into the wall directly above his head. Anything small or light in his bedroom lifted from its place, pulled into the building suction of her vortex. A tissue box went flying by, several pens and pencils, and then the single bottle of aftershave he kept on his bureau. Darien let her mind free, and the calling of the winds seemed natural to her. She dissipated into the flow of air as it drew her up and through the house. She moved above the murky gray fog that resembled a giant abscessed sore ready to burst and release a great uncontrollable ooze of corruption on the city that rested innocently below. Darien continued her dissipation into the winds as she became like the spinning tornado that were the guardians themselves, and as fast as lightning flashes to set the night aglow, so did the warmth of the guardian which she was becoming carry her to where she needed to be.

Darien came down through an old brick building, reassembling herself as her descent ended. The first thing that she recognized was the odor of teriyaki used in oriental cooking. The first thing she saw was the large red dragon that decorated one entire wall of the restaurant, appropriately named the Red Dragon. She walked over to the painted dragon and touched the tail, and feeling the painting under her fingertips, she could almost believe that there was an actual texture, the uneven feeling of scales. Starting at the tail, she walked down the length of the painted picture, letting her hand trail along the ups and downs of the decorated oriental dragon. Its mouth hung open, and fire spilled out from the opening in a great flare of bright yellow, which highlighted the entire wall, and then fell back into the deep red body. Darien touched the fire, and was not at all surprised to find that it was warm under her fingers. The eyes of the dragon followed her across the room, and the large mural shimmered then wavered as the dragon began to disconnect itself from the wall. She felt no fear as the great head turned and readied itself to send the fire after her.

"So it's to be a battle is it?"

The dragon's head rolled back and forth like it was laughing at her, and the front legs moved to lift the mighty painted dragon from the wall as it took on a three-dimensional appearance.

"Not a battle, little guardian, but for you a gift of strength and a gift of power."

Taken by surprise the startled Darien turned and saw that a small oriental man entered into the restaurant.

He could see her! How was that possible?

The elderly gentleman stopped near the bar and put his hand out to steady himself; clearly he was not well, and his face showed a pained expression.

"I am Chenn Yenn, the owner of the Red Dragon." He placed his hand on the dragon that had ambled up beside him.

"His strength is our gift to you because the journey you are taking will affect us all." The old man talked slowly, and needed to stop frequently to catch his breath. These pauses allowed Darien to observe the elder. She loved his long braid, and the silk kimono that he wore over the black pants and dark slippers. He hid a mystery inside of his wisdom and he smiled at Darien as if he could read her mind, but the smile could not hide his physical pain.

"I can see you, little angel, because we have always been aware of your coming, almost as long as your guardians have known that one day they too would have need of you. Come here and sit beside me, I don't think that I can walk the distance to you." Darien obeyed this man, immediately taking a great liking to him and a great interest in what he had to say. She cautiously walked by the dragon that watched her with great solemn eyes, and she sat on the barstool next to the elderly man. She bowed to him, as she knew it was a display of courtesy, and an acknowledgment of respect. His smile was genuine.

"I am a simple man, with a simple wish, and that is to find peace among my people. I own many Red Dragons, young guardian, and the families who work for me are free from the oppression of any outside interference. The problem is that I have grown old, and my time to change things has ended. My life within this world is almost over. However (and he raised his finger slightly from its resting place to allow the importance of what he was saying to come across to Darien), my concern is not for me." The old man bowed his head, and Darien watched with growing alarm, as he had to fight with his body for every breath.

"There is no more time." He placed his hand upon the dragon, and then motioned to Darien. She stood up and away from the bar, suddenly afraid as the old man collapsed onto the floor. The dragon stood and moved towards her. One part of it kept walking towards her, disembodying itself from the original, and a somewhat lesser red dragon returned to the wall. The newly formed dragon walked across the room and stood directly in front of Darien. She needed no words; she needed no explanation because she knew the gift was going to become a part of her. Darien spread her arms out to her side, and allowed the dragon to step slowly into her soul. She felt the fierce fire of the dragon as it secured itself to her, the power of its massive legs and chest, the strength needed to stand in battle, and the quiet conviction in the goodness of its learned ancient wisdom. When she was at last able to open her eyes, Master Yenn lay quietly on the floor, and if Darien had called his name a hundred times, he would not have been able to answer. His breathing was very shallow and she knew beyond any doubts that without any help, he would not survive long.

From over her head, there came loud voices and unmistakable shouts of anger. Darien looked at the ceiling, released herself to float upwards through the room, and she passed unseen into the upstairs storage area of the Red Dragon. Once Darien readjusted her body, her eyes widened in surprise when she realized why she was there. Chenn Yenn lived a clean, industrious life, giving to his people a sense of purpose and an inner peace of freedom. Master Yenn, however, had not been able to do that for his Americanized grandson. As she listened it became clear that Brian Yenn belonged to a very powerful gang of young men in Chinatown. How easy it had become for her to traverse cities, states, countries, and continents in a matter of seconds!

Her thoughts returned to the present; she remembered reading how gang rivalries and gang wars were escalating to become the only way of life for these young adults. This terrible rivalry was also spreading like a disease across the whole country. The young people encouraged racism, bigotry, hate and they were murdering each other at an alarming rate. Brian Yenn had the capabilities to change so many things, to lead his generation into a new era, but he needed the guidance of his wise grandfather. It seemed to Darien that the entire world was about to enter an age where the events that were supposed to change them into a new and better race of beings were continually sabotaged.

She watched as Brian Yenn polished his rifle with almost a loving quality. Sweat beaded up along his forehead, and she could see nervous perspiration stains spreading under his arms. Darien had a feeling that even if Brian wanted to back out of his position as leader, the other members would stop him. The rest of the young men in his gang sat around the storage room equally nervous and equally excited. Darien saw rifles, handguns, knives, hand grenades and even a rocket launcher. They all wore black boots, red T-shirts, with every one having the same haircut, and they all boasted the same red dragon tattoo on the lower inside of their forearm. One of the boys stood and announced that he was ready, prompting several more to do the same, and lastly Brian Yenn stood to gather his men to him. The gang was solid, strong, eager, and determined to take back the part of Chinatown that belonged to them.

Darien hid among the shadows, walking in the background around these young men, and she followed them as they started down the stairs. "Brian," she called to him softly, speaking directly into his ear.

"What?" He turned around, and the boy behind him looked startled.

"I didn't say anything. You hearin' things, man."

Darien moved quickly in and out of the shadows, going back to check on the grandfather, whose breathing was barely noticeable and then quickly back beside Brian.

"Brian."

"What? Damn it! Who the fuck is calling me?" He walked into the dining room looking around to see if one of the servers was in early, and that was when he spotted his grandfather lying on the floor.

"Grandfather!" He ran quickly to the elderly man, bent down, and gently rolled him over. At first, he thought that he died, but then the old man's chest slowly rose. In the meantime, the other men with him had followed Brian through the swinging doors.

"Call an ambulance, hurry." One of the young men left to go to the phone while the others crowded around him. A hand appeared and handed Brian his "Dragons" jacket, which he proceeded to fold up and place under the old man's head.

"Grandfather, can you hear me?" There was no response, and despite the fact that he was the leader of one of the most notorious gangs on the east coast, Brian Yenn at that moment, felt like crying because he dearly loved his grandfather. Brian looked up as his friend Mike returned to the dining room.

"The ambulance is on its way." He looked at Brian as he bent over his ancient grandfather.

"We have to get going, man, it's time. Li here can stay with your grandfather." Brian looked up and saw that the cook had left the kitchen and joined them in the dining room. Brian Yenn put his hand around his grandfather's, remembering that it was only two days ago when his grandfather had asked him not to do this terrible thing, and of how they had argued over right and wrong.

"There is too much hatred," he had said to Brian. "Too much dying, and not just the people, my grandson, but the whole world is dying as well. Make a difference with your life, do something good for your family, for your friends."

Brian was not ashamed anymore of the tears that flooded his eyes when he turned and said, "I'm staying with my grandfather." He felt a light squeeze from his grandfather's hand on his, and they all heard the siren loudly announcing the ambulance's arrival.

Darien sat patiently in the shadows, sitting on the window seat in the front of the restaurant. She looked at the piece of paper that she held in her hand, and read down the list of all the familiar takeout foods that was so typical of any oriental restaurant. It amused her to see that no matter where you went, the fast food "Chinese cuisine" were almost all the same. She thought of how she found the best part of typical oriental takeout to be the brown juice in the bottom of the little silver-handled quart box. The consistent smells of the restaurant were comforting in a world filled with constant change, and it was good to know that from the east coast to the west some things always remained the same.

Chenn Yenn smiled weakly at her from his stretcher as she walked calmly over, staying in between the attendants and standing out of sight right next to Brian. She was in his shadow, hidden in a world that he could not open his eyes to see. Darien kissed the old man's cheek, and whispered a thank you in his ear for the gift of the dragon whose strength and power were now a part of her along with the shining light found only in the goodness of the guardians. He gave a weak pull on her arm, and she lowered her ear until it was close enough so that she could clearly hear his weakened whisper. "He is your dragon, your strength, he has always been yours, and you will need him."

Darien slowly closed her eyes and called the winds. Her body began to dissipate into the warm breeze just as she heard Brian ask his grandfather what he said. The old man slept peacefully as she made her final dispersion into the wind, and Darien suddenly found herself back in Tanner's living room where he was sitting patiently drinking his coffee waiting for her return. She barely finished reassembling herself when he spoke to her.

"They've been standing outside for hours watching this apartment, and they have also been extending themselves into creeping black things that are spreading out across the building, growing like some kind of dark poison ivy."

Darien remembered the two impeccably dressed men that had been at the diner when she had helped little Manny, when she had breathed life back into Henry and when she had allowed Thomas's soul its passage through her body. They stood in wait at Tanner's diner and they had taken Charlie Tanner to the Titobind. She knew that they would be the ones who would take her too, and she was suddenly terrified. She wanted to go home, back to her home with Jack before any of this had started, even to the time before David came. These past eight years had been such a tumultuous time in her life, and she wondered now if perhaps it would have been better if she, or rather if they had allowed her to float free, to fly away as she wanted to. Those eight years ago when she cut herself off from her friends and from her family, how she grew passive and taken a back seat to watch the world pass her by. She remained belittled by the constant verbal beatings from her husband and her children, which caused her to lose the stubbornness, resolve, and determination that made her a strong and independent person.

Sometimes people can become so lost, so alone, that it seems like they can never find their way back, and she knew there were many who did not. Those lost souls wandered the streets homeless, without direction, without purpose. Was her life really been better back then? Maybe it was just that it was different, but she had lacked reason, her life lacked a purpose, or so Darien thought as she continuously searched for one. Now she had one, a sense of purpose to continue with her life as she tried to find the right path. How strange that her way never seemed as clear as it did now, or as hazy. In a time of her life when she was having the greatest doubts, she was finding that her life was going to have the greatest meaning.

So Darien sat on the bed and puzzled and puzzled, till her puzzler was sore (she remembered that line from Dr. Suess's *Grinch*), and then she came to understand. She saw herself sitting alone in the dark with that little light bulb coming on over her head and then all the guardians clapping as she stood up and bowed because she finally solved part of the puzzle.

David, it appears, had a larger purpose then just saving Darien from herself; he also needed to save her for this, because the guardians knew from the beginning that she would be needed to face the Titobind. Paul, the greatest and noblest of all the guardians, knew! Great and noble my ass! He had knowledge, from the very first day, and he secured Darien through David. The next question in her never-ending line of queries was, did David know? Did he know that Paul groomed, recruited, and used her for this purpose? Did he tell her of his love so that she would become so emotionally dependant on him that as a result, there would never be another? In this respect, was it to give her the strength, resolve, and conviction that she needed to venture forth on the quest they had set up for her? Because of this recruitment, was she as bound to the guardians as they were to the Titobind?

Darien doubted everything, and now she doubted most of all the love she had for David. She looked directly at Tanner, and it felt as if everything she believed in for the past eight years was shattering her inside. The great emotional sadness was near to actually pulling her heart in two. Scientists say that your heart does nothing more than pump your blood and that your mind creates your emotions. But Darien never held any truth in that saying, because right now she could feel the tearing of her heart as she realized they all used her! Her mind teetered on the edge, her sanity set to shatter.

In a great gusting of hurricane-force winds, Paul appeared and gathered Darien to him as her protests of "Noooo!" went unheard. He swept Tanner along as a mere afterthought, with the man barely clinging to the guardian's robe. The immortal guardian spiraled though the roof and spun them away, and with the last of his strength, he took her to the haven that he carved deep inside the mountains of their home, hiding from Titobind in the land beyond the mirrors. Darien's anguished sobs caused great upheavals in the ground on which they stood, and it threatened to rend the mountain itself from around them. Paul held her close while the force of her grief threatened to pull the light of life from her soul. Slowly her cries abated, and all she could do was shiver inside the warmth that Paul generated for her. Tanner, as he had been for the past four days, stood stoically by her side watching them intently, studying every move that Paul made. Finally not able to stand it any longer he walked over to Paul and pried Darien from him, forcing her to look at him, and he saw eyes that held a vast emptiness. Tyler Tanner was a gift to Darien, a man who could see beneath the surface straight into what she was. He took her by the shoulders and he told her exactly what he saw.

"I have watched you for four days now, Darien, which is not a long time to know you, but I have become involved in what is happening, and because of that I feel it is time for me to speak. From what you have told me and from what I have observed, you have created and lived in a make-believe world, taking refuge in a self-imposed sanction while becoming oblivious to everything else around you. When are you going to stop feeling sorry for yourself? You told me, with your own words, how you almost destroyed David with your suffocating greed for him, yet it was not enough for you. It has become apparent to me that nothing ever is. You crave love; you crave approval like most addicts crave their drug. Don't you see, don't you understand, they (the guardians) have given you all the love you could possibly ever need and still you demand more. Look inside, Darien, and tell me, what more could you possibly want?" He opened her arms and touched her chest, then said softly, "More important, what is in there?" She could not answer him, because she had gone numb inside.

"You can't answer can you? Do you know how lucky you are? How privileged? I have seen greater tragedies than you could ever imagine, and still you cannot see beyond your own narrow little world."

"I trusted them, Tanner, I trusted them all."

"And how have they betrayed you? They sent David to love you, and that was what he did and how did you repay him? You nearly destroyed him with your petty, clinging ways. His duty is to guide and to help you, not to become your personal love slave. Can't you see what a selfish woman you are?"

"They used me, Tanner." He snapped his head back from her verbal slap.

"And you didn't? My God, Darien, wake up and see what you've become. If you truly want to find happiness, then release yourself from your self-imposed demons and see what is truly inside of you." She looked so small and so fragile, so afraid, Tanner was almost sorry for what he had said.

"What is inside of me, Tanner?" she whispered.

"The guardians gave you something more beautiful than anyone has ever received; hell, even I can see that." Darien looked from Tanner to

Paul and then back to Tanner again. She looked above her head at the ceiling of the cave, feeling a warm glow inside begin to release, and then Paul spoke.

"David's love for you was, is real, Darien. How could you have ever doubted him? Yes, we needed you, but your calling made him real, and his love grew out of your need for him. You carry the most precious gift inside of you, a gift that no one of the human race has ever been privileged to have." Darien knew, she had always known. She knew that day at Tanner's when she released the small sun that came from the night at the hotel when she was showered and bathed with the bright lights that fell from the sky. She absorbed it inside her soul, the very same light that holds a guardian together, the light that gives them power, was now blossoming inside of her. It was keeping the dark reaching blackness of the Titobind at bay, which was why the twins could not been able to touch her. How could she have been so blind?

"I am sorry, Paul, for my foolishness."

Paul could not answer her because he was dissipating, becoming as a mist in the wind, and they watched as the darkness circled him and his last words to her came as a whisper on the wind: "Don't let him take your memories from you, Darien; he is very clever at that, and you must remember your love for David and the strengths hidden inside you." Then he was gone. All that they could hear were the anguished cries of the guardians. Had Tianato Morebind finally captured the last and the strongest of all the guardians? Darien called the winds, and before the Titobind's darkness could reach for her, she swept Tanner and herself back to their own world.

They emerged just outside the diner into the murky gray fog, which immediately penetrated them like the stinging of a thousand needles. Tanner gritted his teeth against the obvious pain, while Darien merely brushed it aside. She was strong now, growing with the responsibility because the fate of guardian and human alike was now hers. Darien continued coming into her own, following the path set before her on the day she was born.

How could she have ever doubted David's love? And Tanner, despite his pain, drew Darien to him, to the safety of his arms and as Darien looked up at him, she wondered if she would ever doubt the new love that she was finding inside the mystery called Tanner. They entered the diner, leaving the pain of the fog to the creatures who craved the darkness of the Titobind.

# CHAPTER EIGHT

# RICHARD AND RACHEL

Richard Williams stood alone in his living room.

He stared quietly out of the large double window in a stance that portrayed protectiveness, courage, and caution. His legs were firmly planted on the strong hardwood floor in the large family home that his Da lovingly provided for his family. He crossed his arms over his chest, and it was only the bulge of his veins from the intense grip on his arms that portrayed his concern as he watched the gray fog advance across his property. Rachel tip-toed down the stairs, causing the old boards to creak, which in turn gave way to her whereabouts in the old farmhouse.

"Richard, where are you?" she whispered as if she was not supposed to speak any louder in her own home.

"I'm here." His eyes never left the windows as his wife entered the living room, and found him gazing at the mysterious fog. He heard his favorite horse nicker loudly announcing its fear, and the sound of his hooves on the hard Texas ground was thunderous in the quiet that seemed to roll in with the mysterious dark fog. Richard's eyes lifted to watch as Willie Bear cleared the fence on the corral, running ahead of the advancing fog. The shriek that followed came from Cindy Lou, Rachel's horse, and the sound caused the hairs to stand up on the back of his neck; still he never moved. Rachel stood by her husband as one by one, the rest of the horses bolted out of the advancing fog, clearing the fence as cleanly as Willie Bear. Their reverberating hooves beat the ground hard enough for Rachel and Richard to feel it inside the house.

"Richard, we paid a small fortune for those horses, are we just going to let them bolt like that?" Rachel looked up at the face of her husband, and she followed his gaze outside as he tried to see what was out of sight, lost inside the fog.

"Let them go" was all that he said, knowing their instinct for survival drove them to flee the danger of the fog. They both watched the advancing thick vaporous mist move forward like it had a life of its own. It billowed out from nothing to fill sails of heavy gray and move forward as it self-procreated. They continued watching as the fog grew right in front of them, expanding every few minutes to cover a few more feet.

"Honey, this is going to sound weird, but it looks to me like that fog is alive."

"Not so weird, Rach, seems the same to me." Rachel stood next to the quiet man that she fell in love with when she was only eight years old. She recalled how they had met, and of how Richard told her that he knew from first glance she belonged to him.

Her mother and father moved to Texas from a large city up north; "business" her father said in offering an explanation. During the first weekend after school let out for the summer Rachel's parents decided to take her to the country 4-H fair. It was Rachel's first time at a fair that featured farmers and their livestock instead of rides and carnival games.

Richard Williams was in his pre-appointed mini-corral, meticulously grooming the farm animals he was preparing for competition. The farm work developed his physique early; he was muscular even then, strong for a boy of twelve, and the pride of his already chosen lifestyle showed in the way he handled himself and his livestock. Richard's red hair shone brightly in the morning sun, and he stopped working long enough to watch her as she walked by. Rachel in turn watched him with wide curious eyes that looked in great wonder at the small country fair. The part of her that caught Richard's attention the most were her big blue eyes, and the thick dark lashes that emphasized her innocence.

"She hit you, Ritchie lad?" The big strong Irishman who boasted the same shock of bright red hair soundly slapped his son on the back. Richard looked quietly up at his Da and shook his head yes while saying:

"Aye, Da, she did." He looked back to Rachel as she continued to walk by his corral area. The Williams were farm folk, always had been, and probably always would be. Marrying young to help with the farming was not unusual, however, Richard's Da saw the young girl with his eyes, not with his heart.

"She'll be too small to be working on the farm, and besides, Ritchie, she's way too young for you to be a waitin' on." Richard continued to groom Barr, his prize-winning bull, while still staring at Rachel, but also listening to every word that his Da said.

At the same time, Patrick Williams watched his son, and he thought about how difficult times were, and of how hard it was becoming for him to hold onto the farm. His two older sons had moved away, attending college in the city, having decided on a more exciting life. The simple way of living that Patrick knew was changing, and although he was disappointed, the large Irishman supported his sons' choices. Both older boys were doing well, Brian and Chris, and they made it a point to come home on every holiday. Brian, who maintained an extremely high grade point average, had already received offers from several large corporations back east. He told his Da that the farm would always be his home, but he was very excited about moving into a very different structured world. Chris, the middle son, was also doing well, and making plans that extended beyond life on the farm. He recently brought his fiancée home, and together the two of them studied to be attorneys. Patrick Williams was extremely proud of all his sons, with the youngest, Richard, remaining somewhat of a puzzle to him. When they were all home, the house filled with boisterous laughter, and Richard would be happy when they were all together; however, he remained reserved. The youngest son would wake early, long before his Da, and Patrick would inevitably find him hard at work, greeting the morning just as dawn brought the first light of day. His grades at school reflected his quiet determination to do well, and after the completion of his homework in the late afternoon hours, he would return once again to the outdoors and complete his chores. There was not a single fence broken, not even one with as much as a cracked board. Patrick worried at one point that this solitary life was not good for his youngest son. When the others were growing they attended parties, dances when they were older, normal things any child would want to do. At one time Patrick expressed these concerns to Richard, and the boy smiled at his Da. His eyes filled with an unusual light, his entire face radiating an inner glow as he very quietly walked out onto the front porch beckoning his father to follow him. They stood together outside, and the two of them looked out over the farm's wide expanse of land. Patrick looked to his youngest son, watching the way he gazed at the earth before him, and the inner light that glowed from Richard could only have come from the very depths of his soul.

"I love the land, Da." It was a simple answer, but the conviction of his belief in the land, his love for the way of life set before him, made Patrick never question him again. Richard did have several interests that continued to surprise his Da and his mother Becky. He was very partial to music, but it was not just any music. When others his own age (and his brothers as well) listened to whatever popular music was playing on the radio at the time, Richard would make a hasty retreat to the sanctity of the barn. His pleasure lay in the created music of concert composers, and in the solitude of being with his animals. His preference in his music, he once told his mother, raised the spirit of his soul. It would also bring a smile to his face when the barn door opened, and his Da would join him.

Richard Williams, quiet, determined, knew that he was meant to be with Rachel Bowman from the first time that he saw her. There was only one answer to give to his Da when he had commented about Rachel being too small and too young for him. It was an answer as simple as the way Richard saw life.

"She will grow." This answer caused Patrick to release great resounding laughs of pure delight in his son's matter-of-fact reasoning. For Richard, life was just as he saw it, and for him it was enough. He really did make it simple. He saw how others made their lives so complicated, and the quiet young boy would grow to become the quiet, strong young man, and he would hold to life as clean and as uncomplicated as it was meant to be. There was of course turmoil from the outside world that he would do battle with because it would seem that there would always be a determination to take that simple life from him. Richard would find respite from this turmoil in the sweet simplicity of Rachel Bowman, who would, at the right time, become Rachel Williams.

The country fair brought to the young girl so many new sights plus new sounds along with new events, and the most amazing discovery into the wonderfully sweet taste of the spun pink sugar that the vendor served on a paper cone. Rachel was raised in a bustling city by parents who, through a fluke of nature, brought forth Rachel late in their lives. Stephanie and Hugh Bowman were a mild, conservative couple keeping to themselves, and they went about raising Rachel in the same conservative way. They loved her dearly, and it was an acceptance in miracles when God blessed them with the gift of a warm, loving child. While living in the city they had kept her very sheltered, so the country 4-H fair in Brisco, Texas, was like Christmas in July, and her eyes reflected all that was new to her.

She saw the red hair first, which made her little heart skip a beat, and for just a moment Rachel was afraid that it wasn't going to start again. Richard observed her with quiet reserve, and Rachel dropped her gaze to the ground under his extensive scrutiny. She followed dutifully along behind her parents while sneaking quick glances at the boy who continued to groom his bull in learned motions. His gaze never left her as she continued to walk by.

"Come along, Rachel, don't dally." Her mother turned around, and followed Rachel's stare.

"It's a really big cow isn't it, Momma?" Stephanie Bowman put her arm around her daughter's shoulders.

"It's not a cow, dear, it's a bull, and that means it's a boy." Richard's Da joined him in the pen, and the quiet boy absently handed him the brush. He jumped over the top rail on the small enclosure, and walked straight up to Rachel's mother.

"If it's alright with you, ma'am, I could take her a little closer."

"I don't know, young man. Do you think it's safe, Hugh?" Richard, however, never waited for an answer as he took Rachel's hand in his own.

"She'll always be safe with me." Rachel let Richard lead her back to the pen, and his Da opened the gate. Patrick walked over to the Bowmans to introduce himself and his rather strong-willed son. He did this out of courtesy and the fact that he knew, as well as he knew his son, that in ten years' time Rachel Bowman would be married to his son. In the meantime, Richard held his hand over Rachel's, guiding the brush until she felt comfortable. The young girl developed an instant love for the animals, their warm soft fur, the big brown eyes, and their infinite trust in man. She also fell in love with the way life might be on a farm with Richard. At age eight, she too instinctively knew that she would someday belong with him.

Twelve years later, they stood together in their living room; determined not to lose the farm that Patrick and Becky Williams had left to their quiet son.

"I can't see beyond the fog, Rach, I can't remember ever seeing a fog like this before. Look over there, see the way it rolls and tries to pull itself along the ground, if I didn't know better I would say that there is something more than just the fog being alive." They continued watching the slow-moving mist that already covered half of their barn, and a fear began to grow as it crept along their property, knowing it would soon reach their farmhouse. Richard looked up, and saw the door to the loft still open, and his fear combined with his protective nature.

"Rachel, go in the kitchen and take a quick count of our supplies. We need to make sure that we can survive if the power goes out." She looked anxiously at her husband, who gently laid his strong hands on her shoulders.

"We'll be okay, Rach, don't worry. I'll take care of you, I always have. Remember that time when you were twelve, and I bloodied the noses of the three boys who were bullying you? Or how about the time you got that flat tire on your bike riding home from work? It was late that night and creepy Stu Burton tired to give you a ride home. I knew that you needed me, Rachel, and I came for you. I will always come for you, and I promised then and I promise now to never let anything hurt you."

"How can you fight a fog, Richard?" She was right of course; there was no way he could physically fight something you cannot hold. Richard walked over to the gun case, and for the second time in fifteen years, he touched his shotgun. His Da gave him the rifle when he was nine and Richard, as always, started going over the reasons as to why and why not he should have a gun. After careful consideration, he placed the rifle inside the gun case, and there it stayed until today. He opened the barrel and slid the shells into place in the same way that he remembered seeing his father and brothers do. The fog moved slowly, seemingly with a mind all its own, knowing that eventually it would get to where it was going. Suddenly Rachel's loud scream pierced the silence.

"Richard!" He bolted to the kitchen and found Rachel staring at the kitchen window.

Tap tap tap tap tap tap tap tap tap tap tap tap tap tap. It seemed to be knocking.

"What is that thing?"

Tap Tap.

"I have no idea what the hell it is."

Tap Tap.

"Damn it, Rachel, they're trying to get in!" Another black appendage appeared at the bottom of the window, and with suction-cup action, it pulled itself along behind the black shadow that proceeded to flatten itself against the window exactly like the first. The two of them, in exact precise rhythm raised a black appendage and between them, there came an eerie rhythm.

Taptap Taptap Taptap Taptap Taptap Taptap Taptap.

"Oh God, I think I left a window open upstairs. We can't let those things in!" Richard left the kitchen and ran up the stairs, taking them two at a time. The door to the newly decorated bedroom stood open, and Richard entered the room at the exact same moment that the fog rolled across the open window. One of the creepy window tappers fell into the bedroom, and immediately blended in with the shadows on the wall.

"Son of a bitch! Where did it go?" Richard walked over and closed the window just before another shadow fell inside. When it could not gain entrance, it flattened itself against the window, and began the same maddening rhythm.

Tap Tap Tap Tap Tap Tap Tap Tap Tap Tap Tap Tap Tap Tap Tap.

Richard felt a cold draft circle around his feet and looking down he watched in stunned horror as the shadow wrapped around his ankles and the cold from the darkness penetrated his skin.

Tap Tap Tap.

He looked back to the window where more of the creepy crawlies landed and all were extending an appendage requesting an invitation inside at triple time.

Taptaptap taptaptap taptaptap taptaptap taptaptap taptaptap.

The shadow clung to Richard as he tried to step away, and the tap-tapping, endless rapping was making his nerves jump and twitch with a fear that began to cut deeper.

Tap Tap Tap Tap Tap.

He began to shake first one foot, and then the other in a new kind of shake step shake step. The shadow, the little flat creepy crawlie extended itself up the outside of his leg and started to wrap itself around his calf. Richard could see the pincers inside the shadow and it held before him a darkness that would eat away at his soul. Rachel screamed from somewhere downstairs.

"Close the shutters, Rachel; latch down everything!" Patrick Williams built his home right in the middle of the tornado belt, and after his first lesson with the roaring winds, he had reinforced the windows with wood shutters, reinforced the doorways with extra-thick headers and built a secured survival area in the basement. Richard could hear his wife downstairs as she closed the heavy shutters, latching them tight against the encroaching fog while upstairs Richard's terror was still growing.

"Christ, how do I fight this thing?" It was holding to his feet, winding up around his leg, following his movements in the mimicking of normal shadow. The gray fog descended on the home of Richard and Rachel Williams, completely blocking out the sun and plunging them into a darkness of unnatural night. Richard's feet became numb with cold; almost all feelings were gone, and then he realized the cold was spreading up his legs. Rachel suddenly appeared in the doorway shining their brightest flashlight directly onto her husband. The advancing shadow quickly uncurled from around his feet, and skittered off into the corners finding another shadow in which to hide.

"Can you kill it, Richard?"

"I'm not sure, but I'm damned sure it can kill us." He stomped his feet trying to ease the prickling sensation as the warm blood flowed to revive his sleeping nerves. He eyed the corner where the creepy crawlie was hiding, and slowly backed out of the room, watching carefully to see if it followed, and then he slammed the door shut. Once the light disappeared, he heard a resounding plop then they heard the noise that was beginning to do its own dance on their nerves.

Tap Tap Tap Tap Tap Tap Tap.

They heard it as it slithered up the door, suction-cupping its way around the room, dancing in the night, exuberant at being exiled in the dark, tap-tapping its hunger.

"How can we keep it from coming under the door? The fog is making it so dark outside, and there are shadows everywhere."

"We'll go downstairs, Rachel, and build a circle of light in the living room. That should keep us safe for now. As long as we can keep the shadows away, we'll be safe. I still have to go out to the barn and check on the rest of the animals, and on the way back we'll get wood for the fireplace."

He didn't tell her how he had felt when the shadow had touched him, and he didn't tell her how it had clung to him, spreading out over his feet or of how it started to climb up his legs. He didn't want her to know that it was strong in the dark, stronger than he was, and he definitely didn't tell her that he was afraid the creepy crawlies might be feasting on what was left of their livestock.

"Come on, we'll go downstairs and get the big lanterns that are in the cellar way. We need to close the loft, Rachel, but before we do that, we'll turn on every light in the house."

"Richard, what if the power goes out?" He looked at her as if the power going out was actually a startling revelation. They went down the stairs in silence, and for the first time since they were children, the two became lost to each other as the fear of this unknown enemy crept into their minds. Richard made his way to the cellar door, opened it, and then handed Rachel the kerosene lantern that was twin to his own. They lit them with old-fashioned wooden matches found in the ever-needy junk drawer. Rachel slowly put her hand onto Richard's arm, and he looked down at her trusting face.

"Don't worry, Rachel, if the power goes out we'll take refuge in the storm cellar and just wait for the fog to burn off with sunrise." Rachel started to open her mouth to remind Richard that the sun was shining when the fog rolled in. Without another word between them, the young couple moved quickly from room to room illuminating the entire house while carefully watching the shadows. Without verbalizing their feelings, they knew that the creepy crawlies still hid somewhere inside their house, keeping out of sight in the shadows. Both of them forgot that the flue in the chimney was partly open, and they forgot how dark it was inside.

Tap Tap.

Richard cautiously opened the back door bringing the kerosene lamp out in front of him. The fog drew back but not nearly enough to help him feel safe. Rachel walked out next to him on the porch, and in a silent synchronization, they turned up the flames on the lanterns. The fog rolled back just a little more, however, they both knew that turning up the flame would only cause the lamps to burn out faster. They stepped completely off the porch, away from the relative safety of their home. Richard took the first step forward.

It was apparent that the fog was going to roll away with the advancement of the light, but they could not stop it from rolling in behind. Rachel could feel the cold nipping at her heels, a cold, wet dampness like someone left a window open during a late fall misting rain. She shivered uncontrollably, realizing that the farther they moved away from the house the lower the temperature became. Richard took hold of her hand, finding it to be as cold as his own. When they reached the barn door, he unlatched it and pushed it open. They held up their lanterns and it was easy to see that they were too late to help any of the animals trapped inside because the things from the shadows were already feeding. The light fell on the tappers, sending them scurrying away into the corners where they quickly blended with the dark. Rachel turned around and looked back towards the house where the comforting security of the inside brightness was barely discernable through the darkening mist. There was a sudden sharp pain in her right shoulder and Rachel reached around to her back, her hand touching what felt like a fluffy piece of cotton. She felt another shock of pain as she tore the tiny pincered piece of fog off her already cold body. As she separated it from her skin, it emitted a strangled cry, sounding like a very tiny "eeeeeeee."

"Richard, it is alive!"

"I'm beginning to think that leaving the house was a stupid idea." The strong Irishman held up his lamp and watched the shadows move just outside the reach of their lanterns' light.

"Look at them, Rachel, the shadows are dancing."

"Dancing with happiness because we're about to become their next meal." Unlike Rachel, Richard Williams did not want to show his fear, but how does someone fight a shadow? They are things without substance, a reflection of an object, which is a reflection in light. One of the black shapeless crawlies raised an appendage and began to pull itself up along the side of one the cow stalls. The young couple could not see inside the stall and they did not hear anything from the mother or the newborn calf that they knew were inside. For the first time in his life, Richard raised his rifle and fired. The sound ricocheted through the barn and Rachel raised her lantern even higher, allowing them a better look.

Nothing could have prepared them for what happened.

The watched in silence as the crawlie flew apart, and instantly a dozen different pieces began a dozen more tappings.

"Rachel?"

"Oh shit."

"Come on!" Richard grabbed her hand, and they began to run. The air filled with hundreds of tap-tappings as their small sprint through the yard turned into a race for life. The house loomed ahead while the fog rolled and moved after them, billowing and puffing, reaching out to steal the warmth from their bodies. Richard lunged forward against the door, and they flew into a welcomed, but sudden brightness that took them by surprise. Rachel watched as her husband continued with his forward momentum, flying into the kitchen table. She slammed the door shut behind them, and Richard turned around while the two of them gulped for air.

Rachel did not even realize her body was trembling until Richard asked her if she was okay. Rachel slowly placed her lantern on the counter as she answered, "I think so, you?"

"Yeah." He pushed himself up off the floor and stood trembling violently but not from fear, it was from the cold that tried to violate his body. Richard looked to his beautiful wife, and both of them opened their eyes wide when the light from his lantern began to flicker. Then the tapping began. It was very light at first, the same as before, a soft…Tap Tap Tap Tap Tap Tap Tap Tap Tap. Then it stopped for a few seconds only to begin again.

Tap Tap Tap Tap. It was louder now, and it beat a strange rhythm as more of them joined in. The taps became louder, quicker, blending until there was nothing but their continuous begging for food.

Tap Taptap TapTapTap Taptaptaptaptaptap TAPTAPTAP TAP!

It reached a level loud enough to make Rachel cover her ears. Without any warning, or any slowing down, the tapping suddenly stopped, and the stillness was so unexpected that at first they didn't recognize the silence. They heard a very wet-sounding plop exactly like the sounds they had heard out in the barn, and from upstairs there came another plop, and then another in quick secession until the plopping also became a continuous maddening sound. The tapping started again, doubling then tripling in rhythm. The lights flickered, then dimmed and in all the corners of the room, the shadows danced with a desire for food. In sudden realization, Richard spoke to this wife.

"Oh God, Rach, I forgot the chimney!" They raced for the living room and found an undulating black mass of creepy crawlies covering their entire living room floor. The lights went out, and the sudden drop in temperature caused them both to shiver. Rachel screamed as she felt the cold wrap itself around her ankles. Richard lowered the lantern to her feet, which in turn increased the darkness over their heads, and the shadows crawled along the ceiling.

"We need candles; where are they?"

"They will only make more shadows; we need to get to the basement!" Rachel's lantern sputtered and went out. The cold dark immediately penetrated their bodies, producing a chill so instantaneously deep that their bodies went from shivering to numb.

"I'm so cold, Richard," she whispered, afraid that if she spoke loudly that somehow the shadows would understand.

"Me too," he whispered back through the darkness. For the first time in Richard's life, he did not have an answer. Downstairs in the storm cellar there was no light and it was possible that it even if they made it there the shadows were waiting. He looked to Rachel, the person whom he loved from the first time he saw her, and he saw his own fear reflected in her face. He looked across the room to where he could still make out the shape of the wood carrier and wondered if they would even be able to make it outside, much less back again. Rachel's hand squeezed his tightly and when she spoke, her voice was full of pain.

"It's hurting me, Richard, the dark is hurting me." He felt so helpless and Rachel leaned into him while together they watched the creepy crawlies from the shadows attach themselves to their feet and being their upward climb.

"I'm sorry, Rachel; I thought I could always protect you." She looked up to him with the big blue eyes that made him melt, and they were filled with so much love and so much trust that he thought his heart would shatter with the intensity of his feelings.

"You cccan't ffight this, Richard, no one cccannn." She slowly sat down, leaned back against the wall, and the quiet son joined her in acceptance of the inevitable. They were too numb to move, too numb to feel as the things penetrated further into their skin. The shadows generated a trance-like state and the young couple would first lose their sense of self, and then the darkness would start to feed. The creepy crawlies that only moments before lay as a black undulating carpet across their floor now gathered themselves into one huge pulsating mass that started to raise itself towards the ceiling. As hard as it was to understand, it was obvious that there was some kind of intelligence guiding its movements. The lights flickered back on for a just a few moments, and the shadow thing shrank back from the sudden brightness. Then the lights went out for the last time and the strange formation in shadow advanced towards the sleeping forms of Rachel and Richard.

Then it began.

At first it went unnoticed as it began to push back the cold darkness that had violently invaded their home.

A gentle breeze.

A light, warm wind that slowly covered their faces, and then it swirled around their bodies bringing back the life-giving warmth where only moments before there had been none.

"Rachel." It spoke to her in a small soft voice, calling her name, sounding directly into her ear, and she slowly opened her eyes.

"Richard." It was woman's voice, and the voice sounded as if she were sitting right next to him on the floor. He opened his eyes, and without a moment's hesitation, he reached immediately for Rachel's hand. They watched quietly as a swirling vortex began to emerge in the middle of their living room, gathering the shadow into itself. As the shadows swirled and twirled, Rachel felt the heat that began to radiate all around them, while in the middle of the vortex a light started to shine. They stared in amazement as it became brighter and the Williams welcomed the unexplained warmth with smiles.

"Close the flue," Rachel said softly while nudging her husband towards the chimney. The quiet man stood on legs that were still unsteady, stomping from foot to foot to regain feeling. He traversed the small obstacle course stepping precariously between the small whirling tornado, and the lingering shadows still dancing on the walls. Richard reached up inside the old red brick chimney, and the instant drop in temperature hurt his hand. He quickly clasped the flue, pulled it shut, and then turned around just in time to see a small woman step from inside the light. She held out her hand to Rachel, uncurled her fist one finger at a time, and revealed a tiny sun. She released the mini-star, giving it freedom of movement, and they watched it rise towards the ceiling, casting its bright light into every corner, slowly turning night into day. The visitor smiled and addressed the young couple.

"It will shine for as long as you need." Rachel, along with her husband, and their strange visitor watched as the sun rose higher and higher, glowing ever brighter as it affixed itself to the ceiling. The light spilled out into the hallway, down to the kitchen and up the stairs. It kept expanding until it replaced all of the horrifying darkness with life-giving light.

"Who are you?" Richard could not help himself.

"My name is Darien."

"What are you?"

"Ssh, Richard, don't ask her that." Rachel did not want to offend whomever it was that had come to help them, afraid that she would leave and take the light with her. Rachel had no doubt whatsoever that they were in the presence of a miracle.

Darien advanced towards her and took both her hands into her own, and with a soft caring voice whispered softly to her, "Rachel, don't worry, you're going to be okay." Rachel burst into tears, her safety seemingly secured, along with the safety of her unborn child. The glow from Darien's vortex began to dim. Her calling here was finished while the cries of a thousand other desperate souls clamored for her help. Slowly she re-started the spin, turning around and around in a small, tight circle that allowed her to begin the dissipation enabling her to ride inside the mini-tornado, while letting the winds carry her back to Tanner.

"Keep him safe, Rachel; raise him to become as strong and as honest as his parents are because he is destined to become one of the greatest leaders this country will ever know." The vortex disappeared, and their entire house shone bright with the light of the miniature sun. As the last edge of cold left the young mother-to-be she immediately raised her hands and protectively covered her lower abdomen. Rachel felt the happiness spread inside her, already nurturing the young growing fetus and the smile she gave her husband was one of pure delight.

"I wasn't sure, Richard. I had thought that maybe, but now I have no doubts."

He was completely surprised. "A baby?"

She nodded her head, and he swept her up into her arms, spinning her around and around laughing with the pleasure of the moment.

"Patrick Darien Williams," she whispered in her husband's ear, and then she added that their son was indeed destined for greatness.

"This miracle came to us, Richard; our son is truly blessed." Richard put her gently back down on the floor, then walked over and opened the shutters to gaze out on their enemy. No one could explain where the fog had come from or why, and now as he looked at it, it suddenly seemed angry. Richard turned around, surprised to find Rachel standing it the middle of their living room spinning in her own little circle.

"Rachel, what are you doing?" She looked up at the sun that cast so much warmth and brightness. Rachel raised her arms up from her sides remembering how they used to spin around in circles on the school playground.

"She came out of nowhere, Richard." Rachel continued her spinning until her husband walked over to her and placed his hands on her shoulders to stop her turning.

"A light warm wind, a gentle breeze is how it all begins."

"Rach?"

"Darien," she whispered. "Our own special guardian angel."

# CHAPTER NINE

# GOING DOWN

"I can't stay with you, Tanner." Darien sighed in exasperation.

"You can." He knew she could not stay, even if she wanted to. It had become a never-ending night outside, where only the worst degenerates among man dared to walk the streets, and where the only place the sun shone was at Tanner's diner. The few customers who dared to come out only two days ago to partake of the laughter at Tanner's finally became too frightened of the murky gray fog. Now that Tanner himself could see the evil tendrils creeping everywhere he felt even stronger about wanting Darien to stay with him. He watched her from across the room as she slowly turned herself around; bringing just enough of the warm winds to lift Tanner's apron like a flutter in a soft breeze.

"How many lives have you already saved, Darien? You can't save them all, no matter how hard you try."

"Oh, Tanner, if only you could see, if only you could hear them, then you would understand why I can't say no. I like the spinning that allows me to ride the winds, and the capture of all their smiles inside my heart makes this unequal in anything else I could ever do."

"You still have to face that thing?"

"You already know the answer to that. These past few weeks with you have been wonderful, you have supported me, stayed by my side, and that is more than I could have hoped for. And now it's time to go and find him because I don't hear any more words of encouragement from Paul, and I'm afraid that the monster took him too. This disease is spreading faster than any plague, and the cries of pain that we both hear are real."

"Your ears are bleeding again." He left the room and returned with two clean towels. "This is the third time in two weeks." Darien held the towels to her ears and closed her mind against the relentless calls for salvation

"It's not just the guardians that are inside my thoughts; I can hear the whole world dying all around me. Titobind doesn't care who or what it destroys, as long as in the end, he wins. I think he sees himself as some kind of god, a creator in a world of darkness, ruler of an evil world, a world full of torture that he can laugh at and be proud that he made as twisted as he is. It makes one wonder, Tanner, when did humankind become so debased to have contributed to something so bad?"

"I can't possibly answer that question. All I know is that I don't want you to go. If that makes me selfish, then I'm selfish and I don't care." She remembered that David had also once said the very same words to her. Darien stood facing Tanner holding the towels to her ears while she again closed her mind to the relentless calls of a dying world.

"Even the ground we walk on is dying. Can you hear it? Every living thing that makes up our world is being destroyed." She looked at him with such sadness that Tanner could do nothing else but go to her, gather her into his arms and hold her tightly, in much the way as David did on the first meeting all those long years ago. She leaned into Tanner, thinking of how much he was like David. As Tanner held her so close and whispered how much he had come to care for her.

"I know. This is why it's making it so hard for me to leave."

"How are you going to find that thing?"

"Jack will take me to the twins, and they will take me to the Titobind. The two of them have been following me for weeks so I'm sure they won't be hard to find. They hide in the shadows, in much the same way as the guardians, while continuing to play the waiting game. It's such a fine line between good and evil and Titobind knows that I come from the opposite side of where he exists. I have to get close enough to convince him of my intentions to join him instead of letting him into my thoughts where I hide the reason for destroying what he is. This is the only way that I can win, and if I can't, then everyone loses. We will all become a part of his dark world, creeping and crawling through the night, feasting on each other to ease our burning hunger."

"A world of monsters."

"Of our own creation. We will either step into a new generation, evolve with a better and higher understanding of each other, or…"

"Or?"

"Or we, as an entire race of people, will cease to be."

\* \* \*

Darien turned around and around spinning a vortex that would carry her safely through the stinging gray fog back to the small room she rented at the Triple Dove Hotel. She emerged from the warm winds into an empty lobby, where she immediately realized that there were no customers, and the girls who bring the men their pleasures were nowhere to be seen. Darien found this to be somewhat amusing because she had thought that no matter what happened, man could not exist without satisfying his libido. She looked towards Jimmy's cage, and saw that it too was empty. Where was he? Jimmy hardly ever left his place except to use the john, or to get something to eat. Darien stopped to listen as the television reporter droned on about "the intense fog covering Corral, Texas, that is now spreading outward across the state in all directions. The strangest thing about this fog is that it seems to have a life of its own. It has an ability to cling to people's skin with what appears to be hundreds of tiny pincers. There is no scientific explanation for the thick mysterious gray mist, and researchers are attempting to analyze its properties. So far without much success. They are also studying the possibility of counteracting the fog with various chemicals. Authorities are asking people to leave their homes before the fog reaches them or if they are already trapped to stay inside…"

The newscaster continued with her report as Darien walked away, mumbling under her breath "chemicals my ass" as she went down the hallway towards the emergency exit. She reached the end of the passage and found Jimmy Bigslee's apartment door partially open. Every part of her body was screaming, "Don't go in there!" but she didn't listen, no one ever does. She pushed the door all the way open.

Darien gasped when she saw the multitude of dark shapes that moved and undulated throughout the room. The smell was sickly and repulsive, like death itself, and when Darien inadvertently inhaled the revolting odors, she began having difficulty breathing. She immediately began to spin as the dark shapes came for her, building a safe barrier to keep them from being able to touch her. She watched in horror as the shapeless creatures played with pieces of a body she could only guess at this point used to be Jimmy Bigslee. One of the shapes extended itself into the vague resemblance of something human, and placed Jimmy's head on the stump of its neck. The eyes popped open as did its mouth, and from somewhere beyond this time Jimmy called for her.

"Help me die, Darien, God please, the pain!" A gurgled scream followed his plea and fresh blood flowed from Darien's ears.

"God help him, God help me." Darien prayed.

"God cannot help what he cannot control." It was Paul! With the last of his strength, Paul had secured the room against the moving putrid shapes that belonged to the Titobind. He lay exhausted on the floor, gasping for each labored breath. He grasped Darien's hand with a strength that surprised her.

"I am done for, Darien, he comes for me."

"No, Paul, he can't!"

"I'm not strong enough to fight him, Darien, not anymore." He looked at her with so much love and so much understanding that it would bring even the strongest of men to their knees.

"You have always belonged to the guardians, Darien. Your destiny was determined before you were even born, and now it is time for you to make it happen. This is how it must be for there is no other way. We are one, Darien, take me inside of you, and let me be the final piece that makes you strong enough to take on this evil."

Tears streamed down Darien's face as Paul closed his eyes, and the light that is the great guardian's shone out through him, directly into

Darien. Paul dispersed into a thousand spheres of tiny suns, and rose into the air bathing the room in healing warmth. The shapes that moved inside the shadows had nowhere left to hide, and they shriveled up from the heat, burned into extinction. Bubbles of light fell from over her head, and into her body. Darien's entire body stiffened as she laid her head backwards and slowly extended her arms out from her sides. The light lifted her body from the ground turning her slowly as Paul entered, and became a living part of her. Her anguish in losing him was nearly as great as the joy she experienced absorbing him into her soul.

Finally, Darien lay exhausted on the floor, sweating and shivering in a room where the temperature rose to well over a hundred degrees. She stood on legs that barely supported her, and she reluctantly left Jimmy's room, heading back down to the lobby. She was not surprised when she turned the corner and found Jack waiting for her.

He had just pulling off the last few pieces of fog clinging to his neatly pressed suit jacket, and he was as impeccably dressed as the twins, looking as if he had just finished a meeting with important clients. His hand came up quickly under her chin, and he grasped it firmly, holding her steady with his grip.

"You should have been waiting for me. Your master is very upset with his little whore. You have not been here for him in almost three weeks. Where have you been hiding, Darien?" As he spoke, he was also dragging her up the stairs, pulling her roughly by her chin.

"I asked you a question, Darien!" his voice commanded, strong, harsh and for the first time Darien felt afraid for her life.

"I was working, Jack. I got a job at Tanner's diner. His place has been really busy, and I've been putting in a lot of hours and he let me sleep upstairs a couple of times because I was so tired." She saw the sudden glare of anger flare in his face, and Darien knew that she needed to slip into the role of submissive; she needed to release Mary, the only one who could deal with Jack. Darien needed to keep deliberately splintering her mind, most of all to hide Sibby, while giving free rein to the rest of her personalities.

"Nothing happened, Jack, he's my boss, I was tired and it was late when we closed up. Besides it's been pretty spooky out there," she nodded towards the door, "and I didn't want to walk home alone, so when Tanner offered me his sofa I accepted, that's all." Well, at least ninety percent was true, actually aside from the guardian she was becoming, all of it was true. She slept with Tanner close beside her, without physical interaction, but the deepening of their feelings for each other grew. Darien, however, could not give love to Tanner knowing that she would have to face Jack and more. There was only one person that could hold Darien, one person that she would give her life for, and she still carried that love deep inside of her. Jack let go of her chin just long enough to get a better grasp on her arm so he could drag her upstairs.

"You are mine and as such, you don't stay with anyone else, ever. Do you understand?"

"Yes, sir." She immediately humbled herself as was expected of her, even though Darien was strong enough to easily overpower him and walk away. In the same perverse way, she was finding herself becoming excited, while at the same time realizing that she actually missed him. Jack went over to her dresser drawer, opened it, and took out the devices he put inside.

While she watched him Darien wondered how was it possible for her to feel for Tanner, love David so deeply, and yet want the pain and excitement that Jack empowered in her. How could she enjoy this while it happened, and hate it when he was done?

(There was a guardian named David, from a time when she was born, who had once questioned Paul, the elder, about the small piece of dark that hid inside the newly born child. The elder's response was that one day she would need the darkness to overcome the tasks that were going to be set before her.)

"When did you bring those in here?"

"I didn't say that you could speak, but since you asked, last Tuesday I called and left a message on your answering machine. Obviously, you never showed up. You have a lot of time to make up for." She looked at Jack, and felt the beginning of fear, which only served to add to the growing excitement.

"Get on your knees and crawl over here to me."

Darien had a low tolerance when it came to being told what to do, but despite being resistant, she followed his command. She crawled slowly, seductively over to Jack almost cat like, flexing her body as she went. Sibby had done this once, a long time ago, in another life, and it was a time that Darien did not like to remember. Sibby, the weak, sick part inside Darien, and the last thing she wanted was to do battle with the whining, sniveling, little coward that was better off being nonexistent, a non-person. The side she really needed to release was Mary, and she never thought that she would be purposely calling upon her mental disorder for help.

"I am your master, take off my shoes and socks, kiss my feet, beg for my forgiveness, and maybe I will go easy on your punishment."

Darien stayed in her kneeling position, removed Jack's shoes and socks in the way he had ordered, while at the same time being extremely grateful for the fact that his feet were very clean and manicured. She placed her lips on the top of his foot, and kissed softly there, first one and then the other.

"I am sorry, sir, please forgive me." She kissed his feet again then sat back on her haunches with head down, and staring at the dark blue carpet. She imagined she saw little creatures down among the fibers, living their own little lives, swinging through the fibers of life safe within their own little world. Then she saw herself swinging on the same fibers, but on this little world, in a slowly unraveling, but never-ending universe.

*What tiny beings we truly are,* she thought to herself.

"Look at me."

Darien raised her eyes, and was unprepared for the slap that knocked her over sideways. Her hand came up and touched the spot already hot and reddening, and she could feel welts rising in the form of Jack's handprint. Jack came at her, lifting her completely off the floor, and throwing her on the bed. He pulled her over to the side of the bed, pinned her against his knees while punishing her with a leather strap taken from the drawer. Welts rose quickly on her buttocks as well as on the backs of her legs, and she cried loudly against him. Jack did not stop until he drew blood. The master then picked up a small red ball, which he proceeded to force into her mouth. He affixed the leather straps around the back of her head, handling her roughly, seeking to punish her, going beyond ordinary anger, because she was not there for him. He pulled her halfway off the bed and mounted her from behind, driving deep inside of her, slapping her bottom with his hand on top of the bleeding welts.

Her scream of pain remained muffled behind the ball that filled her mouth.

"Shut up. You like this and you know it!"

Darien's pain poured out in a torrent of tears as he opened her from behind and pushed deep inside her back end, causing her to bleed from the forced violation. She tried to relax against him but he was tearing her apart. Finally, he pulled away, and she collapsed on the bed, shuddering with relief. She rolled away from him and lay on her side quietly crying, trying to contain the bit of saliva escaping from under the ball and falling on her chin. Darien felt the pressure on the bed as he climbed in next to her, and pulled her over one more time. He leaned over her, licking and biting her neck, then sucking deeply on her skin. It was completely unexpected when Jack grabbed her hair and wrenched her head back. The glare in his eyes was one of dominant pleasure as he licked at the escaped saliva.

"You like pain, little slut, you know you do. Look at it!" Her eyes widened when she saw how big he was, and he pulled her head towards the swollen tip of his penis. He undid the chinstrap and the ball fell from her mouth.

"Look at it. That is your pleasure, this is your place, and you will have no other. Do you understand?"

Her mouth was dry; her voice came in a raspy response. "Yes, sir."

"Take a deep breath." He pushed his swollen member into her mouth. Darien gagged and could feel her stomach heave upwards.

"Don't you fucking puke on me!" He took himself out of her mouth until she stopped gagging.

Darien had barely caught her breath when he pushed himself back between her lips. She was in a perfect position to cause some major damage if she chose to; instead she managed to relax her mouth and accept most of his member. She spread her legs as Jack leaned over her, first targeting her large mounds of fleshy breasts, biting and kneading them harshly. He moved his body downward, his mouth traveling lower, and he opened her labia with his hands, bathing his fingers in her sweet juice. Her body stiffened, and then she relaxed, becoming completely at ease with his movement in her mouth. She felt his hot breath between her legs as his mouth slowly moved closer to her excitement, and finally he pushed his tongue up inside of her. Darien moaned as her pleasure betrayed her initial refusal of him. His slid his tongue up between her labia centering on her clitoris, and it was there that he expertly teased her until she could no longer hold still. Her body deceived her as her hips came off the bed, and she tried to draw him even deeper inside of herself. Unable to hold back any longer she finally climaxed as he pushed his face into her as far as he could. Darien felt his testes tighten in her hand, and she prepared for the initial taste of the first spurt, which would warn of the full ejaculation to follow. The taste of Jack was bitter, and she scrunched her face up against the sourness, but kept him inside her mouth until his ejaculation finished. He stayed above her for several minutes while she lapped his member clean, still holding herself against the vomit that threatened to come. Darien remembered how much she loved David's taste, and how much she enjoyed giving him this pleasure. She felt that she could still enjoy sex if not forced on her; unfortunately even though the enjoyment was not there (or was it?) she had to be extremely convincing, otherwise she would do just as well to give up.

(Sometimes giving up seemed to be a damn good idea).

Jack rolled off her and she breathed a sigh of relief, which he mistook for satisfied passion. She could almost see his smile, and she envisioned the mini-Jacks rolling the wheels around in his head helping him to formulate new tortures. His hand came up between her legs, which she automatically moved apart, and he expertly played with her until she was ready for him again.

"My little slut, you love every minute of this don't you?"

"Yes," she answered thoroughly humbled.

"And you would do anything to please your master wouldn't you?"

"Yes." Darien was very much into the role she was playing as she answered him with a small tiny voice, allowing Mary full rein.

"You are my little whore, now go and get the vibrators from the dresser, both of them, and don't forget the new paddle I bought."

"Please, master, my back end is so sore now." He moved up into her face so quickly that she wished she could disappear inside the bed.

"Do you think that I give a damn how you feel? Do I even give a fuck if your poor little ass is sore?" And he pinched her bottom roughly to prove his point.

*I guess not, you bastard,* she said to herself, and then aloud she said to him: "I am sorry, sir." She obediently got up off the bed retrieving the items that he wanted.

"Play with yourself, I want to watch." He lit a joint while Darien complied with his wishes. His eyes closed halfway, and he watched her though a haze of smoke. Jack offered her a hit on his joint, and Darien obeyed as she inhaled the pungent aroma and slowly relaxed into the high. She watched his pleasure harden through the cloud of bluish-colored smoke, and she reached for his desire. His hand grasped hers with a vise-like grip, and he spoke sternly through clenched teeth.

"You didn't say may I?"

"Master, may I?"

"Yes you may." She smiled a little evil smile of her own, and she looked at his relaxed face, knowing he too felt the effects from the joint.

"I am alert, Darien, don't get any ideas."

"But my master, I do have lots of ideas." She slowly rubbed the vibrator up over his leg, and he watched with renewed interest.

"Who do you love, Darien?"

"Only my master." And at the moment, she meant it.

"And later tonight when your punishment really begins who will you love then?"

"No one but my master." True to his word, when the punishment began, her body responded to Jack, the master. He delivered her into the lowest places of human bondage, and not once did Darien ask him to stop.

Jack stood at the door ready to leave her room, watching Darien as she slept. One minute her face would be relaxed, and then the next minute it would show signs of extreme pain. She performed well for him last night, and Jack felt that she was ready to move on to the next phase. He would induct her into the underground bar called the Pit. For those who were not aware, the nightclub appeared normal on the outside, but hidden inside were the secrets of man's darkest fantasies. It was fairly close to what he and Darien had experimented with, until you cross over to the deepest side of a dominant-submissive relationship learning to go into the depths of whatever the master demanded. It was total mind control where the actions of the master were without question, and the sub becomes slave, succumbing to all demands, no matter the outcome. Jack heard rumors once that someone actually filmed a snuff video within the hidden rooms of torture. Of course he had never actually seen one of these done; however, considering some of the things he experienced, he did not doubt their existence.

Jack buttoned his shirt, and smiled as his mind replayed the way Darien pleased him only a few hours earlier. He had a slight suspicion that she was hiding something from him with her diner job, but he could not figure out what it was. Her body suddenly twitched under the sheets, and then she settled down once again, almost as if she sensed him standing there quietly watching her.

(Watch out for the quiet ones.)

Jack tried to understand what he saw in the diminutive woman. She certainly is not a beautiful woman, and he definitely had his share of those. Her body with its funny shape, well not exactly funny, but more over-shaped. She stands less than five feet tall, but with the largest breasts he ever saw on a woman her height. Her stomach is flabby; a result of not having exercised after having had her children; Jack knew this from the size of her stretch marks. So what did he see in Darien that drew him to her? Her extreme passion was something that he counted on, and she is sweet. The best part is that she pleases him and everything that she does, she does with only his pleasure in mind. That makes all the difference.

Jack finished buttoning up his shirt and put on his jacket. Darien slowly turned over allowing him had a full view of her gentle sleeping face. Someone else might not see it, but suddenly to Jack, Darien was beautiful. He walked over to the bed and let his hand rest on her cheek and in her sleep, Darien touched Jack's hand and brought it to her lips. Jack pulled back his hand, and left Darien to the shadows and to her dreams.

She dreamed of Tanner, and of his kindness to her, while parts of her dream captured David, letting her relive their times together, and in her subconscious, she drank deeply of his love. She slipped into nightmares that brought the twins, and the appearance of Titobind caused her to wake in a dark, empty, silent room. Darien shivered from the cold that invaded her warm little world, and she was unaware that just outside her hotel, the twins trapped Jack between them. They filled him with more twisted thoughts, delivering him to the harsh brutalities that would then descend to Darien, and eventually bring her to the Pit and to Tianato Morebind.

Jack shook, dancing like a puppet as they slowly unwound from the shadows, and penetrated into his mouth, and up inside his nose. They melted the darkness of themselves into his eyes and ears as he shuddered with their unwelcome entrance. When they finished, they let him go, retreating into the shadows where they hid with Jack's last sane thought. They watched as the fog covered him, and Jack took his last uncontrolled step, as he too became slave to the Titobind.

And Titobind had them all.

The guardians squirmed and entwined in and amongst each other, looking for a weakness in the black that held them bound without mercy. He tormented them with nightmares of his darkest thoughts while the cries for help from the human world continued to go unanswered.

It was this alone that continued to cause their greatest anguish. Even with his final conquering of the guardians (which to all truths be known, had not given Titobind the satisfaction he sought), Titobind remained restless in his pursuit for the one called Darien. He knew also of her attachment to the guardian named David. Titobind attempted repeatedly to make David's thoughts of Darien along with the thoughts of the other guardians known to him, but this was one bind among the guardians that he could not break. However, he made plans for David. When his children finally presented Darien to him, Titobind would take the one that she called David, and he would suffer untold indignities. His torture would be endless, and then he would unwind Darien herself, and find out what it was about this small human that made even the guardians themselves call to her. He sat within his mothering liquid night and let the black womb rock him softly into a hideous sleep that would renew his twisted torso, and help him keep his demons alive.

Darien woke suddenly. She did not move or startle herself, but her eyes flew open and she was instantly aware. She watched the silent dance of shadows that moved in the darkness of her room, and she knew that the shadow caused her to wake. They were afraid to approach her, and she also remembered what kept her safe.

Two wonderful guardians fell into her soul, allowing her their light and their strength to form an invisible, unbreakable barrier of safety. She had the smile of little Manny, of Gladys and Henry, and the smile of the small and gentle Chenn Yenn along with Hester of South Africa who so bravely put herself into the line of fire to save her little brother. And she would never forget the home of Richard and Rachel. All of this along with the countless others that Darien saved was helping to keep her safe.

She watched the creatures moving and creeping along the walls, edging a little bit closer to her, and then slowly backing away, while entwining into each other with an endless dance of madness. The gray fog covering the city turned a few shades lighter than the dark night, but no sun could break through the despairing cover. She rose slowly to a sitting position, and felt the morning's urge to pee push heavily into her bladder. A sudden knock on her door startled Darien, and she was afraid. She knew it wasn't Jack, but who? And what time is it? She thought for a moment that she slept through a whole day, and Jack had actually returned. There came another knock, however, this time the knocker lost his patience, and the door burst inward. Tanner! Darien quickly turned her back to him. How could she face the gentle man who had become her own protector after what she let Jack do to her? Even though she had to allow Jack his pleasures in order to free the guardians, she felt herself unworthy of Tanner's kindness.

"Darien," he said softly.

She still refused to answer or to look at him, but she did hear him enter all the way into the room. Her eyes filled with tears, and she sat quietly pulling the sheet up around her body, still unable to turn around.

"Don't, Tanner, I can't see you."

"Let me help you. I can, you know, if you'll just let me."

"You don't know, Tanner, you can't possibly understand, and now you must stay away. You are risking your own life by coming here. Go back, please, and open the diner. You have to make an attempt to bring some goodness and light into this mess."

"Darien, go look outside."

"Why? What's the point? Nothing has changed since yesterday."

"Just go and look outside."

Darien sighed, and then winced as she swung her legs over the side of the bed. The sheet fell away revealing a back covered with welts, reminiscence of the previous night's pleasures. Tanner made a funny noise when he saw how deep the marks of the strap traveled into her flesh. Darien quickly gathered the sheet around her shoulders, and with the light cotton covering trailing behind her she stood and walked to the window. Her eyes opened wide in horror as she gazed at the dark gray fog that seemed to have come alive. It folded and rolled into itself, making swirling patterns in the sky. Two days ago, Darien could see the street below, but now the street was but a remembered picture in her mind. She turned around and looked at Tanner, who stood in the doorway watching her, wondering what he could do to help, yet knowing all the time that he could not. Instead he tried to explain the evil as he understood it.

"The disease that thing is releasing is still spreading, and it's attacking people when they try to walk outside, almost like it's feeding off of them. People are dying, Darien, and not just out in the fog. Ambulances can't get through to the emergencies, to the ones who need the hospital, even normal everyday accidents are hurting people so severely that they are dying. The fog burns wherever it touches, and if you try to remove it, it breaks off, leaving a part of it clinging to your clothes, to your skin." Tanner watched Darien as she turned back around to gaze out at the murderous disease of the Titobind.

"Something inside the fog is alive. It moves against you, into you, and you can feel pinpricks, almost pincer-like as it buries itself into your skin. It's growing, spreading outwards, the television news station say it's reached Pikesville, and there are reports of it starting to settle into Union City." Tanner took a deep breath and then continued. "Do you know what else?"

"What else?" she asked sarcastically.

"The animals are dying, and so are the vegetables in people's gardens. Fresh produce is shriveling up before it can be unloaded from the trucks, and from most of what I can see, even going to the store is a death sentence."

"What do you want from me, Tanner? I cannot force his hand. He has to believe that I come willingly to his side. The only element that I have to use against him is to take him by surprise, and the only way that I can do that is to convince him that I am his, and then he will let his guard down and allow me to see."

"To see what?"

"To see the little twisted being that would play at being a God. Regardless of what his wretched mind thinks he is and what he thinks he knows Titobind is a very self-centered, evil little child. He is playing in a game that he does not fully understand."

"Now I don't understand."

"Titobind, Tianato Morebind, is born of the despair taken from this world. It took him centuries to grow, to become aware, to reason and then to plot. When he was strong enough, had learned enough, had evolved enough to know reason, he attacked and bound the guardians. In spite of this self-learning what he doesn't know is the sum total of the enormous amount of power he has gathered to himself. If I cannot release the guardians to help bring him down, then as a species, we are doomed. He has drawn enough strength to destroy our entire world."

"And he doesn't know this?"

"Titobind knows the guardians are strong, he just doesn't realize how ancient they are in mind and in power. They have a wisdom that is as old as time is old, and they have watched hundreds of civilizations thrive and grow throughout entire universes. The guardians that are in this world are but a mere fraction of what survives in all the galaxies. Do you honestly think that the guardians of the universe will allow this child to continue perpetuating an evil disease? Do you honestly think they will allow its evil to spread out among the stars?" The sum total of what Darien said hit Tanner with the force of well-rounded punch.

"You're telling me that the other guardians will destroy our world?"

"What is one world to them, Tanner, if our demise means the survival of a thousand others?" Her voice became quiet, a whisper of awe when she said to him: "It would not be the guardians themselves who would exact the final destruction, but more it would be the 'Hand of God.'" They both stood in silence, and Darien with her back to Tanner whispered, "What a foolish race of humans we have become." Darien dropped her sheet all the way off her body, and Tanner's eyes filled with tears as he looked at her bruised and beaten form.

"And what small price is this," she whispered softly, "if it will save millions of lives?" She turned around to face him unashamed by her naked tortured body.

"I cannot fail, Tanner, because for the first time in my life, I feel as though I have a purpose for living." She bent to pick up the sheet, and Tyler moved quickly across the room, helped her gather it up, and gently covered her scarred body. Darien melted into him, and he was afraid that no matter where he touched, it would hurt her.

"Touch me anyway; I need your gentleness to help me through this." Slowly he put his arms up around her, and he was so gentle with his enfolding arms that Darien did not feel pain. What she did feel was a tremendous amount of gratitude, and the first small persuasion of something deeper. They stood together for a long time, and then Tanner picked Darien up and carried her to bed. He lay beside her, and as before, held her close while she slept peacefully, and without fear.

When she woke, the clock cubes said four, zero, and a block halfway to two, then with a loud click she watched it fall into place. She was not sure if it was p.m. or a.m. and the first thing she became aware of was the wonderful aroma of coffee. Darien sat up to exit her bed, and the second thing she noticed was that Tanner had put a nightgown on her. She smiled wondering if he was able to sleep at all, her own private little Taylor guardian. Darien saw a hidden inner strength in humans that seemed to make them guardians of their own. She also saw a covered dish and a hot cup of coffee sitting on a serving tray by her bed, and just as she reached for her coffee, the phone rang. Tanner.

"Hello?"

"It's still hot isn't it?"

She smiled. "Yes, it's still hot. Why didn't you stay?"

"Because I no longer trust my feelings, and I don't think I can be near you again without wanting to kill Jack for hurting you. Do you want that?"

"No, I don't. I guess you're right to stay away."

"I just wanted to see if you were okay. There are a few customers here so I have to go. Listen, if you need me just call and I'll come."

"I know."

"Darien?"

"Yes?"

He hesitated but Darien already knew what he was going to say. "I think I'm falling in love with you."

Darien's voice was nearly a whisper when she answered him. "I know that too."

Tanner hung up the phone without even saying goodbye, and Darien returned hers to the handset. She looked around at the clean little room, and suddenly she remembered how she last saw Jimmy.

"Oh God, Jimmy, I'm so sorry," she said aloud. The mention of his name sent the creepy crawlies into a frenzied dance along the walls of her room. She thought of Jack and wondered what he would bring her tonight, and this thought caused Darien to release the sensuous side of her nature. She let it begin; she was ready for Jack to take her down to the center of despair. She sipped on her coffee as the personality of Mary took over, the one who liked submission, the one who could deal with Jack. Darien removed herself, detaching herself from who she was; shivering with delight. The thought of the master of pain brought every part of her body alive, and she began to need his punishment, she wanted him to give her all of the pain. Jack's little whore, his little slut, wanted it all.

"Take me down, Jack," she said in a voice filled with deep sensuous emotions. "Take me down, to where I need to be."

# CHAPTER TEN

# LOOKING FOR THE OTHER SIDE

"Where are we going?"

Darien played with Jack, flirting on the edge of disaster, wanting Jack to punish her, to make her pay for all of the things she had done wrong in her life. Darien's awareness was still there but it was an awareness into a reality that was slowly becoming as depraved as Jack. She hoped that by releasing the submissive side of her nature it would not cause the rebirth of the sniveling, whining Sibby. That would probably be the worst thing that could happen. If Sibby came out while they were in the middle of something that only the strongest part of her had the capabilities to handle, then of course they would all lose again. It seemed to Darien that the whole thing had turned into a lose-lose situation, and if she took the time to think about what she was preparing to do, then perhaps the world would inevitably die. Considering the way most people treat each other, she wondered if that would be so bad. Maybe they could start over again; after all, man did possess some good qualities, although the arguments among the guardians had been quite strong to the contrary. She did not really want to think about it anymore because deliberately dividing herself had brought the headaches back, and those damnable things alone were enough to make her evil.

Jack watched while she dressed, and he watched with growing anticipation because he knew they were about to participate in something that he had been waiting most impatiently for. He thought, more than once, of keeping Darien for himself. But it remained just a thought. He rose out of the small hotel room chair and walked over to Darien just as she started to put on her bra. He quietly positioned himself directly behind her. Jack surprised her as he grabbed her ample hips, and violently pushed her head down towards the bed. At the same time he pushed her feet apart with his own and pulled her panties from her, exposing all of her from behind. Darien vividly recalled the cruelty of Dr. Marris.

"Don't move," he commanded, and she stood silently, bent over in the degrading position he placed her in. She heard the drawer open, and then a few seconds later, she felt something hard and cold pressing against her opening. Jack rubbed the vibrator all over her nether region, wetting it enough for entry. Darien gasped at the harshness with which he thrust it in and out of her. He removed the well-lubricated vibrator, and suddenly slapped her bottom with it. Darien swayed sideways with the force of it.

"Don't fucking move!" She stood still as still as possible hoping that he would not see the tears fill her eyes. The forceful slaps were no longer tolerable, even for Darien, and they came to her with such power that it bordered the harsh side of masochism. She released Mary, her body immediately relaxing into the role.

"What do you say to me? Your master is waiting."

"I'm sorry, I won't move, sir." He pulled her open, and re-introduced the vibrator back into her, and her strong side had to suppress the urge to fight back. Jack knelt behind her and then reaching around, he brutally pinched her clitoris, and still sore from the night before, her nipples received the same brutal treatment. He expertly moved the vibrator in and out, making her anxious with his administrations, and sweet, sensuous Mary secretly wished for the whip.

(Despite the pain he was inflicting, despite her urge to fight back, inside of Darien, the dark place was growing. Her acceptance of Jack's brutalities was bringing an excitement that she could not control; this in turn would cause her to take the next step into the very dark dangerous place. Like a drug addict, Darien started craving this pain.)

Jack brought alive every part of her, brutally, without thought to her feelings or to the pain. He opened her and slid his fingers inside, pulling every part of her over to the side that she needed to embrace. He removed the vibrator, threw it on the bed, and then introduced his own member inside of her, nearly splitting her with his size. He used both hands to put pressure on her shoulders while he drove himself into her mercilessly. His thrusts became wild, so uninhibited that she knew he was completely losing himself to the moment. Jack reached around to knead her breasts again, and then he leaned over to bite her back, leaving angry teeth marks that nearly drew blood. His voice was harsh, nearly a growl, and when he spoke, it was with bitter sarcasm:

"Who do you love?"

"You, Jack, and only you." Darien's consciousness disappeared. The next time she looked up her eyes glazed over, and she hid her sane thoughts in a far away place. Her body came fully alive to the pleasures of the pain, which Darien alone would have never been able to accept. Jack continued to build himself into a wild frenzy, biting and thrusting, knowing that his slave enjoyed every minute of it. He pulled himself out and plunged again, watching the movement of his member. Jack knew without any doubts, that this little slut still wanted more. Mary came fully into the role, accepting without question the master's pain, absolved to this end and nothing more.

"Fuck me, Jack, punish me, I have been bad. Do it, fuck me, Jack! Come on, Jack; fuck me harder. Fuck me!" He exploded into her and she did the same on him. Jack held onto her hair pulling her head back as he rocked and released into Darien. At last, he fell on top of her, his penis deflated and for just a moment he resembled the deflated Dr. Marris.

"Roll over and clean me." He stood up and Darien knelt down in front of him to wash him with her mouth.

"My little whore, who do want now, more than anyone?"

"I want you, Jack," she said between tastes.

"Who do you love, Darien?"

"You, Jack, my one and only master."

"And who do you serve?"

There wasn't even a moment's hesitation when Darien answered. "I serve the Titobind."

Jack slapped her face even as she cleaned him, and she narrowly missed clamping down on him with her teeth.

"Where have you heard this name?"

"I don't know, I just heard."

Jack's instructions were to present Darien to the twins; however, even Jack himself dared not to say the name of the thing that made this request known to him.

"What have you heard?"

"That if someone desires to walk the finest line between pleasure and pain, then he would be the one to look for."

Jack walked away thinking about what she said, and a part of him wanted her to run, to get away as fast as she could. However, he knew that if that happened, then he himself would be tortured with endless pain and suffering. Jack also knew that the punishment would be so ruthless, so intense, that in the end, he would welcome death. He had feelings for her, of that there was no doubt, but Jack also was a coward. He wanted to continue to live within a relative margin of safety, which would enable him to keep on indulging in his little fantasies. So in the choice between giving Darien to the twins, or keeping her for himself, Jack chose the one that was in his best interests.

"Get dressed, Darien."

"You're going to take me out? Not too many people are out in this fog, Jack. Doesn't it bother you?"

"No."

"And there really is a place open for business?"

"For your kind of business, yes, and if you don't shut up and get dressed, then maybe slapping your mouth shut will hurry you along." Darien gazed directly at him, and he felt a small tingle of fear creep around his heart. She looked up at him with eyes as cold and as unfeeling as the creepy crawlies that patiently lurked in the shadows.

"Be careful, Jack, because for now I am your whore, but don't push me too far, or I will give you the pain as well as I accept it, perhaps even better than you." Her words were like a verbal slap, and Jack recoiled from them. She sauntered over to him, half-naked, her breasts bouncing slowly against her fat little belly. She took his hands and helped to squeeze them tightly around her fully rounded oversized mounds of fleshy fat.

"I have only given you what I have wanted you to have, that much and no more. Don't think for one moment that you have ever been in control. You have never had any control over any of this, and you are nothing more than a pawn in the same game as I. Oh and Jack, in case you didn't realize it yet, whether you live or die in this game, is a choice that you will never have to make. Your fate was decided long ago." Jack would never admit to Darien that her words gave birth to a deep-seated fear that nearly took his breath away, so instead he retaliated with anger. He pushed her down on to the floor, and using his foot, he ground her face into the carpet while reaching for the small whip.

"And who is going to make this decision, you?" He quickly gave her a taste of the stinging rawhide, and Darien responded by rolling over onto her back and spreading her legs.

"Do it again, Jack, you know how much I love it. Don't you realize that you can't hurt me anymore? The punishment that I desire now is something that you are no longer capable of giving me."

Jack descended on her, whipping her open wetness with the flat palm of his hand, and as he brutally punished her, she encouraged him to be even stronger. Her feet came up under her and she pushed her hips up off the floor begging for more. Jack stood up and stared at the women who lay open before him, a woman he no longer knew. He suddenly realized that this stronger Darien caused him to great arousal. It was a strange thought that popped into his head when he wanted to say aloud, "Who is this masked woman?" He gave himself a little shake inside, and wondered where those stupid dumb thoughts came from. His eyes were wide with a newfound excitement and fear, and suddenly Jack wasn't sure of anything anymore. He put the whip on the bed and reached down to close her legs. Darien stood and faced the man who helped take her down to the center of depravity, and the hidden dark inside spread like an untamed wild fire.

"Who are you, Darien?"

The laughter that came from her did not fit the sorrowful woman that he knew, and then the sound changed, becoming low, and coarse, more like a growl than a laugh.

"Ah Jack, that is the biggest secret of them all." She turned, and looked in the mirror and saw many different faces, all resembling Darien, and it was there, just for a moment, that she almost remembered what it was about mirrors that fascinated her. Then as quickly as it had come to her, it was gone, and Darien calmly returned to the bed so she could finish dressing. She replaced the tattered torn underwear that barely clung to her hips with a brand-new pair, her body still extremely sore, and sensitive as she slide the panties up and over her fresh bruises. This pain that Darien dealt with would have to become nothing more than a minor inconvenience for her. She began to wonder just how much farther she should let Jack go, before he would need to be completely humbled. There was no more room for indecision, she was running out of time, and she decided that Jack simply was not worthy of her, not anymore. Out of the corner of her eye, she saw Jack watch her with a growing fascination, along with another part that he could not keep down. How could she begin to cope with all that was yet to come when the path before her was still so vague?

In all of her life, in all of her fantasies, in all of her inner conflicts, and in all of her love-hate relationships with men, nothing could have prepared her for the love that David released from her. It was for the guardians that she would face Titobind. However, the fate of the rest of the world also rested on two very small shoulders. Through it all, there was the spot where she had locked David away. If you were to ask Darien, she would answer, with the greatest conviction and without hesitation, that she was doing it all because of her love for David.

* * *

When they left the room Darien saw no need to lock her door, there was no one in the building that neither needed nor wanted anything from her. She stopped for just a moment at the bottom of the stairs, and looked down the hallway to where Jimmy used to live. She felt a great sadness at having lost yet another friend. She said a soft gentle prayer for her friend in the hopes that he would somehow find his home, while the wild side of Darien, the lover of pain that she had become, simply shrugged it off. This hardened woman did not become weepy at births, deaths, or at all of the exciting little things in between that mean so much to so many. When would the world wake up and realize that families everywhere are the same. They become excited at little Janet's first step, or Harold's first time without training wheels or Harold's first time with other things. There is a constant excitement being generated in different places, however, from one end of the world to the other, no matter the way of life, it was all for the same reasons. If one really stopped to think about man as a whole, there really is no difference. When their race expires, becoming as extinct as so many other species that had come and gone on this small planet, there will be no exceptions for anyone. Nothing would matter, not race, or color, or names, dead is dead and all dem bones make the same rattle.

Jack opened the door to the outside and the gray fog immediately surrounded him with a kind of familiarity. He opened his arms to enter willingly, and the strange invading fog welcomed him as he disappeared inside. The master of pain emerged a few minutes later covered with gray murk that clung to him with the tenacity of a leech, and he held out his hand to draw Darien to him. She reached for him and began pulling the pieces of fog off his body, listening to it scream, replicating the sound of a hundred dying sirens. Not unlike Moses who parted the Red Sea, Darien parted the gray miasma. However, it was not just her presence that caused it to separate. It gave way in a silent acknowledgment of a deeper power that she carried. It caused the fog to move voluntarily away from Jack and Darien, while the things that hid inside crept back away trying to stay out of her sight.

The heavy cloud of the Titobind rolled back upon itself, and Darien gasped in horror at the number of bodies that lay inside the gloom and despair covering Corral. Some of them began waking as if they had been in the deepest slumber, but most were not waking at all, and every one of them had been food for the fog. She watched as a young woman stood on shaking legs only to find that there were empty spaces where parts of her feet should have been. There was no blood, bone, or jagged tissue; it simply looked as if her foot had grown that way. The same thing had happened to all of the other people lost inside the fog. They were missing pieces of their arms, legs, and in the case of one elderly man, an entire section of his back was gone. The man kept folding over sideways every time he tried to stand. "How is that even possible?" But Darien knew as soon as she walked past them, and the fog rolled back in, the lost souls would fall back into the same trance. The living diseased grayness would continue to feed upon them until there was nothing left to consume.

The fog stayed active on either side of her, rolling and moving as Jack followed behind her, thoroughly humbled in her wake. Darien raised her hands and parted the fog above her head, allowing the all-powerful healing warmth of the sun to spread its warmth inside of her. She drew deeply on the bright rays of hope, and she delighted in the ability to pull inside the healing qualities of its life-giving rays. Darien continued walking down the street, and as the fog closed back over the sky and the people who had been stranded fell back into their sleep.

*Better unaware than to feel the fog eating away at their bodies,* Jack said to himself. He came around next to Darien so that he could walk beside her, having become more than cautious with these new events.

"Do you know where you're going?"

"Of course, Jack," she lied, but then she also knew that something guided her steps. "But I'm curious, where do you think I'm going?"

"To the Pit?" The new and improved Darien mesmerized him.

"Exactly." And to herself she added, *What the fuck is the Pit?*

Darien suddenly stopped as a small whimpering sound caught her attention. It came from off to her right, and she made a small temporary step away from her inevitable fated path. A small child, not more than three, was sitting alone in the fog, and he was already missing his left ear. There were also dozens of red bumps where he had been trying to pull it off to keep it from feeding. Too young to understand, the fog had not been able to lull him into a trance-like state, so the boy sat down while at the same time he tried to pull off the painful puffs. As Darien came near him, the child reached for her, and she immediately picked him up, cradling him, bathing him with her healing warmth. When she looked at him again, he was whole, right down to his new ear.

"Wait," Jack said looking at the boy's replaced ear, "how is that possible?"

"Feel your head, Jack." He was mute in the realization finding the side of his head flat, like his ear never existed.

"Can you still hear me, Jack?"

"Yes," he answered barely audible.

"Well then, why would you have need of two, when this handsome little fellow needs it so much more than you?"

The boy's mother came stumbling through the fog right to Darien, and she cried aloud when she saw that her son was safe. The little boy quickly transferred himself to his mother's arms, and graced Darien with a huge smile. If this mother could safely get her son out of Corral, then Gregory Daniels would grow to become the prominent scientist he was destined to be. Darien opened her hand and a tiny sun danced merrily in her palm. She gave the happy little sun to Gregory, and it began doing exactly what suns are supposed to do, lighting their way back home.

"Let it stay with the boy, and you'll be safe," she said softly as she gently touched the woman's hair. The mother said thank you and quickly followed the lighted path to her home. Darien's actions totally entranced Jack, even more so by the little sun that had seemed to be happy to do her bidding.

"Do you want to tell me what that was?"

Darien smiled a cool, calculated smile back at Jack. "That is none of your business."

They continued walking through the fog, and Darien continued to part it as she went. When they first entered into the gray leeching murk, she forced it apart with their intrusion, made it allow her passage, but now it seemed to be getting stronger, and resentful. It began rolling and boiling much quicker than before, and to Darien, it appeared as though it was becoming very angry. Darien and Jack stood still and watched while it advanced on them, ready to attack, and then sensing the hidden strength in Darien, it retreated. But it did not give up. Darien watched this with a pretended indifference, while all the time she studied it, searching for a weakness. Despite her hopes, it quickly became apparent that the damn stuff had no weakness. How could she fight something that wasn't even solid?

The body count continued piling up as she moved deeper into the center of the fog, and soon they found only body pieces instead of entire corpses. There was a hand here, a nose there, and she found out just how easy it is to pop an eye when you stepped on one. Pieces of people littered the pavement, and it slowed their steps just when Darien wished they were moving faster. She knew someone watched their progress, and Darien was not surprised to see the fog roll back to reveal the Titobind's children decorating either side of a huge black open doorway. A tiny red neon sign blinked on and off above the door as it subtly advertised "The Pit."

"Well fuck me," she said under her breath. "'Bout time that damn blinking sign showed up"

The twins' bodies were stiff and hard as if rigor mortis attacked them, and as Darien drew closer, she saw that it was true. The Titobind's children resembled petrified wood, hard to the touch, and without life. Titobind gave them the ability to live, to breathe, but when they did not accomplish the task of bringing Darien to him, when they failed, he proceeded to take back that life. The strange blank eyes slowly rolled up to reveal the white parts, yet they turned their heads as if they could see Darien's approach. A putrid smell assaulted her as she neared the open doorway, making her gag with nausea from the stench of their death. The twins were rotting. Pieces of flesh hung loosely from their decaying frames. Darien watched with growing apprehension as swelling rancid abscesses grew huge on their already diseased bodies. Titobind promised them memories of nightmares if they failed and for this purpose, they had. Their mouths opened in silent screams while their skin continued to melt away. The abscesses broke open, and little black things without any discernable human shape emerged from their bodies. These black things, covered in goo from being newly reborn, fell with a wet noisy "plop" down onto the pavement. The little shapeless abnormalities quickly lurched and rolled, already instinctively knowing that they needed to hide inside the shadows. As much as she didn't want the memory, it brought to mind the first time that she saw David. He too approached her as a shapeless blob of a shadow.

(Guardians have the ability to hide in shadow.)

Darien looked up towards the black doorway to the Pit that seemed to be growing into a tremendous yawn, and it started to resemble an open mouth.

"Looks like your friend might be hungry." Jack's feeble attempt at humor was lost at this point.

"My friend, huh? So tell me Jack, does this place always greet customers with a growing mouth decorated on each side with rancid statues?"

"Who knows?" answered Jack. "I'm always high when I come here, so it's hard to say. But high or straight, you'd have to be crazy to walk into an open mouth. It's looks too fucking scary in there."

"This never bothered you before?"

"It never looked this bad."

"So what do you say, Jack, shall we go forward?" As she spoke, the volcanic-type holes that were left of the twins still erupted their night monsters at Darien. The shapeless black creepies kept bubbling up from inside of them, and Jack watched with morbid fascination as the twins dissolved right in front of them. Darien smiled and turned around to look at Jack.

"Well, I'm certainly glad he's not my father." Jack's startled look made Darien laugh while the black waterfalls slowed to a gurgle and the last of the shadow creatures literally stepped from inside the remains of the twins. Still Darien hesitated to take the final step over the threshold. Right here, right now, for a few brief seconds she thought there was still time to turn back, to change her mind, but unfortunately turning back was no longer an option. She took one step up towards the cavernous mouth that continued expanding even as they watched. Darien turned back to face Jack.

"I think we might have been safer if we stayed in the fog." Jack turned around and watched the roll and tumble of the gray murk as it closed in on them with an alarming acceleration of speed. He turned back to face Darien.

"Well that seems kind of iffy too, take a look." He gave her hand a small tug and she lifted her face up to watch the advancing gray that had grown huge arms and legs, which it was pumping furiously as it raced to catch them.

"It appears that there is only one way to go." Darien took another step forward and put all of her senses on alert. She looked one more time at Jack and her face emptied of all emotions. The only resemblance to the former Darien was in features only, and even those seemed to have altered slightly. Her eyes scared him the most because what he saw there was nothing less than an expectation of degrading delight that she wanted to find inside the Pit. She licked her lips, smiled a small crooked smile, and said to Jack, "I don't think that you need to be here, so why don't you take your yellow tail, curl it between your legs to protect that precious bone of yours, and get the hell out of here while you still can."

He needed no other coaxing and Jack retreated into the waiting fog. Darien looked, watched, and wondered as the heavy oppressive thickness of the gray fog rolled in around him, just how far Jack would be able to go before succumbing to the same trance-like qualities. His voice echoed all around her and she laughed aloud when his question came at her out of the darkness, "Hey, Darien, who the hell are you anyway?"

She never actually answered him, instead she whispered softly, "Oh, Jack, I really wish I knew."

She took a deep breath and stepped over the doorway, coming instantly into darkness so devoid of light that it seemed blindness was inevitable. Darien turned back around and watched the fog as it hung outside the windows and doors of the surrounding buildings, trying very hard, but not being able to penetrate into anything. She could see the little black things that hid inside, and she watched as they walked through the fog, finding handholds and footholds that helped them climb up to the windows of apartments and businesses. They plastered themselves against the windows and tap tapped for acceptance. Darien smiled a whimsical smile as she briefly released a memory of the little girl who had lived next door to her in a world far removed from this one. This little girl would come to visit Darien and with little tap taps on her back door window, and vocalize quiet loudly, "Let me out, let me out!" of course all the time meaning "Let me in." Darien listened now to the small demons of the night vocalizing in a chorus of screeches, "Let me in, let me in!" The difference was that they had not come to visit; these newborns came because they are hungry. They flattened themselves like pancakes against the glass, they wiggled and they squirmed, and they made sucking noises, while at the same time the extended appendage continued with its maddening tap-tapping noises. As hungry as these things were, she had to wonder just how long Jack would really live.

Darien turned back around to face the pit and she knew, without looking, that the outside world had disappeared, and she was alone in the dark; a black as dark as the cavern she toured with her family when she was a little girl. The guide put out the lights, and let them stand inside the underground where it is always night. He even went so far as to instruct them to hold a hand up in front of their faces, then asked if they were sure it was there, because even if you touched your face with it, you still could not see. A total deprivation of light, and Darien knew if left alone in this dark she would soon be in doubt if there was solid ground under her, or if she was going to float forever without body or mind.

A light appeared off in the distance, a single star shining in this darkest of dark, and Darien had no choice but to watch as it jiggled and bounced its way through the never-ending night of despair. The jiggle came closer and closer until it rested directly in front of her. It was a miniature lantern and holding the lantern was an equally miniature hand, and she watched curiously as another small hand came out of the darkness to turn up the fire. Darien was face to face with a dwarf who dressed like a court jester, and she felt as if she should know this little man. It appeared that the Titobind was not without a sense of humor. The pint-sized jester proceeded to shake the light at her, to claim her full attention, as if there was something else in the dark that could.

"Time, little queen, to play the game, pleasure/pain, pleasure/pain, all the same, all the same."

Darien rolled her eyes in total aversion, she hated stupid fucking riddles and she had been plagued with the same one all of her life and as far as "playing the game," that was for Sibby and she refused to let her out! The pint-sized jester chuckled and shook the light as he watched the changes taking place in Darien. Was it possible that Tianato Morebind knew about the separate personalities that still lived inside of Darien? He bound their bodies to him, but did he bind their thoughts as well?

"David," she prayed silently, "if ever you needed to guard your thoughts and the others as well, do it now before Sibby comes out, because I believe that is who Titobind is looking for, my weakest side. If he releases Sibby, she will tell him what I hide inside. Do it, David, Keep Him Out!"

The jester suddenly looked confused, as if he had lost his train of thought, then just as quickly his face brightened in the lantern light as he smiled and said, "Darien, Darien, where for art thou, sweet Darien?" There began a tremendous struggle inside of her as the personalities once again began their internal battle for dominance.

"Mary, Mary, quite contrary, how dost thou pussy weep?" The jester danced from foot to foot, taking great delight in the dazed woman before him.

"Sibby Sibby bo bibby, banana nana fo fibby, me my mo mibi, come out come out wherever you are." Tears fell from her eyes and Sibby began her eternal weeping in great exasperation "Little slut, little slut, whom so ever pulls the sword from the stone shall be king, oh no I mean queen." Darien fell to her knees releasing great gasps for air as she struggled to breathe through the engulfing darkness.

"What did you think, what did you think, Little Miss Pink, Little Miss Pink, that the master would be so easy? That he would say 'come and get me, here I am, here I go,' and you win? I think not! He thinks not! Time to learn, time to stay and play the game!"

Darien pulled from herself an inner strength, shook her head to clear her thoughts, and turned to face the silly court jester. Her strength was part guardian, part red dragon, or maybe it came from the healing powers of the smiles so generously shared. Or maybe it was because Tanner emerged from the darkness, grabbed the little gnat by the scruff of the neck, and lifted him off his feet. The jester's arms and legs swung wildly and Darien said with hatred, "Squash him like a little bug, Tanner, the annoying pest that he is." Tanner tossed him away into the darkness, but not before he took the lantern from his sweaty little hand. They heard a tremendous cracking come out of the night, and the jester's yell of terror was cut off mid-scream.

"Sounds like someone stepped on the little bugger."

Tanner did not have time to answer her. A large hook suddenly appeared out of the night, picked him up by the back of his shirt, to carry him away, and in the darkness she heard him cry out, "Daaiirreennn!" Then he was gone.

A small sob escaped from Darien as she stood alone again in the impenetrable perpetual night. Almost immediately, another light came bouncing through the gloom, bobbing and weaving directly towards her, exactly like the first one. She barely had time to say, "Oh God, Tanner, I'm so sorry," when another court jester stood before her quickly bringing an intense feeling of déjà vu.

"It's time, little queen, to play the game, pleasure/pain, pleasure/pain, all the same, all the..."

He never finished because Darien screamed at him, "Shut up, you little fuck!" And she punched him squarely in the mouth, knocking him back into the black night that spit him out. Darien triumphantly bent down and picked up his little lantern.

"How's that for pain, you little bastard." She held up the light in her hand, and began moving forward when the floor unexpectedly dropped out from under her. She fell down as it turned into a kind of cold hard slide. Darien slowly spiraled downwards on the huge metal ramp, her hand holding tight to a lantern she didn't want to lose. She moved around to gain comfortable seating, because her descent was at such an angle that it allowed her slide a leisurely pace. It also gave her time to search for something to hold onto, but her attempts at stopping the slide failed when she found nothing to grab. There was only slick, cold metal everywhere she touched. The only thing Darien could do was to sit, enjoy the ride, and pray that Tanner would be okay.

\* \* \*

Suspended from a hook by the back of his shirt, an invisible pulley carried Tanner forward through the night. He lost track of time, and just when the pressure of hanging became almost unbearable, it suddenly came to a quick stop. His arms and legs swung from side the side, the resulting reaction to the jerking motion from the hook. He remembered his sixth-grade science class and his teacher Mr. Roy Oblique who stood in front of the class, reciting to them:

"For each and every action, there is always an equal and opposite reaction."

Basic science, basic school when everything had been so uncomplicated, or was it? He remembered so much, so many things came back to him as he hung swinging with reaction. Some of the things that came back to him were surprising in the fact that he even remembered them at all.

Little Tyler was outside playing in his backyard sandbox with his newly acquired dump trucks, while his mother watched him from the kitchen window. It was nearing 5:00 p.m., and she busily prepared food for dinner, expecting Charlie Tanner to arrive home very shortly. The young mother looked up causally from her potato peeling, and to her horror, Elizabeth saw a huge German shepherd wander into their backyard. The dog walked funny, sort've staggering as if it had been on a drinking binge, having become quite tipsy. It turned its muzzle up towards the window, and she saw the white foam hanging from its mouth as the dog curled its lips back to expose sharp canine fangs.

"Tyler!" she screamed. "Oh my God, rabies!" Elizabeth flung open the cellar door, ran down several steps, and grabbed Charlie's ax off the wall. She ran back upstairs, panting heavily as she opened the back door just in time to see everything happen in slow motion. Tyler automatically raised his arms for protection, and the dog clamped its drooling fangs down on his arm. The young child let loose with a blood-curdling scream filled with such pure terror that it made his mother's hair stand on end. Charlie Tanner was just pulling into the driveway when he heard the scream.

"What the hell?" escaped from his mouth and his heart started to beat faster as he recognized that the scream came from Tyler. Charlie's run around the corner of his house caused his immaculately placed hair to fly askew in the wind, and his tie flopped up over his shoulder. He heard his wife scream along with his son, and his heart beat faster than he ever thought possible. It began a fear that no parent or spouse ever wants to feel.

His wife shouted, "Let him go, you son of a bitch!" Then he head a sound that he would hear every day for the rest of his life, and it was the sound of metal crunching bone. Charlie Tanner came around the corner of his simple ranch-style home and saw his wife trying to pry the dog's mouth off his son's arm. There was so much blood that Charlie couldn't tell if it belonged to his son, his wife, or the dog.

"Jesus, criminy."

"Oh, God, Charlie, help me." He walked over to her, not sure if he was getting any closer until he knelt down beside them. Little Tyler stopped screaming, and moving, capable of only lying still, with eyes wide open, unblinking, unseeing.

"He's going into shock, Lizzy," Charlie said, and then he looked at the dog that held the same wide-eyed stare as his son. The dog's paws twitched and jumped, the nerves still reacting from the ax blow. Tyler could hear the approaching sirens, but he lay unblinking as his parents pulled the dog's jaws off his arm.

Elizabeth started sobbing hysterically after they were in their car, and on their way to the hospital, she tried to talk between the sobs: "I'm, I'm sss sa sa sorry, Char-(hic)-lee."

"It's okay, Elizabeth, you couldn't know. You did what you had to do and Tyler will be okay." The siren that had carried him to the hospital slowly faded from his thoughts into the background and Tanner became aware again of where he was. He blinked his eyes, finding that he had been staring at the little pinpoints of scarring that remained on his arm.

"Damn, I had totally forgotten about that." His voice echoed around him, seeming to bounce off an oppressive black, a thickness of night that was almost liquid in its content. He jerked his head up as he heard a noise, unmistakable in its sound, the firing of a single machine gun, the way he remembered it, bursting to life in the quiet of the jungle. He felt the bite of the bullet as it entered his upper thigh, the sting of another one hitting his shoulder and then one more grazed his side.

"God!" he cried between clenched teeth as the bullets bit deep with a red-hot fire of penetration.

A sudden bright glare caused Tanner to cover his eyes until they could adjust to the light. Slowly he parted his fingers, allowing the light in a little at a time, while at the same moment he sensed commotion below his feet. He hesitantly looked downwards. The same scream of ultimate terror escaped from his throat as when he had been that small child of three.

Hundreds of Vietnamese stared up at him from the pit where Tanner, unable to get away, dangled like an oversized piece of bait. He saw withered old women, young mothers, children, infants, pregnant women, and enemy soldiers, all reaching for the baited American. Tanner screamed again as the bodies below him began to rise. They climbed over and on top of one another trying to get to the symbol that brought so much death and destruction to their country. There were so many of them, and as Tanner looked down he found that his clothes had mysteriously become army fatigues. He dripped blood down onto the clamoring people below and just as a skeletal hand grabbed for his foot, Tanner pulled it up quickly, taking the person's bony hand with it. Then he saw that they were dead, all of them were dead! He could see more of them now, with rotted decaying skin pulled back to reveal bone. His instinct for survival outweighed the pain of the bleeding bullet wounds and Tanner kicked wildly, connecting with someone's head, and he watched it go flying off the dead thing's shoulders leaving behind a long spray of bugs and maggots. The queen screamed inside his mind, from a play long forgotten, "Off with his head!" Well, yes it seemed appropriate. There were so many, so many, climbing over each other, and falling apart right in front of him. Tanner's mind shifted into overdrive and he raised a rifle that he didn't know he had until now, and he fired for the preservation of own life.

The lights abruptly went out, except for one brightly lit star shining off in the distance. Tanner breathed in deep scared breaths, trembling violently as the aftershock passed through him. The little star that was so far away bobbed closer and closer until it was right next to his face. Tanner felt firmness under his feet but was afraid for the hook to let him go.

"What if it was another illusion and the ground's not there, and I'm still hanging over a real pit?"

A hand appeared out of the darkness and turned up the light on the lantern. It was the same jester and his mouth curved up with a funny little smile as he began to sing to Tanner: "Somethin's happening here." Tanner remembered that song, he remembered Kent State University at the height of the Vietnam war and the righteous protestors that didn't have to watch their friends die.

"What it is ain't exactly clear." He remembered King's march on the White House, the man who stood bravely for peace and equality among all men.

"Stop, heeeyyy, what's that sound, everybody look what's goin' down." A thousand voices raised in protest against all the indignities imposed on a helpless population by a few power-hungry dictators.

"Shut up, you little fuck." His anger took shape in his fist, and he punched the jester square in the face. The little dwarf went flying backwards, once again dropping his little lantern.

"For each and every action." He picked up the lantern and turned up the light as bright as it would go to push back the thickening night; however, it wasn't much help because aside from lighting the immediate area, Tanner still couldn't see. It was as if an invisible wall of dark kept stopping the light. Without any warning, the ground dropped out from under him and he fell down to his knees, while at the same time he began to move downwards on a spiraling slide. It was not a steep slide, because he was moving very slowly and it became obvious as he searched for something to grab onto to try to stop his slow descent, there wasn't anything. He pulled his feet up under himself and tried to plant them firmly on the slide. It stopped him temporarily but then he started to turn sideways, and he would soon be going down backwards.

"This is not good; I have to face forward to see where I'm going." Tanner put his legs straight again, and although it stopped his turning, he realized that he was powerless to do anything except sit back, enjoy the ride, and take in as much of his immediate predicament as possible.

Tanner put his hands palms down on each side of his body to let them take in the texture of the slide. He found it to be as smooth as glass and as slippery as ice. It was cool to the touch and felt like metal, perhaps sheet metal, except much stronger. He did not dare to reach over and touch the sides because Tanner could see that they were razor sharp and besides, right now, he was probably in the safest position he could be in. There was no telling what would happen if he fell off the side, or what could possibly be waiting below.

\* \* \*

Darien laid her hands palms down on the slide feeling the cool slickness of the metal. Her pant legs rose uncomfortably from the continuous downward spiral, and she could not move enough to correct the situation. This continued for an undetermined period until the angle of the slide slowly tapered off, finally becoming level, and Darien stopped moving downwards. A strange illumination came on in a small room right next to the slide, jumping into view, becoming an instantaneous creation just for her. Darien was surprised at how, even with her own little lantern, the room stayed hidden, her light never penetrating beyond the boundaries of the slide. The light inside the room glowed with a soft red luminescence, and it gave an odd uneasiness to the strange objects hanging on the wall. Darien recognized some of them, while some of the others gave her no clue as to their purpose, and she was not sure if she wanted to find out.

A young girl walked into the room dressed like one of the models in Darien's "forbidden" magazine. Her tightly laced corset caused her young breasts to bulge upwards over the top, leaving barely enough material to cover the nipples. The girl wore red lace nylons held up by black lace garters. The corset ended just over her hips, and there was nothing after that except the projected little girl innocence that the shaving provided. The young girl walked smoothly, naturally in high, red spiked heels, surprising Darien by the ease in which she handled the extremely high shoe. The only place she had seen shoes like that was in a Fredrick's of Hollywood catalog, and now she watched someone actually walking in them! Darien always believed that no one except cartoon characters could walk in spike heels, which brought to mind a quick flash picture of Jessica Rabbit.

This memory brought about a brief sultry smile that quickly vanished when two muscular men entered the room dragging an elderly man between them. From what Darien could see, he had already been through his own extreme tortures. The burly bodyguards hung the old man between two posts, bound him with heavy chains, and he never even raised his head or opened his mouth to protest. His strength seemed to be gone as he sagged against his restraints. The young woman walked over to the wall and picked up a whip compiled of at least twenty straps of leather all bound tightly together into the handle. Darien's eyes widened as the young woman took the handle, rubbed it down between her legs, and then brought it up under the man's nose. If laughing had been acceptable at this point, then Darien would have laughed herself silly when she saw the man's head jerk backwards as the woman's natural vaginal scent reacted on him like smelling salts.

(Darien knew deep inside that this was the pivotal turning point in her need for acceptance into Titobind's world. This final masochistic education into the bottom depths of despair and desperation began here, now. Jack was just a small taste of what was to come, but nothing could have prepared her for the events that would nearly tear her apart.)

The pathway to the room was easily accessible from where Darien sat, and as interested as she was in participating, for the moment, she chose voyeurism. The old man stuck out his tongue and began to lick the handle of the whip, drooling with excitement. Darien found it incredible that he wanted to have more when the obvious abuse portrayed itself in a multitude of bruises and in many places, dried blood. The young woman suddenly jerked the handle away, turned the whip around, and in one clean motion, flogged him several times across the chest. He never cried out, and Darien saw his apparent excitement. He loved this. The tormentor placed her spiked heel on his leg, balancing expertly on one foot while she nudged his testes with the toe of her shoe. She started to put pressure on him, and Darien cringed when she saw the old man's body stiffen with pleasure.

She closed her eyes, and when she opened them again, Darien was looking out through the eyes of the young woman. Her body felt young and supple, no stretch marks, no flabby belly, just a young, beautiful, perfect body. She felt so new, coming alive with hidden desires, a need for the punishment that Jack taught her. Her body tingled with anticipation. There was a whole array of tools for her to choose from, and the first one she picked up was a knife to cut away the old man's black leather bikinis. With every touch, his wrinkled body responded with increasing excitement. His penis stood straight up, as hard as any young man. Darien walked back to the wall and picked up a dildo with two attached straps, and hanging from the end of those straps were two small clamps. The old man watched her with alert eyes waiting anxiously for the pleasure of his pain. Darien lifted her leg, balancing herself as expertly as the young girl before and she let him see her wide open and wet. The old man licked his lips, and Darien closed her eyes letting the feelings grow inside of her.

When she opened her eyes again, she found herself sitting back on the slide and feeling a tremendous loss at the displacement. She watched as the young woman diligently fitted the dildo in place, and she was in the process of fitting the clamps to his testicles when the slide started to slope downwards again. The descent caused Darien to resume the same downward spiral as slowly and as purposely as before. Her body felt flushed with excited as the feelings of power that she experienced over the elderly man traveled through her. The true reasons for her being there were slowly slipping away *(he can take your memories, Darien)* and all she wanted now was the physical satisfaction. She fidgeted on the cool metal as her descent continued, and the jester's words of pleasure/pain mixed with a rhyme from a riddle told to her so many years ago.

Unless you remain to be seen, through pleasure-pain for little queen.

Unknown to her on the other side of the room, Tanner sat watching everything that Darien did, with one exception; he abhorred the events unfolding in front of him, but was helpless to stop them. Together they continued moving downwards, and Darien could not contain her anxiousness at wanting to participate.

The slide leveled off again, another room opened much the same as before, and this time it was a man who entered first. His features remained hidden behind a leather mask, but his perfect flawless physique was tauntingly visible. She wondered briefly about the face under the mask; however, her curiosity about his features was quickly forgotten when he beckoned for Darien to come forward. Her mind slipped away, her sane thoughts replaced by the need burning inside, and she responded. The man silently directed her to remove her clothes, and she obeyed. She stood before him, unashamed, her feet slightly apart, her head bowed in submission, exactly as Jack had taught her to do. The leather-faced man approached her and then lifted her head with the handle of the whip, allowing the black leather straps to touch lightly over her breasts. She trembled from his touch, excited beyond the ability to think and to reason, wanting only to experience the biting edge of the pain that would bring her the pleasure.

The pain giver, the master of the pit, fastened a wide leather belt around her waist, and then he methodically threaded chains through the loops on each side. These he securely linked to the chains fastened to the brackets on the wall. Darien felt the sting of the whip on her legs, and she obediently moved them further apart. The man bent down, locked ankle cuffs into place, and then threaded chains through them, securing them to the wall as well. Her bonds were not overly tight, she would be able to move, but unless deliberately released, Darien would not be able to get away. The man in front of her expertly flipped the whip up between her legs, and three possibly four of the leather straps hit their mark causing her head to fly back in an unexpected reaction, releasing an immediate desire for more.

"Whom do you love, Darien?" His voice was even, smooth, strong and masculine, bringing about an even deeper need.

She lifted her head to see her new master and her face filled with the deep-seated desire for his complete domination. She answered him throatily, "I love the Giver of Pain."

"And whom do you serve, sweet Darien?"

Her face changed to one of total acceptance, total submission, completing her role into what she was becoming. She looked at him from under a mask of learned capitulation, and answered with all the honesty she could summon. "I serve no one but the Titobind."

Screeching laughter filled the darkness along with Tanner's sighing refusal to accept what was happening while his quiet protest of "No, Darien" went unheard. Darien breathed heavily, her breasts swelling with every gasp of air as she spoke to the Giver of Pain, quietly begging for more.

Inside the pyramid that floated on the cold fires fueled by the evil Titobind, he entwined and wound the weeping guardians, pulling them to him. He wove and rebound them with the ever-growing black extensions of his disease. The world outside of his world lay covered in a fog that continued growing and spreading, becoming all consuming until it had nearly covered the great state of Texas. Tianato Morebind assured himself of an easy victory, and yet was still somewhat suspicious. For a strange inexplicable reason, he had not expected the conquering of Darien to have been so easy. He could watch her if he wished, participate in her pain if he so desired, or he could reach out and bind her to him now. However, he did not want to bind her too soon, as the pleasure and the fun he was deriving from this particular game was far too enjoyable. He was so certain of an easy victory that he decided to let Darien come to him. After all, he knew where to find her, realizing that a dark desire began to grow on the day of her conception.

Darien arched her neck against the sting of the whip while the man held tight to the chain that led to the clamps he placed on her erect nipples. Her passion rose to heights she never experienced before, and her body shook with an intense tension that screamed of needing release from her sexual prison. There was nothing left in Darien save a desire for the little queen's pleasure/pain.

"Give me more," she said between clenched teeth and she spread her legs wide waiting for her pleasure. It came as she felt the pressure of something entering inside of her. The Pain Giver filled her from behind, and her body quivered against the physical restraints. The man stood in front of her, ready to bring her fully into their world. Blister burns from the hot wax dotted her skin, criss-cross marks from the whip swelled bright red, and numerous other tortures revealed damages to her body, but despite this, Darien continued to desire pain. The deliverer of her punishment began pushing his member up inside of her, and her body rocked with mounting orgasm.

"Who am I?" he asked as his erection entered her.

"You are the Giver of Pain." She hissed as she realized it had started.

"You serve the Titobind, Darien, why?" He was fully into her now, thrusting up inside of her body.

"Because there is no one else to serve, but the Titobind."

Her body rocked and he lifted her completely off the ground. She wrapped herself around the Pain Giver as she came into her own, stiffening with a release unlike any other she ever experienced. Tanner could not bear to watch as he turned his head away, unashamed in the tears he wept for Darien. The slide that he was standing on now showed him stairs, but Tanner refused to leave and he closed his eyes away from her. When he opened them again, he was standing directly in front of Darien, having taken the place of her torturer. His body nearly crumpled to the floor with the sudden impact of her added weight, along with the awareness of waking in the place of the Pain Giver. The guardians gave to Tanner the very last bit of the strength that they used to fight Titobind against their capture, for Darien.

"I am here," he whispered softly in her ear. "Don't be afraid."

"Oh God, Tanner." She trembled and wept against him. "Promise me you won't leave."

"I will stay, Darien, forever if you need." He set her slowly back on her feet and undid her bindings. She collapsed to the floor with exhaustion, and was immediately sorry that she made him promise to stay. Tanner needed to survive and she needed him to be stronger than she could ever be. For this reason, she realized that she had to ask him to go back. Darien slowly stood, grateful as Tanner patiently helped her to dress. His touch was the gentle touch of a true love, and Darien took his hand, guided it to her mouth, kissing it softly. He softly caressed her face, one of the few parts of her body that was not bruised and aching. Darien looked at Tanner, drinking in his scruffy features, the thin haggard look from too many years of smoking, the clear blue eyes and above that his small receding hairline. She placed herself deep inside his long arms pressing her face against his small hard chest. He knew before she asked what was going to happen, and he knew that he would do whatever it took to help Darien win in the evil game that they knowingly played. The dim light in the room of pain became steadily dimmer, and soon they would again be in total darkness. Then as unexpectedly as before, a small sliver of light appeared off in the distance, weaving and bobbing its way towards them.

"I think if all the lights came on we would find ourselves in a very genuine labyrinth," Tanner whispered to Darien as he helped steady her on legs that remained somewhat shaky.

"What makes you say that?"

"From what I can tell, even in the darkness, we were on opposite sides of these rooms, on different slides, but moving in the same direction.

That light is coming towards us is from a different angle, but will eventually reach us. In a labyrinth there are many different paths that cross and intersect which is what seems to be going on in here."

"That light up ahead can mean only one thing."

"Yep, our friend is back."

A small hand reached out of the darkness and turned up the light on his lantern, and it showed them both that Jester had indeed returned. He stood grinning at them and it was all Darien could do to resist the urge to take the ends of his pointy little hat, wrap it around his neck, and strangle the little bastard.

"It's the end of the world as we know it," it was singing again.

"It's the end of the world as we know it and I…" Tanner drew back his fist.

"Wait, don't hit him." He looked at her, a bit puzzled with her sudden change of heart.

"Tanner, I'm sorry I asked you to stay, but you already know that I have to go on by myself. We both know it. So maybe if we make nice with the little toad he'll show you the way out. Then all that I will have to do is convince him to show me the rest of the way in."

"It's the end of the world as we know it." The jester started doing his own little dance.

"And I feel fine."

"Hey, Jester, do you think you could show my friend Tanner the way out of here?" Darien asked him. Jester stopped doing his little dance and looked up at the two prisoners.

"They're coming to take me away, ha ha. They're coming to take us away, ha ha."

"Oh good, now look at what you've done," Tanner said in exasperation.

"I haven't done anything. Come on, you've got to try and go somewhere."

"To the Funny Farm." The jester grinned evilly and continued dancing. He turned around, proceeded to lift one foot up and put it down, then he followed with the other foot, lifting it up high and then putting it down. The rhythm continued faster and harder until he had started to dance away into Tanner's preconceived labyrinth.

"They're coming to take me away, ha ha." His light was disappearing quickly as he moved into the darkness.

"Go, Tanner, quickly, follow him, hurry!" Darien could not disguise the urgency in her voice as she pushed him away. Tanner looked back only once to see Darien's little face staring at him as he moved to catch up to the jester.

"To the funny farm." They disappeared into the darkness, leaving Darien with a fading glow of red that barely illuminated a new room of pain and the return of a Pain Giver. He stood in the doorway again beckoning her to enter.

"Ha ha he he ho ho," came echoing out of the darkness, followed by a gravelly voice strained and full of emotion.

"....careful....I....you." Darien filled in the blanks, and in her mind, there was "Be careful, I love you."

She hugged her body close, looked down at her toes, and smiled. Darien wiggled them as she were burying them in the warm sand before turning around to see if the Pain Giver still watched her. He was watching, and he walked over to the doorway to stand directly in front of her. She could smell his maleness, which caused her excitement to rise once more. He gestured for her to return, beckoning with his finger, and God help her, without wanting to, her body responded. She closed her eyes, took a deep breath, and then extended her hand to him. Darien heard the voice then; it came to her like a bomb going off inside her head, and she thought for a minute that her eyes were going to explode out of her face. Her ears were bleeding, as were her eyes and nose, along with a trickle of blood from her mouth. She fell to the ground, crumbling like a rag doll that had no structure to support its body. The Pain Giver was gone, and in his place were swirling pieces of the Titobind's black extensions.

He was so close, the coldness of his black heart forming an invisible barrier around her already battered body.

She staggered to her feet, shaking from the effort of trying to keep his presence out of her head. She heard its laughter, a hideous sound grotesquely twisted, a match for the misshapen body, and the eternally evil mind.

Suddenly the laughter was gone, Darien felt it pull away, but she also felt that as it retreated, it tried to grab pieces of her in an effort to drag away her secrets. Unfortunately as it retreated, it also took what little bit of light had been left and darkness fell upon Darien. If it was this close, why didn't it just take her? The absolute dark disorientated her perceptions, and she could not tell if she was sitting, standing, or lying down. However, she was lying on the ground, too scared to move, not sure what to do, not even sure at first if the light that appeared off in the distance was real. It moved up and down as it came closer and then she heard a humming with the light. Out of the darkness came the same chubby hand and it turned up the flame to melt away the perpetual night. Darien lay on the ground, so afraid she could not stop shaking, and the jester started to dance and laugh. He turned a grotesquely ugly face to her and recited:

"Fe fi fo fum, I smell the blood of Darien dumb."

"Be she live...." The face was changing, growing out of proportion, twisting into an evil thing.

"Or be she dead..." Jester was growing huge sharp fangs honed to razor sharpness and dripping with salvia.

"I'll grind her bones...." His mouth widened into a huge cavernous door like the one they entered into and found this living nightmare.

"And slip her the wonderful weenie!" Jester broke into great roars of laughter; Darien screamed and closed her eyes. The next time her eyes opened and her mind could remember, the scream was all she heard, and the face that she saw was that of the Jester turned to Pain Giver.

Darien screamed in terror.

She screamed from the intense pain that moved inside of her, while every part of her body trembled.

Not one part of her body remained free of bruises or bleeding. Through clenched teeth and with a body soaked through with perspiration and blood, Darien looked with hatred at the Pain Giver. Through the pain, through the growing hatred of the Titobind, she made herself speak precisely and clearly, and most empathetically when she humbly begged:

"Please, sir, may I have some more?"

# CHAPTER ELEVEN

# SEEK AND YE SHALL FIND

Jester kept court near the prone form of Darien.

She labored for each breath, her body shaking with each exhausting effort to pull in the thick air. The jester had assessed her injuries and concluded that there were two ribs possibly broken, and several were cracked for sure. If they snapped and punctured a lung, then Jester would be at a loss, and Darien Dumb would become Darien Dead. The small court comedian lit several lanterns to try to shed enough light and provide some warmth to her shivering body.

"I could lay a blanket for her." The voice that came out of the darkness was low and menacing, even as it offered help.

"Forgive me, sir, but she needs to be warmed, not made to freeze under the blanket of cold that you would provide."

"I could squash you with one small squeeze between my thumb and forefinger, like the tiny little bug that you are, so take care what you say."

*It's not like you haven't already done that,* the jester said to himself.

"The light will warm her, provide us with more." There was no response to jester's request, and as the minutes ticked by, he gave up on receiving the requested light. At the same time he tried to massage warmth back into her body, but there were not too many places he could touch that did not cause her to cry out from the pain. Suddenly an answer to his previously asked question penetrated the darkness.

"I cannot provide the light or the warmth, the night is my mother and it is from the nurturing of her cold ebony love that I am strong. When Darien comes to me, and I make her a permanent part of the night, she will no longer need the warmth."

Jester felt its evil presence retreat from their immediate surroundings but he could not be sure if he was completely gone. Darien opened her eyes only to close them again, and Jester moved along the small cot-like table until he stood right next to her face.

"Are you awake?"

She shook her head with a yes response, as she ran her tongue over cracked and swollen lips.

"Water, please," she croaked out. The dwarf disappeared and returned immediately with a small glass of water. He dipped his fingertips in the water and ran the wart-covered, stunted fingers over her lips. She gratefully opened her mouth so that a few drops of water fell inside. Jester repeated this several times until Darien fully opened her eyes and kept them open. Her body ached with the effort it took just to perform this simple task, and she knew despite the pain, she needed to continue. With concentrated effort, she tried to sit up. Her arms trembled and threatened to collapse under her until Jester touched her. He helped her as gently as possible into a sitting position, wincing when she winced as the pain became overwhelming to her senses. Her hand reached out for the glass of water, but it shook so badly the water threatened to spill over the side. The new and improved jester placed his misshapen hand over hers, helping Darien to bring the glass to her mouth. She drank greedily, which caused some of the water to escape from the corner of her mouth. She continued to drink as the water ran down her chin, and she didn't stop until she felt it spill onto her lap. After pushing the glass aside, Darien managed to speak through chattering teeth.

"It's so cold hhere."

"You should know by now that there is no warmth in Titobind." Darien watched as the jester very tenderly rubbed one of her legs and then the other, trying to restore some circulation to her body. Her hands touched the bandage around her middle, the one that kept her ribs from causing her excruciating pain.

"Why are you helping me?"

"It is his wish that I tend you, so that you may yet serve him." Darien fell quiet to think about her situation, and to decide what her next move would be. The Titobind was playing his hand at leisure, in a game that was still the basis of the riddle.

"Help me, Jester, here." Darien tried to swing her legs over the side of the table.

"I'm still inside the Pit aren't I?" It came across more as a statement than a question.

"Yes." Jester picked up her legs and keeping them together, he moved them over the side of the table. Darien let out a huge moan as her sore body rebelled against what she forced it to do.

"Please help me undo these bandages." Jester proceeded to do as Darien requested.

"I must be free of restraints in order to heal."

"He waits for you to come; he thinks he has won."

"I know this, Jester, what do you think all of this was for? You can't really believe that I did all this for my own pleasure." While she waited for an answer, Darien wondered if the Jester, who is obviously a part of the Titobind, was inadvertently allowing the monster privy to their conversation. She voiced her concerns.

"Do you have a mind of your own, or are your thoughts his thoughts? Do I betray myself as I speak to you?"

"He is gone from both our minds."

"Titobind does not enter me."

"You think not?"

"He cannot, not completely." Jester finished removing her bandages and her hand automatically went to her side, putting pressure back on her ribs. She slowly let out the air that she had unknowingly been holding inside.

"Whom do you serve, Jester?"

"I serve the Titobind and no one else."

"Will you lead me to him?"

"No, you must find the way yourself."

"Why?"

"Because those are the rules." This was maddening for Darien, there is no line of reasoning, only do and don't do, no why or why not and certainly no answers.

"Whose fucking rules?" Darien watched, and observed Jester and she could almost see inside him as he calculated an answer.

"I don't know whose fucking rules. I only know that they are."

"What are you really doing here, Jester?" It must have been hard for him to try to reason this in his mind because his brow became more furrowed than it already was, and it looked as if making him think physically hurt him. Darien studied the jester, his gnarled wrinkled face, the strange way his body seemed to be twisted to one side, and the short pudgy hands covered with hairy growths of tremendous size.

(There was a crooked man.)

The thought was there, and then just as quickly; gone.

"Are you a part of your twisted master, Jester?"

"Yes, he made me; it's all just a part of playing the game his way. It always has been. I'm surprised that you didn't figure this out." The jester stood looking up at her as she shivered in the cold and Darien started to think that maybe "Darien Dumb" was a good way to refer to her. She slowly opened her hand and then closed her eyes, as she drew from the strength that she kept hidden.

"You are about to see and experience a wonderful thing, Jester, and even though you serve the Titobind, you must keep this secret from him. If you can do this for me and for all the guardians, then in the end you will be set free." Jester nodded his head so vigorously in agreement that Darien practically saw the little fuckers with their fire hammers go rolling off to the side. She smiled down at the jester, and at that moment, despite her plainness, the beauty inside shone through, and she opened her hand to reveal merrily dancing light radiating warmth from a tiny sun. It was part of the goodness from the absorbed guardian. Darien raised her hand slowly above her head, and the light grew brighter, warmer, until it filled the entire room in a glory of healing warmth. It penetrated her body, and Jester watched in amazed wonder as the bruises began to fade. Her hand came away from her side, and the pain that had been so obvious on her face before was now gone. Darien's head went back, and she raised her other hand to take back the sun and to draw the power of the guardian once more into hiding. A soft warm breeze wound its way around them, and when she looked at Jester it was with eyes that sparkled with laughter, her face softened with endless love for all that lived, and her smile showed all the gentle goodness of the guardians themselves. This wonderful warm light continued to fade until once again all that was left was the light from Jester's little lantern, along with the look of astonishment frozen in place on his misshapen features.

"The power you carry is very strong, Darien, but I do not know if it will be enough to defeat the Titobind. That is why you have come isn't it, to try and defeat the evil?"

Darien slid off the table back to her feet, bending and stretching her arms and legs trying pushing the muscles back into flexibility so that she could move again without the pain. "You can be set free, Jester, if you truly want it, and if I win the game."

He was quiet one more time as he put back on his thinking face, a face that could not hide the grinding of wheels and gears inside his little mind. Darien was surprised at his answer but she understood his reasoning.

"I belong to the night, I always have. Things like me are things that people like you do not like to see. We remind them of how they would look if the outside could sometimes reflect the inside." His answer also brought tears to her eyes because the words he spoke carried truth.

"Is it always worth it, Darien, to seek the absolute truth? Sometimes the answers we receive are not the ones we want, and in the end you will face what you are."

"It is what I have wanted from the beginning to know who and what I am."

"The divine plan?"

"Yes," she answered quietly.

"Then I have but one thing to say to you."

"And what would that be?"

"Seek and ye shall find." Jester handed Darien his little lantern, and slowly danced away into the darkness. She watched as he disappeared into the perpetual night, the little man who was a strange enigma in this whole perplexing, continually unfolding living nightmare.

Darien shivered against the cold that enveloped her again, but she was not nearly as cold as she was before, and this caused her concern. Was she was becoming used to the cold? Or was it because the coldness of the evil Titobind was finally seeping into and becoming a real part of what she was. The woman sent on the quest raised the lantern, and was not surprised when the darkness allowed the light only a few feet of penetration. Darien reasoned that it was so she could not tell what she was walking into. Another part of their stupid game. She tried to relax and open her mind for a feel of intuition, or perhaps a nudge in the right direction. Instead of a needed guidance, all that came to her were images of the Pain Giver, and the tortures that he inflicted on her when she was before him, bound in helpless submission.

She remembered crying for him to stop, and screaming for him to be merciful. However, in the end she looked at him without fear, with a lust unmatched by anyone, and the truth was there when she had asked, "Please, sir, can I have some more?" And it is a truth that she did not want to admit to.

It was happening right now. She felt it growing. Darien needed the punishment, and she wanted the pain. The lust grew, consuming her like a live demon inside. Her body screamed, "Feed me!", and she ran forward into the night as if she knew the labyrinth by heart.

Up and down the stairs, in and out through the alcoves, Darien ran as the fire and the lust continued to grow, threatening to consume her completely. The light from Jester's lantern shone only a few feet in front of her, and she ran through the twists and turns knowing where they were before she reached them. She passed rooms filled with unspeakable evils, horrifying tortures, and sometimes she would slow down to see what was ultimately waiting for her at the end of her quest.

"These are my rooms of dreams now, all of them are mine." Her voice was thick, full of emotions, and her body strained against the conflicting desires. A light came on to her left, and a Pain Giver stood in the middle of the room releasing a whip that crackled with sparks of electricity. A white streak of lightning escaped from the strap and it made the tortured person strain against his bonds, rigid against the electrical charge that entered his body.

Darien licked her lips in envy.

The whip cracked again, this time striking the tip of the man's hard penis and the man bellowed with the pleasure of his pain. Another room off to her right lit up and she jerked her head around to watch a woman inside being strapped to the table, and the pain givers using gleaming wires as sharp as razors that tore through her soft pink skin. Darien wanted to go into that room and lap the blood that flowed from her wounds while accepting and inflicting the same pain.

More lights came on, blue, red, green, and then starting again with red, each glow illuminating another room of pain, another room of torture. It was above her, below her, to her left and to her right. Some showed barely visible in her peripheral vision, and she turned in full circle to capture them all. Darien bled from her ears, her eyes, and from between her legs. There was no coldness now, only the fire of her lust, and the need for the pleasure/pain running through her veins like the need for a liquid fix. The lighted rooms flashed on and off, resembling the black lights at a nightclub, and Darien began to draw on the victims' pains, she drew on their tortures, and she felt the evil that crawled and moved over the floor. The shapeless extensions of the Titobind were clinging and binding themselves to her feet, and the pain she craved became all she knew, all she wanted. She raised her hands and saw that they were covered in blood, and she cried aloud for relief. The truth that spilled from her now was one that she finally accepted. She opened her mouth and spoke in a whisper and all eyes turned to her as a hushed and rapt audience listened to her when she said, "Please, sir, I want some more."

Laughter erupted through the night, and unexpectedly something raised Darien off her feet, lifting her high into a sea of watery blackness that hurled her though the perpetual obscurity. Locked away in a room of truth with her last choice taken away, she would finally have to find what she ran from most of her life, herself.

Waking came slowly for her. Darien first became aware of the cold that penetrated into all of the fibers that held her together. It reminded her of the bone-chilling cold that a person can get when they have stayed too long outside in the winter wearing clothes soaked with snow. Your teeth chatter, and you shake without control, until someone throws a blanket over your shoulders, and there appears like magic a wonderful mug of hot chocolate with a swirl of whipped cream on top. You continue to shake, but with less force, and as the warmth penetrates the cold, the shaking subsides altogether. However, Darien was not shaking, her teeth were not chattering, but her skin was cold to the touch. So much of the warmth had left her body; it felt as though she had died.

She lay there on her side for the longest time, trying to decide if she was still capable of movement. She laid her hand flat upon the ground, assured for the time being that there actually was ground underneath her. It felt smooth to the touch, and as she moved her hand over the surface, she could not feel any cracks, seams, or patterns on the floor. For a moment, she thought that something returned her to the slide so she could continue her descent into Hell. Her eyes were wide open and she knew this, because she had put her hand up to her face to make sure. Darien touched her body and felt the blood, knowing without seeing that it covered every part of her. She remembered the lights going on and off in the rooms of pain, and she remembered entering into all of them. She could not remember when she shed her clothes; however, she knew that she lay naked. The darkness that surrounded her was heavy and oppressive, covering her like a blanket, and yet there were moments when it was also oddly comforting. Darien pulled the darkness around her, wrapping herself in a blanket of liquid cold.

"The night is my mother," she said aloud, "and it keeps me safe in its dark womb."

Darker shapes moved around her, shadows among the shadows, and they danced for her and they did obscene things to each other for her to see. Darien raised her hand, and opened it with a gesture for the shadow thing to come closer. It danced, swirled, and moved towards her. It flattened its appendages against the floor as it suctioned-cupped its way over to her. While it moved, it also changed, warping in and out of different shapes. It reached her hand, and she quickly closed her fist around it, pulling it off the floor, making it make popping noises as its suctioned parts reluctantly relinquished their hold. Darien hugged it to her naked chest, and the shadow spread itself over the top of her body shaking, wiggling its way over her chest, and then down between her legs. She smiled as its coldness attached itself to her, and she rolled onto her back while the hundreds of tiny pincers clung to her skin. It continued to grow in size below her waist, and she spread her legs wide, wanting to carry and cradle the evil deep inside her womb. It was splitting her apart, and she cried aloud with the never before experienced intensity that was delivered in the pain. The remaining shadows danced furiously with the excitement she generated, and the black shadow she placed on her body spread over her entire form. She felt the cold hardness between her legs, and her body responded in a way she never thought possible. It released more pincers into her body and this time when it penetrated her, she screamed.

Darien erupted blood from every possible part of her body. It dripped down the side of her face from the hair pores on her head. It dripped onto the floor where its abnormal warmth sizzled against the cold of the stone marble. A small glow of white light started to shine, and it became brighter by degrees, as if someone stood in shadows and slowly turned up a dimmer switch. Underneath this light was an old-fashioned mirror framed in weathered oak, mounted on a three-legged stand, and fastened in the middle by wooden pegs. A part of her wanted to go to the mirror, but she could not remember why this obsession was always so constant. What was it about mirrors that fascinated her? In the meantime, the capturing of her mind continued as Darien prepared to accept the real and true evil child, Tianato Morebind.

A veil dropped over her thoughts, and she became lost in a sea of emotions. Suddenly there was no room for darkness; no room for the penetrating shadow of cold. Her mind filled with an emotional overload, bringing her memories of David, his clear soft brown eyes that spoke only of the love he still carried for her; and there was Paul, who knowingly groomed Darien from the day she was born to accept this final step. The words that David spoke to her now were words of his truth, and she felt this with her heart as well as her mind.

"In all that we have done, in everything that is to come, remember that no one carries a greater love for you than I." She was crying now, with tears of unimaginable sorrow, and through those tears, she was able to reach down and rend the dark entity from her body. The loss in separation of this shadow thing caused severe pain, as if she was tearing away a part of her own skin. She rolled over onto her knees, and screamed, feeling the shadow's emptiness as well as her own. Despite her deliverance into this world of pleasure/pain, and wanting to remain a part of the never-ending rooms of ecstasy, Darien forced herself to her feet and staggered towards the mirror. Her image abhorred her and it looked back at her without recognition. Her hair hung wet with perspiration and blood, and there was not one part of her body where she could see her skin. Fresh and dried blood hid her human form with wounds that seemed to pulse with a life of their own. She watched in horror as a black crawlie emerged from a large gaping wound just above her knee and it fell to the ground with a resounding "plop."

"Oh God," she croaked. "What are you, Darien?" Her mirror image seemed to laugh at her and then, much to her surprise it began to mimic her.

"What are you, Darien?" It laughed at her.

"What's the matter, Darien? Don't you like what you see?" Her skin tore and ripped as more of the black things burned their way through her body, escaping from various slashes they themselves created. One emerged from between her legs and clung persistently to her thigh.

"I am you, Darien, this is what you are." She reached down, plucked the shapeless little creepie from her thigh, and threw it into the darkness.

"This is not what I am," she bitterly said back to her mirror image.

"Of course it is, you only see what you think you are, but you cannot hide from this truth." Darien stared at herself, at the thing in the mirror who told her that this lover of pain, lover of humiliating and degrading acts showed her true self. Her mirror image, the ugly truth of Darien, the ugly truth that we all sometimes hide. The time came for her final decision, and it would be the last chance she would have to change her image, to become the person she really wanted to be.

She remembered the birth of her daughters, and the love of being a mother that nurtured and watched them grow. Darien remembered his gentle breeze, his warmth of wind that brought her his kind, understanding smile. Shortly thereafter, a complete form arrived, an entity, and then a man who loved her despite her flaws and her imperfections. Then her selfishness, her insecurities, and her inability to accept his generous love turned her ugly, greedy, and insecure. She ended up with an emptiness she thought she deserved. It led her to become the person standing before her now, covered in blood, succumbing to tortures of the mind and body. This person no longer needed to exist. She raised her fists, and stepped closer to the mirror.

"I hate you; I hate what you've become!" With both fists, she pummeled the mirror. It cracked, and then shattered inwards creating a huge suctioning vacuum. Darien put both hands on the sides of the mirror, and held on while the vacuum sucked in the shadows that squealed with delight as the Master called them home. Finally, exhausted, and unable to fight against the pull from the opened junction, Darien let go. Her instantaneous disappearance flipped the mirror into a spin, circling around and around on the pegs that held it in place, and when it stopped the lights came back on. The party continued in the Pit, the well-known palace of pleasure and pain. Jester picked up a cloth and a bottle of window cleaner and limped-walked his twisted body over to the mirror. He sprayed and wiped, and sprayed and wiped until all traces of Darien's blood were gone. He whistled while he worked, scrubbing here and scrubbing there, and then he started to sing softly as he worked.

"Scrub, scrub here, and a scrub scrub there and a couple of la ti daas, it's how we laugh the Game away in the Miserable Land of..." Jester did not finish because he caught sight of the silver rose that Darien wore around her neck, the one that David gave her in his declaration of love. David, the amazing guardian who opened her to feelings that ultimately became unparalleled in their strength and convictions. Jester was able to feel all of this as he placed the small necklace in his pocket. He gave one final swipe at the mirror and said softly, "Seek, my dearest Darien, and ye shall find."

# CHAPTER TWELVE

# TANNER TANNER BO BANNER

Her little white face was the last thing he could see of Darien.

She sat staring mournfully at him through the fading light while Jester still danced in front of him with a zest for foot stomping that Tanner had never seen before. They walked through the dark, around corners, up and down endless stairs, and through short tunnels. Tanner could tell when they went through the shorter tunnels because it actually became a little less dark. Jester turned around and presented his smooth clean face to Tanner. It looked as if he had just stepped from the shower, all scrubbed and fresh with little cherub features that gave him an angelic appearance. His big puffy cheeks were made for pinching, and his beautiful sparkling green eyes put Tanner on edge. He was also wearing the same pointed hat that all the jesters had worn. Tanner wondered why all jesters who appeared to him looked just a little bit different each time, and he couldn't stop wondering where the hell they were all coming from.

It was also becoming apparent to Tanner that they were no closer to finding the entrance to the pit than they were to finding an exit. This new jester was taking him on a merry walk through a labyrinth that he could not see, and it seemed as though they walked for hours. He felt his anger rise with the seemingly random walking through these endless passages with this poor imitation of a man. Even the thought of talking to him nearly caused Tanner to knock him down, take his lantern, and find his own way out. He wanted to strike out at someone, take his frustrations out on anything, and the overwhelming feeling of helplessness threatened to overflow and replace his sanity. Finally unable to stand the incessant foot stomping dance, Tanner yelled, "Stop! For crying out loud, just fucking stop!"

Jester turned to him with a look of great confusion on his round cherubic face, not understanding the sudden outburst of Tanner's growing frustrations. Jester began to open his mouth to speak but Tanner quickly placed his hand over it.

"No more rhymes, no more mysteries, no more stupid riddles, you little piece of shit, understood?"

"There is no need to use profanity, Mr. Tanner." Now it was Tanner's turn to look surprised.

"So you are intelligent after all, you twisted little piece of fucking nothing."

"Well, your intelligence is definitely showing," the jester answered sarcastically.

"Sometimes, little man, swearing can be quite appropriate in its rendition."

"Are we to have a battle of words and wits, Mr. Tanner? You would fail you know."

"Not necessarily, just because I think you're fucking nothing doesn't automatically mean I have no intelligence."

"And just because I sometimes appear with my body twisted out of shape, doesn't mean that I am a fucking nothing. We cannot always control our fate, and if I am nothing and worth nothing, then dispose of me now and be done with it."

"Touché. Besides, I do keep disposing of you, little man and I emphasize the 'do,' but for some reason, you keep coming back, and I can't figure out why."

"It's all part of his game. He can create ten of us for every one that you dispose of. He has become God-like, breathing life into things that had none before."

"He gives birth to twisted, evil things."

"You're wrong, Tanner; he only feeds on the despair that is already there. Even now, as we speak, he prepares for the binding of Darien."

"You know his thoughts?" Tanner was astonished.

"His thoughts are my thoughts; we are all bound to him by different degrees of despair and hopelessness. There is no one living, that at times, has not given vent to those feelings, and those feelings become the property of Tianato Morebind."

"He'll not bind Darien."

"Oh but he will, and she will succumb willingly and with great pleasure." Tanner felt his anger rise, and he approached the seemingly innocent little Jester whose features began to change. His hand captured the little man, and his anger gave way to strength as he lifted him off his feet, and spoke not to Jester, but to the evil that was his master.

"Those are only his hopeful thoughts, you will listen to me, Titobind, if you are in there. Darien won't be won so easily, she is very strong, stronger than what you realize." He opened his fist, dropped the little twisted man, who bounced as if manufactured from a rubbery synthetic material. When the bouncing slowed, his reaction became one of rocking back and forth, slower and slower, and then he stopped. The jester lay on his side, elbow on the ground while his little fisted hand held up his face. He was looking at Tanner, who remained somewhat perplexed in the way the events were unfolding for him. Some questions came to him since he began walking with this little cherub, so he sat down across from the jester, not realizing just how tired he was. Tanner sighed and silently wished for a cigarette.

"You said a few moments ago that this is a game."

"All children play games, Tanner."

"Children? You mean to tell me Titobind is a child or are you making a definite reference to the fact that he is a child, but there is more than one?"

"You hear more than what I say. Yes, compared to the guardians, he is but a child and I only likened him to other children in the fact that he likes to play games. Be aware, however, that in terms of years, the Titobind is a few millenniums in age, while the guardians have been forever."

"You know all of this because you are a part of Titobind."

"Now you're catching on."

"Then why are you setting me free?"

Jester looked at Tanner and rolled his eyes, having become bored with his incessant babbling.

"You do have a thought process, Tanner; my suggestion at this point in time would be for you to use it. I'll wait as I have no impending meeting at this time."

"You are quite the sarcastic little bastard aren't you?" The jester smiled, and kept on smiling as Tanner puzzled over the riddles again. It was not really so much a riddle this time as it was simple common sense and reasoning, and the conclusion he came to was one he didn't want to have.

"You're not setting me free." The jester stood up, and Tanner watched him with a growing apprehension trying to suppress the urge to get up and start running, because suddenly the jester started to grow. His body elongated; stretching into a shadow creature, extending his appendages into the surrounding darkness. Tanner's body stiffened as he felt the initial penetration of the pincers that would wind their way into him, binding themselves to his side until his entire body succumbed to the cold. He would then be bound to Titobind the same as the guardians themselves. There was, however, one slight difference. The guardians, who are as old as time is old, are able to withstand the pain and harshness of the binding, while Tanner, who is a mere mortal, would not.

"Tanner Tanner Bo Banner

Banana nana fo fanner

Me my mo manner…"

And softer, from farther away: "Tanner."

Then the rhyme came again even farther away than the first time.

"Tanner Tanner Bo Banner

Banana nana fo fanner

Me my mo manner…"

And then again just barely audible:

"Tanner."

He felt the warmest wind, a soft gentle breeze on his face, and a voice he knew said again:

"Tanner." Sing-songy sounds, repeating the name as if someone was actually singing the lyrics to the old tune.

"Tanner."

Somehow, he found the strength from inside to break the binds that held him to the twisted evil entity that was yet a child. Tanner started to run through the expanding darkness, stepping into a perpetual night that could abruptly end. He ran until exhaustion overtook him, finally stopping, thoroughly convinced that if he took just one more step he would walk right into a great vast void and die inside an endless fall into darkness. Which, if he considered the alternative, might not be such a bad thing; at the very least, it would be quicker and less painful. Tanner stood quietly in the dark and off in the distance there appeared a small light, shining like a miniature star.

"Oh Lord," he muttered, "here we go again." The light moved closer, bobbing up and down as it came to him. A hand came out of the darkness, and it was a hand that was gnarled and warty, the same as the face that appeared when the flame increased in a feeble effort to stem the encroaching darkness.

"It's the end of the world as we know it."

Tanner immediately decided as he drew back his fist that he preferred the darkness to the singing. Then Jester shook his head from side to side in a quiet "no" and put his finger to his lips telling Tanner to hush, then immediately motioned for him to follow him.

"It's the end of the world as we know it." Tanner started to walk after the shrunken form of a man because he realized, quite simply, that he had no other choice.

"Twiddle Dum and Tweedle Dee
Sat beneath the willow tree
Counting berries that they'd pick
Eating every other one they'd lick."

"What the hell are you talking about?" Again, the jester turned and put his finger to his lips for silence, and then he cupped his hand to his ear. Tanner dutifully shut his mouth and listened to the crooked little man.

320

"Tweedle Dum and Tweedle Dee
Sat beneath the willow tree
Counting berries that they'd picked
Eating every other one, they'd licked.

You could not tell Dee from the dother
Face to face, one was his brother
There was no mirror to be found
As Tweedle Dee to Dum was bound

A mirror image has its place
When looked upon you have to face
As Dee to Dum and Dum to Dee
A lesson in reality."

"What the fuck is this thing telling me?"

Jester turned around and looked at Tanner with a face softened by the caring of Darien. Even as the shattered mirror had replaced itself, and warty old Jester scrubbed scrubbed here and scrubbed scrubbed there, a little warmth and tenderness of what Darien was touched a part of his shriveled body. In this touch she brought warmth to him, warmth that he never knew before, and the result of this touch was that he came to help Tanner. At the same time Jester needed to hide that fact from Titobind, because after all, the jester's mind and his thoughts were not completely his own. He again looked to Tanner and this time held up one finger to his face and then cupped his ear as if listening again. Jester walked backwards so that he could face Tanner, and he repeated to him the riddle that would confuse Titobind, however, Jester hoped that he could make it clear to Tanner that Darien had found the way.

"Tweedle Dum and Tweedle Dee
Sat beneath the willow tree
Counting berries that they'd picked
Eating every other one they'd licked.

You could not tell Dee from the dother
Face to face one was his brother
There was no mirror to be found
As Tweedle Dee to Dum was bound

A mirror image has its place,
When looked upon one has to face
As Dee to Dum and Dum to Dee
A lesson in reality"

(Jester said the next lines very slowly and very clearly for emphasis.)

"We are, we are what we've been made
A lot of light, a piece of shade
So look and face what you've become
There lies your strength to overcome
To face the loss, a life redone
Empty hands that hold the sun."

Jester stood still as he held open his hand and drew out the little bit of warmth that Darien had given him, he drew on her strength, and on her ultimate commitment until a minute piece of her little sun bounced merrily in his hand. Tanner reached out to touch it, but in order for it not to lose its warmth, Jester pulled it quickly back inside. Now Tanner was not stupid, but like Darien, he was very bad at riddles, and this one had him completely stumped. He knew well enough that it was a message about Darien, but now more than ever, even though Jester was only trying to help, he wanted to strangle the little bastard. God, he hated damned fucking riddles.

Jester turned back around but not before placing his finger back to his lips motioning Tanner once more to silence. Tanner was not about to babble on about how perturbing he had found Jester's riddle. The little crooked man was trying to let him know where Darien was while protecting them both at the same time, and Tanner had no choice again but to continue following him, and believe that Jester was only trying to help.

"It's the end of the world as we know it."

"Fe Fi Fo Fum,"

"Mary, Mary quite contrary," and then "Little queen, little queen, pleasure/pain, to play the game." This last part disturbed Tanner, even more than the riddle, and his concern grew that Darien would not survive without him. He remembered when she accidentally wakened him while practicing to bring the winds. He remembered her apparent fascination with mirrors, and how she would always raise her hand to touch the image that looked back at her. That memory brought to Tanner part of the answer to the riddle. It was just too simple, Dee to Dum and Dum to Dee, one was his brother. Of course, when anyone looks into a mirror you have to face what you are. You are bound to what you see there merely because it is your own reflection, a twin so to speak.

"Think, Tanner, damn it, what's the rest of it?" he verbally but quietly chastised himself.

"Wait, that's it, exactly! Darien saw herself, her piece of reality." Suddenly Tanner knew. He had seen Darien touch the mirror as she tried to remember, and he had wondered on more than one occasion why she was so fascinated with her mirror's own reflection. Tanner also knew of her love for David, and that it was this love that drew her on this quest. He humphed as the thought about her having said that she was "saving the world."

"And well, if that other one, that David, just happens to come along, well how can she deny that?" If ever there was a time to take a trip into the horrifying, Tanner knew where to find the door. He also knew where Darien was; she went through a mirror. He stopped walking and when Jester turned around, he said to him, "Take me there."

"It's the end of the world as we know it."

"Jester, I'm warning you." Jester changed so quickly, and in less time than it takes to blink an eye, he loomed above Tanner larger than what a thought could allow. His body changed, expanding, becoming transparent, allowing Tanner to see through to what lay beyond. It was the doorway back to his home, his safe little diner in Corral, and if nothing else, it is still his home. Images flooded his mind of the old man who came to his place day after day, afraid to tell Tanner that he was his father. The sudden pain of his loss caused him to feel a great emptiness, and a longing to hold close the comfortable body of sweet Darien. Her soft yielding flesh that was so generous, along with a smile charged with genuine undeniable pleasure when she looked at Tanner. He really had fallen in love with that woman, and he was not going to lose her.

"Close the door, Jester, I'm not leaving."

The door from the Pit that would lead him into the dense gray fog remained open, and Jester's voice came at him, projected from somewhere over Tanner's head. "You have no choice, Tanner, you must leave, or you will die."

"Take me to the mirror."

"I cannot, it is for Darien alone."

Tanner felt so defeated, so helpless. His next words were a plea. "Let me stay, Jester, she might need me." The lights came on so unexpectedly that Tanner barely had time to shade his eyes against the sudden onslaught of brightness. A violent blast of music accosted his ears, and a din that came from a multitude of screams and harsh commanding voices. Tanner hesitantly removed his hand from his eyes and was sickened at the sights that he saw. They were the same rooms that Darien had so willingly stepped into and participated in. The sights that greeted him were nauseating ones, and of course Tanner could only guess at her becoming one of these depraved human beings.

The psychedelic lights flashed back and forth, red, green, blue, white, yellow, and they were as vivid in color as a crayon in a Crayola box as they repeatedly illuminated each room with an intense glow. Each time a different room became visible, Tanner could see horrendous rituals being carried out, most of them too nightmarish to watch. The cannibalism was the worst, because even as he watched, the victims fell prey to the worst possible death. He saw a young man strapped to a table slowly consumed by fanged zombie-type women migrating about the table.

His Pain Givers.

With faces totally devoid of emotion, they hovered over and around the young man as they mechanically took bite after bite, pulling large pieces of flesh off his body. The boy's screams stayed alive in Tanner's head, echoing in his thoughts, bringing the world to life in a true fantasy of terror. It was not the act itself turning Tanner's stomach; it was more the look of pleasure on the boy's face, especially when his eyes met Tanner's. The boy drew back his lips and smiled a large, self-satisfied smile, and then he started to laugh. Suddenly that laugh turned into another scream, as his tormentors tore another chunk of flesh from his body. The smile repeated itself and again followed by his hideous scream. At one point Tanner remembered seeing the ejaculation of the boy's excitement, and then that part of his body disappeared as well. Lights flashed again and Tanner felt as though he was watching the filming of snuff movies that had moved into his new reality, one that he definitely did not want. When Jester spoke to him, Tanner became angry, wanting to keep the warty man from invading his mind. Having that thing know his private thoughts could put Darien at an even greater risk.

"Everyone has to feel their own beat of life, and eventually we all have to face the decisions that we have made. Some are good, Tanner, you know this, and some are not so good. You faced yours over the pit of death that has held you prisoner inside yourself all of these years. Darien has had to face the person that has held her prisoner, the same as you and that is all I can tell you." There was a pause before he continued.

"Tyler Tanner, it is time for you to leave, because the rooms that you see before you are not a part of your fate." The dark fog outside the open door seemed thicker than before, and the quiet that hung over the once busy town of Corral scared him as much as Darien's downward journey to find the Titobind.

"It's spreading you know, every day it goes farther and farther, and he is becoming all encompassing in his ability to reach and to control. The strength he feeds upon comes from the guardians themselves, and they grow weaker every day, until soon, there will only be hopelessness, and the Titobind. The world as you know it will be plunged into total despair, then desolation, and finally he will be responsible for the death of an entire species."

"So, Jester, what will he feed upon when there is no one left?"

"Tanner, you told me yourself that you are an intelligent man, but it seems that you lack somewhat in the reasoning department. He desires the annihilation of your species because it will set him free. He will gain enough in knowledge and power to flee the confines and constrictions of his earthly bounds to travel as an all-powerful energy throughout the universe. He will create and then he will destroy. He will consume and he will continue to grow. Titobind has but one goal and one goal only."

Tanner digested all of this information while Jester looked on with the eyes of his master. He also could feel Darien's presence and knew that for now, she was safe on the other side of the mirror. This new information was far more than he needed and Tanner felt the goose bumps begin to rise on his body. Tianato Morebind is an evil greedy child, who like all evil greedy children, never have enough. Tanner could see what was happening, and no matter what he said or what he did, it would not change the course of the path that was leading them. Darien was the only one who could. He remembered her saying the same words to him, and that he was not aware of his true power.

"He will continue to grow and become as a guardian himself, won't he?" The question went unanswered because Tanner already knew that he was right.

"He will become a God of unbelievable strength and power, enough to destroy an entire universe. A God, damn it, and all there is to stop him is one small woman."

"You have solved the puzzle, Tanner. Now go, and hope you will live to see another day."

"Why did I forget the reason? She told me, I knew the answer all along." Tyler remembered her words, and somehow he knew that the Titobind can take the memories, he can do anything he wants to do. Tanner looked to the jester, suddenly feeling a great pity for the twisted, misshapen midget.

"There are pieces missing you know, the one she was sent to find, the good piece, the last piece."

"She has but to look inside, because the strength of your whole species is based on love."

"She is but one woman."

"Take comfort in knowing that she is not alone, and that for now, I can keep our conversation from him."

Tanner put his head down and stepped through the door to go back to his little diner, and wait for his death or for his life. He took one last look into the semi-dark rooms that he was leaving behind.

"May the guardians speed my love to you, my little Darien." The murky grayness quickly swallowed the diner owner, and it reeked with the stench of death, while in the meantime, sitting in the darkness an entire world away, Darien felt the words of Tanner and the honesty of the feelings that they carried. A truth of real love, not one contrived, not one only made to fill a needed desire, but a truth and a loyalty that went beyond words. It was the same as David's ideals which he so desperately tried to convey to her during her never-ending self-pitying tirades of why me?

There were so many who helped make her strong. The captured smiles of the ones she helped, the guardians who entered and become a part of her, and the generous gift of the great red dragon.. The truth in all that she was seeking floated just below the surface of her life, and circumstances were giving rise to a quiet beauty inside not found in actual real words. Echoes of "look inside" reverberated all around her, penetrating her head in a chorus of understanding.

"Look inside" were two words leading to a place where Darien never wanted to go. The entire world reflects what we are, and as a species, what we have done. In these reflections are the terrors of wars, the finality of death, and the wonders of birth followed by rebirth. All of our destinies are predetermined, but it is up to us, as individuals, to choose the path as to how we get there.

"Look inside, look inside." Darien stood up from where she had sat on the ground rocking and hugging herself. She had been cast down, beaten, and mentally tied with the thoughts in her head that kept her defeated. Her mind and body opened to what she was, it opened to what she could become, and what she had to do. She opened her mouth and whispered, "Tanner."

Tanner stood lost in the living fog of his world, in his reality. It clung to him with its pincers, and held him in a grip of death while it fed upon his flesh. It stuck to him like a thousand leeches sucking away at his life. Her voice arrived with a force and power unlike anything Tanner ever felt before, and the fog itself screamed as it died upon his body.

"Tanner," came a whisper so strong that it made the fog fall and roll away. Exhausted and drained Tyler Tanner fell to the ground on top of corpses hidden inside the feeding frenzy of the killing fog. He put his hand out to steady and lift himself back to his feet, when unexpectedly his entire hand penetrated through a rotting corpse, hitting the pavement underneath. Tanner vomited as he pulled his hand back out the way it had entered, and as he did so it created a small vacuum-type suction trying to make him a part of its death.

"Get up, Tanner." The diner owner rose unsteadily to his feet, wiping the vomit from his mouth with his clean hand while shaking his other hand as free as possible of blood and rotting flesh. His voice was the same whisper as hers and it carried his answer back to her.

"Darien, oh God, Darien." The fog rolled back farther and wider to reveal a massive sea of dead bodies covering the street, a feeding ground for Titobind's misery.

"I am here, Tanner. We can't help those who already lie in death, but you can find your way home and wait for me there."

"Bring me to you instead," he said softly.

"I cannot." Tanner stepped forward placing each foot carefully down between the bodies. Some parts of them he moved aside with the toe of his boot, and at times he stepped on them when he had no other choice. The sanctity of his diner finally came into view and he breathed out a much-needed sigh of relief.

"Stay strong for me, Darien, and I will wait for you return." He stepped from the death of the fog into the light of his diner, and so he saw Darien step from the self-imposed prison of her mind. Her strength issued from the growing guardian light within. It allowed her true beauty to rise to the surface, and she spread her arms wide, placing her feet firmly in the world of good and bad. Her heart filled with the love of her guardians, the love of her children, and the truth of herself.

"I know you," she said aloud, "I remember it all, I remember Darien." She smiled and then she laughed into the darkness. Darien saw the tall thin man stand in the doorway of his diner, the man who had helped lead her to find the truth.

"What is truth, Tanner? What have I found?" Her voice was loud in the strange dark land.

"I have found me, Tanner!" He heard her voice; he heard the genuine happiness unfolding from the silver rose that David gifted her with so long ago. In a voice as soft as a whisper in the wind, she spoke to him and the sound came across the dimensions to sound directly into his ear.

"I do love you, Tanner."

"I know," he said quietly and stepped into the total safety of his home to wait for her return. Darien in that moment had truly become his.

Hidden safely away in the atmosphere of liquid night, a new awareness besieged the Titobind, which caused a new emotion to twist his evil form into different painful positions as he tried to understand exactly what the new feeling was. The guardians knew what he was learning, because Titobind had instilled the same feeling in them.

David also knew, together they brought to their capturer a name for what he was learning, and it was called fear.

# CHAPTER THIRTEEN

# THE OTHER SIDE

## PART ONE

Darien watched from the other side of the mirror.

She gazed upon a world encompassed in a vast grayness, a world that brought only death to those who dared challenge the twisted mind that lurked in the shadows. She could not remember how long she had been sitting there with her knees hugged to her chest, and the rocking motion that she maintained, to some degree, comforted her. She watched a tall thin man, with an outwardly scraggy appearance, step somewhat reluctantly into a small diner. It seemed to Darien as if she had always belonged here and she merely wandered about on the other side until at last she came home through this mirror. How quickly her past was fading, and if she was not careful, soon she would have no memories at all.

Titobind can do that.

He can take away memories and leave one's mind empty, or he could overload her with memories of continuous nightmares, filled with unspeakable horror, as he did with his own children. Darien continued watching the man as he moved about his diner, seemingly lost in its familiarity.

Tanner knew that there would be no more customers, at least not until the fog lifted, and he knew there would never be any more customers ever, if the fog stayed. He felt lost without Darien and a song unasked for popped into his head.

"I believe in miracles, where you from, you sexy thing." He smiled as he "saw" Darien. Her short, small-framed body accentuated by the few extra pounds of child bearing and the general filling out as one grows older, her bright eyes, her generous pouty lips, and this picture brought a need to him. Tanner never had time for women who doted on their looks and obsessed about their wrinkles. Darien was real, she was someone he could touch and hold and not have to worry about moving a few hairs out of place or making a smudge in her make-up. He smiled because he could almost feel her warm supple body pressed against his, and it was not so long ago that she lay trustingly beside him. He wanted more than once to pull her to him and make love to her, but after seeing the extent of the bruises and burns on her body and then entering the Pit, Tanner wondered if she would ever again want someone to touch her. There was not too much more he could do, except hope for his sake, and for the sake of the entire human race, that this one, very small, very little woman could defeat an evil grown to monstrous proportions. Despite the danger from Titobind, and its threat, his thoughts were on one more person.

David.

The first time Darien relaxed in Tanner's diner and told him the story of the guardians, she also told him of David; after all, he was the main focal point of her transition. If it had not been for him coming to her and convincing her that suicide was not the way, then the entire world would already be at the mercy of Titobind. It could still happen, and Tanner hoped and prayed that it would not. But for the diner owner, there was still the risk that even if Darien won, he could lose. She might not return if the choice she made was to remain with David. Tanner saw a strange irony in playing these games with winning and losing. The jester pulled him along in the maze, baffled him with the riddle, while in the meantime Titobind pulled out all the stops, making his own rules as he went along. It had become a brutal competition between Darien and Titobind. She had to stop the spoiled little child who played a fierce game with only one option, to win.

Now Tanner is not a stupid man, and he possesses a knowledge that can only come with life's experiences, and he knew that some people can and do fall in love many times over in one lifetime. He fell for Darien with a soft gentle love, and could not imagine his life continuing without her. On the other hand, Tanner is fully aware of the love that comes along booming like a clap of thunder followed by a lightning strike that goes deep into the core of someone's soul. This kind of love holds strength beyond believability, a bond never to be broken, and this is the love David and Darien share. Tanner fears their bond more than a slow death at the hands of Titobind.

The tired owner of the small diner slowly trudged up the stairs to his apartment with each step harder to manage than the last, until finally upon reaching the landing, he stopped to catch his breath before going inside. The air is oppressive, difficult to breathe, almost like it too is becoming liquid in its context. Tanner did not know that as Titobind extended his reach, he was also changing the world so that it would be inhabitable for him. He spread the extensions of the evil obscurity from safe inside his liquid womb, and out of this perpetual night, he would send the ramifications of his own madness along with the release of his dark disease.

Tanner slowly walked over to his favorite armchair and sat quietly pondering all the events until his stomach rolled extensively to verbalize its resentment at having gone too long without food. He had no idea of how long he wandered in the Pit, and could not remember the last time he had enjoyed a good solid meal. Tanner pushed his bony frame from the chair and he walked into the bathroom where he proceeded to turn on the water to wash his face. It wasn't until he stood with a thoroughly soaped face that he realized the wounds he suffered when suspended over the pit had disappeared. He wondered then if they had ever really existed. Vietnam was a very real place of his past, but as happens sometimes in memories of things gone by, they occasionally became more like dreams than past realities. Was his time in the Pit reality, or was it dream? He cupped his hands under the warm running water, filled them to overflowing, and then splashed it over his worn-out features. He wiped his face and stared into the mirror looking intently at his image while at the same time trying to see through to the other side. He put his hand up and touched his fingertips lightly to the mirror, and unknown to Tanner, Darien watched him from the other side.

"Are you there, Darien?" Darien answered almost before he finished.

"I am here." His hand moved around the mirror, and she followed his hand with hers. She saw the man's eyes fill with tears, genuine care, love from a man who had lived too many years without.

"Be careful."

"I will." And that was all he said. He picked up the towel and patted his face dry as Darien watched him with mild curiosity, having already lost the memory, and feeling that she somehow knew this man. In fact, she was sure of it. His name began with a T, of that much she was certain. She frowned deeply as she watched him drop the towel on the sink, leave the room, and walk into the bedroom. Tanner lay on his side, and despite his hunger, was soon falling into his own dreams becoming lost in sleep. Suddenly there was movement in the shadows, and the creepy things that hid inside the darkness reached for him. Darien quickly searched her memory trying to remember why this person was so important to her, and she screamed aloud as the dark things reached for him. Tanner! It was Tanner; she pulled hard on her memory and brought him into focus.

He can take your memories.

"You bastard Titobind, stay out of my head!" There was no answer but then Darien had not expected one. The monster induced waking nightmares into her mind, taking away her memories, the shadows she thought she saw were not there, and Tanner slept safely in his bed. Darien as always was puzzled. How could what happened to Tanner affect her if Titobind took away her memory of him? Of course, Darien did not want to see anyone hurt, but everything she just saw and remembered quickly faded again, and her thoughts were already becoming fuzzy. She shook her head as if trying to shake out whatever bad notion might be lurking there, and suddenly everything repeated itself as if it had never happened. Tanner was back at the mirror putting his hand up to match Darien's and he asked her, "Are you there, Darien?"

And she answered almost before he finished. "I am here."

"Be careful" was all he said, but it was all she needed.

"I will." Darien took one last look at Tanner, and then turned away from the mirror.

\* \* \*

It was not as dark as she thought it would be.

It was more like an endless dusk, and Darien did not know if being able to see everything was a good thing. She slowly turned around, becoming tuned with the immediate area, and was surprised when she heard the barest sound of running water. She walked off into the general direction of the familiar sound, and the mirror that brought her life's revelations slowly disappeared behind her.

Marsh grass appeared in front of her, blocking her line of sight from left to right, and it was just high enough to keep her from seeing what lay beyond. Darien knew that going to the left would be the same as going to the right with either way presenting an endless border of high flowing marsh grass. Throwing all caution aside, she just plunged straight ahead following her sense of hearing. She stopped when she felt something drop onto her neck, and after touching the dampness, Darien knew that her ears were bleeding again. She pulled out the handkerchief that Tanner gave her, dabbed it to her ears, and then continued with her trek through the swamp. Without any warning of a thinning out, the marsh grass suddenly stopped, and she stepped out onto a slick gray surface. The ground beneath her feet was as hard as ice and just as slippery, resembling very closely the moving slide that she rode in the Pit. Darien caught her breath at the sight that greeted her.

A vast purplish-black emptiness stretched before her, and in the middle of this vast expanse of barren land there was a single blade of grass. Perched on this blade of grass was the largest barn owl that she ever saw. The owl was nearly twice her size, and the thin reed of grass should never have been capable of holding the weight of the oversized bird, but it held nonetheless. She walked closer, and it watched her with big wise owl eyes blinking slowly as she approached. The sound of moving water became more distinct the closer she came, and suddenly a great rushing river came into view. It ran in one direction, and it continued as far as she could see. An amazing river comprised of three distinct canals of spellbinding colors that flowed upwards into a mountain range just barely visible under the purple sky. It brought to mind a river that her daughter drew in first grade many years ago. She remembered asking her about it, and the child had answered that it was a place from her dreams. The river that was in front of Darien ran its upward course, and the individual canals' colors were comprised of blue, silver, and gold. Exactly the same three colors that were in her daughter's drawing. Appearing through the haze, docked at the river's bank waiting for her, was a Chinese junk, whose pilots were none other than the twins. Titobind's continuing reminder of the simplicity in rebirth to evil.

The twins turned their blank eyes to look upon her as they waited patiently for Darien to join them. As she approached them, the owl lifted its great wings and pulled itself off the grass, creating a great gusting of wind that nearly picked Darien off her feet. It settled back down on the ground, blocking her way by extending its wings to hide her from the view of the twins. The mammoth bird looked down at her and then spoke with the voice of the wisest and oldest guardian of them all.

"It is a great and noble thing that you do, Darien."

Rather than wanting to receive its words of encouragement Darien replied, "Owls can't talk."

"You see things not as they are, but as you think they should be. Why have you not leaned to accept what is?"

"I have accepted what I have to do."

"But you have not accepted who you are."

"I am nothing more than a person who has stepped through a mirror to do battle with an evil monster. This quest, or whatever you want to call it, was decided for me long before I was born. I have accepted what I have to do without knowing why the Gods chose me. As to who I am, that is a question I never had an answer for."

"And now?"

"And now I stand here talking to an oversized barnyard owl, about to fight an evil monstrosity grown from the despair of the human race, or so I've been told. I have also been told that he is a titan of corruption who has taken over the council of guardians and bound them all to itself."

"You will not win unless you understand." Darien had heard enough and she lost her temper.

"What is there to understand? Look, Mr. Owl, I have gone through too much to stand here and play stupid fucking riddle games with you. I am tired of fighting, I am tired of having to figure things out, and I am sick and fucking tired of the same old stupid questions. Don't you see, I don't want to understand I just want it to be over!" She looked at him with a sudden blaze of temper that matched the lashing of her words.

"Stupid fucking owl, stupid fucking backward river, fucking twins, fuck everything!" She screamed all of this into the land beyond the mirrors while the owl stood quietly watching her tirade.

"Are you done?"

"Yes."

"Do you know who I am?"

"No and I don't give a damn."

"That's not true."

"True, not true, who am I? Who are you? Up down in out around about. I just want it all to stop." She could hear her heart pounding and blood was seeping from both ears as the owl's voice boomed inside her head. It began to grow, first doubling and then tripling its size. The guardians screamed, the great owl laughed out loud, and Darien fell to her knees in pain, as the blood continued to flow freely from her nose and ears, quickly soaking though her shirt.

"I am that which you fear the most, Darien. I am the truth of what you are." The owl flew off in a great rush of air, and in its place the twins held Darien.

*How can an owl be the truth in what I am? God, this is fucking confusing!*

The touch of the twins allowed her to see inside the darkness of their minds, and Darien began to scream, and she kept on screaming until she could make no more sounds. But even then, she kept opening her mouth in mute attempts, unable to stop the images or the twins as they carried her aboard the Chinese junk.

Titobind's evil children dropped her onto the mat that lay on the bottom of the boat. They proceeded to untie the junk, unfurl the huge sails, and then let the movement of the river begin their journey. The boat slowly turned away from the land, and moved out into the silver canal of water. One of the twins reached down into the silver wetness, and it coated his hand like a thin layer of paint, sparkling brightly in the endless dusk. He held his hand over Darien's face and let two drops fall. It reacted like an electrical charge jumping through her body. Her temperature plummeted; she immediately sat up and began to shiver. Cold ruled in Titobind, and everything he touched became just as cold.

Darien watched with the same numbness learned from her time in the Pit as the twins started to disrobe. She waited with learned reflexes, and when they stood naked before her, she was able to feel his touch spreading inside of her, turning her mind as well as her body to ice. Darien was becoming as empty inside as the twins, as empty inside as the nightmare she was chasing, and this time when the twins touched her, she did not scream.

Darien welcomed their darkness into her heart.

They began to bring her to their side, in the same slow, painful process that Darien had become accustomed to, and she welcomed the pain as part of what she was to become. The first twin erupted semen as dark as the shadows that he hid in. It poured from him like a burning liquid, and Darien lay underneath as he drenched her in a shower of decay. Everywhere it touched Darien's flesh gave way to the hot fire, and she watched in horror as her skin began to melt, staring more in awe than in pain as it bubbled, blistered, and then fell away. The Chinese junk sailed on, slowly changed course, and as it moved towards the gold canal, it began to pick up speed.

The twin who burned her started to laugh, issuing forth a deep-throated twisted sound that came from being born from the worst in humankind. The other twin stood at the helm, and turned its empty eyes upon her, and Darien smiled over at him as she began a slow seductive crawl along the bottom of the boat. At first, she lay submissively at his feet, and then she began to caress him with her mouth, licking her way up between his legs while he stared impassively ahead. His skin glowed in the dusk, and he stood like an ebony statue, perfection in sculpting. Titobind allowed no pleasures to the children he created, until now. Being directly linked with them allowed him to participate in the new experience. Titobind sighed with satisfaction when Darien slid her mouth around the twin's erection, and then he felt a deeper arousal even more when the impassive ebon form swatted her away with the back of his hand. She lay again in the bottom of the boat while the pale twin proceeded to tie her down, his exquisite form towering over her. He spread her legs and arms as far apart as possible, and then he secured her with rope while she felt the force of the oppressive monster that waited for her. The extensions of Titobind, his children, settled down around her and began to enjoy her desperate attempts to struggle uselessly against him.

The pale twin bit her and drew her blood, which he proceeded to suck into his soul. The twin at the helm decided that they were far enough into the river to leave the pull of the boat to the water's undulations, and he joined his brother. The children of Titobind did extreme damage to Darien with tortuous undoing learned from their creator; they left her barely able to move her body. The twisted black entity felt the ejaculations of their pleasure, and it shook the existence of all that was on of his side of the mirror. He was so close to escaping this world, so close to capturing and destroying an entire race of people and his pleasure with this woman was making her even more desirable.

Darien drew deeply on the rancid air and her body shuddered involuntarily finding the warmth of her body nearly gone. The twins turned their vacant, expressionless eyes to look at her and then returned to watch the horizon. They had to take the junk upstream into the mountains where the great paddle wheel in the purple sky turned the time for an entire dimension and sealed the gate to Tanner and Darien's world. The small tortured woman turned on her side moaning out loud as she moved her battered and beaten body so that she could gaze up at the paddle wheel watching as it turned slower and slower. If it stopped completely, the invisible gates that held him would open, and Titobind would surge forth on a tide of darkness and the cries unto heaven would be a chorus of pain unlike anything ever heard before.

There would be a silence for all eternity and man would never again walk on any world.

"Darien," the whisper came, but it was not a whisper of the guardians, they had stopped calling to her long ago.

"Darien," it came again. She reached up and grasped the rope that just a short time ago had been her bonds, and now hung loosely from the side of the boat. She pulled herself over to the side of the slow-moving junk and gritted her teeth as her body screamed silently from the pain in her movements. Her eyes were swollen shut to the point where they were only slits for her to see through, and she slowly maneuvered herself into a position where she could see into the river.

"Darien," came the call again, and the twins seemed oblivious to her as they gazed unblinking to the mountains. As she looked over the side of the boat Darien could see where the silver water ran parallel to the gold, and there was movement in the water. Darien watched closer and began to make out the shapes of things that somewhat resembled humans.

They swam through the water like fish and while some had the features of people, others had fish features, with arms instead of fins. Despite the oddness she was finding in these canal-dwelling creatures, all of the beings cut gracefully through the water much like dolphins and seals, keeping pace with the boat that sailed Darien closer to her destiny.

"What are you?" she gasped with a raspy voice.

A head popped up through the gold water, barely discernable in the dusky light, because it too was as gold as the river it lived in.

"We are…" It disappeared and another one popped up different than the first.

"…the souls…" Then a third head appeared.

"…of all the goodness…" With a gentle plink it too was gone and just as quickly the first one reappeared.

"…that he could not bind or kill." The water went quiet, no waves, no movement, and Darien against all protests, leaned farther over the side of the boat so that she could gaze directly into the swirling waters below. The voices came to her in small whispers on the waves.

"Give us your hand, Darien."

"Yes, give us your hand."

"Give us your hand, Darien."

"Yes, give us your hand."

"Give us your hand, Darien."

"Yes, give us your hand."

Hypnotically she extended her hand until her fingertips grazed the crest of the small waves and the souls immediately surrounded her, pulling on her arm until half of her body submerged under the water, and Darien stared straight into the eyes of the gold souls of goodness.

That was where they first entered her, through her eyes.

They filled her mouth, her nose, her ears, and she started to struggle fiercely to free herself because they were taking her breath away. The twins watched emotionlessly as she struggled for her life, and then they tuned their empty faces away. Titobind did not care; he already told them that her soul was his no matter how she died, be it by his hand or her own. There was only his way, Darien belonged to him, and he was looking forward to binding her soul for a hundred lifetimes. Her movements in the water slowed, and then stopped as Darien's body hung lifeless half in the gold water and half in the boat. The pale twin walked over to her, and placing his hand on her side, he inserted his fingers through her body, creating a handle to pull her back inside. He dumped her back onto the floor of the boat, and returned to his brother. The water continued to pull them upwards, always upstream toward the mountains. Darien lay still in her death while the gold souls from the river continued to spread into her body. The goodness flooded her still form, and there could be only one choice left to Darien after her death.

A resurrection into a new and different life, but to serve the Titobind, or as savior to humanity?

Her body glittered from the bright scales that resembled a simple goldfish. Her mouth opened and she pulled in a deep breath, and as before, her wounds began to heal themselves. Her body shimmered in the permanent dusk of the world of mirror images, and Titobind was again aware of her, not realizing the full extent of her recovery. One of the twins approached her, picking her up off the bottom of the boat, and holding her upside down by her foot over the part of the river that ran silver and boasted the coldness of Titobind's heart. She squirmed like a worm on a hook, and its child threatened to let her go into the river when suddenly a waterspout erupted from the gold water and came down on the twin. His body twitched and jumped as he flung Darien back into the boat.

Titobind screamed as he encountered his first real experience with excruciating pain.

The twin dissolved into the waterspout that quickly returned to the gold water carrying the ebony son of Titobind. The other twin merely watched with undisguised indifference as his twin brother melted into the waters, and then on command that only he could hear, the pale twin dove into the silver water as his father called him home. As for Darien, she lay quietly, exhausted, and bit anxious waiting for the boat to dock. In the meantime, the Titobind could not disguise his surprise at the souls in the river.

Darien brought to him so many new emotions, fear, uncertainty, pain and now curiosity. He did not understand how this one little human could carry such tremendous strength. With just one small gesture of his finger, he was sure that he could easily nap her into small pieces, but Tianato Morebind wanted to know more about this woman. She is a mystery that he needs to take apart, to understand, and then to bind through all the eons as he dominates and spreads among the stars. He wants her to ride on his shoulder and watch him conquer universe after universe, to feel the power as he becomes a god. But for now, she rides alone on the Chinese junk, heading straight up into the mountain to the paddle wheel of time. Let her come then, let her come willingly, ready to absorb all of his depravity, and become as evil as Titobind.

Titobind in all of his youthful arrogance did not realize that there were things he did not understand. He did not know how the good souls survived in the gold river, nor did he care now that they were gone. However, there continued a small nagging thought at the corner of his mind about Paul, and why he could not find him. The guardians bound by his leeching tentacles suddenly become excited with Titobind's thoughts of Paul, and their movements could not disguise their excitement. The pain of their capture forgotten, and their struggle to be free, strengthened.

"Neither Darien or Paul can free you," he said quietly into the womb that still provided his nourishment. His words spread out, causing a rippling effect in the darkness from which he would soon be free, and it caused the guardians greater agitation. Titobind expanded and then pulled them further into him, causing them to emit a great cry of agony that reverberated out around them. Suddenly, through their screams of pain Titobind heard her. Her voice was quieting the guardians, and she eased their pain with a comforting sound.

Darien was singing.

She was singing without words and she was singing with the voice of an angel.

"I am not afraid of one puny human." The vibrations of his voice met with the quiet force of hers and she stopped singing just long enough to reply. Her eyes narrowed, her voice became hard, menacing, the gift of power she claimed to her soul brought fierce projection to her voice, and through the dark of his world, she reached him:

"You should be."

The boat sailed on, and Titobind unwilling to admit that the fear he felt earlier began spreading, and along with that fear, the beginning of building anger caused by her arrogance.

\* \* \*

The proportions of the paddle at the end of the wheel were so large that they stretched beyond where she could see. Darien could barely tell where the giant paddle connected to the arm, while the connection of the arm to the hub in the middle was left to her imagination. She sat down in the boat and watched the paddles turn, studying them to see if there was a way she could climb up on one of them. It had become another puzzle for her to solve.

The upper half of her body shimmered with gold iridescence because the remaining fish scales shone as bright as the river the souls put her in. Her heart was light and she sang the same wordless song that issued from deep inside, where everything she absorbed lay buried. The Chinese junk took her all the way to the end of the river, becoming nearly vertical in its final ascent rising up the tri-colored waterfall to the mountains until it crested the top of the waterfall. It reminded Darien of riding up the incline on a steep roller coaster, and then coming slowly up over the top, but instead of falling downwards into the shock of that first deep drop, the boat leveled off into a glacier-type lake hiding between the mountains.

This was where the three colors blended into one; the water becoming white, like a giant pool of milk. Darien wondered if the water tasted like milk, and then as her newly acquired gold fish-scaled body glinted in the strange dusk, she wondered if this was going to be a permanent look in her life. She could also feel the souls inside of her and knew that even with all that she had absorbed, there was still the uncertainty that she would not be able to destroy him. She looked down at her body and talked to herself.

"It must be getting kind of crowded in there isn't it, fellas? Damn, I wish there was someone, something instead of this vast emptiness. Has this thing ever known anything other than darkness?"

Darien felt a lurch as the boat hit the embankment. She walked to the end, stepped slowly over the side, and was very careful not to touch the white milky water because she could see where parts of silver dotted the edge. She stood comfortably on a large flat rock as she gazed out over the barren hills that lay before her. A thin puff of smoke started to issue forth from a small fissure in the rocks. Darien watched quietly, with inquisitive amusement, as the smoke began to take on the shape of a small lizard. Once solidly formed, it sat down on a rock directly across from her. The lizard leaned back, took a deep breath, and relaxed as he crossed ankle to knee, in the resemblance of human posture. Of course, like the owl, she expected him to speak and she was not disappointed because such is the way of things in the world of Titobind. Darien decided to save him the effort.

"Don't bother because I am sick of your riddles and sick of your games."

The lizard watched her, turning his head to one side, studying her, and then moving its head back to watch her again. "The Titobind says you are hiding something."

"I have hid nothing."

"Your lying words cannot disguise the truth in your eyes."

"Fuck you."

The lizard thought this to be extremely funny, and his laughter caused him to bounce so much that he could barely keep his precarious balance on the rock.

"Such bad language."

"Oh balls, lizard, I say it all the time, as in fuck you, fuck him, fuck me and just plain old let's fuck. You should know all about 'let's fuck,' I did it often enough back in the Pit. You wanted to bring me down, and now you have what you wanted. I have sunk about as low as one person can become. I have had sex in every way imaginable, I have been whipped, beaten, bit, kicked, burned, drowned and now I am here. What more could you want to know so that you will see that I have come to be with Titobind, with a right I have earned."

The lizard reached into a hidden pouch on the side of his skin and proceeded to produce, of all things, a pipe, and with this pipe, some tobacco. He sifted the tobacco from the pouch and packed it into the pipe, which he then placed in his mouth. He proceeded to tap his sides looking for a light. The search finally produced a single wooden match, which he scratched onto a rock, one, two, three times, before it burst into flame. Darien watched the lizard expertly puff his pipe, allowing the tobacco to catch the burn, which briefly reminded her of her grandfather. He had been, to Darien, a great bear of a man, and he used to light his pipe in much the same way. She briefly recalled how protected she always felt in his company. The memory came, and went so quickly that Darien just sat and blinked her eyes. Had that time of her life ever been real? The lizard puffed away relaxing on the rock, and then brought his gaze directly into contact with hers.

"He wants to know the real reason behind your seeking him, and you cannot lie because in the same way as the great guardians, he knows your heart, Darien."

*Protect them, Darien.*

"He lies, he knows shit, lizard." The lizard continued to smoke his pipe while he quietly abandoned all train of thought until she could not stand it anymore.

"What do you want Titobind? What more can I do to prove that I belong with you?"

"The paddle wheel of time slows, Darien, and soon it will stop. When that happens the gates between the dimensions will be breached and he will be free."

"I know this, lizard, answer my question."

When the lizard spoke next, it was not the Titobind she heard.

"He is taking your memories. Do you remember Tanner, or Jack or Jimmy Bigslee or little Manny? What about Hestor Green?" Do you remember the bike messenger Tommy?" These names sounded like a foreign language to her, and she could not remember the significance of them or their importance to her. It was not Paul, so who was this lizard?

"Whether you go to fight him or to join him is your choice, it has always been your choice; we can only hope that when you do face him, it will be for the goodness of the guardians." The lizard tapped the burnt-out pipe on the rock next to him and he returned it to the invisible pouch pocket. He slowly dissipated back into the smoke that he came from, becoming nothing more than another puzzle, and Darien looked up startled as a familiar voice called to her.

"Give me your hand!" The voice was indeed familiar but she could not place where or when she had heard it before, and as Jester reached down for her the huge paddle slowly moved by, creating a small tailwind in its passing.

When had it moved so close? When had she moved closer to it?

Darien jumped across the large rocks and started to run across the rugged terrain, oblivious to the small sharp stones that pierced her soft bare feet. Their hands were nearly touching now and even though she was running, twice as fast as the wheel was turning, she still could not catch it.

"Darien! See that stone up ahead? The one that is jutting from the crest of the mountain?" He shouted this to her, and from her exhausted running all she could was to nod her head yes.

"You must leap from that rock. The wheel will be turning upward; do not hesitate because if you miss all is lost. Do you understand?" Again she nodded her head yes.

"You must believe in who you are and why you are here. You must have faith." Darien's pace suddenly slowed, the wheel slowed even more, and Jester's face became horrified.

"You must believe!" he shouted down at her, and a smile suddenly came to her, the smile of baby Manuel, the little one she saved from suffocating in what seemed like a hundred years ago. Her stamina surged and she ran full out, slapping the rock with her bare feet, and then she leapt off the crest of the mountain, suspended in midair, and into the empty purple sky.

So much flashed through her mind, but the most prominent thought was of finally flying, all of those times that Darien had wanted nothing more than to be free. Her hand reached up, and her hair blew hard away from her face as the tailwind swept her upwards towards the passing paddle. Jester's hand came down and he clasped her firmly by her forearm, and she clenched his arm in the exact same place. Darien hung precariously with nothing between her and oblivion except one gnarly, very old, very twisted court jester. The strain of hoisting her up to the paddle showed in his face as he pulled her up towards the giant paddle wheel of time.

"Look...for...hand...holds," he gasped and Darien saw small indentations in the paddle. As he pulled her up, she was able to grasp one of the indents. It was there that she hung as Jester gasped for breath, and the wheel continued its slow upward turn. Darien looked out over the murky land, and as far as she could see was an endless purple sky that met in the distance with a gray and desolate land.

"No wonder he draws us to him and craves our souls," she said more to herself than to Jester. The paddle came up under her and her feet magically found foot indents and Jester was finally able to let go.

"Follow me; we need to get to the hub before it circles around." Hand over hand, very cautiously; she followed the dwarf across the paddle, making sure each new grasp was secure before letting go of the previous one. Slowly they made their way to where the huge arm was secured to the paddle, and climbed out onto it. When the arm was almost horizontal with the hub, the jester started to trot down the connection, which was nearly as wide as a suburban sidewalk. It reminded her of when she was a child and used to watch her older brother create projects with wooden sticks and dowels called Tinker Toys.

"Hurry, you must hurry." The paddle started into its upward swing, and Darien lifted her head when she noticed a slight shift in the wind. Quickly gathering her thoughts, she followed the jester down the arm almost overtaking the small dwarf, whose movements were obscenely accentuated by his twisted body. Up ahead Darien saw a large stake driven into the wooden arm, and attached to the stake was a rope leading down inside the hub. The wheel circled, moving higher into the sky, and the wind picked up speed, blowing against her, causing her to stumble. Without so much as a second thought, she reached for the rope to secure her hold on the wheel.

"The wind will get stronger!" Jester shouted against the mounting gusts. "We must hurry." Darien nodded her head in understanding because the building wind already buffeted against her hold on the rope. They moved towards the hub of the paddle wheel straining for the dark opening that led inside. The wind roared around them with hurricane force, and it was all they could do to hang on. It tried to loosen their hold on the rope as the temperature dropped, and Darien found herself suddenly wishing for a coat, or at the very least, a sweater. Jester entered the darkened doorway, and then reached back out for Darien, who most graciously accepted the knotted, warty hand. With one mighty tug, Jester yanked her inside just as a huge gust of wind drove by with a force that would most assuredly dislodge her hold. Darien's hands were raw and bleeding, and she shivered repeatedly from the prolonged exposure to the cold.

"Come with me." Jester walked down a small hallway, and Darien pushed herself up off the floor to follow him for the short distance. The dark interior suddenly opened into an oversized room, kept warm by a large red rock that glowed on top of a mini volcano-type mountain. Darien slumped immediately to the floor, and Jester moved through the room, opening small cabinets, taking out various bottles and bandages and placing them on a crude wooden tray. He returned to where the exhausted, battered women sat quietly on the floor. The twisted man placed a raggedy old blanket around her shoulders and Darien quickly drew it around her half-naked body. Jester carefully opened her hands, and she cringed, but held her tongue as he placed a soothing gel (which he had made from the various bottles) over the raw open cuts. Amazingly, the burning stopped, and Darien watched another magical healing process. Jester wrapped marsh grass around her hands as bandages and then placed her thumbs on the grass to secure the wrappings.

"They will heal quickly," he whispered as he put the tray aside and returned with two mugs that held a steaming beverage.

"Tea?" she asked.

"As close as you'll find here," he answered. He sipped his cup, and laughed when Darien sampled the liquid, quickly scrunching her face up with the bitterness of its taste. The tea generated heat throughout her body, and was as instantaneous in its healing properties as the strange gel. She watched Jester remove his cap (how it even hung onto his head in that wind was a miracle in itself) and hang it on a peg almost out of her sight. He then returned to sit on a small wooden chair directly across from her. There was more going on here than what she could see, that was obvious, but she wasn't sure of what she needed to know or where she was supposed to go or just how she was supposed to get there. Jester, it seemed, was not only a healer, but a mind reader, as well, and he began to answer her unasked questions.

"I can tell you most of what you need to know, however, there are some answers you will still have to find for yourself. First, let me tell you who I am. I am the Keeper of the Wheel of Time. The jesters that you met in the pit were merely clones that Titobind created to confuse you and your friend."

"I don't remember."

"That is because he keeps erasing your memories; you must fight him on this, as well as everything else. Before you ask me how I know this, let me explain that I have been here almost since earth began. I am not quite as old as the guardians, for they are close to being forever, and I will not live as long as they will. However, I will abide for as long as the earth planet abides. If the wheel stops then the gates between the worlds will be weak enough to allow him to break free, and the despair that made him will destroy everything in your world. Already he is spreading further into your land his shadow moving slowly, but it covers almost a thousand miles in all directions. In the affected areas there is no food left, and those that have survived are leaving the sanctity of their homes in search of it." Here he shrugged his shoulders before continuing, and then took deep breath.

"The obvious is that they die, but it won't matter much who lives and who dies, because if the wheel stops, no one will survive." He let his words sink into Darien, and then after a few moments he continued.

"I keep the time, but I also help keep the rhythm of the worlds in balance, however even I couldn't fight against the despair from your world that fed him for all of these centuries."

"Is it true that he is but a child?" Jester smiled at her and Darien had to smile back because the pleasure of his indulgence with her innocence softened his harsh features.

"In the great expanse of time," he held his arms out and gestured to encompass all the worlds, "he is but a small child, and a very evil one. His twisted black soul makes him strong, but his lack of wisdom makes him vulnerable. Tianato Morebind believes he is immortal, beyond destruction, and therein lies his weakness. You can defeat him, if you desire it deeply enough. Do you desire it deeply enough?" She cocked her head to one side as if she was seeing Jester for the first time and was having trouble remembering what they had just talked about.

"He is blanketing your mind, stealing your memories, taking them from you. You must not let him! Think, concentrate, and remember the pain that he gave you in the Pit. Remember the sick desires that he caused you to feel. Remember Jack taking you down, Jimmy's death, remember Tanner. You have children out there; focus on keeping them, and on keeping all the children away from him. Darien, look at me." She lifted her head and gazed into Jester's eyes, looking beyond the stare that he placed on her.

"Darien, remember David." Her eyes squeezed shut as memories flooded her mind, coming in like a crashing tidal wave. She remembered how warm and comforting her children were when they were placed in her arms for the first time, and of how the surge of protective love took her breath away. She remembered her own tumultuous childhood, and the teen years that continuously came back to haunt her, and of how she had isolated herself while dealing with her fears and inadequacies. Then there was David.

Sweet, beautiful, gentle David, whom she had nearly destroyed with her self-centered, over-bearing, endless tirade of depressive obsessions. David held captive along with the rest of the guardians, and suffering the endless tortures from the clinging leeches of pain who bury themselves deep inside their innocent souls. All of this and more came breaking though the barriers that Darien put up around herself for the past ten years of her life, and she was finally able to see the truth of who she is. Darien stood up, stretched her hands up towards the heavens, and slowly opened her eyes looking to the ancient Keeper of Time.

"I remember." Her gold scales began to glow with her awareness while the understanding of her own self-worth finally emerged.

"I remember," she said again, with more conviction and more confidence. Darien looked at Jester, and she smiled at him while the glow of the gold river souls that had been outside was now evident inside. Her love filled the room.

"Keeper of Time, Guardian of the Gate, know that I speak true when I say to you I remember. The beauty of the inside is often hidden by what is outside, I see to the inside of who you are and the riddle has been solved."

*There was a crooked man...*

"I always knew we would meet again, Mr. Toady Face."

Toady Face could not hide his relief, and the smile he gifted her with was one of true friendship.

"How have you been, Darien?"

"To tell the truth, I've had better decades." Their laughter rang out through the mirror world, laughing until they cried; falling happily into each other's arms and the laughter in their reunion caused Titobind tremors of fear that spread through his twisted torso.

# THE OTHER SIDE
## PART TWO

Darien followed Mr. Toady Face's gaze upwards.

"The winds will be strongest as the paddle crests the top of the wheel, and it is here where only your faith will be able to keep you. If you time the release correctly, the winds will carry you to the vortex; if not, well if not, then there will be certain death, and the Titobind will capture your soul."

"I understand what you're telling me."

"I can't come with you, I'm not strong enough anymore to hold my own against the wind, and my body has grown a little older since the dinosaurs called this planet home."

"You lived with the dinosaurs?"

"Let's save that story for another time." Darien grinned at him, and she made ready to step out onto the arm that would lead her down to the paddle while the winds were already trying to make her loose her balance.

"Once you hit the vortex that leads the way into the mountains, don't move, because the slightest rupture in the swirls around you can cause a rend in the warp and you'll be spinning so far out of control, that maybe he won't even be able to find your soul."

"Don't be so encouraging, my friend."

"Guard your thoughts, your memories, they are your strength, do not let him take them from you again. Go now, Darien, and take with you the blessings of the guardians, and of myself."

Darien stepped out onto the arm, and the strong wind immediately swept off her feet and she held desperately to the rope. Little by little, she pulled her way down the arm until suddenly the wind was gone, and the sudden release of its hold caused her to fall down. Darien stood up, quickly jogged down the arm to the paddle to where she expertly found indentations, and climbed out onto the paddle. The wheel turned slowly upwards but before the winds could become strong again, she dug in as hard as she could right near the topmost part. Jester told her to let go just as the paddle topped the wheel, giving her a mere split second before beginning its downward descent. There would be no time for reasons, no time for questions; there was only what she had to do. Darien watched over the edge trying to gauge where she had come from, and where she was going. The only thing Darien saw that she could do was when she reached a horizontal position, with the hub directly below her, then it would be the exact moment to let go.

The wind steadily increased in strength, pulling against her body with every intention of tearing her from the wheel. This only increased her grip, and she hung on praying that when she could see the vortex, it would be easy to let go. At times, she was not even sure if she still held onto the paddle because the feelings had long since departed from her numb fingers. She lifted her head to face the continuous gusts of cold wind, and then opened her eyes to see if she could look over the rim of the paddle. Even though Jester had explained the vortex to her, there was not any way that he could have prepared her for the sight that greeted her.

A funnel opened into a sky that boiled and rolled with dark purple tumultuous clouds. She could see the extreme pull of the swirling vortex before she could feel it. Her eyes began to tear, and Darien had never before experienced the hopeless or the ultimate in despair that she felt at this time. She could not imagine having to let go and fly through the air with only a shred of hope that she would enter the vortex at the right angle. How could anyone do this?

Oh sure, "have faith," he said, "trust and believe in yourself," he said; "What a bunch of bullshit," she said out loud. If she missed the vortex she died, when and if she faced Titobind, she might die, and even if she made it through all of this, she still might not make it back. So it would end up being, not a test of faith, but more like, "Oh what the hell, I'm going to die anyway and there is no other way for me to go." Her body was almost horizontal on the paddle, and her hands were so numb that they lost all feeling, and did not seem a part of her body anymore. She managed to release one hand, and the force of the wind was so strong that it kept her flattened to the paddle. Darien dropped her arm down to her side, and she stood there with nothing more than centrifugal force holding her onto the flat paddle. She opened and closed her fists very quickly, forcing feeling back into her hands, and then Darien reached up, and very slowly climbed towards the top of the paddle until she was up to her waist over the edge. The wind suddenly stopped and her body was straight up and down to the width of the paddle. It was here that she needed to lift free, but where was the wind that was going to take her? Jester (she preferred that name now as opposed to Toady-Face) had told her to just to let go, but there was supposed to be wind. Okay, so where was her faith now?

"This was crazy, I'm crazy, and there's no way I can get back home from here." Yet she did not want to leap into certain death. At the very least, if she hung onto the paddle, it would go around again. She pulled herself all the way up and straddled the paddle one leg on each side, with her feet anchored securely in the indents. The view was nothing short of sitting on the edge of heaven with a gaze into the hell that waited for her. Darien suddenly remembered an adventure movie that she loved; after all, who not could love Sean Connery and Harrison Ford? It was the third adventure of Indiana Jones, and she could see him standing in an opening inside a cave while looking out over a huge abyss. He was gazing to the other side of the chasm where there was another doorway. However, there was no way to get across. Harrison Ford stood transfixed in the doorway, and his father's voice (Sean Connery) was imposed over his own as "a leap of faith," replayed in his thoughts. His father was dying, and Indiana Jones would not be able to save him unless he took a leap of faith. Darien did not face the choice of saving her father; instead, she needed to save the entire human race.

"And if that doesn't deserve a leap of faith, then I guess nothing does." She brought one leg up over the side, and sat fully on top of the paddle facing the madness in front of her. She gazed once more around the purple sky, not even daring to look below. She placed the bottoms of her feet on the paddle in a very precarious balance. If she leaned forward and pushed off at the same time, she would at least have made the jump. Just then, the paddle crested the hub; Darien closed her eyes and pushed.

An upward draft immediately caught her body and the breeze from the paddle pushed her in slow motion towards the violent storm of the vortex. Darien was finally flying, in a way that she never expected. She entered the pull of the vortex, and the temperature immediately dropped and her body shivered despite the raggedy blanket she fashioned into a substantial covering. Darien closed her eyes; the cold crept into her body and so great was the infusion that her skin color began to change.

"Let me through this, please, in one piece." And she graciously succumbed to cold deep sleep.

* * *

Darien's awareness came slowly. She kept her eyes closed, but listened carefully until the muffled sounds she heard entered clarity and with the clarity came an understanding of the words. Being in the mirror's world, she lost all track of time and was suddenly aware of how hungry she was. There was also warmth, and softness on top of her as well as below. Her best guess about the warmth and softness was that it felt like cozy fleece comforters. She could hear the familiar pop and crackle of a fireplace, and she thought immediately of David, and their private room of dreams. The voices became clearer, and their discussion was one of personal interest between two females who were chatting about, why of all things, men! First on Darien's mind was finding out what happened, and where in the hell she was. She opened her eyes and saw two very attractive young women across the room placing hot steaming food on a small table. They giggled as they discussed their respective male partners, and Darien smiled as she recognized the patterns of young love. One of the women turned around and saw Darien watching them.

"How are you feeling?" one of the girls asked as she placed a bowl of steaming soup on the table. The young woman wore a light blue gauze gown cinched at the waist with a dark blue cord, and it pulled the gown down in such a way as to accentuate her full, round breasts. Protruding from each side of her forehead, peeking through her short boyish hair, were two small red horns. The second young woman was dressed identically to the first, except her gown was yellow, and she turned around to face Darien. She also boasted the same small red horns on her forehead. Their clothing made Darien think of the old black-and-white movies about old Roman days and the way the women dressed in togas.

"I'm feeling quite warm, thank you," Darien said smiling, and she slowly sat up, forgetting everything for the moment except her hunger. She threw off the comforters and tried to stand, finding that her legs were not quite ready to support her weight and she stumbled back onto the bed. The two horned girls giggled as they picked up the tray table and carried it over to her. They set it down close enough for the odors to assault her sense of smell, and her stomach voiced its displeasure loudly at having been empty for so long. Darien looked down at the long white nightgown that covered her body, barely. It seemed to be made of a lightweight fabric resembling gauze and it was close to being see-through. First, she wanted to eat, deciding that the questions she had could wait until later. Blue girl and yellow girl (as she had named them) sat down in chairs across the room and patiently watched her eat. The fire blazed warmly in the fireplace, and Darien ate until she felt that she would burst, and then immediately became drowsy. She lay back upon the pillow, falling again into a deep and dreamless slumber. When she woke again, she was no longer in a warm bed; instead, she was sitting in a huge oversized wooden chair that made her feel dwarfish in size. Sitting directly across from her was not two young giggling ladies, but instead a giant horned devil waited for her to wake.

"Welcome, Darien. Welcome to my home. You have arrived safely through the vortex, and now sit in the underground home of the Mountain King. I understand that you have had the pleasure of meeting my two daughters." He gestured to the shadows and Darien saw the two young girls standing quietly in the background.

"And outside this room abides my small meager realm." He saw the puzzled look on her face, and she shook her head trying to clear the last cobwebs of sleep from her mind.

"Let me explain to you about the place where you have arrived. When you leapt from the wheel of time into the vortex, you entered into a warp between the Keeper of Time and my kingdom under the mountains, or maybe I should say deep inside the mountains. All of us who dwell on this side of the mirror know of Titobind and his capture of the guardians, and we have awaited your arrival. You shouldn't have any trouble recognizing me because there are many stories written that depict my escapades down through all the centuries. Every now and then, when I become tired in the roasting of the flesh here, I will step into your world and pick apart a few of the souls there. I am as much a part of your world as the guardians are. We offset one another, so to speak, matching quotas, which at times, might tilt a little more in their favor. It's simply a system of checks and balances. Whenever your species is in danger of overrunning each other, I might step in and play a hand or two. Most often, however, I take my 'share' in larger doses, such as a plane crash, a war, sometimes a bombing, hurricane, tornado... well, you get the drift. I threw them a curve with Hestor Green though; I didn't think you were going to make it. Sometimes I do smaller things like inhabiting humans who have too much too drink, or I might cause their temper to flare to a point of fatality. Now and then a drowning, a jump off a bridge, parachutes that fail to open. I do have a flair for the dramatic, and you, Darien, you have made for a much more interesting game."

He stood up, stretching to his full height and girth, and Darien suddenly felt as small and as insignificant as the dwarf who had helped her. The horned beast's great cloven hoofs raised mini dust storms as he stomped and shook his giant red torso. His daughters giggled, and gave away the pretense of his seemingly frightening gestures. As always, Darien was full of questions.

"You roast our flesh, cause our deaths, play these games, and then you let me live? It seems to me that you would work well with Titobind against our world. So, great devil, what need could you have of me?" He laughed then, loud and long and the flesh that was roasting in the depthless pit of the Mountain King, known in the world of Darien as Satan, screamed their agonies loud when they heard his laughter. When he at last looked upon her, she felt herself shrivel inside, and when he did speak, his voice became grave and very serious.

"We are not (Titobind and myself) on the same side, Darien, nor am I on the side of the guardians. Titobind wishes total domination and then total destruction as he spreads his evil out into the universe. I am merely a player in the same game; I am the evil that balances the good that is within all men. If Titobind escapes, he will also destroy my daughters, my mountain, and me as well, for although my power is great it is no match for his. Simply put, Darien, I enjoy playing my role only too well to give it up to him, and I am not strong enough to win in battle."

"Oh, and in the role that I am playing, I'm strong enough? A mere mortal, and a woman at that, I'm strong enough?" This caused the Mountain King even greater delight and he roared with laughter, expressing his amusement.

"You don't know your role yet, Darien? You haven't figured out how he played the game? Look at how you're dressed. What are you wearing?"

"A nightgown."

"That is all you see? You still don't know how the puzzle pieces together. One of Titobind's favorite games is fitting together the pieces in his never-ending puzzles, and then watching the results. Yours has been the greatest puzzle of all because he has not yet figured out who you really are, Darien, but he knows what you will become."

"And that is?"

"Attired in the see-through night dress of the softest white, who else could you be, Darien, who else but his bride?"

Her thoughts ran rampant through her mind.

*So that was it, the bride of fucking Titobind. He is going to have me with or without my permission, if not with a body then he will have my soul, but either way he is going to have me.*

"Bullshit," Darien said aloud. The daughter in blue stood up and walked with pride and respect over to where her father was standing.

"We are the true children of the Mountain King, ruler in this small empire. As a devil to your people, he portrays an evil and scary being, but as father and ruler, he is a fair and just king, and an excellent parent. He does set the balance between our worlds, much as the Keeper of Time watches the gates. In the entire universe one must continually seek balance, because without balance, kingdoms topple and worlds come to an end." She took her hands and positioned them as a scale to symbolize the balance between the two.

"The gates are breached..." She raised her right hand and lowered her left. "He escapes..."

She made an even greater distance between her hands.

"We cease to exist, and Titobind flees the confines of this world." She moves her hands as far apart as possible then brings them together with a resounding slap, and her sister slaps her hands together immediately afterwards. Darien watches as the great emperor known as the devil, known to his daughters as the wise and noble Mountain King, bring his hands slowly together with strength, and a crash strong enough to shake the halls in which they stood.

"Upset the balance and you have oblivion for every living thing in this universe and beyond." Darien stood up in the oversized chair, and she seemed to become even smaller as the two daughters of the Mountain King reached their full size, standing almost shoulder to shoulder with the mighty entity.

"I guess," said Darien, "that I am destined to attend a wedding and to be, such as it is, a bride." Her final acceptance into her role, her play in the game would decide the fate of entire human race.

* * *

Darien sat quietly while the daughter in blue slowly poured the warm water over her back. Her legs were pulled up to her chest, and she laid her cheek upon her knees as she watched the daughter in yellow sprinkle her gown with lightly scented water that made it sparkle in the glowing embers of the fireplace.

"You must have names," Darien said quietly.

"I am Meara," answered the one who bathed her. "I was given life nearly three centuries ago by a woman from your world."

"I am Mimba, and I was given life only a short century ago, also by a woman of your world."

"How is it in all of our histories there is no mention of the daughters of Satan?"

"Because, Darien, we have never entered your world, never caused fear to strike in the hearts of your people, never entered a human's soul and caused them to do dark things. To be honest with you neither has the Mountain King; because it is the darkness of the human soul that calls to him. Unfortunately there is a flaw inside your creation, but my sister and I have always remained here, safe and with our father."

"I have so many questions I would like to ask, but don't know where to begin."

"There is no time, Darien, for questions or answers, there is only what you must do." Mimba held out a towel for her and Darien stepped from the tub to the heated stone floor, wrapping herself in the delicious warmth of the towel.

"Everything is so warm here, so comforting."

Meara laughed. "Not so bad for the home of the devil is it?"

Darien smiled at the two girls who giggled like ten-year-olds, yet had already lived for centuries, and suddenly she missed her daughters with a great empty longing. "No," she said aloud, "not so bad."

The girls left her alone as she dried off the remaining beads of water, and then she slipped the clean nightgown over her head. Darien turned around looking for a mirror, however, was not surprised when she found none. She ran her fingers casually though her hair, tousling it just a little. Unaware at first of what escaped from her lips. Even though Darien could never carry a tune, she began to sing, a wordless song, but one that lifted on notes of unequaled quality and beauty. She felt the good souls ripple though her body; she remembered the gracious grateful smiles that she took to her heart, and lastly the strength of the guardian that Paul put to rest inside her own soul. Her voice gathered momentum, and spread through the great halls of the Mountain King, and the devil himself had to stop torturing the poor serial killer who lay on the dining table for his amusement.

Her voice carried with such exquisite notes of tenderness, that even the fires of hell ceased to move, and deep in the womb, secured in the liquid darkness of despair, Titobind opened his eyes. In the darkness, her melody hurt his twisted soul, and feeling her pain was becoming one of a learned experience.

\* \* \*

The diner was open, but no one came in, and all the radios had stopped broadcasting. Tanner sat diligently for the past four hours in the storage area at the back of the store with his ham radio on, trying to pick up any transmission he could find. He was trying to contact someone, anyone, just to make sure that he was not the only one left alive in Texas, or in the whole country for that matter. The voice that he finally contacted scared him so much that he jumped up while leaping backward, falling over his chair.

"She comes to me, Tanner." He stared in terror at the radio, expecting at any moment to see the horror that belonged to the voice reach through the radio to take him to the place of his death.

"Maybe it would be better to end it quickly," he said aloud, "to let me join her, if death is the only thing that waits for us."

"It waits, yes, Tanner, it waits, but she is mine. Your death will not be swift, and it will be yours alone."

Tanner picked himself up off the floor and walked quickly into the diner, thinking that he might find a place to hide. The gray murky fog pressed tightly against the windows, and Tanner moved quickly about the diner, trying to contain the mounting panic, which was threatening to replace his common sense. In the final realization of the hopeless futility of the situation, Tanner took a deep breath and sat down at the counter trying to ease into an acceptance of what was. He reached for his cigarettes, and tried to take some peace of mind in the inevitable as he drew the smoke deep into his lungs. The smoke from the cigarette drifted up towards his face and he exhaled on the draw, watching more in curiosity than in fear as the shadows shifted in the corners of his diner. It seemed to Tanner that the shadows played within the safe confines of one another, hiding inside shadows cast from normal objects. They weaved patterns of duplicity, complicated and then simple. He inhaled once more on his cigarette and continued watching them dance.

Darien stood quietly before the mountain king as he reached down, opened his palm and allowed Darien to climb into his giant red hand. She had no idea of how she was going to arrive at the pyramid that sat atop the great cold fire, which was home to the Titobind. As sure as she was that the devil wanted to survive, she was sure that he would make certain that her arrival to Titobind's home would be a safe one. She pulled up her nightgown just enough so it would not catch around her neck as she settled into the comforting warmth of his heat.

"Take as much as you need, Darien, because you will find no warmth in his home." The Mountain King walked with huge strides through his great halls. They passed table after table laden with souls abiding inside their tortured flesh, until finally Darien had to close her eyes and her ears to their cries.

"He is a monster, Mountain King, but you are not much better." The devil found her statement amusing, and he proceeded to laugh most generously. Slowly he brought his hand up until Darien could see his face, and when he spoke to her, his voice was serious as he told of the tortures they passed.

"Darien, they are the ones from your world who did not deserve a second chance at life. Despite your religious beliefs in life after death, there is also the truth of reincarnation. The humans who earn that right, the right to return, are good people, who led good lives, and had a good death. When ready, they return to either complete or continue their education until they can move to a higher plane of learning. You or they can make the conscious choice to return to another world, where there is a more advanced intelligence, or one can also return to the same world, if there is more to do before completing their life cycle. On occasion, if someone has been slightly remiss in the performance of his or her life, one can return as a lower life form to begin over again. They will have to earn the level of human, and then eventually evolve to become a civilization of higher learning like the Vinsiba on the world of Sibanon in a galaxy a hundred light years away." Somehow, this all made sense to Darien; she did not even understand why it made sense, except that it just seemed the right way to be.

"The souls below you became lost, and committed the most atrocious crimes, like the taking of a life, or more than one life. I have been working on the dictator from your World War II for over a half a century, and he has presented quite a challenge for me. Of course, I must keep him in one piece until his crimes against humankind are paid. On the other hand, innocents immediately continue on, or to rest if that is what they prefer. We do not question why or why not, it is just an acceptance in what is and in this way, we keep the balance.

"We?"

"Of course, the guardians, and myself."

"Is there a singular God? One who is all powerful, all knowing, and who has a plan for each and every one of us?"

He stopped walking then, his huge cloven feet coming down onto the ground in great thunderous vibrations. He brought her up very close to his face and looked upon her with a combination of marvelous wisdom and profound sadness. She was not sure at first, if he was going to answer her, but he did.

"Yes, Darien, there is a God, a creator of the entire known and unknown universe, and that is all I can tell you." The devil reached down and picked up a large stick that had squirming souls all skewered neatly in a row.

"People kabob." He opened his mouth, and despite their screams of terror, he entered them into his cavernous maw. He closed his mouth and when the notorious Mountain King pulled the stick back out, it was clean. He belched his pleasure loudly, and Darien closed her eyes.

"Don't pity them, Darien, they took no pity on their victims, and besides I'll shit their souls tomorrow, and make more plans for their divine tortures, providing there is a tomorrow." He began to walk quicker now, taking her deep into the heart of the mountain. It seemed as if his quickened pace signaled that time was running out, and Darien shivered in fear for what was to come and suddenly she cried out as she saw the shadows reach for Tanner.

The shadows moved in and around, doubling back and folding into themselves as Tanner casually smoked his cigarette and watched. The front of the store drew his attention as a black shapeless mass appeared on the window, quickly followed by countless others. All of them extended an appendage and began a rhythmic tap tapping for acceptance. He watched as the plate-glass windows bent inwards under their weight, and the shadows already inside the room began to grow. Tanner's self-preservation took over as he jumped from the stool and ran upstairs to his apartment.

"Don't worry about Tanner, Darien, I've sent him some help. He'll be safe for the moment and then the rest will depend on you." The Mountain King had to bend himself nearly in half to get through the doorway and he set Darien on the ground. Old-fashioned torches set in sconces mounted on the walls and they lit the room to bring about their own dancing shadows.

"This is the last doorway that you will need, bride of Titobind." The torches flared and she turned around to find the final way to Titobind. Covering the entire back wall were a dozen gilt-framed mirrors that reflected back a dozen Dariens.

"Only one will lead you directly to him, the others are rooms that resemble much of what you experienced in the pit; however, those tortures in the pit were executed by man. In these rooms you will face his tortures." The Mountain King brought himself down in size, until they were comfortably face-to-face.

"These mirrors hold a riddle, one of his quirky little puzzles, and word has it that you're not that good at solving riddles, but in this case I think that you better get it right." The Mountain King leaned in, and whispered softly in her ear.

"I don't think you will survive the tortures he will give you if you take three, four, or five chances on solving this puzzle." The Mountain King leaned back and looked at her with solemn affection. "I wish you success, now come here, and let me give you some warmth to take with you." He held out his arms, and Darien graciously accepted his hug. The Mountain King began to fade away even as he held her, and she drew on his warmth until he was gone. Darien was alone once again. She slowly turned around and faced the mirrors.

Tanner opened the door to his apartment and stepped quickly inside making it to safety just as the plate-glass window below crashed inwards, and the dark twisted minions of Titobind came for him. The entire apartment filled with the sounds of the black things tap tapping for entrance. They were in the walls, under his feet in the floor, tap tapping on the ceiling below, and from up above he heard a different sound, one that sounded more like a squealing than like a tap tapping.

"Jesus Christ, what the hell is that?" He stared up at the ceiling.

Far away in the underground hall of the Mountain King Darien was having one of those weird song moments as she tried to solve the riddle of the mirrors.

"I am woman, hear me roar," Helen Reddy blasted into her head.

"Oh, brother," she said aloud.

Tanner looked over his head as the squealing noises grew louder while the noise of things flying in his diner tried to drown out the noise from above.

"How did fucking birds get in my crawlspace?" The ladder in the kitchen ceiling flew open, and his entire apartment was flooded with noisy squealing bats! He barely had time to utter a "What the fuck?" when suddenly the apartment and his diner downstairs became a battleground for bats versus black crawly things. God, Tanner hated bats, but he watched in fascination as the tiny mouse-like creatures fiercely attacked and drove back the certain shadow death of Titobind. All Tanner could do was to stand, grin, and watch. It also let him know that Darien was still alive. He extended his arm and one of the tiny fur-covered bats landed on him, and as he looked at its pushed-up piggish nose, he could not stop grinning. Without conscious thought Tanner brought his arm around in front of him and with his other hand, he gingerly scratched the bat between its ears. The bat closed its eyes and made grunting noises that Tanner hoped were sounds of contentment. Several more bats joined the first, and Tanner carefully approached the open door that led down the stairs to his small diner.

He stared in amazement finding the bats were everywhere. They invaded his house by the thousands. He did not care how she had gotten them, he was just thankful that she did. Tanner stood perfectly still as more and more of them landed on his clothes, until they covered him from head to toe, thoroughly encasing him with their protection. His mind drifted briefly to the thoughts of lice and fleas, but he quickly decided that his life would be worth a good delousing afterwards.

"Mmmm, I'm the original Batman." He walked slowly down the stairs, not wanting to disturb the ones that were hanging on him just in case one of them became a little nervous and decided to take a bite. He stood in awe as he reached the bottom of his stairs and stared at the upside-down rodents that hung everywhere. They dangled from his pots and pans, the light fixtures, underneath his counter, from the chairs, and the most amazing thing was the way they encased each other. Tanner looked towards the front of the diner and stood in stunned silence when he saw the intricate bat blockage they formed across his shattered front windows. The mouse-like creatures had intertwined and locked themselves around each other's bodies to form a protective barrier, keeping out the fog as well as attacking whatever grew inside.

"It won't last long," a strange eerie voice addressed the diner owner. Without even having been aware that it was there, a figure stepped from the shadows and spoke to him.

"You may have your life for now." The voice issued from a world that Tanner could not see, but he could feel the immediate drop in temperature when the figure addressed him. The shadow wavered in and out like a picture trying to focus and when it was solid, it finished the sentence it had started. "But not for long." The figure became like a popsicle on a hot summer's day and melted into a liquid black, dripping to the floor where it beaded up and rejoined forces with the active invaders in the shadows.

One of the bats up near Tanner's face yawned sleepily and licked the scruffiness on his neck. This small act wrenched at his heart for it proved how close Darien remained, and it reminded him of how far she had gone. In knowing this, he did not attempt to stop the tears. He turned carefully around, and walked slowly to the stairway in the back. The bats squealed in the other room, and he heard a brief commotion before they settled back down. Tanner stopped to watch one of the bats wrestle with one of the things it caught in its mouth. What the bat did not consume dragged itself off into the corner where it immediately blended back into the dancing shadows. The recently fed bat flew to Tanner, nestled itself onto his shoulder and for the first time in his life Tanner spoke to God.

"I believe, sir," he said looking upwards, "without a doubt that you do indeed work in mysterious ways."

Darien faced the twelve mirrors, and the possibility of eleven tortures that waited for her if she guessed wrong. There were no clues, there were no more rhymes, and there were no pieces left for her to fit together.

"How can I interlock the pieces to solve the puzzle if they have taken all the pieces away?" She walked up to the mirrors and watched the twelve reflections stare back at her. She put her hands up in front of her and gazed at the gold ring that never left her hand. She tried once before to go without the wedding band but of course, her finger felt naked, and she missed what that simple band signified. A life shared with someone, a commitment to each other of love and honor. She had never felt those things with her husband; Darien had never really understood the concept of real love. As she stood before the mirrors, she made the decision that there was no reason for her to continue with a ring that meant nothing to her. She slipped it easily from her finger, and stood ready to face the Titobind along with whatever he had waiting for her. She tossed the ring towards the mirrors, and just as it hit the glass the doorways opened, all twelve of them, and there before her was the answer all along.

Twelve mirrors opened,

Twelve doorways revealed, but how to choose?

No more missing pieces, the entire puzzle solved, here and now.

Behind each doorway waited the same outcome. A consummation, a completion of her life as it was meant to be.

Darien began to turn.

Slowly at first, spinning around in circles, as she and her sister had done when they were small. She turned around and around seeing pictures in her mind of her children as they had done the same thing when they too were small. She remembered that the best part had always been in trying to walk straight afterwards. Darien smiled as she saw them take a few sideways steps and fall down, unable to keep their balance. Life is life that, take a few steps, giggle, fall down, then get up and start again. She raised her arms straight out from her body, bringing to herself the warm winds that would dissipate her body and carry her to the pyramid of the Titobind. She turned faster and faster creating a mini-tornado, a whirling vortex, and she felt the same sensations that had become so familiar and yet remained so strange.

Darien's body entered all twelve of the mirrors, and she would fit all the pieces together again on the other side.

# THE OTHER SIDE
# CONCLUDES IN PART THREE

It was dark here, as dark as it had been in the Pit.

The stinging bite of the extreme cold inhibited her reassembling, and it became apparent why the Mountain King offered her all the warmth that she could carry. It brought her some comfort to know that she could still tap into the heat stored safely inside, and Darien smiled at the irony of actually having to thank Satan for his help. Suddenly she missed Meara and Mimba, wishing she were back under the warm soft blanket.

She was having trouble breathing the thick air because it was so close to being the same consistency as water. Darien caused the air to ripple outwards from her body as if she had become the stone cast into a lake. Suddenly she started to panic, and began panic-like gasping. The air was drowning her! She desperately tried to draw in life-giving air, but there was no air for her, there was no air! Darien fell to the cold hard ground, down to her knees, and then quickly onto all fours. Saliva dripped from her wide-open mouth, her chest expanded to its fullest and choking noises issued from her throat.

"Relax," came the voice that cut a path through the liquid night.

"Relax," it said as it penetrated her mind.

"Relax," it came again, and Darien felt herself go loose and her lungs stopped heaving.

"Relax," it was hypnotic in its effect as her breathing slowed, and she found herself able to utilize the fluid air.

"Relax," came the voice again, and she felt the tension leave her body as the liquid night became easier and easier to breathe. Finally Darien stood up with her white gown glowing in the darkness, and the night slowly pulled back to allow the barest hint of light to surround her in an aura that made her look angelic.

"You are quite an enigma, Darien, do you realize that?" The voice that spoke was garbled to the point of being unintelligible. Maybe it was just the way sound traveled through the liquid air, and Darien suddenly realized she could breathe the liquid dark without any more difficulty. The same blackness that she pulled into her lungs slowly seeped into the rest of her body. She found that opening herself to its evil was quite exciting, and the power she felt was overwhelming in the effect it generated.

Its voice brought to her a deep, diseased desire.

She felt him probing at the corners of her consciousness, and she let her mind fly away to the corridors of safety within the confines of her memories of David. David, who came to her as a small and gentle voice, and spoke quietly in her ear.

"Darien," he said and for a long time it was all he ever said. It started from a time when she was barely old enough to remember, his voice was there, his voice softly saying: "Darien." Despite the fact that it was one word, it had saved her many times from walking into self-destructive situations. She remembered how easy it was to be self-destructive when all the years of struggling to survive suddenly came crashing down around her.

Thoughts of betrayal were first becoming linked with David, and then with Paul. She began slipping away into another place, a different reality, and Darien felt her emotions turning back to thoughts of destruction and pain. Pain was what she desired, pain was all she deserved. Her entire life had been built on what the guardians had led her to believe was the way her life was supposed to be.

They lied.

All of them lied, and they made David lie. David, who said that he

369

loved her, and then left and Darien, at that time, could not see that it was her own fault. Now, finally, with Titobind's help she could see how wrong that was.

Darien was a very bad girl.

Darien needed punishment for all the damage she caused. Poor David almost died; she deserted her children, and she was the cause of her husband's alienation and abuse. And she left Tanner behind, a man who waited patiently for someone who did not deserve him.

Oh yes, Darien was a very bad girl.

"Are you ready to take your punishment?" She heard the same garbled voice speak again; however, she found that some of it started to make sense. Darien moved her head around, feeling the strange resistance of the liquid dark, and then she turned her body around, watching herself flow within the confines of her watery prison. She marveled at the rippling effect she was having, the same as before, like a stone's rippling effect when thrown into the water.

"How will you take your punishment?"

"Is being your bride not punishment enough?" Darien moved and turned like she was under water, and then out of curiosity she curled down into a ball and sprang upwards, arms extended, leaping from the bottom of a pool. Her body sliced through the night, in the same way a swimmer slices through water. She hung suspended in air waving her arms to keep herself afloat in this endless dark sea, and then ever so slowly she waved them in the opposite direction to help force her body back down, until her feet were once again touching solid ground. She recognized the same smooth surface that was in the Pit.

"I have considered your answer." The voice was clear now and she cringed away as it made her insides shake like an earthquake was at hand.

"You are mine no matter if it is willing or otherwise, the game ends here, Darien, and as always I am again the winner, and as the winner I am ready to claim my prize. Are you ready to become the bride of a God? Shall I take you down to where you need to be? You should be grateful, Darien, that I even take the time to ask."

"How can I oppose the will of a God? Yes, I am ready to be your bride and to accept my punishment, whichever is to come first, but I will ask one thing before we begin."

"And that would be?"

Darien peered into the semi-darkness that moved before her, knowing that he stood hidden inside those shadows. "If I am to be your bride, then I think it's only fair that I see you." She heard a scratching sound, a thousand tiny scratches building as it were, a thousand tiny souls trying to escape the confines of their Darien prison. Her mind screamed for them to be quiet less the Titobind become aware that buried deep inside of her, she carried an army of good souls to fight for all of humankind. They called to her, filling her mind with echoes of "Darien, let us free, Darien."

"SSShhhh," she begged them to be quiet. He was not trusting in her yet, and Darien must keep the souls of the gold river a secret.

"SSShhhh," she told them again as their voices became more insistent.

"Darien, Darien, let us free, Darien." They were growing louder and more impatient as they struggled to be let out to face the Titobind. He was aware of their activity, but not quite certain what it consisted of, or exactly where it came from.

"Not yet, it is not time yet." She spoke vehemently so that they would settle back down, and Darien felt probes from Titobind.

"Are you hiding something from me, Darien?"

She felt him pushing against her consciousness; filling her with such painful agony that it lifted her from the ground. Darien screamed as he held her suspended in midair and the torment coursed through her body. The blood erupted from her orifices, and the guardians he bound to him reeled in despair for wanting to help her. Unexpectedly Titobind suddenly released her, and she fell back though the darkness, the same as a stone sinking deeply into the pond. Darien lay on her back on the cold hard floor where her blood spattered across the smooth surface. She coughed up more blood and then moved quickly, rolling onto her side, as she did not want to drown in her own vomit. The darkness that she lay in began to change, becoming a lighter shade, resembling the same dusk that she found when first entering this land beyond the mirrors. With shaking arms, she raised herself into a half-sitting position, her body nearly shattered, and her mind holding onto the barest edge of sanity. The white gown she wore was the color of the blood torn from her body, and she could barely see through the dripping tears of red. The liquid black womb drew back away from her, and a grayish circle crept in around the Titobind. Darien looked up and saw what no other human had ever seen.

"Do you still think that you can destroy me?" She looked up and wiped the blood from around her eyes as she stared at the thing bent on the destruction of her world and of all the worlds, he could find after that.

He stood before her at least four times the size of the Mountain King with eyes the shape of giant ovals, shining bright with a deep green color, like true and natural emeralds. He had no discernable nose and if he had not spoken, she would not know where his mouth was.

"Is this what you wanted to see?" His entire body was twisted into a shape as far from human as possible. His legs used to be planted firmly in the ground, and Darien could see where he had slowly been dislodging himself. The darkness moved around him with a myriad of appendages, all twisting and turning in and among themselves, and she could see that bound to his misshapen torso, held securely in place by the pincers on his appendages, were the guardians themselves. They moaned in agony when he moved the dark twisted extensions that drove the pincers into the helpless victims of his aggression. Darien could see where their lives, all of their lives, were going to end, and Titobind revealed for her a smile of triumph.

"Your race of people has made me what I am; you are all responsible for my creation."

"So you have decided to be responsible for their deaths. You will be responsible for the death of an entire universe and I have yet to understand why." He ignored her last remarks and gazed down upon the tiny bloody form that lay shivering in the cold, the cold provided by what he was.

"What are hiding from me, Darien?" This time Darien chose to ignore the Titobind as she curled herself into a small ball trying to escape from his gaze.

"At this point in time to defy me is useless, there is no place for you to go; there is no place for you to hide. You can look around and see that there is nothing here but me, and all of your options are gone. I am all that remains." To prove his point Titobind sent his appendages after her, and they closed around Darien, bringing her more agony than she ever thought a human body could withstand. She opened her mouth to scream, and he filled it with his cold, hard darkness. She lay on her side still curled into a ball, her breathing slowed, and blood trickled from her ears and eyes. It was next to the impossible that she was still breathing at all, and Titobind withdrew himself from her to watch her die. The great paddle wheel slowed across the dimension, and the Keeper of Time sat inside, waiting for his death while the Mountain King drew his daughters to himself so that they would all be together when the mountain came down.

Darien stared at Titobind with unblinking eyes and her body shook continuously until finally that too became as slow as her breathing. The motion of the wheel became almost nonexistent as it turned slower and slower, and the wind roared throughout the entire dimension. The existence of every living creature arrived at the point of extinction.

"You still live, Darien, and I am so impatient waiting for your soul. It is time to sit beside a God, and continue on forever into the canyons of time as partner and soul taker with Tianato Morebind. I will be ruler and destroyer of a thousand cultures, a thousand worlds, and you, sweet Darien, will hold their souls with me forever. It is time to extinguish your human body, and join me in eternity because you have lost everything, and all of you is mine to take and to torture and to do with as I will." A great silence filled the pyramid, and even the moans of the guardians were no longer audible. The Titobind was drawing the last loose part of his twisted evil form from the ground and he looked once again to the shivering woman below him.

"Have you nothing to say to me before your body dies?" Darien slowly uncurled herself from the fetal position she was in and pushed herself up to her knees. She rested for a moment until she was able to gather enough strength to stagger upright to her feet. She pulled from herself the fire of the red dragon, the faith of an ancient wise race, and it gave her the strength to look straight into the green eyes of the monstrous evil that was Titobind and say to him:

"I say that if it pleases the Titobind, may I have some more?"

He immediately recoiled from her, stunned and shocked that Darien regained her feet, much less answered him. This was not possible! By all human standards, Darien should be dead, and Tianato Morebind should be consuming her flesh and at the same time, absorbing her soul. While he watched, she dropped down to one knee, never releasing him from the steady gaze of her blood-streaked eyes. It was the evil monstrosity's turn to watch in awe, and to experience the multitude of emotions that she brought to him. Curiosity for what she thought she was doing, pain that he suffered when she sang in the halls of the Mountain King, and fear as the one emotion he has come to resent the most.

His triumphant attitude was waning.

Titobind was at a loss at what to do, and his appendages disobeyed him, the guardians were moving and struggling violently against him, while the liquid womb that nurtured him would not respond to his commands to settle back down around him. He looked at Darien as she struggled to hold command over her weakened body, and he heard the paddle wheel turn again with a resounding "click, click, click, click." The gates of time were once more reinforcing the barriers, and the winds that had blown her cold death towards him were now retreating. Titobind looked down one more time at the tiny blood-soaked figure that still fought to hold her ground, and now it was too late, when he finally heard the cries of the souls begging Darien, "Release us now!"

Terror hit home, and he opened his green oval eyes wide in total fear and spoke to her for the last time.

"Who are you, Darien?"

She rose from her crouched position to stand straight and strong and her eyes held no fear as she gazed at the twisted, bent, evil, black form of the Titobind. When she spoke to him, her body began generating a power of light that emanated from the selfsame places which moments ago had erupted with her life-sustaining blood. As she spoke, she rose higher into the air, casting light and warmth in every direction.

"Know you not who I am, Tianato Morebind?

"I am the brightness in the light that finds its way into the hearts of all people.

"I am one with the earth that survives despite the horror you have cast upon it.

"Look at me, Titobind; behold the light of all that is good inside, for I have become all things clean and pure.

"You have no more power, and now we command you,
"RELEASE THE SERAPHIMS OF PAUL!"

Darien rose before him surrounded by the brightness of the tiny suns that escaped from inside her, the light of the guardian who had fallen to earth when they were first betrayed. Hundreds of gold souls erupted in an explosion of righteousness for all that is fair and honest, and the gold river rose with them, erupting from inside of Darien, spewing forth like a cascade of virtuous baptismal waters! They became one in a chorus of triumph as they rejoined, and then rained down upon the evil. Darien threw the darkness back, suspended by the light that came from deep inside where the never-ending love and understanding that was Paul had lain quiet and dormant. She had forgotten.

He hid his own soul inside of Darien!

The light that surrounded her now came together as one large brightness, and there in the very center, back into his ethereal form, was the guardian Paul, along with the mighty red dragon that breathed his hot flames to help destroy the malformed monster. Then Darien with the voice of all that she had endured, and all that she had come to love, released a song of such exquisite beauty that Titobind continued to shrink before their eyes.

Titobind screamed as the extensions of his own evil were torn from his body, and the guardians themselves swelled into the light, breaking free from the constricting binds that he cast upon them. Darien watched with tears flowing freely down her face while the golden river rainbow combined with the powerful dragon and the everlasting goodness in the light that was Paul, and together they all melted into, and then shattered what remained of the evil that had been so corrupt in its origin.

Darien began to fall. The light that carried her had gone to Paul and to the other guardians as they spun their warm tornado winds with their exhilaration at being free.

Bursting through the light he came for her, reaching, and gathering her into the strength and glory of his soul. David caught, held her, and then carried her away, leaving the guardians to re-light their dimension so that they would never be in the darkness of despair again.

David stood in the corner near the fireplace that brought so much warmth into the empty life of Darien. This is her room of dreams, the one where David first brought to her the presents of the double roses. Suspended on the chain around her neck, he watched the rise and fall of the small silver rose with her level, yet shallow breathing. The Jester stood nearby, as did the Mountain King and of course Paul. David thanked the Jester for his return of the necklace, assuring them that he would let her know they came to see her, and then he returned to his vigil by her side. Jester along with the Mountain King bid their respects to Paul, and then took their leave, returning to their respective realms. David's heart went out to her and despite all of his teachings, and all of his learnings, there was one fact that he could never deny, and that was his true feelings for her. Paul quietly returned to the room, bringing a sudden rush of warmth, striding slowly and purposefully over to David accompanying him in his silent watch over the quiet sleeping savior.

"She is my smallest angel," he said softly.

David turned to look at his elder, and asked, "They are all free aren't they, Paul?" It was more a statement than a question, and Paul answered yes with a slight nod of his head, then he looked at David with great affection, placing his hand on his shoulder.

"We must never again allow darkness or despair to grow and replace the light that is our life. What is done is done, and now they must rebuild."

"Do you know how far he was able to reach over there in their world, how much he destroyed?" Paul breathed a great sigh, and relinquished with much anguish the exact number of deaths, the sum total of souls that Titobind removed from their earthly bonds.

"That many? It appears that the Mountain King will have a glorious century."

"Indeed, but it will quickly pass as the humans return to procreate. You have checked on Tanner, and found him well?"

"He waits patiently, and of course seeing the evil withdraw from their world, he realizes that she has survived."

They stood in silence watching her healing process, and without warning her body began a series of tremendous dry heaving. David was immediately by her side as the evil that Titobind used to corrupt her came pouring from her mouth. A black, foul-smelling thick sludge trying desperately to reassemble into some kind of human shape. David looked to Paul in amazement as he gathered the sludge into a box that the souls had fashioned from the gold river. Through the course of their conflict, the tri-colored river re-routed itself to flow around the home of the guardians, and it surrounded them with an even stronger barrier against evil.

"He still lives? I don't understand how."

"David, parts of him will always live; there will always be some degree of evil floating within the universes, keeping pace throughout all of time. Maybe one day we will fully understand the reasons for it to exist, but for now, we will continue to do as we have always done. There will, however, be one exception; this time when we release the despair brought over from the human side, we will contain it inside the shell boxes provided by the souls of the gold river."

"Did you know of them, Paul?"

"I can't answer that question, because it will only lead to more questions, many of which will be unanswerable. You should understand by now, David, that even with thousands of years of learning, we still do not have all the answers."

"The flame that held his home in the sky, is it also completely gone?"

Paul smiled at David, he was so much like Darien, so much like small children, and to Paul, they always would be. He shook his head, looking at David knowing they were all only children playing an elaborate game designed by a power they would never see.

"Why don't you go and look with the others, David. I have sent several groups out across the expanse between our dwelling and where Titobind's home used to be. All remaining traces of Titobind are to be captured, contained, and put where he can no longer come together. Doing this for yourself should, at the very least, put to rest some of your questions and no doubt relieve me from having to answer them all." David smiled at Paul and his small glow of white light expanded with his relief, until he looked upon the small body sleeping soundly under the blankets.

"I will watch over her. Don't worry, David, she will heal. It will just take a little longer now that we have all left her."

"And then?"

"David, you are close to exasperating me, just go and join the others and put your lingering fears to rest, and we will address other things later." David smiled again as he picked up the gold box that was now heavy with the evil secured inside.

"Don't forget to dispose of that."

"No," he answered as he began to spin, "I won't."

He dispersed into the mini-whirlwind and let it carry him up and out of their home, far away across the vast expanse to join the others. He found them searching and containing shattered pieces of the pyramid that had floated on the cold flame of Titobind's black heart. The guardians walked the bare ground, dislodging little black shadow things that emitted eerie little "eeeessss" as they dissolved into pools of liquid black that were quickly absorbed into the ground. David found the stench alone to be overwhelming as he helped the other guardians proceed with the gathering. One of the older ones, almost as old as Paul himself, started to chant as he worked. His deep-throated baritone voice made the horrendous task less tedious, and the others took up the rhythm of the labor. They raised their voices in song, singing in beauty with the light of their world, a light that would always flow inside the great guardians.

Tyler Tanner opened the door to his dinner, and watched with a mournful heart as the Red Cross trucks tried to maneuver around the piles of corpses. He had expected to see and prepared himself for a few bodies, but even this great number caused his stomach to turn. There were dead people everywhere, corpses piled upon corpses, raising the unmistakable stench of decay and rot that permeates into everything; it's an odor no one gets used to. In some of the spots, where the bodies were piled two and three deep, the ones underneath ended up being just pieces. He felt a great deal of pity for the armed forces that came in, the men who had to roll the corpses and search them for identification. Tanner could still hear the screams as children braved the fog looking for parents who became lost in a desperate search for food. He remembered how the fog parted for Darien and of the people who made the unfortunate decisions to venture outside and ended up being food for the shadows. He recalled how they lay in a fog-induced stupor while the shapeless myrmidons of Titobind feasted upon their zombie-like bodies.

Tanner wondered if the surviving populace would ever understand what really happened. He could already see the headlines in the papers, as those who survived would blame it on everything from a new disease to the inevitable alien invasion. Tanner snorted his displeasure at the inadequacies of man to accept something as simple as good against evil. There would of course be the few who would know, the few who believed, and there would be the newly converted. Would this religious fervor last? There was no way anyone could predict the next step. Tanner would still be a non-believer had he not experienced firsthand the arrival of the bats and their protectiveness of him. Even at night, they stayed protectively by his side, hovering over him. He knew the morning he woke and they were no longer in his home, that Darien had freed the guardians. Tanner also knew that somewhere someone was sitting and waiting to make the next move in this gigantic amusing game.

"Excuse me, sir?" The "sir" came out as a southern drawl, and sounded more like "suuh," bringing Tanner out of his wandering thoughts. He looked up to see a good ole boy wearing army fatigues, and his face bore the pain of someone totally despaired with the job he was doing. Tanner's thoughts were ironic when he looked down and said, The guardians are needed now more than ever to clean up a world united in despair.

The young soldier spoke again: "If'n we tote you in some supplies, do ya all think that you could cook us up somethin' to eat?"

"You hungry after smelling and movin' that stench, boy?"

"Yes, suh, I am that."

"Red Cross givin' you anything?"

"Coffee, suh, and a donut or two, but we need something a little more'n that."

"Bring 'em on; I'll do the best I can."

"Yes, suh." He smiled like a child who hit the jackpot on some giant candy machine, and it appeared as though he was not much older than that. The boy-soldier ran, skidding around piles of corpses, yelling his relief, and Tanner grinned at the happy sounds. They were alive, the whole world was alive! The sun was shining again, and Darien would be coming home! He walked into his diner and happily put his apron back on as he turned the flames up under the grill and the deep fryers.

The soldiers piled into the diner until it couldn't hold any more, and then the overflow spilled out onto the street. They put the grave task on hold while they ate, laughed, and brought the joy of living back into the diner, and into Tanner's life. He flipped burgers and deep-fried potatoes until all the supplies were gone. The diner emptied out slowly as the soldiers ate the last of the food, and Tanner could see the reluctance on the young faces at having to go back outside. He was picking up dishes and wiping down the tables when the southern boy came out of the men's room. He startled Tanner, who dropped the dish he was holding, shattering it into far too many pieces. The soldier bent to help him pick up the shards, and then the two worked together in silence, clearing the diner from top to bottom until finally they sat down with two fresh cups of coffee. The soldier addressed Tanner.

"Corbin Bennett." He held out his hand and Tanner shook it.

"Tyler Tanner, but Tanner's fine."

"Sounds like one of those soap opry names." Tanner laughed at this statement because his mother would never have turned on one of those senseless programs.

"When I was growing up there was a show on television called *Circus Boy*, and I think that Mickey Dolenz of the music group the Monkees played the kid star."

"Hey, I heard of them."

"Most people have. Anyway, this boy traveled with a circus, and was always getting into all sorts of scraps, you know, making up the stories for the weekly series. In the show this kid's name was Toby Tyler and my mom said she named me after him. You know what the funny part is?" The soldier boy shook his head no.

"The funny part is that I ended up a lot like this kid, getting into trouble but always coming out on top, been like that most of my life."

"You were in Nam, right?"

"Shows that much?"

"To another soldier, yes, suh." He paused for a minute as if he was trying to pull his thoughts together and Tanner could see that his brain was hard at work, trying to get the words to come out just right. It reminded him of an obnoxious little jester.

"If you've got a question, son, the best way to get an answer is to ask it."

"Well, suh, you survived right in the middle of all this mess, and you and I both know that the odds of that happening are extremely low. I get the feeling that you know a little more about what happened here then you might be willing to talk about."

Tanner sipped on his coffee studying the young man, whose intelligence had been somewhat diminished in Tanner's eyes by his young appearance. He lit a cigarette and pulled on it deeply, taking the cancerous smoke deep into his lungs where the nicotine addiction scrapped along his nerves. He expunged the gray smoke and raised his eyebrows at the similarity in color of the gray fog that had surrounded them with death and the gray smoke that he pushed from his body. He put the cigarette out; it was his last.

"I know."

The soldier nodded his head, rose up off his stool, and headed towards the door, but before leaving, he turned to Tanner and said, "Do you know if it's over?"

Tanner looked out past Corbin Bennett at the brightness of day that was lighting the world once again with hope. "My best guess would be yes, for now."

"I was kinda hoping that would be your answer."

Corbin returned to the empty streets of Corral, Texas, to help finish cleaning the remains, and to finish searching the houses for possible survivors. Tanner started to light another cigarette, stopped and put it back into the pack. Instead, he poured himself another cup of coffee as he watched the news on the television, extremely thankful that the utility workers had already restored his electricity. Censuses of the number of deaths were not finished, but so far, the best guess reached well into the thousands. Titobind's short hold in this world had resulted in nothing less than devastation. It stretched as far west as California, east to the Mississippi and north as far as the southern part of South Dakota.

"So many," he whispered under his breath. "Was such a harsh lesson really needed? It won't change that much, you know, a few more will acknowledge you, maybe even make a permanent change in their lives, but was it necessary to take so many lives to convert so few? As your children, are we that ignorant of our own doings?" He walked around to the counter to where the grill was and picked up the stone he used to scrape it clean.

"Come home soon, Darien, I am desperate to hold you close." Tanner laid the stone back down without cleaning anything, and went up to his apartment. He was glad that it was finally empty of bats and of black shapeless blobs, but a part of him would always scrutinize the shadowed corners.

Darien opened her eyes, frightened at first, until she realized the sanctity of the home that she rested in, and she pulled the blankets up close around her. David and Paul stood nearby smiling down on her.

"Leave us, David."

"Paul, she has just wakened."

"David, this is not easy for me either, you may see her when I'm done. Why don't you go and prepare some food, and I'm sure Darien is thirsty." David bowed to Paul then retreated from the room, but not before he gave Darien a quick smile. Paul walked over, and sat on the bed beside her, covering her hand with his own.

"How are you, Darien?" His concerns, genuine, his dept of compassion, overwhelming.

"Cold, Paul. I'm still cold, and I feel like part of him is still hiding inside, the way I knew you were in me, without realizing it was you. I'm not sure, but it does feel the same.

"You body is nearly cleansed, Darien, but you could be right, a part of him might be still be hiding inside. We will summon one of the gold souls tomorrow to help you export the last of his evil." Darien nodded in agreement.

"My back feels strange. Is something wrong?"

"Nothing is wrong so to speak, your left shoulder and your entire back is transformed into an everlasting part of the river souls, and the gold scales that covered you in the water are now a permanent part of your body."

"You have got to be kidding!" she said incredulously.

"Guardians don't kid."

"Damn."

David returned with hot soup, bread, fresh fruit, and a pitcher of water. After setting the tray down, he gently folded his hand around hers, and this time Paul retreated to the far side of the room.

"How are you really?"

She raised her free hand and tenderly touched the face she so dearly loved. "I'm okay, David." He brought her hand to his lips and kissed her as softly as he could, letting his lips drink in once again, her texture, her smell, her softness.

"David," Paul said softly.

David turned and looked at Paul, then with great reluctance he left the room whispering to her, "I'll be back shortly." Darien gave him a weak half-smile. Paul stayed on the far side of the room watching Darien as she ate.

"Please don't stare. If you have something to say, the best way to get it out is to just say it." Paul recognized her simplistic way of getting straight to the point, and he smiled.

"I have never seen such a tying bind between two people before, well between human and guardian. Let me rephrase that, between two of anything." Darien laughed at his statement and Paul smiled, knowing how much laughter would help speed her recovery.

"Darien, we need to talk about more serious matters."

"I know. Say what you have to."

"You don't make this easy, but then you never did. I cannot, we cannot make you completely as we are, and you already know that this is not possible. You also know that you cannot stay here with us."

"Who makes up these damn rules anyway?"

"You can be quite exasperating but I do understand the connection you have with David and there is a solution to the problem. We can't help you to become a guardian that you will eventually become on your own; however, we can send David back with you as human." Paul's words stunned Darien because no one ever told her that this was even a possibility. And her mind ran back to the first part of what the he said.

*I am going to become a true guardian? When is that going to happen?* She kept this thought to herself, even though the words pushed her into a hundred more excited questions, let alone the fact that David could come back with her! Paul continued talking as if what he said about her being guardian should have no bearing at all.

"Before you become quick to answer consider the consequences not to you, but to David. He has no idea what it would be like to live among you. David has the greatest love for all living creatures, and his purpose as guardian is one he treasures above all else, for he knows no other way. You have sacrificed so much for us, for your race of people, and through the experiences you have had you will return to see everything in a different way. You have grown into such a beautiful, understanding woman, and have so much to offer your world. However, despite all of the love David has for you, he needs to exist here with us. He needs to fulfill his duties as guardian, as he has done for thousands of years. Do you understand what I am saying to you?"

"You want me to say goodbye to David and you want me to make it the last goodbye."

"Yes, and Tanner waits for you; he is a good man, Darien, and his love for you is strong and true."

"But not as deep, nor does it evoke the all-encompassing power of feelings that David generates within me. What if David wants to come with me?"

"He will want to at first, then with great reluctance and relief he will let you go."

"Without your influence."

"Of course, I would not dare."

"Oh, please, you tried to erase me from his memory once before."

"You have both come a long way since then, Darien. You have both grown together to understand and accept what can never be a healthy relationship for either one of you. Desperation is not a good reason to cling together, and you have seen the type of destruction it can cause.

"Aren't you exaggerating this just a little?"

"Am I?"

"Don't make me think so hard, it's not fair." It was Paul's turn to laugh.

"When you take the time to really think about it, you'll see that I'm right." Paul walked from the room dispersing into the winds, and David stood in his place.

"May I come in?"

"Of course, David, always." He entered the room, slowly approached the bed, and proceeded to climb in gently beside her. Darien immediately laid her head on his chest and he folded her back into the arms she loved to have around her. He kissed the top of her head, and she snuggled into David's chest then closed her eyes. The next time Darien woke, David was still holding her. It was twelve hours later and neither one of them had moved.

Several days later Darien found that she was feeling much better, and was actually able to get to her feet on her own, even if she was still a little wobbly. She picked up her gown and briskly rubbed then shook her legs, trying to get some circulation going again. She dropped her gown back down over her legs, and ran her hands over the downy softness of the material they had draped over her.

"Everything here is so warm and good." David smiled at her. "You dressed me, David, bathed me?"

"No one else was allowed to touch you."

"Touch me again, David." She walked over to the bed. "Touch me again. I have missed your soft caresses more than I have missed anything else in my life."

Darien walked over to the bed, lifting her gown over her head and dropping it to the floor. She turned suddenly as the flash of gold scales glared in the mirror on the wall. She turned and studied her back; scrutinizing the way the scales overlapped and fit into each other all way up over her right shoulder. She expected them to feel fish-like, and possibly even smell fish-like. Darien was surprised and pleased when she found them to be as soft as velvet to the touch. Now the test was the smell. She brought her fingers to her nose and breathed in just a little and then more deeply as her nose filled with the sweet smell of the cool, clean gold river that they evolved from.

"Darien, you look wonderful."

"Well, it is quite the fashion statement." She walked over to the bed and climbed back in next to David. She kneeled before him and let herself sit backward on her legs resting her arms on her thighs. Unexpectedly she felt a slight movement on her back, finding that the scales were rippling with her breathing. Darien opened her mouth, took a deep breath, and was delighted to feel the movement of the scales as they fully expanded and then relaxed. She repeated this three or four times, finding that the breathing released an exotic smell into the room, except the odor changed slightly, leaning towards more of a musk.

"It's changing with my mood isn't it, David."

"That's how it seems to be working, but this is something new to me also, Darien, I didn't even know about the gold river, or the good souls."

"Let me guess who did though, maybe Paul? Maybe the selfsame all-encompassing entity who started this damn game in the first place, trying to appease his eternal boredom?" Her scales rippled rapidly, becoming tinted with a light hue of red as her anger grew along with the cutting edge of her endless sarcasm.

"Darien, don't do this, don't become angry. It has been so long since I have seen you, and I would rather make love to you than argue about things that are beyond our control."

*Is this what Paul meant by an unhealthy relationship? My anger, my jealousy?*

Darien looked at David, at the most exquisite man ever to enter her life. A man who could touch and turn any area of her body into sensual pleasures, a man who gave her only kindness, caring, and an understanding that Darien still abused, without understanding the consequences of her greedy consumption. She looked into his beautiful brown eyes, and saw only the same love that had always been. David rose up to his knees and reached out to take her arm and pull her back up to her knees, and then ever so slowly he took his hand and covered her breast. He closed his eyes while he held her and caressed her nipple with his thumb, and his touch was like a spark that sent charges of arousal through her body. Darien covered his hand with hers and David opened his eyes to smile down upon her, then together they leaned forward until their lips met, and Darien shuddered under his touch while tears sprang from beneath her closed eyes, making little puddles under her lashes. A small cry of emotion issued from her throat directly into David's mouth, and she broke the kiss throwing her arms around him while crying silently into his neck. He held her close as she purged herself of all the past events, grateful that everything was finally over.

"I miss my children, so much, more than what I thought I would."

"You can go and see them; nothing is stopping you from doing that."

"I know."

"Look at me, Darien." She did as he requested. "You are their mother, and no matter what happens they will always need you, and I know that they miss you just as much, if not more." He touched her face tenderly, kissed her, and the familiarity of his kiss brought a sudden rush of feelings, which the guardian could never fully control.

"I wish that I could hold you forever," he whispered in her ear, his voice husky and deep with emotions.

Darien's passion was building from nothing more than the simplicity of knowing his touch. The newly attached velvety scales released a heavier concentration of the musk while David became fully aroused. He caught her breasts in both of his hands and looked at her while he teased them. Darien brought her legs up from under her and stood up over him. David held onto her thighs and buried his face deep between her legs, filling his face with her sweet juice. She steadied herself on his shoulders as his mouth and tongue teased her until her body trembled for release. He took his mouth away, pulled her slowly down to the bed where he could kiss her deeply, taking pleasure in the sharing of their tastes. His mouth left her mouth, and he once again explored her with his tongue, moving down her chest, laying his face on the softness of her breasts while he played and aroused her nipples with his tongue. Darien shivered with excitement and David loved his ability to create such pleasure for her. He moved his hand down her side to caress her thigh while at the same time pushing her leg gently backwards. He slipped his fingers inside her wetness, and she gasped gratefully as he filled her. Suddenly Darien held his hand, taking it from inside her. She wanted to taste him, to rouse him to the same level of excitement that she had reached. She slid around on the bed until she was directly underneath him and Darien gently licked at the testes that hung above her face. She encouraged him to move backwards so she could consume David with her mouth and she did this to bring him the greatest gift of all, the complete trust and faith that they had in each other. David slowly removed himself from her mouth and mounted her, parting her sweet velvety labia with the hot hard tip of his penis. She pulled in her breath as he pushed onto her clitoris, making her cry out for release. He let himself side down to where he could penetrate her and Darien locked David inside of her as she threw her legs up over his hips, and he buried his head into her neck while at the same time pushed deep inside of her. He shuddered and they climaxed together in a great cry of pleasure and relief at the same time, and then they lay in each other's arms where they rested, made love, and rested once more.

Four times that night, their passion returned knowing that it could be their last night together, but they were happy despite this because they were truly safe with their common enemy defeated. David enfolded Darien into the warm winds of the vortex that the guardians summoned when they traveled, so that he could take her to the places that previously brought them pleasure. He made love to her in the cozy winter cabin where he emerged from the shadows cast on the walls by the blazing fire in the huge stone fireplace. They sat together under a heavy winter blanket sipping hot chocolate and watching the clean white snow blanket the mountain. They walked outside into the midst of the snowstorm, and David melted the snow around them revealing nature's soft green grass underneath. They lay down and made sweet delicious love in the midst of a roaring winter storm that never touched them.

David took her to the sandy beach where he first taught her total body pleasure and he re-entered all the places that made her cry out in complete fulfillment, while the physical pleasure she bequeathed on David fell just short of being miraculous. He held her close when she needed, and they were able to lie together for hours, touching, relearning, and burning themselves fiercely into each other's minds and souls. He took her to the guardians' sanctuary where she was able to watch through the mirrors and make sure her children were cared for, and she was mildly surprised to see her "husband" with a girlfriend.

"He deserved more happiness than what I gave him," she whispered to David. "I hope he finds it with her and I hope she is a better wife to him than I was." Darien felt a kind of sadness for her and for Jack, an emptiness that spanned through twenty years of her life, years with a sickness that made their lives miserable. Her velvety scales rippled into a bluish tint; the odor that emanated seemed to be a spicy, piney, woodsy odor, and she learned the scent of her own sadness.

With great reluctance, they returned to the room of Darien's dreams, and made love one more time; because both of them knew it was time for her to return home. How could they face separation again? Darien's scales remained blue as her sadness increased, and she could not bear to look at David because she felt, inside her heart, there would never be any mending. Paul quietly entered the room, and they were unaware of his ethereal presence until he spoke to them.

"Have the two of you discussed your options?"

David looked at Paul with eyes that held a sadness so great that it pulled on Paul as well, turning his emotions into a sudden turmoil of misgivings.

*What options, Paul; you really didn't give us any.* She wanted to voice those feelings, but instead she said matter-of-factly: "I want to stay, but I know I can't."

David kneeled before her with tears and tenderness and whispered softly to her.

"Let me come with you, please, Darien."

She looked to Paul, who shook his head no, and then he looked away so she would not see the tears in his eyes or the pain that he was feeling at their separation as well. Darien touched the soft skin of David's face, and with choked emotions spoke to him of her love, of her burning desires for him, and of how she longed to have him come with her. However, deep in her heart of hearts she knew that without his calling, without being able to express his love of all the people that even with her love, he would wither and die inside. She could not, would not be responsible, there was too much between them to allow that to happen.

"Take from me, my beloved David, a part of my love for you." She returned to him his small token of love, the silver rose he gave her.

"If ever you have need of me, send the rose through the mirror, and I will find a way back to you, this is a promise that I will never break." He threw himself onto her lap, holding her tightly, and at that moment Darien knew she was making the right decision.

"I love you, David, I have always loved you, through the centuries, throughout all of time. Have faith in us and that we will find a way to be together." David looked up at her, with a face wet with tears, and kissed her deeply pulling her into him. The warm winds came, dispersing their bodies to travel back to the other side, while Paul looked on his own heart aching at her departure.

# CHAPTER FOURTEEN

# GOING HOME

The road leading into Corral, Texas, was deserted.

After all, who would want to go into a place where so much destruction had originated? The quiet, however, would not be long lived because soon there would be the curious thrill seekers, the reporters, the scientists and of course let us not forget our infamous and various government agencies. It would not surprise Darien if some innovative person took pictures along the way, and was going to charge admission into the Corral Museum, "Where Devastation Originates." In her mind she saw them swarming down the road like a great giant colony of ants, and for those who had thought that they knew so much, how humbled they would be to find they knew so little. David sat nearby on a large flat rock watching her gaze out around the empty desert. She turned around to face him while the space between them became wider by the second.

"How does it feel knowing that you saved your species and thousands of others throughout the galaxy as well?"

"It feels like it never happened."

"It will become real to you again after you enter the deserted town, and the emptiness of his destruction can actually be seen. I did keep you a few extra days so by the time you arrived at Tanner's diner, all the cleanup would be done. I didn't want you to come back and see all of the death that it caused."

"I appreciate your concern, but tell me, is that the only reason you kept me there?" She grinned at him and he gave her a half-smile. David, one of God's greatest gifts to the human world, looked at Darien with a face full of wonder, and she knew that even with everything that had happened, his soul remained pure.

She thought to herself, *How human he looks, so much like a sweet little boy.*

"I didn't ask you, Darien, I was a little afraid to, but when the gold souls came to take you, to purge the last of the evil from inside, did it go well?" This was probably the one thing that Darien would never share with anyone, ever, because being taken down into the gold river where the souls without homes float endlessly through time, was more overwhelming than having to face the Titobind. They clamored over her body, begging for a place inside of her, raising such a din of desire that Darien was afraid they were going to tear her apart in their eagerness to touch and be inside as a part of her.

In the end, to be free of his evil, she let them in, and the pain of doing that was greater than the sum total of all the past three months. They entered every part of her, down to every cell, scraping her body from the inside, chasing away the last part of its existence. It seemed strange to her, however, that as thorough as the good souls had been, it felt like there was a part of him creeping around inside, hiding and waiting.

"It went fine." He looked as if he did not believe her.

"You will watch over me?"

"You don't need me to watch over you anymore. Your body and mind are strong, and you are still learning the powers of the guardians. This has always been your destiny, part human, part guardian, and a part of the gold souls."

"Say yes anyway." She walked over to where he sat on the rock and wrapped her arms fiercely around him and they melded so perfectly together. Why did something that felt so right have to end?

"Yes," he whispered softly in her ear.

"I will never love again, as much as I have loved you. You are my life forever, through all of time." David's answer came in the form of the tear she felt drop on her neck, and in the kiss of love he placed upon her lips, and in the quiet strength with which he held her. They stood linked together until, in just a few moments' time, Darien stood alone as David dissipated to return to his world. The wind blew warm gently around her, and his words came as soft as they had always been, and he spoke directly into her ear assuring her that he would always walk beside her.

"Always and ever my beloved Darien."

There was nothing left for her to do except go into town and find Tanner. Paul told her that he would be waiting at the diner. In a strange and wonderful way, she loved him as well. There were different kinds of love and David brought a burning desire that Tanner could never equal; still she did love him, and she would make her earthly home with him. Darien shivered despite the ninety-five-degree heat in the Texas desert, and it was becoming apparent that some of the Titobind's sludge had escaped the purging. She could feel a little piece of his black soul running rampant through her system, hiding and laughing at the gold soul's ineptitude at finding it. There was time to worry about that later, but right now all she wanted was something real, something she could hold onto, something that was not going to disappear, and that something was Tanner. Darien turned and started to walk towards town feeling somewhat apprehensive at what waited for her beyond the comfort that she knew within the boundaries of the guardians. She was also confused, as always, with the question of why had it become so easy for her to let David go. Was it because she knew that Tanner was waiting for her? Maybe it was because she knew she would not be alone. Was she so shallow that she could slide so easily from one man's arms to another?

Darien wanted to believe, between the two of them, they filled her with a love she never knew before and between the two, they taught her the simple respect and deep commitment that came with unquestionable faith.

Darien felt a drop fall onto her upper lip and she glanced upwards to the sky. Was it raining? She put her hand up on her lip, and touched a drop of blood with her fingertip.

"Oh God, is it starting again? It's supposed to be over damn it!" Suddenly there were a thousand cries of terror and confusion exploding inside of her head, and blood poured from her ears and nose, driving Darien to her knees.

And then it was gone. As unexpectedly as it started, it stopped. She gagged on the remains of blood that lodged in her throat, and she vomited red so that she could breathe. Darien heard the sound of a motorcycle engine, and she knew without looking that Tanner would be the driver.

She did not have the strength to lift her head from the sudden torrent of the pained voices, but Tanner was there, and she felt his arms go around her as he lifted her off the ground. She gratefully hugged his neck as he held her close to him.

"I thought it would be over," he said softly to her.

"Me too" was all she could squeak out.

"Can you stand?"

"Yeah, I'll be okay." He set her back on her feet then quickly removed his shirt and put it around her. Darien dropped the soft nightdress off her body, and Tanner buttoned his shirt around her. She had become so small from her ordeal that his shirt fit like a dress, and she was lost inside of it. It was a good, safe feeling. Tanner went over to turn the bike around and Darien climbed on behind him, grateful beyond words that he was there. She put her arms around his waist and laid her cheek on his back while he started the bike. He pulled up the kickstand and headed back towards town at a speed that would close the distance for them in just a few short minutes.

A small tumbleweed blew by the discarded nightgown followed by a mini swirling tornado. A large hand came out of the passing vortex, scooping up the soft material, and a gentle voice came from within.

"Ever and always my beloved Darien."

Darien, like Tanner, was not ready to accept what she saw. The sound of the motorcycle's engine was huge against the deserted streets, and its noise bounced off the walls of the empty buildings. She expected to find a few people, but she was not prepared to find the extreme quiet that accompanied an empty, deserted town. The soldiers' detail was over, and they were back at their respective stations, their cleanup duties completed. Erected on the outskirts of the city were large red posts to mark the mass graves. The soldiers hung lists of all the known dead or missing at city hall, just as they were ordered to do. Darien squeezed Tanner's arm and pointed to the large brick building where the last of the details were climbing into traditional green army jeeps. She watched them drive away knowing how anxious they must be to leave the town where so much death originated. Tanner cut the engine and jockeyed the bike backward onto its stand while Darien waited patiently for him to dismount.

"What could you possibly expect to find here, Darien?"

"I have to see, Tanner, I have to know."

"Why? Nothing you could have done would have made it better or easier. My God, Darien, a whole world would be dead right now if it weren't for you. Isn't that enough?"

"It should be, Tanner, I want it to be, but somehow it's not. Please come inside with me."

"Darien, I lived through this, I watched them die."

"And I have seen so much more, please." She held out her hand to him, and Tanner could not argue with her reasoning or the look on her face that melted his heart. He took her hand inside of his and helped her up the stairs. Greeting them inside was page after page of papers lining the corridors with the names of the deceased. These were the voices Darien heard cry out when she arrived; the torment of all of thousands of souls who were now fair game for the Mountain King and it would be for him, beyond any doubt, a most glorious century.

"So many, Tanner, so many." She turned around and looked at the man who still waited ever so patiently for her.

"There would not be a list if it were not for you, because no one would ever see the names in the death of entire world."

She whispered under her breath as she turned to look back at the wall, "It was so much more than just us." Then to Tanner she said softly, "You are right; I don't need to be here. Please take me home." They quietly left the building, leaving it to the echoes of their footsteps, and Darien thought for a moment, a small glancing moment, that she saw movement in the shadows.

The diner looked the same as before she left, and Darien could not understand why she had expected everything to look different, but she did and this surprised her.

"Hungry?"

She nodded her head. "Starving."

"You go on upstairs and wash the rest of that mess off of you and I'll fix you something to eat." She gratefully accepted his offer and headed up the back stairs.

"Tanner?" He looked up at her. "Don't be long; I don't want to be alone, okay?"

"Don't worry." He grinned at her; she smiled back, and then went upstairs.

Darien quickly lost track of time as the hot water beat down on her head until Tanner opened the door and good-naturedly admonished her to get out of the water before she turned into a prune. It was ironic as to how many times, when as children, they had sworn up and down they would never end up saying things like their parents, and yet. Tanner turned on the TV, finding that the only broadcast was the news. What else could there be? Darien picked up the plate of bacon, eggs, home fries, and toast in one hand, her cup of coffee in the other, and joined Tanner in the living room. He watched her sit down cross-legged balancing her plate in her lap, and then setting her cup of coffee on the end table.

"Where'd you get food?" she asked as the taste of the eggs and bacon became like a brand-new eating experience.

"The army left me with some supplies until we can get more or until we get out, whichever comes first." He watched her eat out of the corner of his eyes, and made a few grunting comments at her appetite.

"Don't they eat over there?"

"They fed me, but this food is the good stuff." He watched her finish her plate, followed by a resounding belch.

"Oh I'm sorry; it's just that it all tasted really good."

"It's okay." Darien set her dishes aside, and moved over on the sofa where she laid her head softly against Tanner's small, hard chest. She had never even kissed Tanner, not at any length, how did she know that they would even be compatible? She rose from her leaning position and sat on his lap, positioning herself directly in front of him.

"Is there something I can do for you?" he asked playfully.

"Well for starters you can kiss me."

"I've wanted to kiss every part of you, for a very long time."

Darien gently brushed his lips with hers and said softly, "I think then maybe it's time you did." He held onto her hips and leaned over Darien until she lay underneath him on the sofa.

"Are you absolutely sure this is what you want?"

"Tanner, it's one of the few things that I am sure of." He brought his lips down to hers, and his kiss was as tender and as sweet as any that had been David's. She responded to him, as he was Tanner, but a part of her responded to him like he was David. His touch was as soft as the clothes the guardians covered her in, and his attention to her responses was astonishing. Tanner slowly unbuttoned the clean shirt she had put on after her shower, and he opened it fully so he could look at all of her, from the small erect pink nipples, to the light brown hair that covered her below. He traced the train-tracked scars from surgeries that had occurred in a life that was forever ago. Tenderly he kissed the scar marks on her body that still caused her to jump with a remembrance of pain. His mouth traveled lower and he parted her legs with soft licks of his tongue. Her body fairly trembled as Tanner wakened all the desires she still held for David.

He picked her up and carried her into the bedroom where she waited for him to undress, and out of impatience, she stopped him and started to undress him herself. Darien wanted her mouth to touch him everywhere; she wanted to know how he felt under her and over her, and especially deep inside of her. Her back released the musk smell of her excitement and Tanner noticed the delectable aroma. Darien slid the shirt that she wore from her shoulders, revealing the cascade of interlocking gold-colored scales that trailed down her back. Tanner nearly jumped from the bed when he saw her, and she watched his eyes flare with an anger that she never saw before.

"Oh God, what the hell did they do to you?" Tears sprang uncontrollably to her eyes, and she was afraid to answer him, not sure of how to explain it all to him.

"They helped me survive." He took her fiercely in his arms, and held her so close that she was losing her breath.

"Never again," he said to her. "Never again will anyone take you from me." The words were unsaid but she knew, for Tanner, the love was there. He loved her deeply, without question, and he made love to her tenderly, waking his own deep raw passion.

Tanner held her close as he slept, making sure that she was safe and secure in his arms, and Darien lay fitted to him like a piece to a never-ending puzzle. She watched the far corner of the room with calm serenity and knew that even when she could not see them, the shadows danced against the wall, and they only danced for her. She closed her eyes.

"If it's okay with you, I'd like to see my children," she said quietly the next morning as they sat in the diner. Tanner propped the doors open even though they were the only two living souls in all of Corral, Texas.

"I figured that you might." He sipped his coffee and absently reached for a cigarette and placed it between his lips, but never made the move to light it. Darien looked at the cigarette and shuddered involuntarily as she remembered her time in the pit and the burns made deep into her tortured body. There was limited scarring appearing on the surface to reflect Darien's ordeal; most of the scarring she carried inside, and for that much, she was grateful.

"Pack your bags, take what you need, and I'll go and find a nice comfortable car for us to ride in. Connecticut you said, right? Shouldn't take us more'n a week even if we take our time."

"You're coming?"

"I'm not letting you go alone."

"Thanks. I didn't really want to go alone, but I was a little afraid to ask you." She looked around the diner, walked over to the open door, and leaned up against the doorjamb.

"I did say that I wasn't going to lose you again; it was the truth, Darien."

"Tanner?" He looked over at her. "What do you think we're going to find out there? I mean what do you think is left? Parts of him have gone so far and cut so deep into the lives of so many. I'm a little afraid to leave here. I mean I want to, you know, see my kids, but I am a little scared to leave. I guess in a funny kind of way, despite all that has happened I feel safe here with you." Tanner walked over to where she stood and put his arms around her, drawing her into him and he softly kissed the top of her head.

"It's understandable that you don't want to see any more of the damage it caused." She leaned into him for support and he held her without question, knowing, as he had right from the beginning, that it was all Darien needed. The loving touch of another person can bring more healing than all the pills in the world. Darien was not surprised when she felt his hardness against her belly and this began to excite her as well, it also pleased her to know that she could bring this excitement to him.

"Come on, let's go upstairs," he said to her.

"We don't have to, Tanner; we have a whole city before us that we can make love in, to explore each other and to learn."

"Every day is an adventure with you, isn't it?"

"What fun would life be if it wasn't?" Tanner had made a quiet understanding with his own life and this reconciliation began to ease inside Darien. He brought her a sense of peace that she had not felt in a long time.

"Do you think that someday you will be able to tell me what happened out there, in the world on the other side of the mirror?"

Darien thought of the Keeper of Time, who was older than time itself, her friend Mr. Toady Face, and she wondered briefly if she would ever see him again. She brought up images of the Mountain King and his tortures of the wayward souls, along with the innocence of Meara and Mimba. She thought of the lovely palace of the guardians that sat on the purple mountains, and of the gold river that now ran rich and pure through the center of their home. She remembered the river rainbow, and how the good souls, along with the strength of the dragon had entered and hid inside of her.

She remembered the pain and worse yet,

She remembered that somewhere, to some degree of the insanity that been instilled inside of her that she liked, ands at times, welcomed the pain.

And then she wondered about all the cloned jesters. Did they survive, and where was the doorway to the Pit now? Should they go and look for it, was it a real place? Did it still need to be destroyed? She sighed against Tanner and drew on the quiet solace he so willingly offered.

"Maybe, someday," she finally answered. He humphed against her, a kind of deep growling inside his chest. She noticed that his excitement was gone, but she also knew that she could get it back and with that thought, she smiled.

"What do you say to going and finding a nice comfortable Cadillac or maybe a Mercedes and then maybe we'll find a nice hotel suite or we could even have some fun right on the ground-floor lobby. At the very least we don't have to worry about anyone watching us." Darien knew that the happiness that Tanner brought her was going to be long lasting.

"Do you want to take a walk?"

"Sure." They stepped outside into the hot sun and if not for the deserted streets, everything else seemed normal. They knew without speaking that to talk about or even dwell on all the deaths that had occurred in Corral would bring nothing less than painful mental agony. It was done, over with, and now they needed to move on. The news station kept them informed as to how far his reach had been, and Darien was not surprised to hear that all of Texas and the closer neighboring states had taken the worst of its madness. After that, people fled before the fog, but the amount of deaths that it caused was still staggering.

"Wait a minute, hon, I'm going back to get a couple of bottles of water." Tanner stepped back inside the diner, and Darien stood alone in the empty town. She felt her scales ripple, and then they separated on her back. She slowly raised her arms out from her sides. She began turning in a circle, feeling as though there was a kind of disconnection.

She also felt good, entering a kind of drug-induced high; maybe a part of it was from the erotic odor she released through the scales on her back.

Darien knew, she recognized what it was.

She was free.

Free to fly.

She could call the winds, and she could travel beyond the boundaries of this world.

She was spinning faster and faster and the warm winds were coming.

"Darien!" came a cry through her self-induced high.

"Darien!" came the cry from a loved one, a plea to return.

"Darien!" came the call of a man who loved her more than anyone else in his life, and Darien knew that she needed him as her lover and her friend. She let the winds relax, reforming the beginnings of her dissipation until she was complete. The light from the guardians shone around her, and the awareness beyond her immediate boundaries had become so acute that she could hear the chirping of a cricket nearly two blocks away. Her love for Tanner and for life itself filled her to overflowing, and she raised her arms to him.

"Darien, don't leave me."

"Oh, Tanner, how could I leave you when I love you so much." He walked over to her and picked her up off her feet in a giant bear hug.

"You have their powers, the strengths of the guardians?"

"I have it all, Tanner, and so much more." He set her back down on the ground. "There is so much more for us to discover, so much for us to do, and I can't do it alone. I need you by my side, as my lover, as my partner, as a part of me."

"You will have all of that and more." He kissed her deeply, and vowed to remain with her as long as she needed and wanted.

"So we are off on a new adventure?" Tanner said matter-of-factly.

"Life, my dearest Tanner, is the greatest adventure."

"Then let's go find ours." They clasped each other's hands and turned to face wherever their new path would lead them.

Behind them, in the darkest corners of Tanner's storage cabinets, the shadows danced. They would follow her through the night, through the deepest black, and they would dance, always dance for sweet Darien. And she would fight, every day for the rest of her life, against the piece of dark it left behind.

# THE RIDDLE

A light warm wind, a gentle breeze
Is how it all begins
Then it will come as shadows creep
And bind the Seraphims

Do not fear the shadows dark
They can be brushed away
Fear more the twisted evil thoughts
You think have come to stay

In the past you've made a few mistakes
For which you will atone
But they must not rule the here and now
Stop hiding in the zone

A destiny still waits for you
Of good and bad beware
To reach out and find the truest path
And stop the binding in its lair

For if the sun should fade away and die
The world would breathe an empty sigh
In a silent realm devoid of light
An evil grows from endless night

Unless you remain to be seen
Through pleasure/pain for little queen
The endless night becomes the day
And all of humankind will pay

The suffering bequeathed will know no bounds
And screams in pain, unholy sounds
Become the light you are meant to be
A savior for humanity

Save them, Darien, save them all
A crumbling empire set to fall
The light flows out from within
The release of Paul's sweet Seraphims.

By Claudia Syx